# A FRAGILE PEACE

Born in Essex, Teresa Crane still lives in a village in the north of the county. Married with two grown-up children, she began writing thirteen years ago. Her first novel, *Spider's Web*, was published in 1980 and was followed by *Molly*, *A Fragile Peace*, *The Rose Stone*, *Sweet Songbird*, *The Hawthorne Heritage*, *Tomorrow, Jerusalem* and *Green and Pleasant Land*.

# TERESA CRANE

# A Fragile Peace

Fontana
*An Imprint of HarperCollinsPublishers*

Fontana
An Imprint of HarperCollins*Publishers*,
77–85 Fulham Palace Road,
Hammersmith, London W6 8JB

Published by Fontana 1984
10 12 14 16 18 20 19 17 15 13 11

First published in Great Britain by
Collins 1984

Set in Plantin

Printed in Great Britain

## PART ONE

## SUMMER 1936

# CHAPTER ONE

There was absolutely nothing in the pleasant, late summer afternoon to prepare the Jordan family for the shock that was to come. The garden party in full swing on the lawns of Ashdown could already, in the first hour, be counted a success, and even the weather, uncertain for a week, had chosen to be kind. It probably, thought Allie Jordan just a little tartly, had not dared to be otherwise. The party was in aid of the fund set up by her mother towards the cost of repairing the fast-decaying roof of the village church: caught between Myra Jordan and God, Allie felt, not even the weather would dare to misbehave.

From the leaf-shielded sanctuary of her hiding place, she watched the activity on the wide lawns beneath her, as she sat tucked into the familiar, armchair-like niche where she had spent so many of the timeless hours of childhood, her back to the trunk of the ancient tree, her long legs stretched out along a branch. It still surprised her to see how far her feet reached – it now required considerable effort to wedge herself into a space in which, when first she had discovered this refuge, she had been able to curl up like a small squirrel. She leaned her head back, half-closing her eyes, letting little flickering darts of sunshine make rainbows through her lashes. The sound of voices and laughter rose and fell in the garden beneath her. Teacups rattled in their saucers. From across the river, the church clock struck the half hour. She smiled. She loved the sound of that old clock. It had been her constant companion ever since she could remember – it had brought a small girl home from the surrounding woods and fields in time for tea, had counted and comforted through the occasional sleepless nights of childish illness, had struck the hours, the days, the years of her young life with a steady, kindly regularity that spoke of changelessness and security. She stirred a little. It was easy in this drowsy, rustling world of green to dream of being a child again. Easy to push away thoughts of the future, of coming adulthood, of independence and responsibility. Easy to ignore for the moment the awful stirrings and buried fears of a young womanhood towards which one part of her yearned and from which, confusingly, another shrank—

As the sound of the clock's chimes died, she allowed herself to slip towards that enjoyable, melancholic nostalgia that is peculiar to the very young. Under this tree, on summer nights that now seemed a million years distant, her father had spent hours reading to her and her brother Richard – Libby, her elder sister, had never been able to sit still long enough to get through a chapter, let alone a whole book. Allie treasured the sound of his pleasant voice in the still evening air, saw the rapt look on the young Richard's face as he lived the dramas of *Coral Island* and *Tom Brown's Schooldays*. Richard was at Cambridge now, had been there a year, was no longer the skinny, scruffy companion-in-mischief of their very young days, or the hero-worshipped leader of school holiday pranks, but a young man who lived in a world in which she had no real part . . .

The sudden, booming voice from beneath her nearly knocked her off her perch.

'—but my dear, you can't possibly mean it?' Allie recognized Mrs Angus MacKenzie, her plump jowls pink and faintly sheened with sweat beneath a flower-trimmed, improbably girlish hat. 'A *progressive* school?' – she invested the adjective with a kind of dismissive distaste – 'Surely not?'

The little woman to whom she was speaking opened her mouth to reply.

Mrs MacKenzie steamrollered severely on. 'Dear Angus

says – and I'm bound to say that I agree with him wholeheartedly – that these establishments will be the certain ruin of an otherwise excellent educational system. I do beg you to think again, my dear. There's no discipline, you realize? Absolutely none—'

'Well . . .'

'For your daughter's sake, my dear, I do think you'd be very wise to reconsider. Why not let me send you the prospectus for St Hilda's? Now there is a thoroughly excellent establishment. I am able to recommend it personally with an absolutely clear conscience. Our dear Cynthia has done so very well at St Hilda's . . .'

The two women moved away. Allie, her wide mouth turned down expressively, spared a moment to hope, for an unknown girl's sake, that her mother would not be persuaded to force her into the mould – or the company – of dreadful Cynthia MacKenzie.

'—not that I don't feel sorry for some of these unemployed chappies, or anything like that.' A couple of young men in blazers and flannels, Cambridge acquaintances of Richard's, strolled beneath the tree, their voices clear and clipped in the summer air. 'But, dammit, it isn't as if we aren't all suffering to a greater or lesser degree. And one can't help feeling that if these people really wanted to work that badly they'd do something about it and stop wasting everyone's time with this idiotic marching up and down the country . . .'

'Couldn't agree more, old man. As Benjie was saying the other day—'

Whatever Benjie had said was lost in a sudden shout of laughter from the part of the garden where the hoop-la had been set up. Allie's mind dwelt on the provoking scrap of conversation. Could people who lived in warmth, comfort and security truly be so blind to the needs of others? A few months before, she had watched a ragged line of hungermarchers tramp through the streets of London, their grim faces, like their lives, bleakly marked by the helpless destitution forced upon them by the Depression. The sight

7

had affected her deeply. When, just after that, her father had regretfully decided that Jordan Engineering, a small subsidiary of the family firm in the hard-hit North East, must close, she had – to her mother's exasperation – agonized for weeks over the fate of the families of men thrown out of work and onto a parsimonious and totally inadequate dole.

'For heaven's sake, Allie,' Myra Jordan had snapped at last, 'what do you think we can do about it? Do you think your father *wants* to close the wretched place down? It isn't just the men that will suffer, you know. Have you forgotten that poor Uncle Albert has run that part of the business for nearly twenty years? How do you suppose he feels?'

'Uncle Albert's going to the Manchester works, isn't he?' Allie had asked doggedly, wincing at the perilous gleam in her mother's sapphire eyes. 'He isn't losing his job.'

'You're being ridiculously naïve. What do you suggest we do? Keep the Darlington works open at the expense of Manchester and Nottingham? And the new venture in Coventry – what of the men employed there? I doubt many of them are losing sleep about Darlington. They know which side their bread's buttered. Really, darling, it's all very well to be idealistic, but the world simply doesn't run that way. We can't eat fine words and promises, and neither can your Jarrow marchers. It simply doesn't make economic sense to keep Jordan Engineering going, so there must be an end to it. Is it your father's fault – the family's fault – that drastic ills demand drastic remedies? If we are to keep our heads above water in these difficult times, and protect ourselves and the future of Jordan Industries, there are sacrifices to be made . . .'

She had thought then, but had dared not say, and thought again now, remembering, her long mouth wry, that she had not noticed much sacrificing going on at Ashdown, nor yet in the comfortable and well-staffed offices in London from which her father, Robert, ran Jordan Industries. The Bentley still stood on the sweep of the drive; Mrs Welsh, the family cook, still laid on meals for a family of five that Allie suspected might feed twice that number; she herself still attended the same expensive boarding school that her sister had left three years before. If sacrifices were being made, then her common sense told her that someone else was making them. And yet – she knew that in a way her mother was right. For every man that Jordan Industries had lost over the past few years it had kept two in employment. Everyone accepted that her father and the various uncles and cousins who made up the management of the diverse small engineering works that comprised Jordan Industries were reasonable, honest and caring employers, insofar as present conditions allowed. Her own great-grandfather had founded the business in a tiny converted blacksmith's forge in the back streets of Birmingham nearly a century before; two generations of Jordans had worked hard since to establish and successfully expand it. Why shouldn't the family enjoy the profits of its labours? If Uncle Willie wanted to spend his time at Epsom and Newmarket, and cousin Bob had a hankering for fast motor cars, whose business was it but theirs? Who had the right to condemn them? The man who marched on blistered feet for the right to work, to feed his family? The shop steward who had been quietly sacked from the new Coventry works before he could become a troublemaker? She sighed. She did not know the answer. Worse – she had a strong and frustrating suspicion that she had not discovered the right questions . . .

Another shout of laughter, rising from the hoop-la stall, drew her attention back to the present. She craned her neck to look and, as she did so, caught sight of a figure on the terrace outside the french windows that led into the dining room. A tall, slim woman in sapphire-blue silk which glimmered, expensively jewel-like, in the sunshine had come from the house. She stood with graceful authority a little above the crowded lawns, her strong-boned, beautiful face shaded by a hat of exactly the same colour as her dress, her eyes moving slowly over the scene below her, as if looking for someone. Instinctively Allie shrank back against

9

the trunk of the tree. If her mother caught her hiding here, there would be the devil to pay. Worse. There was no doubt in Allie's mind that she would rather take her chances with the devil any day than face the ice-sharp and scathing edge of her mother's rare anger.

She tried to narrow her wide shoulders, contract her long and bony limbs. She felt suddenly enormous, a gawky young giantess, Alice after she had eaten the wrong side of the mushroom. As she felt her mother's brilliant eyes sweep her hiding place, she thanked God – and her sister Libby – that she was wearing, after all, her second-best dress, which was green. Not, she knew, that Libby's insistence that she should not wear her pink had been anything but entirely selfish. Libby herself was wearing a deep rose pink this afternoon and, as she had pointed out with cruel and careless truth, it suited her so much better that it would not have flattered Allie to try to compete. '. . . besides, darling, we'd look like a couple of bookends – a big one and a small one. How silly! Wear your green, love, there's a pet.' Libby had put her silver-blonde head on one side and regarded Allie with tolerant and absolutely genuine affection. 'You're still such a *baby*, darling, do you know that? That wretched school! Navy blue knickers and gym slips at seventeen, honestly, it's too bad! God, how I hated it. Still, it won't be long now, will it? But oh, my Lord—' she had rolled her eyes in remembered agony '—just wait till you get to Switzerland! You'll just *die* when you see the difference between the poor little stick-in-the-mud *anglaises* and *les chic continentales*!'

Allie's retort that she had no intention of going to Switzerland had been wisely bitten back; it had not been the time to precipitate a pitched battle. Now she sat, scarcely breathing, watching her mother and praying that her refuge would not be discovered.

Myra Jordan was well content, on the whole, with what she saw as she scanned the grounds of Ashdown, her swift, bright glance taking in every tiny detail. The afternoon was

10

running smoothly and well – as she knew, with no conceit, was only to be expected from anything in which she invested her time, energy, and considerable organizing ability. The garden looked lovely: the velvet lawns manicured, the rose garden symmetrical in weedless and perfumed beauty, the box hedges trimmed to dark perfection, solid and sweet-smelling. She made a mental note to congratulate Browning, the gardener; he had excelled himself. In the orchard beyond the rose garden, young people strolled, the girls' dresses and hats butterfly-bright in the stippled shade. Through the well-pruned trees she could see the glitter of the river and beyond that the Kentish countryside rolled in a dappled patchwork to the sky. Nearer to hand, beneath the terrace on which she stood, were set chairs and tables. Half a dozen women in dark dresses and snow-white starched aprons moved among the seated guests with trays laden with cakes, tea and lemonade.

Myra's brilliant blue eyes moved across the chattering crowds. Now and again she acknowledged a caught glance or a lifted hand with a smile and a slight inclination of her head. Her husband Robert stood by the fountain in earnest conversation with the vicar and his wife. As he glanced up, she caught his eye and a smiling, private signal passed between them before, soberly attentive, he turned back to his guests. Elizabeth, the elder of their two daughters, was the centre of a noisy group of laughing young people who were trying their hands at the skittles that had been set up on the tennis court. As Myra watched, a dark-haired young man in the regulation flannels and open-necked shirt bowled with a flourish and scattered the wooden ninepins – relics of the young Jordans' childhood – in all directions. Receiving his prize – a battered teddy bear with a glumly ferocious expression – he presented it with an even more picturesque flourish to Libby who, to the young man's obvious mortification, tossed it into the air for one of her friends to catch, glancing as she did so in an oddly challenging way at a solitary figure who leaned, hands in pockets, in the shade of the big oak tree that sheltered the court. Myra's

11

eyes, following her daughter's, chilled perceptibly at the sight of the slight, hard-faced young man who stood watching the bowlers with no trace of expression on his face. He neither acknowledged Libby's provocative look nor moved. Myra's lips tightened. She had disliked Tom Robinson from the instant she had met him, and the past month had done nothing to improve her opinion of the young man. She considered him to be a disruptive influence on her son: she had not until this moment ever considered that he might have an equally disturbing effect on her daughters.

The thought brought to mind the original reason for this mental roll-call of the family. Where was Alexandra? She had been left an hour ago dutifully entertaining the extremely rich if undoubtedly unpleasant Mrs Osbert Ogilvy from whom Myra was attempting to extract a handsome subscription for her church roof fund. At some time during that hour, Allie had disappeared and Myra, discovering the disgruntled and deserted Mrs Ogilvy marching firmly down the drive towards the gates, had been obliged to exert her most tactful charm to guide her back before she and her money disappeared into her rather vulgar limousine, never to return. Fifteen minutes had then been expended upon finding some innocent ignorant enough of the lady's character to engage her in conversation. Meanwhile, of Allie there had been absolutely no sign.

Myra's shining, fashionably pointed shoe tapped with rhythmic impatience upon the pale marble of the terrace. Really, it was high time that the child grew out of this disconcerting habit of disappearing to God knew where for hours at a time. Time, in fact, she added to herself a little grimly, smiling graciously at a passing guest, that Alexandra grew out of a lot of silly habits that she seemed intent upon preserving from a rather awkward childhood – 'Myra, darling!' called a voice from the lawn, 'what a marvellous turn-out! Marvellous!' Myra smiled and waved in acknowledgement – Allie had to learn that with young ladyhood came certain obligations, certain socially accept-

12

able ways of thought and behaviour. She was a nice enough child, of course, but . . .

Myra's glance flicked again to where Libby stood, shining head thrown back in laughter, her every movement prettily graceful, her bright face flower-like in the sunshine. Her mother sighed, imperceptibly. The finishing school in Switzerland had produced in Libby just exactly that style and grace with which a young woman of moderate fortune and position could manipulate the world to her advantage. Myra hoped, with what she herself recognized as more fervency than conviction, that the establishment might work the same alchemy on her younger daughter. She was not unaware of Allie's dislike of the idea, any more than she was ignorant of the fact that her daughter had been toying hopefully with the idea of going to university. But, in her mother's firm opinion, to allow that would only – heaven forbid! – turn the girl into a worse blue stocking than she was already. It would pander to the child's most unbecoming attitudes and ideas, and in particular her regrettable and misguided growing interest in what Myra thought of, quite simply, as 'The Wrong Kind of Politics'.

Myra was not insensitive to the plight of working people, to the distress and anguish caused by the worst depression that the country had ever suffered, but she firmly believed in law, order and the utter rectitude of the English ruling classes. Labour politics appalled her; they could, in her opinion, bring nothing to the country but chaos and destruction. Her eyes wandered again, speculatively, taking in the world around her, the secure, pleasant world over which she held sway and which she would defend to the death. Let the unpleasant little housepainter restore order in Germany by whatever method he wished. Let the comic-opera 'king' of Italy strut as the Emperor of Abyssinia. Let the Spanish tear themselves apart – it was neither the first, nor probably the last time. Let the Wall Street investors scramble as best they might from the pits of greed that they had dug for themselves. Let the unemployed be grateful for those industrious souls who ordered their lives better, paid their

13

taxes and provided the dole. The world had always been thus, and Myra could see no possible argument for change. It infuriated her that two of her children had been tainted by the infection of left-wing politics, for it was Richard even more than Allie who preached what to his mother's ears sounded like sedition and revolution. Richard, indeed, who had first introduced his sister to these dangerous and stupid ideas – as it had been he who had nearly drowned Allie when she had followed him blindly onto the thin ice of the village pond, who had taught her to bowl overarm in a way so successful that, to both their delight and their mother's horror, she had been drafted into the village cricket team . . .

Beneath the old oak tree the solitary figure of Tom Robinson still leaned, motionless. An expression of pure dislike flickered across Myra's lovely face. There stood the real culprit. The infection that fevered Richard and was in danger of afflicting Allie came directly from him. She felt a small spur of anger as she watched him. The boy had not even the common courtesy to appear to be enjoying himself. He was watching the activity around him with an expression of detachment that to Myra's eyes was infuriatingly close to contempt. Tom Robinson, she thought grimly, had out-stayed his welcome. Richard's friend or no, he must be made to understand that his presence at Ashdown was no longer welcome. And he could make, she added to herself, what he wished of that. For all Myra's strongly held views, she was no snob. She had every admiration for a lad who through gruelling hard work and – according to Richard – the application of a brilliant mind had won through from a back street in London's East End to a place in one of the finest universities in the world. Her objections to young Robinson were quite genuinely rooted not in his background but in what she considered to be his disruptive and difficult personality. He was a dangerous and rather disturbing young man, and there was no place in Myra's scheme of things for such a one.

'Myra, darling!' Myra turned, almost into the arms of a

small, vivacious woman in poppy red. 'I've been looking just everywhere for you!'

'Emmie! When did you get back?'

'We docked yesterday, darling. Southampton.' The woman's dark eyes sparkled. 'We left a few days early. I just refused to miss your shindig! New York was unbearable. *Unbearable*. Like a Turkish bath. Hotter.' She tucked a small hand into the crook of Myra's arm, guided her along the terrace. 'I've so much to tell you. We met the Bertie Smythes, you know – oh, what a bore that man is! – but they know so many people that you have to forgive him or no one would ever invite you anywhere. Myra, darling,' she scolded, 'you aren't listening!'

Myra smiled. 'Yes I am. I'm just wondering where Allie's got to, that's all.'

'Oh, never mind that. She's down in the orchard with the other young people, I'll be bound.' Her friend leaned her dark little head confidentially close. 'I'm dying to talk to you about the absolutely *scandalous* reports in the American papers . . .'

'Reports?'

'The King, silly. *The King*. And Mrs Simpson—'

'Oh, come now, Emmie—'

'It's no good "coming now" me. I know they've denied it here, but it's all over the papers in the States. They're cruising together. The King and a married woman! And her husband is going to sue for divorce, or so they say . . .'

Myra's attention was caught at last. 'Divorce? Surely not?'

Emmie laughed delightedly. 'Come and sit down. I positively devoured every report I could find. Memorized them! I'll tell you all about it . . .'

Allie, still in her tree, sighed with relief to see her mother's attention taken from the garden. Her heart was pounding in a quite ridiculous fashion and her every muscle ached. Time, she decided, to escape while the going was good—

'Allie! What in heaven's name are you doing up there?'

She almost fell from the branch in shock. 'Richard, you beast! You scared the life out of me!'

Her brother stood beneath her, looking up, hands on hips, his blue eyes, as brilliant as his mother's, alight with a suppressed excitement that Allie, in her present predicament, at first barely noticed. 'I've been looking all over for you, Pudding. I've something to tell you.'

'Don't call me Pudding.' The tone was irritable. Allie peered down through the screen of leaves. 'What's the matter? Did you win a coconut or something?' she asked ungraciously.

There was more than a touch of his mother, too, in the sudden angry tightening of his lips. 'This is serious, Al. I really do have something to tell you.' His air of tense excitement was unmistakable now; it puzzled and rather perturbed Allie. Richard made as if to turn away.

'Wait. I'm coming.' With remarkable agility the girl twisted her body and swung herself down from the branch, landing lightly beside her brother to the astonishment of an elderly couple who were strolling past. She tossed back her short, brown, wavy hair with a sharp movement of her head. 'Now. What did you want to tell me?'

She tilted her head against the low-slanting sun to look up at him. Richard Jordan was tall and slim and possessed those regular, clear-cut features which, beneath his short fair hair were the very picture of upper-middle-class young English manhood. Yet there was a look about the bright eyes, an undeniable softness in the mouth that belied the decisive line of jaw and cheekbone. It was a face made for ready laughter, a friendly, oddly lazy face, its weakness hidden by the spectacular bone structure he had inherited from his mother. Just now it had about it an almost feverish look. Unusual colour stained his cheekbones and there was a look in his eyes that worried Allie. She had seen that look before, in a shared childhood of scrapes and mischief. It always meant trouble.

'Well?' She eyed him warily.

Richard glanced round, nervously. 'Not here. Come to the old summer house.'

16

She followed him with growing misgiving, into the hot and musty dimness of the disused summer house. Motes of golden dust, disturbed by their coming, hovered and swirled in the slanting, metallic rays of the sun. The small room was a jumble of broken deck chairs, old tennis rackets, discarded toys. As children they had played here. It had been *their* secret place, sacrosanct and private, even from Libby. Allie waited for him to speak and still he did not. Outside the open door she saw a long shadow move.

'Richard, what is it?'

He nibbled his lip, watching her. The air about them was suffocatingly close.

'Richard?'

'I'm – we're – going to Spain.'

The blurted words fell like stones into a well, and in just that way their meaning took full moments to reach Allie's mind. She stared at him. 'But – you can't! There's a—' She stopped. Idiotically she had been about to say, 'There's a war in Spain.'

An intolerable silence lengthened. The shadow beyond the door moved again.

'It's a joke, isn't it? A silly joke?' Allie's voice lifted sharply, barely controlled. 'Richard, honestly, you can be really . . .' the words faded into silence.

He took a long, slow breath. 'No, Pudding. It isn't a joke. We're going. Today. Now. I didn't want to – couldn't – go, without saying goodbye. At least to you. But you've got to promise that you won't tell anyone until we're well away. You know what they are. They'll never understand. They'll try to stop us. Me,' he amended. His voice had an awful, raw edge to it.

'Richard, you can't mean it?' Faintly, through the open door, she could hear the sounds of the garden party, echoes of sanity in a world unexpectedly mad. 'They're killing each other out there! I mean – what do you think you can do? You aren't a soldier! And what about Cambridge? You so much wanted – you worked so hard – Rich, you're out of your mind!' She heard the babbling voice as if it had be-

17

longed to a stranger. Still she searched his face for some sign that the whole thing was some tastelessly awful joke. And knew it was not.

In a silence intensified by the heat, they stared at each other.

Richard half-turned from her. 'I thought you, of all of them, might understand.'

She still felt as if he had hit her. Suddenly the fierce and unexpected temper that had plagued her all her life flared. 'Well, you were wrong. I don't understand. I don't begin to understand. And what's more, I don't think you do, either. You've taken leave of your senses!' She flung past him, making for the door. 'I've never heard anything so lunatic in my life. I'm going to find Mother—' She stopped, her way barred by a long arm across the open doorway. She lifted her head and found herself looking, as she had known she would, into a pair of pale, cool eyes. If Myra Jordan had found her son's friend graceless and disagreeable, she would have been surprised to know that her younger daughter had detested him from the moment he had set foot in the house. Characteristically Allie had hidden it, unwilling to upset her brother or to precipitate unnecessary unpleasantness. At this moment, however, such considerations were a long way beyond her.

'Get out of my way.'

Tom Robinson smiled, very slightly, and with no humour at all. He did not move.

She heard Richard come up behind her, but did not turn to look at him. 'This whole stupid business is your doing, isn't it?' she asked the slight, still form who barred her way, her voice low and shaking with the effort it took to control it. 'Not even Richard would think up something as half-baked as this on his own.'

'The half-baked idea was his, all right.' The flat vowels of London which he made no attempt to disguise in no way detracted from a voice which was surprisingly light and melodic. 'He insisted on kissing his baby sister goodbye.'

Already perspiring in the heat, she flushed hotly. 'And do

you find that so surprising? If you'd been half a man you'd have seen that he said goodbye to his parents too—'

'Half a man? Or half a gentleman, do you mean? The two things aren't necessarily the same, you know.' His voice was softly derisive. 'The one I am – the other I'd never pretend to—'

She stormed on as if he had not spoken, 'But you wouldn't let him do that, would you? Oh no. He might find himself listening to a bit of sense. You might have to find some other idiot to talk into this – this madness.'

He straightened. He was not much taller than Allie. His dark hair was straight and flopped over his eyes, his face thin, hard-eyed. In the fear of losing her brother, she hated him.

'I didn't talk Richard into anything,' he said quietly. 'He doesn't have to come. As a matter of simple fact, that bit was his idea, not mine. I wanted to go alone. I don't give a tinker's cuss what you or your parents or anyone else thinks or does. It's nothing to do with me. I'm going. There's an end. Richard's coming is his own idea and his own business. I even tried to stop him.' His eyes flicked over her shoulder. 'Didn't I?'

'Yes, he did.' There was a kind of humiliation in her brother's voice that made Allie flinch. She turned to look at him. He was watching Tom with a painful intensity. 'Allie, you don't understand,' he said again, 'Tom would have been off on his own a week ago. I kept him here. I wanted to go with him. I have to go with him.'

'*Why?*'

A hand spun her round, holding her wrist. Tom Robinson's voice when he spoke was as stone-hard as his eyes. 'To fight against something, Little Red Riding Hood, that if it isn't stopped by suckers like us will eat up the whole of Europe – including your nice, safe, middle-class corner – and spit out the bones. To make certain that the brown shirts that are flapping on the washing lines of Germany and Italy and Spain don't start blowing in the winds of Kent. Though why the bloody hell I should care about that is beyond me. I'll tell you what I do care about, though. I care about the little Jew-boy who runs our corner shop and gives my Mum tick when she needs it. I care about my Dad who's a union man and proud of it. I care about freedom—'

'I don't think it's that simple.'

'Of course it bloody isn't! Nothing is!'

'You don't have to go to Spain to fight Fascism,' she said, doggedly.

'Where in hell else are we going to do it?'

'Try here. Right here. Try setting your own house in order before you go interfering in other people's problems—'

'Allie . . .' said Richard, miserably.

'—but that's not what you want, is it? You won't get any medals for working in the back streets of London, will you? Or in the mills of Lancashire? Or for standing up against Mosley and his thugs? Those blackshirts aren't as far away as you seem to think. If you care so much for your little Jewish shopkeeper, why don't you stay here and defend him?'

To her insupportable fury, he laughed. 'My dear Allie, perhaps I should leave that task to you. Abie will be in very capable hands. No blackshirt could stand up to such temper.'

'It isn't funny.'

'I didn't intend it to be.' His uncharacteristic spurt of anger appeared to have died entirely, but his fingers around her wrist were still savage. The pain tingled to her fingertips. She felt as if the bones of her wrist were grating together.

'Let go of me.'

For the space of a couple of heartbeats, he held her without relaxing his grip. Then, with a gesture of dismissal, he released her and stepped back. 'So long, then, Rich.' It was calculated, and they all knew it.

'No, Tom – wait!'

'Let him go, Richard!'

Richard's face suffused. 'Shut up, Allie! Will you just shut up!'

She stared at him, tears pricking behind eyes that were dry and burning. Tom stood absolutely still, leaning against the door jamb, a dark figure silhouetted against the brilliance of the fast-setting sun which had dipped to touch the tops of the trees of the orchard, limning them in fire.

'You can't go without me now,' said Richard, unashamedly pleading.

The dark figure shrugged. 'I'm not getting stopped on the dockside by your parents' henchmen.'

Richard turned on Allie. 'I should have gone without telling you. That was what Tom wanted, and he was right. But I tell you this: you won't stop me. I swear it. They can't watch me all the time, can't lock me up. If I'm forced to stay, I will, for now. But I'll go tomorrow. Or the next day, or the next. And I'll never forgive you. Never.'

She flinched.

His voice softened. 'Pudding? Come on, old girl . . .?'

She had lost; each of them knew it. Richard reached for her and pulled her into his arms. Tom watched with still, clear eyes as her brother stroked her hair. She pulled away, her colour high. 'What do you want me to do?'

'Absolutely nothing – just wish me luck. Tom and I'll slip away now. I told Father we were off to a party in town. They won't expect us back tonight. We'll be on the boat tomorrow. I'll send a telegram just before we leave – it'll be too late for them to stop me then. And no one need ever know that you knew. Allie – please – we mustn't part bad friends. Not you and I. Won't you wish me luck?'

She felt faintly sick. 'Luck? You make it sound as if you're off to a cricket match.'

'Of course he does. How else would he make it sound?' Tom's voice was back to normal, light and brutal. 'Now, come on, kiss him goodbye like a good girl and let's get going.' He glanced over his shoulder, out of the door.

Allie clung to Richard. 'Be careful.'

'Of course I will. All this fuss – it'll probably be all over by the time we get there.'

'It certainly will be if we don't get a move on.' Tom stood back and allowed Richard to precede him through the door. Before following him, he paused, looking at Allie who stood very close to him, watching her brother. 'I'll look after him,' he said lightly, and she could not for the life of her tell whether the reassuring note in his voice as honestly meant or mocking. She tilted her head, searching his eyes. For one single moment they stood so. 'Don't I get a kiss for luck too?' he asked then, drily flippant.

'No.'

The straight mouth turned down in arid amusement and he sketched a sloppy salute. Then he moved, light and fast, after Richard who, after pausing to pick up a couple of bags that had been secreted beneath a shrub, was threading his way through the trees of the orchard towards the garden gate. Neither of them looked back.

From the lawns behind the house came the tinkling sound of Libby's laughter and the clatter of teacups.

# CHAPTER TWO

The bombshell of Richard's leaving reverberated through the Jordan household like nothing Allie had ever known before. Myra was first incredulous, then quietly and over-whelmingly furious, her anger spurred by her unspoken but heartfelt fear for her son. For days, the other members of the household, each coming to terms with the shock in his or her different way, moved about Ashdown almost on tiptoe; there were grim times when it seemed to Allie that her brother might already have been struck down by a Falangist bullet. Then, as the realization took hold that nothing could be done to bring him back, Myra charac-teristically erected a wall of cool practicality around her outrage and fear and, as if it were the most natural thing in the world, set about discovering the needs of the men who had chosen to fight in Spain.

Allie had never admired her mother more. For herself, she nursed what she saw as her guilty secret through those fraught weeks and carried it, untold, back with her to school at the start of the new term. Here at St Leonard's another blow awaited her. She had never been one to court general popularity – her affections tended to be fierce and singular – and all of her schooldays had been shared with one particular friend, Sonia Barton. They had spent their first, miserably homesick days together five years before and had been inseparable companions ever since, though Sonia's holidays were mostly spent with her parents in the Far East. Now, unexpectedly and at the last moment, Sonia's mother had decided that she could no longer bear to be parted from her daughter, and Sonia, willy-nilly, had been withdrawn from the school. The letter that awaited Allie bemoaned their parting and swore everlasting friendship. Allie, watching her classmates with their

23

ready-formed allegiances and friendships, swallowed her dismay, resigned herself to a lonely term and wrote a cheerful letter in return.

And so it was to her father that she at last, three long months after Richard's leaving, found herself confiding the secret that had haunted her waking and sleeping hours.

He looked at her, a faint furrow between his straight, dark brows. 'You knew?'

She nodded miserably.

They were walking in the grounds of St Leonard's, the late November air damp and iron-cold. Patches of yellow mist wreathed the desolate woodlands and floated over the waters of the lake, making the small island in the centre a faint, mysterious smudge in the growing darkness. The sky was dull and heavy, and light was seeping from the afternoon very fast. Behind them, cresting the rising parkland, the school – a Queen Anne mansion with sprawling modern additions – glowed with light and warmth, a refuge of familiarity in the oddly primeval chill of the afternoon. Allie pushed her hands deeper into her pockets and buried her chin in her scarf, not looking at her father.

'Just before they left. Daddy, honestly, there was nothing I could do. I've been over and over it in my head. He said that if I told he'd just wait and go another time. He said he'd never forgive me—' A movement of the cold air made her shiver suddenly. She hunched her wide shoulders. 'I didn't know what to do.' The words were as dreary as the landscape.

Robert Jordan stopped walking. His daughter took another step and then also stopped, turning to face him. In a familiar, loving gesture he lifted his arm and, thankfully, she slipped beneath it, allowing the comfort of his embrace to ease her sore heart. 'What if something happens to him?' Her voice was muffled; the agonizing thoughts which had pursued each other around her brain like rats in a cage were not easy to put into words. 'What if he's k-killed? Or crippled? It'll be my fault, won't it? If I'd told you – if I'd said something . . .?' She gulped air awkwardly. He laid his

24

face against the thick wavy hair that swung across her eyes, grazing her cheekbone. His eyes were tender.

'Listen to me.' She had always loved his voice. It was gentle and cultured, always warm. He paused for a moment, marshalling his thoughts. 'Richard is a man. He may not always act like one – which of us ever does?' In her self-centred misery, she missed the rueful note of irony in that. 'But a man nevertheless. He must be allowed to make his own decisions, and learn then to stick to those decisions. If he chooses to go to war, as men have so often chosen before . . .' For a fraction of a second, Robert Jordan hesitated; blood, barbed wire, the deaths of friends hovering in a nightmare that was now almost twenty years old – 'If that's what he chooses, then I'm afraid there's nothing we can do to prevent him. Oh, I know he's under age,' he added in reply to her small, protesting movement, 'and if you had told us, then, yes, I suppose we could have stopped him. But by what means and for how long? If he's half the lad I hope he is—' his arm about her tightened and he half-laughed, quietly, into her hair '—if he's half the lad that I suspect you are yourself – then nothing that you, I or the devil might have done could have stopped him.'

'You forgot to mention Mother,' she said, and was not aware until she said it of the faint twist of humour. She smiled lopsidedly. 'I didn't mean . . .'

'I know what you meant. But no, I don't think even she could have stopped him. This way was the best, my love, believe me. If we'd forced him to escape us, he might have enlisted under another name and we might never have found him, never have heard from him. At least now he writes. We can keep in touch. We'll know . . .' the pause was infinitesimal, but telling '. . . when he's coming home.'

It had not been what he had intended to say. Allie's mind supplied the words with cruel clarity: We'll know if he's killed. She squeezed her eyes tightly together, forcing the tears back. Her father held her for an instant longer, then, gently, he put her from him and they turned and walked on.

'He hates it, doesn't he?' she asked, after a moment in

which the only sound was their footsteps on the rotting carpet of wet leaves that covered the ground and the dreary sound of water dripping from the melancholy trees. 'Don't you feel it? He doesn't say so in so many words, I know, but it's there. All that silly bravado – rah, rah for the chaps and what a jolly good show. He hates it.'

Her father said nothing. Then 'It isn't always easy,' he said quietly, 'to take the right decision at the right time.' He was not looking at her but into the shrouding mist ahead. His dark, firm profile was outlined against the dull sheen of the winter waters of the lake. 'We all find ourselves in-fluenced by circumstances, emotion – passion, even, rather than logic. It's a failing I'm afraid that isn't uniquely characteristic of the young.' Once again her inexperienced ears missed the thread of bitter irony in the words. Her normally acute senses were blinded and deafened by her own feelings of guilt and anxiety. 'I think you're right,' her father continued. 'I think he hates it. I'm not surprised that he does.' Again, faintly, the rumble of a bombardment, the swish and howl of a flying shell. He passed a hand across his face.

'He will be all right, won't he?' Allie knew the stupidity of the question the moment she had blurted it, heard the childishness of it in the uncontrolled lift of her voice. She bit her lip. The years shifted like the November mists, and she was a small girl pleading for reassurance about whatever disaster threatened her safe world – a broken toy, a pet with a hurt foot – saying, 'He will be all right, Daddy, won't he?' 'I'm sorry,' she said now abruptly. 'That was ridiculous.'

Her father laid an arm across her shoulders as they walked.

'You aren't mad at me then? You don't think I could have stopped him?' she asked.

'I think you did exactly the right thing. I just wish you'd talked to me about it earlier and saved yourself a lot of worry.'

She scuffed a pile of leaves with her foot. 'Mother's taken it very well, hasn't she?'

He smiled, his eyes warm. 'How else would you expect her to take it? Your mother is not only the best wife a man could have – she's the most practical. I have never known her to create a fuss about anything that she felt could not be altered. She is at present engaged in organizing some of the ladies of the village to collect for parcels for Richard and his fellows-in-arms. She writes him long, entertaining letters full of happy nothings. On the day that he comes home, having first ascertained that he's hale and undamaged, she'll probably hang, draw and quarter him.'

Allie smiled a little, then sobered.

They walked on until they came to a small clearing beside the lake, a stretch of open bank with a shingle beach which was used for swimming in the summer. It was hard to believe now, Allie thought, looking at the still darkness of the water and feeling the bite of the air on her face, that she had run, laughing, into the water just a few months before at this very spot. Suddenly and inexplicably she felt a wave of sadness. It was as if her childhood had fled from her, leaving her bereft, in limbo, dreadfully vulnerable.

'Let's sit for a bit.' There was a huge fallen tree by the water's edge that had been worn completely smooth by its use as a seat. Allie perched upon it, her legs swinging, her heels catching in the dead undergrowth. Her father leaned beside her, his long legs crossed, his eyes narrowed against the worsening visibility, scanning the still waters of the lake.

Allie bent her head and watched her swinging feet; her sensible school brogues were stained dark with water, her thick, mud-coloured stockings splashed and snagged. 'When I leave school,' she said apparently inconsequentially, 'I'm never going to wear lisle stockings again.'

Robert Jordan smiled slightly and waited.

She took a deep breath. The cold air was sharp in her lungs. 'Talking of which . . .' Her quiet voice seemed lost in the waterlogged, shadowy quiet. She glanced sideways at her father.

'. . . that's the other thing you wanted to talk to me about,' he finished for her.

She nodded.

'Fire away.'

'Mother doesn't want me to go to university.'

'No. She doesn't.'

'And you? How do you feel about it?'

He took a long thoughtful breath. 'I honestly don't know. I'm not trying to dodge the issue, love, truly I'm not. I don't know. As you know, your mother and I have always had the understanding that with regard to the education and up-bringing of yourself and your sister she has the final say, and I have always allowed myself to be guided by her. It may be old-fashioned, but up to now it has worked. I would ask you to consider this: it is against your own interests to dismiss your mother's opinions without thought. She is a perceptive and extremely intelligent person, and she has your best interests at heart at all times.'

'I know that.'

'She is rarely motivated by anything other than that she believes that she knows what is best for you. She cares for you deeply. She cares for all of us deeply.' There was an unfathomable note in his gentle voice. 'I shouldn't like to do anything – I shouldn't like any of us to do anything – that might hurt her. Not at the moment. Not after Richard. Now having said that, let me say that my greatest desire is to see you happy. If you've absolutely set your heart on going, if you're completely certain that it would be right for you, then I'll do my best. All I ask is that you consider carefully before we take up the cudgels and wade into a fight that might take a good deal out of both of us.' The last words were said with that wry twist of humour that Allie so loved in her father. She smiled in acknowledgement of it.

A water bird skimmed from the opaline sky and landed on the lake, sending darkly silvered ripples across the quiet surface to lap at their feet. Allie fought one last battle with herself, weighing and measuring cause and effect in her mind. Then she sighed. The moment had come.

'Actually,' she said, 'I've decided that I don't really want to go.'

He looked at her sharply.

She shrugged. 'I probably wouldn't get in anyway.' She broke off a piece of bark and tossed it into the water, watching the pattern of its movement as if it were the most absorbing thing in the world. 'It was a pretty stupid idea really.' Her heart was thumping in awful, joyous liberation. She sensed her father's relief, his gratitude that unpleasantness and friction had been avoided, that he would not now be forced to take sides with someone he loved dearly against someone, Allie was certain, that he loved even more. She felt the familiar, tranquil glow of warmth that always came when she indulged her own eagerness to please the people about her. In her more mordant moments, she despised herself for it. She jumped from the tree, brushing her coat down. 'That's that settled then.'

Her father did not move. 'Allie, are you sure?'

'Yes, I'm sure.' She took a deep breath. 'But there is something else . . .'

'What's that?'

'I don't want to go to that dreary finishing place that Libby went to. I don't want to go to Switzerland. You won't make me, will you?' They both knew that the pronoun was a euphemistic courtesy and that Allie was referring to her mother.

Her father considered for a long moment. 'Well, that seems fair to me. If you're really set against it.'

'Do you think you could explain to Mother? I'm not sure she'll understand.'

'Of course I can. And of course she will.' His quick smile flashed again. 'Though it does seem strange, my love. Most girls, I'm given to believe, would give their eye teeth for such an opportunity . . .'

'Unfortunately,' she said, a real note of regret in her voice, 'I don't seem to be "most girls".'

'Libby had a wonderful time—'

'I'm not Libby, either.'

'That's true.' The words were a small conspiracy between them, compounded by their exchanged, smiling look.

Allie tucked her hand into her father's pocket as they turned to stroll back to the school, and snuggled close to him. 'She's coming down next Sunday, did you know? She and Celia. They're treating me to tea.'

A long time later she was to remember that it was at that exact moment that her father caught his foot in an exposed tree root and stumbled a little. As he recovered, he spoke neither of her sister nor of her sister's friend. 'Tell me – if you've decided after all not to try for university, and if you don't want to go to Switzerland – what do you want to do?'

She was not quite prepared for that. There was a small silence. She took a breath. 'I'd like to get a job.' She spoke very quickly, not looking at him.

'A job? For heaven's sake – what sort of a job?' He could not quite keep the astonishment from his voice.

She lifted her shoulders. 'Well – I'm not sure. I haven't quite thought that far.'

'I see.' He considered for a moment, with the thought and care that she loved so much in him. 'Well, I must say that we hadn't quite anticipated . . .' He paused. 'Were you thinking of Jordan's? I daresay I could—'

'No.' She squeezed his hand inside his pocket to compensate for the sharpness of the word. How in heaven's name to explain how she felt? The compulsion to *do* something, to be part of a world that she sensed but did not know? 'I don't mean to be awkward, honestly, but I don't want to be the boss's daughter, playing at being a working girl, marking time until a nice, suitable young man asks me to marry him—'

Her father glanced down at her, eyebrows raised, but said nothing.

'—I need something of my own. Something away from the family. You do understand, don't you?'

In the silence, from the direction of the mist-wreathed playing fields came the faint sounds of shouts, and laughter.

'I – think so.'

'I haven't really thought about it yet. I know I can't expect much – jobs don't grow on trees nowadays. But I'd like to try. On my own. I wondered – well – my French is passable, and my German's still very good, thanks to Aunt Margaret and Uncle Otto—' She broke off. 'How are they by the way?' Her mother's sister and her German husband, with whom she and Richard had spent many a happy summer in Germany, had recently settled in England, unable to accept any longer the tainted brutality of Nazi rule.

'They're fine. I've found a place for him in Coventry.'

'I'm so glad they got out. I'd hate anything to happen to them. Those holidays that Richard and I spent with them were so very happy . . .' she paused. '. . . It's hard to believe, isn't it? What's happening over there, I mean. I like the German people. They've never seemed any different to us, the ones I've met. How can they have let that little monster take them over the way they have? And when you think of Spain – it's terrible to think that some of the German boys we met – the Mullers, the Zimmermans – might actually be bombing Richard . . .'

They strolled on in pensive silence.

'It'll be all right, then?' she asked at last. 'About my going to work, I mean. If I can find something.'

'Of course it will. I'll speak to your mother, and we'll talk about it properly when you come home at Christmas.'

'Thank you.'

'But one thing I absolutely insist upon.' He waited until she looked at him, held her eyes with his. 'I know you, my girl. I'm not having any hare-brained schemes about working in a sweat shop or a factory, just to find out what it's like. I have the last say in this, and that's final.'

'Yes, Daddy,' she said, meekly.

Her tone drew his smile. 'You see what happens when you get old? You start to order people about—'

That made her laugh outright, knowing his small conceit, knowing that no one, least of all himself, could seriously think of her father as old. 'Crumpets for tea?' she asked. 'In front of the fire in my room?'

'Do you promise to burn them?'

'To a cinder.' It was a standing joke in the family that her

31

father liked his crumpets practically incinerated. 'I built the fire up specially.'

'Then what are we waiting for?'

As they strode through the gathering darkness towards the welcoming lights of the school, Allie felt suddenly like singing at the top of her voice. It was as if, with the load that her confession had lifted from her heart and a decision about her future taken, a leaden weight had been lifted from her. Life, which had seemed as oppressive and dark as the winter weather, beckoned now with rainbow fingers. She skipped a little to keep up with her father's long-legged stride. He grinned at her and reached for her hand. Laughing like children they ran together the last twenty yards of the gravelled drive.

On Sunday, as promised, Libby and Celia came to take Allie out to tea.

'Darling!' In her swirling, cherry-red coat, a matching bright beret perched on the side of her silver-blonde head, Libby looked as out of place in the swarming corridors of St Leonard's as a bird of paradise in a suburban garden. 'What a lark! We missed one train, and then got on the wrong one – I just utterly forgot my way to this dead-and-alive hole, would you believe it? In the end we had to take a hired car. Well, come on, darling, aren't you ready yet? We're supposed to be taking you out to tea, remember? Even got the Buzzer's permission for it.' Gracelessly she pouched her cheeks and lowered her delicate brows in passable imitation of Miss Busby, the school's principal. '"Why, Elizabeth,"' she boomed, '"I do declare that Switzerland must have been good for you after all. I never thought the day would come when you would ask my permission to do anything."' She pulled a face. 'Old bag. I warned Celia about her. And wasn't she every bit as bad as I said?' she asked.

Celia inclined a shining dark red head, smiling. She was a tallish, slim girl, well groomed and with a striking rather than a pretty face. Her voice when she spoke was a little husky. 'And since she made a point of asking us not to keep Allie out for too long then perhaps we'd better go . . .?'

'Allie isn't ready yet,' said Allie's sister, positively.

'Yes I am.' Allie was not the least bit put out.

'Oh. Are you?' Libby eyed Allie's skirt and jumper in vague surprise. 'Right then. Off we go. I thought we'd go to Plumber's. Sticky buns and things. Marvellous. What do you say?' Typically, before anyone could say anything she had swept down the corridor ahead of them, well aware as she did so of the turned heads and wide eyes of a group of second-formers who were making their decorous way to the music room. She waited for a moment, dramatically posed, for Allie to catch up with her, then tucked her arm into her sister's. 'What's all this I hear about not going to Switzerland, you silly thing? Giving Madame Lascalle's famous establishment *le brush-off*? Whatever next. The poor old bat'll *jette une fit*.' A passing girl giggled and Libby, pleased, threw her a droll look, which had the girl scarlet with the effort of not laughing outright – a pastime strictly forbidden in the corridors of St Leonard's.

Embarrassed, Allie ducked her head. 'I . . .' She wondered for a dismayed moment if Libby were her mother's advance guard.

'Oh, leave the kid alone, Lib,' said Celia good-naturedly. 'We don't all want to be finely polished young ladies, you know. And when it comes down to it, it's none of your jolly business. Now – make yourself useful and lead us to the sticky buns. I'm starving.'

The little tea shop was dark, very warm and quite crowded. The air was heavily fragrant with the yeasty, appetizing smell of baking. A cheerful waitress whose starched cap sat upon her head like an improbably perched, petrified butterfly showed them to a corner table. Allie recognized several acquaintances, pupils from the school being 'treated' by parents, grandparents, aunts, uncles and, in one case, what looked suspiciously like a boyfriend masquerading as a brother, judging by the warm looks and finger touching. She did not miss the eyes that followed Libby's small, striking figure across the room.

'Good Lord.' Once seated Libby reached into her smart little handbag and produced a slim cigarette case. She extracted a cigarette, placed it between her bright lips, lit it, and surveyed the room through a veil of wreathing blue smoke. 'This hasn't changed much, has it?' Her glance, almost proprietary, took in the small leaded glass windows, the cottage furniture, the crisp gingham tablecloths.

Allie smiled slightly. 'It hasn't exactly been a hundred years since you were here.'

Libby blew smoke from her nostrils, smiling wickedly. 'That's true. It only seems like it. This place and its sticky buns was the only oasis of civilization in the dreary desert that was my days at St Leonard's. They do still do them?' she asked, with exaggerated concern.

Allie nodded.

'Good. I'm going to make an utter pig of myself.' She waved a small, marvellously manicured hand. 'Perhaps we should get Plumber's to supply some sticky buns for my party?' she giggled suddenly, like a child.

'Sticky buns and champers,' said Celia, speculatively, 'that'd be something new, wouldn't it?'

Libby threw her head back and laughed, an infectious sound that rang above the buzz of conversation and turned a few smiling faces towards her. 'Spectacular! Oh, it's going to be a wonderful party! The most wonderful party anyone ever had. New Year's Eve and my twenty-first. What a combination! Wasn't I clever to be born on such an appropriate day?'

'I think Mother and Father actually had something to do with that,' said Allie solemnly.

Libby cocked her head on one side, a faint, slightly offended line creasing her brow. 'I do wish you'd be a sport and come for the whole of the Christmas hols, Celia.'

Celia shook her head. 'I've told you, I can't. I do have a family of my own, you know. Mother and Father would be left alone. You know I can't do that. I'll come a couple of days before New Year's.' She turned to Allie, smiling. She had a truly lovely smile that lit her rather severe features like a sudden burst of sunshine. Allie thought it impossible that anyone could resist smiling back. 'Are you looking forward to the party?'

Allie nodded. Libby's coming-of-age had been a subject of anticipation and excitement at Ashdown for the whole of the winter. Only one thing shadowed the thought of it: Richard would not be there. She tried not to think of that. 'Yes, I am.'

They ordered their tea and buns. The waitress remembered Libby. 'Well, miss,' she said with a twinkle in her eye, 'aren't we the smart one now? No climbing out of windows in that outfit, I'll be bound.'

'Climbing out of windows?' Celia raised austerely pencilled brows and widened her rather oddly coloured, sea-green eyes. 'What can she mean? Tales of a misspent youth?'

Libby stubbed out her cigarette. 'Oh, all of us used to do it,' she said, airily. 'We used to break bounds to meet the boys of St Saviour's, down the road. Holding hands and going gooey-eyed over a cold cup of tea. Ugh! The Buzzer used to patrol the place – if you saw her coming, you had to do a rather hurried bunk out of the back window. I did it rather often,' she added, modestly.

'St Saviour's? Wasn't that Richard's school?' asked Celia.

'Yes,' said Allie, and the word came out just a little too quickly.

Celia glanced at her, a gleam of sympathy in her eyes. Libby snorted inelegantly. 'And a fat lot of good it did for him. Don't talk to me about Richard.'

The tea had arrived. Allie ducked her head and tinkered with her teaspoon in her saucer. 'Christmas and the party are going to seem funny without him,' she said in a small voice.

A look of brittle anger flickered across her sister's face. 'Whose fault's that? If the beastly stupid boy and his equally stupid sidekick would rather be in Spain killing people than at my party, then that's their lookout.'

Allie lifted her head, shocked. 'Libby!'

'I hardly think that Richard and Tom went to Spain just to spite you, Lib.' Celia's voice was quiet.

Libby shrugged. 'I think it flatters them both to suggest that they had any logical reason at all,' she snapped.

Celia lifted her dark red head, her eyes fixed on some point at a distance that the small room did not actually afford. '"It is better to die on your feet than to live on your knees,"' she quoted, softly. Then 'A month ago Mosley's blackshirts were attacking Jews in the streets of Whitechapel. Where's the logic in that?'

Libby made a sharp, impatiently angry gesture. 'What's that got to do with us? For God's sake – let's change the subject, shall we?' She snapped open her cigarette case again.

The silence was awkward. Libby's pretty face had set in an arctic mould that Allie recognized all too well. As her sister lit her cigarette with abrupt short temper, Allie glanced in desperation at Celia and was rewarded by that warm, attractive smile.

'I hear that you've decided against university?'

Allie nodded, grateful for the change of subject. She was uncomfortably warm now. She wished that she had taken her coat off. Her fingers were sticky from the buns and she had spilled sugar on her scarf. Ineffectually she tried to brush it off, aware that Celia looked cool, composed and perfectly groomed.

'And you aren't going to Switzerland either?'

'No, I'm not.'

Libby raised caustic eyebrows. 'Two idiots in the family. What did I do to deserve it?'

Celia ignored her. 'What are you going to do then?'

'I – don't know exactly. That is – I want to go to work. But I don't know really what I might be able to do. Daddy offered me a job with Jordan Industries, but that isn't what I want really.' She laughed, a little self-consciously. 'Not that I know what I do want. I just feel that I need to do something different, something of my own. I couldn't bear to do nothing—' She broke off, too late, looking worriedly at her sister.

Libby, who had spent the past year pursuing a little, but not much, ladylike charity work, inspected the fingernails of her small, spread hand. 'Don't be sanctimonious, darling.'

'I'm not being,' Allie said doggedly. 'I'm just saying—'

Celia, unexpectedly, cut her short. 'Correct me if I'm wrong, but don't I recall that you speak German rather well?'

'Well – yes.'

'Then I might be able to help you. If you're interested, of course.'

Both sisters looked at her in surprise.

'In my father's office. He imports wine – you probably know?' Allie nodded. 'I work for him. It's quite interesting – secretary-receptionist stuff. The girl who shares the job with me – we work every other day – is leaving to get married. So we're looking for someone to join us.' She smiled at Allie. 'I really think you might enjoy it, and it would be bliss for Father to have another German speaker around. How about it? Shall I put it to him?'

'I wouldn't want to impose on you.' It was a helpless try. If she had not been able to explain to her father, what hope here? Privilege, unknowing, defended its own. And anyway, what real alternative had she?

'You wouldn't be. On the contrary you'd be doing us a favour. Father would much rather employ someone who's known to him. What do you think, would you be interested?'

Allie smiled, smothered in kindness, helpless to resist. 'Yes. Thank you,' she said, like a small girl offered an apple.

'Right. I'll speak to him and let you know. Now, Libby dear, for heaven's sake,' she added in the same equable, husky voice, 'take that scowl off your face like a good girl and tell us about your party. We promise we won't interrupt you for five whole minutes. Will we?' she appealed to Allie, smiling.

Allie, grinning back, shook her head.

Libby held out for a moment, trying to nurse her ill-humour. Then with a capricious suddenness that was typical of her, she threw back her head and laughed.

'You're an absolute pig, Celia Hinton,' she said. 'And I'm damned if I know why I put up with you.'

'Because I'm the only one who stands up to you, darling,' said Celia. And to Allie it sounded suspiciously like the simple truth.

# CHAPTER THREE

That Christmas at Ashdown was almost entirely dominated by preparations for Libby's party. The comings and goings of caterers and dressmakers, the hiring of the marquee, the ordering of flowers and decorations took precedence over every other activity. Christmas itself came and went as a short lull in the proceedings and very little more. The big house, always spotless, was unnecessarily spring-cleaned by an army of additional help. Mrs Welsh, at first greatly offended by the advent of outside caterers, was soothed by the wholehearted agreement of every member of the family that no one but she should have charge of making the cake – a duty that she took so seriously that it resulted in a total ban on visits to the kitchen. The cake was Mrs Welsh's secret, and not to be seen until the stroke of twelve on New Year's Eve.

And so, with ruffled feelings soothed and a peaceful household restored, the rest of the arrangements were embarked upon. A dance band was hired, complete with a rather precious young man who described himself to Allie as 'dear old England's answer to Crosby, my duck. If you want a singer, you'll have to look elsewhere – I croon.' There were streamers, balloons and bunting by the hundredweight stacked at the back of the garage awaiting the great day. Myra pointed out in some alarm that the guest list appeared to be getting longer every time she looked at it.

Allie enjoyed the excitement thoroughly. She ran errands, checked lists, decorated the big drawing room, took phone calls, ticked off names and stacked boxes of supplies, while Libby changed her mind twice a day about the colour theme for the marquee, the flower decorations for the tables, the order of the dances.

On the day before New Year's Eve, a sudden, odd silence fell upon the house, a stillness accentuated by the heavy, leaden clouds that filled the sky. It was, thought Allie, as she wandered through the lovely, spacious rooms, as if the house were holding its breath. Libby and Celia were upstairs with the dressmaker who was making last-minute adjustments to Libby's dress – a dress that Allie considered with no envy to be the most beautiful she had ever seen. It was of bias-cut white satin, sleek and shining. It clung to every sweet curve of Libby's figure, flared gently, shimmering, from her hips to the floor. It looked – and was – elegant and expensive. Her father had been the only one to ask, innocently, if the dressmaker had forgotten to put the back in it? Allie grinned at the thought. Secretly she was more than a little pleased with her own dress. It too was of satin but of demurer cut than her sister's and in a deep autumnal brown, which suited her less spectacular colouring. She knew that the narrow waist and swirling skirt emphasized her height and slight build. She had spent several very private hours before the mirror in her bedroom, practising the arts of standing and walking gracefully, determined to eliminate the inelegant, hunched stance that the always-too-short St Leonard's uniform seemed to have bequeathed to her. She was tall. She would have to learn to live with it now, or she never would.

While on a Christmas shopping trip she had found and bought a book entitled *The Modern Woman – Beauty, Physical Culture and Hygiene* and had perused it in the privacy of her own room as avidly as if it had been a forbidden romance, jumping guiltily and hiding it beneath her pillow if anyone came into the room. She had arranged her hair a little differently, had experimented tentatively with cosmetics – an effort that had at first prompted her sister to ask her, a little uncharitably, if she had had strawberry jam for breakfast? Celia had then, with Myra's blessing, taken a kindly hand and the results had been far from displeasing. This party was to be Allie's first, real grown-up affair. She could not have been happier had it been her own coming-of-age. She was more than excited; she was almost sick with anticipation. Tomorrow, first thing in the morning, the men would come to erect the great marquee, build the stage for the musicians, set out the tables and chairs. An enormous net of balloons was to be stretched out above the heads of the dancers, to be released at midnight. The marquee itself was to be decorated in pink, silver and white . . .

Tomorrow.

It seemed an age away.

She could not, as everyone else seemed thankful to do, rest. She wandered into the drawing room. Ashdown was a gracious house, built in late Victorian times, the rooms big and high-ceilinged. The drawing room was Allie's favourite. It ran the depth of the house, the long windows at the front overlooking the sweep of the drive and the front lawn upon which she could see now the enormous decorated Christmas tree glittering in a shaft of thin, wintry sunshine that pierced the clouds, while the french windows at the back gave on to a delightful, lofty conservatory, built and stocked by the first owner of the house and one of the passions of Myra Jordan's life. Through the years of Allie's childhood it had always been to her a place of enchantment. She loved the green, filtered light, the soft, damply warm atmosphere. Great palm fronds brushed the yellowish glass of the roof. An old vine curtained the wall, curled in tendrils around the gnarled trunks of other exotic trees and plants. The conservatory had been the main reason why Myra and Robert Jordan had bought the house more than twenty years before. To Allie, its allure had never died; it was a fairy-story corner of green nooks and crannies, warm silence and happy memories. She smiled as she looked at it now. It looked smaller, she thought, remembering the long, fanciful afternoons of childhood. But then, everything did.

She peered through the lacework of leaves into the garden. Tomorrow the marquee would stand there. Tomorrow! In the grip of a swift and irresistible surge of excitement, Allie hugged herself, took a few swift, dancing steps, humming softly to herself a catchy, popular tune. She loved to dance. Tomorrow she would dance every dance. Every single dance. She stopped, the echoes of the tune she had been humming still in her head: Richard's favourite song. As clearly as if he had been in the room, she heard his voice, slightly off key – 'Yes, sir, that's my baby. No, sir, don't mean maybe . . .' She nibbled her lip, the excitement curdling within her. Richard and Tom were in besieged Madrid. The Condor Squadron – German planes, German pilots, German expertise – were bombing and strafing. Practising, some said, for other targets. The pleasurable anticipation of a moment before ebbed from her like a receding tide, leaving her stranded on a familiar, bleak shore of worry. Her hands dropped to her side. In the garden, Browning was clipping the hedge, the sound of his shears sharp and loud in the winter air. From inside the house someone was calling her: 'Allie. Al – lie.'

Pushing her hair from her eyes she went back into the drawing room. 'Coming.'

Inevitably, to begin with, everything went wrong. The men were late in coming to erect the marquee, the flowers were the wrong shade of pink and there weren't enough of them, Libby did not like the way the hairdresser had done her hair and there was no lunch because Mrs Welsh was absorbed in the finishing touches to the cake. By late afternoon it was perfectly obvious that nothing and no one was going to be ready in time. Then, in a final flurry of activity the last pieces of the puzzle dropped into place and, miraculously, all was well.

Just before eight, the family and Celia assembled in the drawing room for a first glass of champagne. The clouds of the previous day had lifted and it was a clear, cold evening. The lanterns that adorned house and garden sparkled in the frosty air. From the marquee came the sound of the band tuning up. There was a crackle of static, then 'One, two, three,' said a man's voice. A piano tinkled, a saxophone played a snatch of tune. Through the double doors of the drawing room, Libby made a well-timed entrance, striking a prettily self-conscious pose, turning slowly to display shimmering perfection. 'Will I do?'

'Darling, you look lovely.' Myra's words were, in fact, an

understatement. Libby looked stunning. Her excitement and pleasure at being the centre of so much attention served to heighten her natural beauty. The dress was a marvel. She picked up her glass and toasted them all, her eyes sparkling. 'Here's to a night to remember.'

On the drive, the scrunch of tyres heralded the first guests.

The problem, Allie thought much later, was not so much that the advice offered by her unknown mentors in *The Modern Woman* had not worked, but that it had worked a little too well, and on entirely the wrong person. Arthur Millson's rather nasal voice and silly, yelping laugh had driven her to distraction ever since they had joined the tennis club together ten years ago. She had been listening to the voice – and the laugh – now for more than an hour. And she had had enough.

'. . . I must say, Al, you're looking quite topping . . .' It must have been, she thought, quite the hundredth time he'd used the word – he applied it to everything from the fishing rod his mother had given him for Christmas to the dance band and the champagne. She smiled politely. 'Bit different from the old tennis shorts, what? Remember the day you fell into those beastly stinging nettles?'

Allie opened her mouth to tell him that, in fact, there were few things that she wanted to remember less, then, trapped as always by her infuriating inability to say anything that might upset anyone, shut it again.

'Who's the chappie that Libby's dancing with?' Arthur craned his neck, rather rudely. 'He's not local, is he? Not one of the crowd? Can't say I've ever seen him before.'

Allie, too, had been watching her sister. The young man with whom Libby was dancing – with whom, indeed, she had danced a noticeable number of times during the evening – was tall, and as fair-headed as she was herself, impeccable in his white tie and tails. They made a striking pair.

'His name's Edward something – Mayhew or Maybury or something. He came with Celia's crowd. He's very good-looking, isn't he?'

'Mm.' Arthur chose not to pursue that. 'Celia? Do I know her?'

'Probably not. Libby met her in Switzerland. They "finished" together. They're great friends – I like her a lot. There she is, dancing over there, by the band. The tall red-headed girl in green.'

'She doesn't look very happy. If Edward what's-his-name came with her, then he's certainly having a better time than she is.'

This was self-evidently true. Celia's thin face was unsmiling, her mouth sombre. She was dancing stiffly, an arm's length away from her partner – a young man whom Allie vaguely remembered being introduced as Peter – her eyes fixed in that disconcerting way that she sometimes had on some point in a distance that no one else could perceive.

The band's rhythm changed. The sleek-haired singer, who reminded Allie irresistibly of a tailor's dummy, confided to the microphone that he was nobody's sweetheart now . . .

'Oh, I say, a quickstep. My favourite. Well . . .' Arthur yelped, self-consciously '. . . actually the only dance I can do. Come on, old girl – I'll give you a turn around the floor.'

Five minutes later, in self-defence, Allie decided that enough was quite enough, good manners notwithstanding. Gently but very firmly indeed, she excused herself and went to join her mother and father who were sitting at a table with Libby, Celia and the two young men. Libby was laughing, flirting quite openly with Edward Maybury, who appeared utterly dazzled by her. He could not take his eyes from her small, vivacious face. Allie had the distinct impression that for him no one else in the room existed. Celia watched with cool eyes in which Allie could discern no expression at all. Certainly there was something amiss with Celia. It was unlike her to be moody. Allie wondered if perhaps she had designs on Edward Maybury herself – if she had, then patently she had lost before the game had truly started. Undoubtedly she was paying no attention to Peter, the young man who sat beside her; she sipped her champagne in silence, her face brooding, a still island in a noisy sea of merriment. Allie was not the only one to notice it.

'Is something wrong, Celia?' Myra's voice was concerned. She was in her favourite blue; she looked almost as beautiful as her elder daughter.

Celia shook her head, then shrugged. 'I've got a bit of a headache to tell the truth. I think I might go and lie down for a while.'

'What a pity,' Myra began. 'Perhaps you should—'

'Nonsense.' Robert Jordan stood up. The band had swung into the melodic 'These Foolish Things'. He extended a hand, smiling. 'We can't have pretty girls headaching on a night like this. Whatever next? Come and treat an old man to a dance.'

Celia hesitated for a moment, then, obviously captive to good manners, rose to dance with her host. In the distance Allie saw Arthur bearing down on her again. 'Dammit!' she said under her breath, but not quite quietly enough. Libby pealed with laughter, Myra frowned repressively. In desperation Allie reached for the deserted Peter's hand. 'I'll be your friend for life if you'll dance with me,' she hissed urgently, aware of her mother's brilliant, astonished eyes. 'Just once round the floor. Please!'

He was too much a gentleman to refuse such an appeal. He stood up smiling, offering his arm and they stepped onto the floor past a perspiring and disappointed-looking Arthur. Allie firmly suppressed her conscience and gave herself up to the pleasure of dancing. She had always loved to dance – and Peter, it soon became apparent, was a very good dancer indeed. It did not matter in the least that he did not attempt to manufacture a conversation as they swept and spun around the floor. On the contrary, she was grateful for his easy silence. It enabled her almost to detach herself from him, to lose herself entirely in the pleasant physical sensation of their shared movement. They danced easily and fluently, carried by the music into an intricate, moving pattern that was a delight to them both. They hardly paused as the music died, changed tempo, lifted again. It was several dances later that the band stopped for quick refreshment and Peter, smiling, offered his escort back to the table.

'Thank you,' he said pleasantly. 'I really enjoyed that.'

Allie flushed. Released from the spell of the music she felt gauche and awkward again, ashamed of the way that she had wished herself upon him. She was suddenly and painfully embarrassed by the sensations that the last minutes had aroused in her, sensations that, quite truthfully, had nothing to do with the particular man with whom she had been dancing, but that stemmed entirely from those magical, sensual moments when his body had moved in perfect harmony with her own. An awful excitement seemed to be thumping through her heart with her blood, disturbing and confusing her. Clumsily she tripped over her own feet as she left the dance floor, blushing violently as Peter good-naturedly took her arm to steer her back to her parents' table. She shivered a little. He laughed.

'Not cold, surely?' The tent was heated with paraffin stoves, and the press of bodies had made the atmosphere almost tropical.

She shook her head. At the table she could see Arthur talking earnestly with her mother, who looked, beneath a veneer of polite interest, very bored indeed. Libby and Edward, her father and Celia were still on the dance floor. As the music started again, Allie caught sight of Celia's face as she drifted past, her expression still distant and unhappy, almost sullen. Allie's mind hardly registered it. She could only see the awful Arthur, waiting for her, with his clammy hands and silly, neighing laugh. Quite incontrovertibly, she knew that under no circumstances could she expose the surprising, frightening, delightful web of emotional and physical sensation that had been so suddenly woven about her to that painfully insensitive gaze. She stopped.

'I need to powder my nose. Tell the others I won't be long, would you?' and she slipped away from him, through the flap of the great tent and out into the freezing night. Clouds had built from the north, and a first, stinging flurry

46

of snow swirled spitefully in the lamplight as she hurried across the rimed grass to the house, the freezing air striking like steel on her warm, damp skin. The house was deserted. The noise of revelry faded behind her as she shut the door. She had had enough champagne to feel pleasantly detached; she had no desire for the moment but to be alone. She hoped to heaven, fervently, that Arthur would not follow her . . .

She wandered into the drawing room. The glasses from which they had drunk earlier were on a small table. One of them was half full. She picked it up and sipped, wrinkling her nose at the taste of flat, warm champagne. She carried the glass into the dim conservatory. Through the curtain of vine leaves the garden with the lantern light glittering on the still-falling snow was like fairyland. Above the faint hubbub of voices, music rose. She folded her arms across her breasts and swayed softly in the darkness, humming.

The drawing-room door opened.

She froze, visions of Arthur Millson's pale and pudgy face filling her mind.

Footsteps approached the conservatory.

Quicker than thought she fled to the farthest corner, slipping into darkness behind a trailing curtain of vine leaves. As she stood, tense as a spring, her heart thumping, memories of a thousand games of hide-and-seek slipped through her mind – 'Ninety-nine, a hundred – *coming* . . .'

Someone entered the conservatory, his footsteps clicking briskly on the tile floor. Then she froze utterly as she heard a second, lighter set of steps, heard, too, a faint, sighing breath, the rustle of their clothing as the two turned into each other's arms. Allie felt a dreadful warmth steal through her body and up into her face. She had read often enough of people wishing that the earth might swallow them up; she had never before experienced it. She shrank back into the shadows. She could not, absolutely could not, reveal herself, could not bring herself to be the cause of such awful embarrassment. Veiled by foliage she could see reflected in the window the shimmering outline of the lovers, the man's head bent, the woman's hand caressing his face. She shut

47

her eyes. There came the sound of a sharp, almost violent movement and a familiar, husky voice said, 'And that, I take it, is supposed to make it all right?'

Celia's voice, instantly recognizable for all its savage harshness. In her surprise Allie almost betrayed herself, and was so taken aback that the shock of recognition of the second voice, even more familiar and distinctive than the first, was delayed by a split second.

'My darling – please – what do you expect? We knew it would be difficult . . .'

Allie reached out a hand and steadied herself against the wall, not believing her ears. Refusing to believe.

Celia uttered a bark of laughter. 'Difficult?' she said bitterly. 'Is that the best you can manage? Try impossible. Try bloody impossible.'

'Celia, Celia . . .' Allie's father's voice was gently pleading. 'You know that we have to be careful. We've both known, all along, that it would be—'

'Difficult,' supplied Celia with brittle acidity. She turned away from him, her shoulders hunched against him, her arms crossed tightly against her breasts, shutting him out. 'Of course.'

'Celia. Darling—' Robert Jordan reached for her. She neither turned nor pulled away but after a moment leaned back into his embrace, her head tilted back onto his shoulder. In the faint light, translucent pearls of moisture glistened on her cheeks. 'I can't stand it,' she said.

Robert cradled her gently, his cheek against her hair, his hands still and strong on her breasts. He said nothing.

'You're right, of course. I know it,' Celia said at last, her voice drained, 'but, Robert, I'm simply not strong enough. I swear it will drive me mad – being in the same house with you, not being able to touch you, talk to you, love you as I want to. When I'm with you there is nothing but pain. When I leave you there is nothing but emptiness. There is no place for me. You are destroying me—'

Roughly Robert spun her to face him, bent his mouth to hers to stop the words. 'Don't!' There was an edge of violence in the word.

In her hiding place Allie, her body clenched like a fist, her face an agony, covered her ears with hands that shook, squeezed her eyes shut until bright stars wheeled about her.

A long time later she lifted her head. She was alone. The lanterns around the marquee were dancing and swinging in a fresh-lifted breeze, the light reflecting on spasmodic flurries of snow. Shadows swayed, grotesque, tentacled plant-shadows that stretched and reached around her as if with life. Her body ached with tension, here eyes were hot and dry. Blindly she left the conservatory, stood for a moment of dazed uncertainty in the drawing room. She could not go back to the party. She could not face her father and Celia. She could not face anyone. From beyond the door she heard the sound of a giggle, a sharp command: 'You be careful now, Maxwell. You drop this and I'll skin you.'

Allie opened the door. Mrs Welsh and one of the young waitresses were bearing with care a huge board upon which rested a most splendid confection of white and silver adorned with an enormous key. On seeing Allie, Mrs Welsh stopped, her face concerned.

'You all right, Miss Allie?'

Allie struggled for a moment. 'I'm – no, I'm not, actually, Welshy. I feel rather unwell.'

'Oh, deary me. Here, Maxwell, get this thing onto the table for a minute—'

'No, really.' Allie held up a hand. The hall light seemed unbearably bright. She could think of nothing but her desire to get away to her own room, to darkness and to peace. 'I just need to rest. Too much champagne, I expect. I'd be pleased if you'd tell Mother that I've gone to bed. But, please, don't worry her. And ask her not to disturb me, would you? I'll be all right in the morning—'

She fled to the stairs, the satin of her dress swishing at each step. She felt Mrs Welsh's worried eyes as they followed her up to the landing. Inside her own room at last, she leaned back on the closed door, her eyes tight shut. In the garden there was a sudden, expectant hush. Then the old church clock began its chime, mellow and musical in the quiet air. *One, two, three* . . .

Allie moved to the window. The brightly lit marquee was quiet for this moment as the revellers listened for that all-important stroke that would usher in the new year and Elizabeth Jordan's twenty-first birthday.

. . . *nine, ten, eleven, twelve*. It was 1937.

There was a tremendous burst of cheering. The band struck up 'Auld Lang Syne'. Voices were raised, roaring the old tune. Shadows leapt and flickered on the canvas walls.

Allie leaned her hot forehead against the cold, misted glass. She could see nothing, hear nothing, but the insistent, terrible tableau of her father and Celia Hinton.

The revelry was at its height now. With stamping, clapping rhythm the guests were serenading Libby: 'For she's a jolly good fellow . . .' Fleetingly Allie wished that she were there to kiss her sister, to give her the small gold locket she had bought for her to commemorate the day. She hoped that Libby would not miss her, knew, with the faintest twist of self-pity, that she would not.

As she watched, a group of rowdy young people, Libby in their midst, burst from the marquee into the pool of light cast by the lanterns onto the snowy lawn. Despite the cold, two of the young men had taken off their jackets and their white shirts blazed brilliantly in the lantern glow. Edward Maybury's bright head shone in the light. He was holding Libby's hand. Laughing and shouting the crowd streamed down the garden towards the river. One of the girls stumbled in her high-heeled shoes, bent to pull them off and toss them into the bushes before shrieking off after the others. They flickered like shadows through the orchard, their young, excited voices echoing in the darkness. Allie heard the splashes as two of the punts were launched, the shouts as the company, at risk of life, limb and expensive apparel, clambered into them.

She left the window, her movements slow, and stretched out upon the bed, the gleaming brown satin of which she had been so proud crumpled about her as she stared with wide, unfocused eyes at the flickering pattern of light and shade that moved upon the high ceiling.

## PART TWO

## SPRING 1937

## CHAPTER FOUR

The same marquee in which Libby had celebrated her twenty-first birthday was re-erected on the lawns of Ashdown in the gentle sunshine of May that same year.

'We were actually rather lucky to get it.' Myra was sitting at the dining-room table, her chin resting upon one well-shaped hand, a pen in the other, her attention on a sheaf of papers in front of her. 'With the weather so good, everyone's had the same idea, I suppose. They've charged us over the odds, of course – but, well, one doesn't cele-brate a coronation every day, does one? It could be thirty years before there's another, so we might as well make a splash of it. And the New Year's affair was such an enormous success . . .' She lifted her head and regarded the still figure of her husband with bright and slightly ex-asperated eyes. 'Am I talking to myself?' she asked mildly.

Robert Jordan was standing with his back to her, looking into the garden, which lay warmly tranquil in the early summer sunshine. Through the open window came the sound of a racket striking a tennis ball, a call, a shout of laughter. 'I'm sorry, my dear. What did you say?'

'I said—' Myra laughed suddenly. 'Oh, it really doesn't matter.' She laid down her pen, pushed her chair back and came to join him at the window, her every movement perfectly graceful, the fine, pale blue wool of her dress complementing marvellously the sheened silver of her hair. As she stood with him watching the young people on the tennis court below the terrace, Allie tossed the ball into the air and served thunderously to Edward, who hastily stuck his racket in the way of the hurtling ball and was rewarded by seeing it shoot skywards, skitter through the branches of the new-leafed oak tree and drop into the flower bed beneath.

'Honestly, Allie! Anyone'd think you were trying for Wimbledon!' Libby's laughing voice rang in the still air. 'We're in danger of our lives on this side of the net!'

Allie gave a small, downturned smile, crossed over to the other court and stood, racket swinging, as she waited for the others to sort themselves out. Her partner gave a silly, yelping laugh and called across to her.

'Bet you a quid you can't do that again.'

'You're on.' Allie lined up her racket.

In mock terror Libby shrieked and scuttled across the court. 'Oh, no you don't. Not at me. Edward, come on, do the gentlemanly thing – I don't give a toss what the rules say – you take it.'

As Edward, clowning terror, moved across the court a movement beneath the oak tree caught Robert's eye and he experienced the familiar, involuntary, almost physical shock that the sight of Celia always produced in him. Her tall, slim figure emerged from the dappled shade of the tree as if materializing from the shadows. She picked up the ball that lay in the flower bed and stood tossing it idly in her hand, smiling a little as she watched the players. Libby waved, and called. Allie, apparently engrossed, ignored her. The ball rose, the racket sang with every aggressive ounce of energy and effort the girl could muster behind it.

Edward stepped back. 'I say, old girl.' He sounded truly aggrieved. 'Steady on!'

Allie laughed, the sound high and a little harsh, and her father's attention was drawn from Celia to his daughter, a straight, thoughtful line drawn between his brows. It struck him, not for the first time, that it had been a long time since he had heard Allie laugh in her old, happily infectious way, a long time, too, since they had spoken together without strain. There had been about her, over these past few months, a brittle and defiant shield that defeated any attempt to pierce it and behind which the Allie he had always known seemed to have disappeared entirely.

He had been utterly astounded when Allie, soon after her eighteenth birthday in February, had announced that she had made up her mind not to return to St Leonard's after the Easter holidays to take her final examinations. Since she was not going to university after all, she had said, taking full advantage of what she well knew was her father's tender conscience over that issue, then she could see no point in continuing her education. No amount of argument would shift her. It had been Myra, practical as always, who, quoting horses and water, had pointed out that it would be a useless exercise to force the girl back to school. And so Allie had stayed home – and sometimes Robert thought it was like having a young stranger in the house. It disturbed and puzzled him, this change in his favourite child. Allie was by turns morosely moody and excessively bright, withdrawn and flamboyantly gay. With certainty, her father sensed, beneath the uncharacteristic and sometimes highly irritating behaviour, a core of bleak pain, the cause of which he could not discover since Allie, when taxed, denied absolutely its existence. Trying to ignore his own hurt at his daughter's oddly changed behaviour, he had waited patiently, unable to believe that, in the end, she would not come to him with her troubles as she always had before. But gradually now he was coming to admit that, for a reason that was totally beyond him, their old, special, easy relationship was gone. Any conversation he had managed to hold with her over the past few months had been, on Allie's side, flippantly inconsequential, peppered with racy slang and silly jokes. Her only interests, it seemed, were dance music and rather silly young men in fast cars.

Just once, a week or so ago, the old Allie had shown herself briefly, only to withdraw again almost immediately. It had been at the end of April, when the reports had come through about the Fascist bombing of a small town in Spain called Guernica. They had all listened, shocked, as the radio announcer's dispassionate voice had described the brutal and fiery death of this small market town. Wave after wave of bombers, German-built and German-piloted, and timed like clockwork to appear every twenty minutes for three hours, swept from the bright springtime sky to destroy the town and machine-gun its fleeing, terrified inhabitants. Libby, her hands to her ears, had left the room before the report was finished. Myra, her face almost expressionless, had heard the bulletin to the end, then, wordless, followed her elder daughter, leaving Robert alone with Allie. Robert, swearing softly, had turned off the wireless with a sharp, angry movement. The silence that ensued had been charged with anger, outrage and, somewhere, buried deep, the first faint stirrings of fear. Allie had been sitting bolt upright on the sofa, her face bone-white, her brown hair veiling one side of her face, her only movement a rhythmic, nervous clenching and relaxing of her left hand. So still was she that it had taken a moment for Robert to realize that her cheeks were shining with tears.

'Allie, darling, you mustn't—'

'Children,' she said. 'Women with babies. Blown to pieces. Machine-gunned. *Machine-gunned!* Oh, Daddy—' She had been in his arms in a second, sobbing, her face buried in his shoulder. 'It's so horrible!'

Briefly and, despite the circumstances, with a lift of happiness, he had held her, stroking her hair. Then, as the storm subsided, he had felt the change in her. In one movement she had stiffened and pulled away from him, turning away, dashing a hand across her face.

'I'm sorry. That was stupid.' Her voice had been harsh, totally withdrawn.

'Allie . . .'

'I'm all right. You know me. I always was a grizzler. I'd better go and do some running repairs on my face. The gang'll be here in a minute.' She had left him, standing alone, with no backward glance.

He watched her now as, the game over, she threw a white cardigan over her tennis dress and strolled with the others towards the house. Celia had disappeared. In a sudden eruption of sound and flying gravel, a small sports car skidded up the drive and came to a screeching halt, horn blaring stridently. It was driven by a young man whom Robert recognized with a lowering of his brows and a slight tightening of his mouth. He had disliked young Ray Cheshire on sight, remarking to Myra that too much money and very little sense was not a combination that appealed to him in his daughter's friends. Allie walked over to the car and stood talking to the driver for a few moments. Robert saw her glance once or twice towards the house as she spoke. Finally she stepped back and the little car, engine growling, leapt forward, made a skidding turn and disappeared down the drive. Allie rejoined her sister and the young men. Robert saw Libby stop, looking at Allie in surprise, obviously startled by something that she had said. Allie shrugged in that odd, defiant way that was becoming all too familiar. Libby's hands lifted to heaven as she appealed to Edward. Allie turned and left them, coming towards the house.

Myra, too, had been watching. 'I wonder what all that was about.' Then, following Robert's own thoughts with uncanny accuracy, 'I can't think where Allie found these new – friends – of hers.'

He shook his head.

Myra walked to the table, stood tinkering absently with the papers upon it. 'Robert?'

'Mm?'

'I think perhaps you ought to have a word with Allie. I'm not at all sure that these people – this "gang" of hers – are altogether suitable.'

The door slammed. They heard Allie's light, quick footsteps as they crossed the hall and she ran up the stairs, two at a time.

'I think, too,' added Myra firmly, 'that the time has come for us to settle Allie's immediate future. It seems to me that we've given her quite enough leeway. Since she shows no interest in anything herself, I feel strongly that we should take a hand. For the child's own good.'

'You mean Sir Brian Hinton's offer?'

'Exactly. I think it most kind of Celia, and of her father. I

55

am of the convinced opinion that Allie should take advantage of Sir Brian's offer. I never thought the day would come when I would say about Alexandra that she needed steadying down – but I'm saying it now.' She lifted her smooth head and waited for her husband's agreement. 'This job with Sir Brian is exactly what she needs.'

Robert cleared his throat. 'I—' He stopped, started afresh. 'Allie – doesn't seem all that keen on the idea.'

Myra's voice sharpened. 'Robert, my dear, I think, extraordinary though it seems, that you'd be hard put to find anything that Allie is "all that keen on" just at the moment, apart from very loud dance music and equally loud young men.' She lifted her hands in a graceful gesture of exasperation and sank into a nearby chair. 'Really, she is the most tiresome and unpredictable child. I can't imagine what's got into her. I almost preferred her socialist phase . . .' She glanced at Robert, a half-smile quirking her pretty mouth. 'All right, that's an exaggeration. Anything would be better than that. But, nevertheless, I am concerned about her. I felt we were wrong to give in to her over Switzerland, and it seems to me that I'm being proved right. We've been too lax with her, Robert, and now we're paying the penalty. I'm absolutely determined that she must be taken in hand. Between Richard and Allie—' she sighed suddenly and laid her head back on the chair '—I really can't see what we've done to deserve this kind of behaviour from them both.'

'Darling, I hardly think—'

She ignored his interruption. 'She must be given no choice in the matter. In fact—' suddenly brisk, she stood up and reached among the papers on the table '—I've written a draft here, a letter to Sir Brian accepting the position he has offered.'

'Isn't that a little high-handed?'

The blue eyes were undisturbed. 'Of course it is. But do you have anything else to suggest?'

He was silent.

'It's settled then,' Myra said crisply. 'There's no need to

56

say anything to Allie yet, of course. We'll leave it for a few days, shall we? Until after the celebrations. I'm sure we can rely on Celia to help us to persuade her that—'

As if conjured up by her name, the door opened to frame Celia against the sunlight that was reflected in a shining pool on the polished floor of the hall. Seeing them, the girl stopped, confused.

'Oh – I'm sorry – I didn't realize there was anyone here . . .'

'Come in, my dear. As a matter of fact we were just talking about you.'

Celia looked startled. Her eyes flickered to Robert and away. 'About me?'

Myra smiled and extended a hand. 'You and I are going to enter a conspiracy.'

'We are?' Celia was dressed in dark green, a colour that suited her well. Her skin, which never took the sun, was a startling alabaster white.

'I think perhaps I'd better leave you to it.' Robert strode past the girl, barely glancing at her. 'I'll see you at lunch.'

Celia watched him to the door, in the depths of her eyes an enigmatic spark that glittered disturbingly for a moment before, her face pleasantly expressionless, she turned back to Myra.

Upstairs, Allie heard the murmur of voices below her, heard the opening and closing of the dining-room door and the sound of her father's firm footsteps in the hall. She was standing at the back window of her bedroom, still in her tennis dress, her racket and cardigan discarded upon the bed. She heard the sound of her father slowly mounting the stairs. She stiffened. The footfalls stopped on the landing outside her room.

'Allie? Allie, are you there?'

She did not reply.

'Allie?'

Almost without thought, she flew across the room and flattened herself against the wall behind the door. A couple of seconds later the door opened a little as her father

57

surveyed the apparently empty room. She stood very still, scarcely breathing. The door closed, softly. She waited until she heard him go back down the stairs before she moved. At last, satisfied that he would not come back, she took up again her position by the window.

The marquee was up. With its swooping, pointed roof, pennants fluttering from each corner and its sloping sides, it looked like something from a medieval masque, requiring only a tilting ground to complete the picture. Her breath misted the glass. She rubbed at it with one finger, imagining knights on caparisoned chargers, their lances glittering in the sun, and graceful ladies offering scarves and gloves as tokens – in a way that was fast becoming a habit, she manufactured inconsequential thoughts and allowed them to crowd her mind in defence against the anxious, almost pleading note she had heard in her father's voice as he had spoken her name. She lifted her chin. He didn't deserve sympathy. He didn't deserve anything. And nothing, nothing in this world, was going to force her to stay for the coronation party tomorrow night. She knew there would be hell to pay when they discovered that she had made other arrangements, but she didn't care. Nothing would induce her to stay, to have the buried and festering memories of that other night revived, to watch her father – and Celia. Her wide, straight mouth hardened. If other people didn't care what they did, what hurt or damage they caused, why should she? By hook or by crook she would go with Ray and the others. And she would have a good time. She would.

With a sudden impatient, distracted movement, she turned from the window and flung herself upon the bed. On the bedside table lay several magazines, on the front of each one a picture of those most unprepared of monarchs – King George VI and his pretty Scots queen, Elizabeth. Allie rolled onto her stomach, her chin propped on her hands. Somewhere in Europe, a lonely man waited to marry the woman he loved, a woman for whom he had sacrificed not just a throne and a lifetime's preparation for that throne but a people's respect and love at a time when Europe trembled again with presentiments of war. Allie wondered if he was happy. If he would ever be happy. Despite the younger generation's general sympathy for the couple – after all, wasn't their story every romantic Hollywood film rolled into one? – Allie had her doubts. She wondered, not for the first time, at the strength of a love that could make such a sacrifice.

And her father? Always it came back to her father. How would he choose, if he were forced? Who – or what – did he truly love? The sense of bitter betrayal that had poisoned her every waking moment since that night in the conservatory rose again, acid in her throat. Until that moment Allie had never questioned, had hardly indeed been aware, that the very basis of her life was her absolute faith in her father and her mother, both separately and together: their separate strengths, perhaps even their weaknesses, their love, their support, their indivisible unity. To deny any one of these things was to deny them all. It was to her young mind perfectly simple: you could not love two people at once. Not in the way that adults were supposed to love one another. So her father, of all people, was living a lie every minute of every day. He and Celia had shattered not only her faith in him but, by association, in everything else as well. Sometimes she felt she hated him for it, though perhaps not surprisingly it was for Celia that she reserved her cold, wholehearted detestation. It had become a game to hide it, to reserve for unexpected moments those quiet barbs that brought to Celia's eyes a sudden, astonished flash of pain. Thinking of it now, Allie tried to feel some satisfaction for the just punishment she had on occasion been able to exact. To her own surprise, instead she buried her face suddenly in her hands to hide the tears.

It was at dinner that evening that Allie broke the news to her parents that she had made other arrangements for Coronation Day. With the echoes of her own too-loud voice still in her ears, she stabbed viciously at a piece of potato, head down, her cheeks bright with hectic colour.

Very precisely Myra laid aside her knife and fork. 'I beg your pardon?'

'I'm – we're – going to London. To watch the procession.'

Myra considered. 'Well, that's all right. I don't see why not. You can be back here perfectly well in time for the evening—'

'Mother, I told you – Ray's got tickets for the Coronation Ball – a dinner-dance thing – at the Ace of Spades. You've heaps of people coming here.' Allie's voice verged on desperation. 'You won't miss me.'

Silence hung, drumming like rain, about the table. Libby stole a glance at her mother. Robert was watching Allie, who resolutely refused to lift her eyes from her dinner plate. At that moment, he thought with a pang, she looked exactly the rebellious child that she was.

Myra took a slow, audible breath. 'Am I to understand that you have made these plans, deliberately, behind our backs? That you never intended . . .' the pause was slight and acid '. . . to grace us with your presence?'

With her mouth set in defiance, Allie gave an almost imperceptible shrug. She did not raise her eyes. Libby, watching her mother, winced.

'Alexandra, you will kindly look at me when I'm speaking to you.'

With an effort Allie lifted her head.

'I have absolutely no objection,' her mother said icily, 'to your going into town tomorrow to watch the procession. On the contrary, in the circumstances, I might say that your absence might be positively beneficial. You will, however, be home here by seven, in good time to ready yourself to receive our guests at eight o'clock. Is that clear?'

The battle in Allie's face was open and painful to watch. 'Yes, Mother,' she said, and lowered her eyes again to her plate.

The rest of the meal was taken almost entirely in silence.

'Right, a few more bubbles of Dutch courage . . .'

Squashed into the telephone box, Allie obediently and a little dizzily tilted her head back and let the warm champagne trickle from the bottle into her mouth. The taste reminded her of something, but she could not for the moment place the memory.

'. . . and off we go. Come on, old thing. You can remember your own telephone number, can't you?'

To Allie's inexpressible relief, it was Mrs Welsh who answered the phone. She pressed the button and the pennies clattered into the box.

'Hello – Welshy? It's me – yes, Allie—' She clamped a hand over the mouthpiece as Ray, champagne bottle held aloft, nuzzled her ear inexpertly. Outside the booth, laughing faces were pressed to the glass, grotesquely distorted. She giggled explosively. 'Sorry, Welshy, I can't hear very well. The noise is awful.' She made furious, dismissive gestures at Ray, who in reply slid his arm around her waist and started on her ear again. 'Look, Welshy, I know it's awful of me but I'm afraid I'm . . .' she hesitated '. . . going to be late,' she finished. Ray growled at her. 'Yes – there's a bus strike, you see, and there are just millions of people about. Taxis are just impossible – oh, yes thanks, it was lovely. The Queen looked marvellous. She's such a dear. What? Oh, no, don't bother.' A note of panic crept into her voice. 'I haven't long, and I haven't any more change, don't call anybody – could you just be a love and tell them that I'm going to be late? I know Mother will be furious, but – oh, thank you, Welshy, you're an angel. We're stuck in Trafalgar Square, and the crowds are really awful – I'll be home as soon as I can. Yes, yes, I will – oh, and Welshy? I'll call again if it looks as if I'm going to be really late, all right? Lovely. Thank you. I will. 'Bye.' She cradled the receiver.

Ray took her hand and kissed it with drunken courtesy. 'You lie like the proverbial trooper, my dear. Something greatly to be admired in a girl, I always say. Your carriage awaits.' He waved his hand at the small MG that led the parade of cars that were parked by the kerb. 'Cinderella, you *shall* go to the ball!'

Much later, when she knew that the party at home would be well under way, Allie telephoned again, from the Ace of Spades roadhouse, the door of the kiosk closed firmly on the revelry outside. The telephone rang for a long time before anyone answered, and then it was a voice that she did not immediately recognize. She pressed the button.

'Hello? Hello, who's that?'

'Bestworth's the name. Did you want one of the Jordans? There's a bit of a shindig on here, but I daresay I could . . .?'

'No, no, Uncle Bertie, don't bother. It's me. Allie.'

'God bless my soul. Allie? Where are you? Your mother and father have been very worried . . .'

'I'm – well, it's perfectly awful, Uncle Bertie. A friend of mine was giving me a lift back from town and his car's broken down. We're stuck in this garage in the middle of nowhere . . .' Suddenly and inexplicably sober, the anxiety in her voice owed nothing to play-acting. 'I know they must be worried. And absolutely furious, I expect. I promised to be home for the party.'

'Don't worry, my dear. Where are you? I'll come and fetch you. We'll have you home in the shake of a guinea-pig's tail, eh?'

For a dreadful moment her mind stopped working altogether.

'Hello? Allie? Are you there?'

'Hello, y-yes, I'm here. Th-there seems to be something wrong with this phone. I can't hear you very well.'

'I said I'd come and fetch you,' bellowed her uncle, almost deafening her. 'Where are you?'

'Oh, no, I couldn't possibly let you do that. It's bad enough that I can't be at the party. Mother'll kill me if I drag you away too. If you'd just tell her – well, explain for me? Tell her I'll be home as soon as I can.' In her sudden, miserably sobered state the whole silly deception seemed shoddy and childish. Desperately Allie found herself wishing that she had never embarked upon it.

'Well, if you're sure?' asked her uncle.

'Yes, I'm sure. I'll see you later, I expect.'

'Perhaps you'd better let me know where you are? Just in case—' His voice was interrupted by the regular pips that denoted that their time was up.

'Sorry, Uncle, I'm out of pennies—' She held the phone and then carefully cradled it, standing for a moment, quite still, staring at the instrument as if expecting it to ring again, summoning her. The little telephone booth was dark. She wanted to go home. Oh, how dreadfully she wanted to go home . . .

As she pushed open the door, a gust of warm, moist air met her like a tangible wall. She wondered, feeling it, why she could not see it, like fog. Through open double doors she could see the great ballroom with its square of polished dance floor beneath flamboyant red, white and blue decorations, its glittering, mirrored lights, its tables littered with the wreckage of finished meals – a shambles of bottles and glasses, discarded, crumpled napkins, empty coffee cups and full ashtrays. The dance floor was crowded. There was a sheen of sweat on faces and on bare shoulders as the dancers jiggled in the scant space. Allie looked down at her own dress. It was the brown satin, smuggled from Ashdown that morning in a paper bag. She had changed in the house of one of Ray's friends in London, and had only realized much later that she had left the bag containing her other clothes behind when they had left for the Ace of Spades. At the time it had seemed rather funny; now she did not think so. If she arrived at Ashdown dressed as she was, they would know that she had planned this, that she had lied.

She caught sight of herself in a long, flatteringly peach-tinted mirror. She was frowning ferociously. She smoothed her expression, fluffed out her hair, peered at her slightly smudged make-up. The corsage that Ray had bought from a street vendor in London looked wilted and dispirited, its scent was sweet and stale.

'Allie! There you are!' A young man she knew only by sight swooped on her. 'Come on! You're missing all the fun!' He grabbed her hand and she allowed herself to be pulled into the hot and crowded ballroom. She was here;

63

she might as well make the best of it. Already the odd mood of a moment before was slipping from her. She laughed as an unknown young man in a red, white and blue boater seized her and gave her a smacking kiss. The band had struck up a rhythmic two-step. Long lines of dancers were linking arms and forming wavering ranks as they stepped and kicked their way, with much raucous laughter, through the Palais Glide. Allie stumbled a little, almost pulled off her feet by a burly, middle-aged man who insisted on stepping to the left when everyone else was stepping to the right. They scrambled through the last few choruses, kissed each other goodbye and at last Allie found herself back at the table she was sharing with Ray and the others.

'All right, old thing?' Ray Cheshire was a tall and very thin young man with floppy straight hair and a rather bad skin. In moments of honesty Allie had to admit to herself that her parents' swift judgement of him came very close to the mark. But he was twenty-one, and was considered, by himself and some of his acquaintances, to be a man of the world. The flattery of his attentions had so far made up for the lack of any real regard or attraction. He was fun to be with. That was enough.

'Yes, thanks,' she said. 'A bit thirsty.'

'More bubbly!' Ray waved a bottle in the air. 'And then more! The old man's excelled himself tonight – he's footing the bill for the lot and no questions asked. So drink up, me hearties—'

'Lucky beggar!' said a girl named Dora and, inevitably, giggled at the entirely inappropriate phrase. Ray's indulgent parents were, more than anything, responsible for his social standing among his peers.

'Come on now, the blessed stuff'll get warm! Down the hatch. Here's to our new king—' Ray drained his glass. Allie followed suit. The champagne bubbled in her throat, deliciously refreshing. She held out her glass for more.

'That's the ticket!' Ray tilted the bottle, raised his glass again. 'And damnation to his enemies! Rule Britannia!'

There was a roar, and the glasses were drained again. In

the gratifying, misty glow of warmth and friendship, Allie felt the last of her unexpected despondency disperse like morning mist in the warmth of the sun. The night became a kaleidoscope of fragmented sensations, pleasantly blurred one into the other as her champagne glass magically emptied and apparently with equal enchantment speedily filled again. She neither noticed nor cared how much she was drinking. Laughter and music and raised, loud voices rushed in her ears like the sound of the sea. She smiled, and nodded, and laughed immoderately at jokes that she could not hear. Bright, flushed faces and open mouths swam about her. Inexplicably, she suddenly found herself sitting on Ray's lap, her arm about his shoulders, his bony hand warm and possessive upon her thigh.

'I want to dance,' she said, but her voice was drowned and no one heard her. She took Ray's ear between finger and thumb and pulled it close to her mouth: '*I want to dance.*'

In the same, easy, miraculous way that she had found herself sitting on his lap, she now found herself in his arms on the dance floor, with apparently neither effort nor thought required from her. She giggled. Ray's arm tightened about her waist. She wriggled, unable to breathe. He grinned down at her, stumbled a little, picked up the rhythm again. Someone had flung open the tall windows, which opened onto a dim-lit terrace and a shimmering pool. The refreshingly cool air that blew through them was delightful. She tilted back her head and breathed deeply and a little dizzily. The current of air grew stronger; when she opened her eyes it was to discover that Ray had steered her expertly off the dance floor and towards the tall, open windows.

She lifted her chin, pouting a little. 'Where are we going? I want to dance.'

'We're going to,' he said, soothingly, 'but wouldn't it be nice to dance outside, where it's cool? Just look at the stars. Come on, Al . . .'

With some reluctance she allowed herself to be led to the

65

windows, stepped across the low sill and onto the paved terrace.

'There,' he said encouragingly, 'isn't that much nicer?' He wrapped his arms about her and drew her very close to him, moving slowly in time to the music, which drifted with the smoke and the laughter on the glimmering night air. She relaxed. Above them the black velvet of the sky was diamond-studded with stars. The terrace and swimming pool were screened and surrounded by wooden trellises covered in rambling roses from whose depths shone hundreds of tiny fairy lights. The air was marvellous after the clammy heat of the overcrowded ballroom. They were alone. Coloured lights danced and shimmered in the waters of the pool. Ray pulled her head gently down onto his shoulder and for a moment they stood, swaying to the music, in silence.

In a pleasant limbo of glittering lights and champagne, Allie's eyes drifted shut. She felt Ray's hand in her hair, felt the insistent pressure of his hand turning her face to his and then was astonished to find his lips on hers, hot and moist. She tried to pull away, but his hand behind her head held her firmly to him. She stood absolutely still, unresponsive, letting him kiss her, her mind all at once uncomfortably and absurdly clear. She felt absolutely nothing apart from a faint revulsion as their wet lips, tainted sweetly, slid against each other. Was this, then, what all the fuss was about? She felt a vague lift of disappointment, a sense of having been cheated. She remembered with quick, awful clarity, her father's head bent above Celia, the movement of Celia's hand on her father's face. Desperate to erase the vision, she pressed suddenly against Ray. She felt his increased excitement. His teeth pressed painfully into her lower lip and with a shock she felt his tongue pushing and probing into her mouth. This time she did manage to pull away, moving her head sideways and onto his shoulder. His enterprising mouth and probing tongue transferred themselves to her ear. She shuddered and buried her face deeper into the curve of his neck, trying to escape the awful, hot wetness.

His hand was on her breast, kneading it clumsily and painfully. She felt the strap of her dress slip from her shoulder, and the hot mouth and sharp teeth were on her bare skin. With all her strength, she pushed him from her.

He stumbled, caught off balance. 'I say—'

At that very moment they were engulfed by a shrieking, laughing crowd of young people.

'What did I say? I *said* they'd be out here . . .'

'Dirty devil, Ray!'

'Cradle snatcher!'

'Looking at the stars, are we?'

Bemused, Allie pushed the strap of her dress back up onto her shoulder. 'We were – dancing . . .'

That brought forth a great shout of laughter. 'Is *that* what they're calling it nowadays?'

'Jolly nice kind of dance if you ask me. Who's going to teach it to me?'

Above the sea of laughing faces, Allie could see Ray; his expression was a weird mixture of hurt surprise at her rebuff and a kind of infantile pride at being singled out for such envious, if misguided, attention. Suddenly she felt sorry for him. He had been kind to her today, his inept lovemaking notwithstanding. She did not want him to think her cold or ungrateful. Cold. The word trickled uncomfortably through her mind. Was that it? Was she – what was the word? – frigid? Was that why she had not enjoyed Ray's advances? He made to turn away, a sullen set to his reddened mouth. She slipped through the laughing crowd and caught his hand. 'Ray – I'm sorry . . .'

Someone pushed a glass into her hand and upended a champagne bottle into it. The liquid overflowed the top of the glass and ran in a golden stream over her hand and down her dress. She lifted the glass to Ray's lips. He hesitated, then, to cheers, he swallowed it awkwardly. In the ballroom the band had struck up a Charleston. Frenetic figures flailed across the dance floor beneath the shifting, mirrored lights. With a shout, a young man grabbed Allie and began to dance. In an instant the terrace was alive with flying feet and clapping, waving hands. Breathlessly Allie passed from one partner to another until she found herself, by accident or design, dancing once more with Ray. His ill-temper forgotten, he caught her hands and swung her round faster and faster until terrace, pool and lighted windows dissolved into a single, swinging ferris wheel of coloured lights. As the music stopped she collapsed into his arms. Several people sank to the floor, fanning themselves.

'Good heavens!' squealed someone. 'Dora! What on earth do you think you're doing?'

'Cooling off.' Plump Dora, with great aplomb, was standing by the pool calmly divesting herself of dress, stockings, suspender belt, shoes.

'Topping idea!' A young man began to pull his jacket off. 'A swim! Just what the doctor ordered!' He dragged his shirt over his head.

Dora, clad only in shining satin underclothes, made a very creditable dive into the water. The young man, stripped to his underpants, jumped in close behind her, causing a tidal wave to break across the poolside. A girl, spattered with water, shrieked.

'What's it like?' called Ray as Dora surfaced.

'Wonderful! Come on in and see! Last one in's a donkey!'

There was a tipsy scramble for the poolside. Shirts, trousers, sparkling dresses and high-heeled shoes were discarded as their wearers scrambled to be the first in the water. Allie stood back. There was a great deal of splashing and shouting.

'Come on, Allie, in we go.' Ray, shirtless but with his trousers and shoes still on, grabbed her hand. He was having some difficulty in standing up straight.

She shook her head. 'No, Ray. I don't want to.'

'Don't be a spoilsport, old thing. Can't have that, you know.'

With sudden and surprising strength, he scooped her from her feet, one bony arm about her shoulders, the other under her long legs, the brown satin of her gown rucked to her thighs.

'Ray, don't be stupid. Put me down.' Growing angry, Allie struggled in his arms. Ray staggered, recovered himself and gripped her tighter. The onlookers whooped and screamed.

'Ray! Will – you – put – me – *down*!'

He teetered on the edge of the pool, swaying, grinning stupidly. Really alarmed now, Allie stopped struggling and clung to him. The noise around them died as the watchers held a drunken breath. Ray half-turned, his eyes unfocused, hesitated for a moment, then with little grace and no sound keeled over into the water, taking Allie with him.

Ashdown was almost entirely in darkness. A single light burned in the window of her father's study beside the front door. Debris from the evening's celebrations skittered in a lifting breeze across the littered, dark lawns. Beyond the house, the silent marquee loomed, deserted and quiet, a faint pale mass in the star-thrown shadows.

A sobered Ray rolled the car to a halt outside the door. 'Would it be better if I came in with you?'

Allie shook her head, her teeth chattering. 'No. It's best for me to go in alone.' They were almost the first words they had spoken to each other on the journey home. She shivered a little. Beneath Ray's dinner jacket, which was draped around her shoulders, her crumpled dress was still chillingly damp. She made to take the jacket off.

Ray lifted a hand. 'Keep it for now. You'll catch cold if you take it off. You can let me have it back another time.'

'Thanks.' She swung her legs from the car, her eyes on the steadily burning light by the front door.

'Allie?'

She turned.

'I'm sorry.'

'It's all right. It was as much my fault as yours, I guess.' She smiled, fleetingly. 'And more the champagne's than anything . . .'

'You're sure you'll be all right?'

'Yes.' She wished she felt as confident as she sounded.

'Will I see you next week?'

She shrugged. She could not think. In all but body she was already facing her father. When, realizing at last the unforgivable lateness of the hour, she had telephoned the house, an hour before, his voice had been more coldly angry than she had ever heard it. 'Perhaps. We'll see.'

He did not press her. As she stepped back from the car, he rolled it forward into a tight turn and, with a lift of his hand, was gone.

She had been right to be apprehensive; one look at her father's face jolted her into something close to panic. She stood just inside the study door, Ray's jacket still draped lopsidedly over her ruined dress, her head up, her face chalk-white in the lamplight.

There was an acid edge to her father's voice when he broke the silence. 'Come in, please, Alexandra, and shut the door behind you. There's no need for the whole household to be disturbed. I've already told them you're safe.'

She did as he bid, remained for a moment leaning against the door. Her still-damp hair clung to her head, tousled and untidy.

'Sit down.'

She crossed the room, forcing her legs to steadiness and keeping her head high. To her mortification, she had, however, less control over her lower lip, which trembled despite all her efforts. She clamped her teeth upon it and looked at her father. He sat behind his desk, his handsome face a stranger's behind a harsh mask of hurt anger, the angled light throwing brutal shadows beneath his eyes and around the straight, well-shaped mouth that was so like Allie's own.

'First, I think that I should tell you that before your belated and almost incomprehensible telephone call of an hour ago we had the police of two counties out looking for you.'

She winced. She had not thought of that. 'I'm sorry,' she said, knowing the total inadequacy of the words.

His eyes travelled over her, taking in every detail of her utter disarray. She withstood his regard as best she could.

70

'Your behaviour tonight,' he said at last, 'has been an absolute and to me totally unbelievable disgrace. You have caused disruption and desperate anxiety to those who love you, cold-bloodedly and with intention. You have humiliated your family in front of our guests. You have disappointed me bitterly. Your mother's feelings I leave you to judge for yourself.'

She did not speak, could think of nothing to say. The atmosphere of the room was very close. After the chill she had experienced in the car, Allie now endured a rising tide of warmth that prickled her skin uncomfortably and brought a scarlet flush of fire to her cheeks. She slipped the jacket from her shoulders and then immediately, beneath her father's outraged eyes, wished that she had not. A bright, red-blue bruise showed on one of her shoulders and the right-hand shoulder strap of her dress was broken.

She looks like a young whore who's been fighting in the gutter – with difficulty Robert Jordan restrained himself from speaking the thought aloud. He stood abruptly, almost knocking over his chair. 'I'm waiting for your explanation,' he said into the heavy silence, 'if you have one.'

'I—' Allie stopped and, at last, broke. She bowed her head and, through a blur of tears, looked at the hands that were twisted together in the lap of her ruined dress.

Relentlessly her father neither moved nor spoke.

Allie gritted her teeth and forced the tears back. When she lifted her head, her flushed face and bright eyes beneath the mop of damp brown hair were dry. 'I went to the Ace of Spades with Ray and the others.'

'Against our express wishes.'

'Yes.'

'And?'

'And we had too much to drink. I fell into the swimming pool.'

'You omit to mention that you also lied. To us, to Mrs Welsh, to your Uncle Bertie . . .'

'Yes. That too.'

'And is that all you have to say?' His voice was perilously quiet.

'No. Of course not. But I know how stupid it sounds if I say that I'm truly sorry if my behaviour has caused trouble for everyone—'

'Trouble? I should damned well think it has!' Unable to contain himself her father crashed his hand painfully on the desk in front of him. 'And if I lay my hands on that young whippersnapper Cheshire, I'll horsewhip him—'

'No.' Allie stood up. 'It wasn't Ray's fault. It was mine. Take your whip to me, Father, if that's what you feel you must do . . .'

At her tone, unstable colour rose in her father's face. 'Perhaps that's exactly what I should do, young lady. Perhaps I should have done it a long time ago.'

A long time ago you wouldn't have needed to, and you know it. You must know it. A long time ago there was no Celia. No lies. No pain . . . She stared at him, daring him, knowing that she had it in her power with a few savage words to revenge herself for these last, hateful months. She opened her mouth.

'Allie, darling—' His sudden cry forestalled her. 'In God's name, what is it? What's wrong? What's changed you so?' The baffled pain in his voice stopped her tongue like a blow. She stared at him dumbly. He came around the desk, stood an arm's length from her, studying her face as if to read there her thoughts. 'Have you any idea what we've been through tonight? We thought you dead – or lost – or Christ only knows what else. And look at the state of you . . .'

'I told you,' she said doggedly, her voice miserably low, 'I drank too much. I fell into the swimming pool. I'm sorry. I'm truly sorry. I didn't realize how late it was. It all got – muddled . . .'

The anger had cleared from her father's face to leave behind an expression that, to Allie, was infinitely harder to bear. It was a look of perplexed and painful defeat. 'I'm sorry,' she whispered again, her shoulders drooping. All at once a dreary exhaustion had her in its grip. She wanted nothing but to lay her swimming head upon a cool, clean pillow and sleep. Already the arid acidity of tomorrow's hangover was on her tongue. She looked at her father, openly pleading. He sighed.

'You'd better get to bed. We'll talk again in the morning. I'm afraid, though, that you must be prepared to find your mother less easy to appease than me.'

She wrapped her arms across her breasts, her fingers biting into her own flesh. The emotional see-saw had tilted again; more than anything she wanted to fling herself into her father's embrace, sob out her misery. 'What do you think she'll do?' she asked, uncertainly.

'I don't know.' He ran a tired hand through his hair. 'But one thing I'm afraid you must come to terms with. You'll be starting work with Sir Brian Hinton next month. Your mother is absolutely determined upon it. Now more than ever.'

'No!' Allie had gone bone-white. 'I can't!'

'You have no choice, I'm afraid.' Her father laid a heavy arm across her shoulders. 'Allie, love, go to bed now. Perhaps tomorrow we can talk? Perhaps, tomorrow, you could bring yourself to tell me what's happened – what's worrying you – whatever it is?'

Blindly she shook her head and walked from beneath his arm out of the room, leaving him looking after her, an unusual brightness in his eyes.

# CHAPTER FIVE

The next few days were truly awful. The household held its breath; even Libby's usual careless high spirits were muted. Not that Myra raised her voice in anger – far from it. The morning following the party, when she with painful clarity told her daughter what she thought of her behaviour, her tone was cool, quiet and had the cutting edge of a honed razor. She refused absolutely to listen to Allie's unhappy, stammered apologies, and instead insisted again that Allie take the position offered by Celia's father.

'Mother – please – I can't – I don't want to . . .' Unable to explain her real reasons, Allie fell back on childish pleading that simply and understandably strengthened her mother's resolve. In the end, hopelessly disadvantaged by her desperate desire to make amends and to heal the rift between herself and her mother, Allie found herself obediently sitting at the writing desk in the dining room, grimly writing a polite letter of acceptance.

The following Sunday morning, she came downstairs to find her sister curled up on the big sofa in the drawing room reading the newspapers. Their parents were still breakfasting. Sunlight shafted through the open windows and the morning was bright with birdsong. Libby, dressed in a pair of silk lounging pyjamas in an attractive shade of lilac that suited her perfectly, looked up and grinned as her sister entered the room.

'Fine morning for a swim,' she said with friendly malice.

'Don't be beastly.' Allie picked up a paper. 'Anything happening?'

'Not so's you'd notice.' Libby stretched, and yawned. 'Mussolini's got the Italian trains running on time – or so they try to tell us, though personally I doubt if God himself could work such a miracle. They're still trying to figure out what happened to the *Hindenburg*. The Führer's made a few more frenzied speeches. Stupid little man. And they're still blowing each other to pieces in Spain, of course. I'm hanged if I can remember what we did for entertainment on a Sunday morning before one half of the world started to hate the other half and Lord Beaverbrook took to reporting it, bless his little heart—'

'Libby!'

'Oh, for God's sake, don't be such a pain, Allie! Don't take everything so *seriously*! I thought you'd seen sense at last. Will there, won't there, will there, won't there, will there be a war? And does it matter? If it comes, we won't survive the first five minutes anyway if you can believe what they say about air raids. So why worry? Why make yourself miserable? Now, if you're interested in some *really* important news . . .?' She paused, inviting question, her face alight with life and mischief.

Allie lowered the newspaper behind which she had taken refuge. 'What is it?'

Libby sprawled elegantly back on the sofa, crossing lilac-clad legs with a whisper of silk and pointing a long, scarlet-tipped finger. 'Guess who popped the question last night?'

'Oh, Libby! He didn't!'

'Oh, Allie, he did! And what's more – after due consideration of course—'

'You accepted! Of course you did! How absolutely marvellous! I'm so happy for you!' Allie was across the room and hugging her sister in a second. 'Mrs Edward Maybury. Sounds super. When's it to be? Has he spoken to Daddy?'

'He has.' Her father had come to the door unnoticed and stood, smiling, watching them. 'And my only reservation was that they should give us time to save up for the occasion! We seem to have had rather a lot of expensive celebrations already lately. Of course . . .' he added, innocently, to his elder daughter '. . . if you fancy just a simple ceremony – a quiet affair with just a few close friends, in the tradition of young love . . .?'

His laughing glance flicked to Allie and, unable to return his smile even under these circumstances, she looked away, but not quickly enough to miss the baffled flicker of hurt in his eyes. They had hardly spoken since their confrontation in the study.

'Don't be absurd, Daddy darling.' Libby sprang to him, stood on tiptoe and kissed his cheek. 'I intend to cost you an absolute fortune! Hundreds of guests, champagne, caviar, the lot. It's going to be the very best wedding anyone ever had, so there. That awful Jesse Warrington is going to be positively *green*. Hello, whoever can that be at this time in the morning?'

They had all heard a car on the drive outside. Libby ran to the window. 'It's a cab. Who on earth . . .? Oh!' Her hand flew to her mouth. 'Oh, good Lord!'

Allie moved to her side, craning her neck. 'Who is it?'

'It's – it's *Richard*!' Libby was at the door as she squealed the name. 'Richard!' she shouted again as she flew to the front door.

For one inarticulate moment, Allie and her father stared at each other, then they too ran into the hall in time to see Myra and Mrs Welsh come from the kitchen.

'What on earth's going on? Robert? What's got into Libby?' Myra stopped speaking and stood like stone as Libby with a triumphant flourish threw open the front door to reveal the tall, very thin and rather shabby figure who stood on the doorstep. Libby threw herself upon him. He caught her and hugged her to him, while above her shining head, his eyes found and held his mother's.

Myra put out a hand to the wall to steady herself. 'Richard?' she said, very softly.

Robert came forward, hand outstretched. 'Welcome home, son. Welcome home, by God!'

With Libby still held fast in one arm, Richard extended his free hand to his father who took it fiercely, covering it with both of his. Richard blinked, smiling. Very composedly Myra walked to him and then, as Robert and Libby stepped back she was in his arms, wordless. He rocked her a little, his thin cheek resting on her hair.

76

Allie stood watching, transfixed with happiness. Richard lifted his head and looked at her. She saw then, with a shock, the changes that marked his boy's face – the shadows in the bright eyes, the new, bitter line of his mouth that no smile could disguise. He looked cruelly tired. He released his mother and held out his hands to his young sister. Allie took them in her own, fighting back tears as she tilted her head to kiss him. 'Welcome home,' she echoed her father, 'oh, welcome home!'

She watched him, later, perched on the arm of his mother's chair and answering the family's excited questions, and studied the differences in him. His narrow hands were thin and restless; they fidgeted upon the plush arm of the chair, plucked at threads, traced the pattern of flowers, never still. His hair was long and shaggily un-kempt. The bones of his face stood out, angular and clear-cut beneath a skin brown as a gypsy's, and his rag-bag clothes hung on his frame like a stick-built scarecrow's. Yet more disturbing than these obvious physical changes were that awful exhausted shadow in his eyes, the bleak set of his mouth in repose, which could, she supposed, be attributed to his obvious and painful weariness, but which spoke to her of something deeper and more damaging.

'. . . haven't slept or eaten properly in something over a week. It's hard to remember exactly. After Tom caught it, we were in the mountains for a few days trying to patch him up enough to get him out. Then we came through at night, over the passes . . .' He stopped, fidgeting a bony hand around his mouth. 'Luckily, we'd been given an address. Once we got to Bordeaux, we were all right.'

'Tom was wounded?'

He nodded. 'I've just come from him. He's in hospital in London. He's going to be all right, thank God.'

'Is it bad?'

He lifted a tired shoulder. 'Bad enough. But he's a tough nut, old Tom. It'll take more than a couple of Fascist bullets to finish him off. Mother, I wanted to ask—'

'And you?' interrupted Myra, looking hard at him. 'Are you all right?'

'Yes.'

'Thank God for that.'

'No, Mother, it's Tom you should thank. He saved my life. Twice. The second time it nearly killed him. He was helping me when he was shot. He could have got clean away, but he wouldn't leave me.' He smiled, a travesty of his old, sudden smile. 'I've discovered that I'm not a very good soldier, I'm afraid.' He hesitated, watching Myra's face. 'Mother – they said at the hospital that Tom would be able to come out in a few weeks if he had somewhere to go, somewhere quiet, to recuperate. There's no way he could afford a nursing home . . .'

Myra stiffened. 'The boy has a home, doesn't he?'

'Two rooms and a shared bathroom.' Richard kept his voice very even. 'He has to sleep in the living room when he's home. His mother works all day . . . Mother, please – it would be so much better for him here. He needs someone around to take care of him, to watch him. I know him – if he's left to his own devices, he'll undo all the good the doctors have done him. He has to rest—'

'I hardly see myself standing over that particular young man with a shotgun in one hand and a cup of beef tea in the other,' Myra demurred, wryly.

'Mother, he saved my life.' He paused. 'And my sanity once or twice as well.'

Myra stood up briskly. 'Well, if you put it like that, then there isn't much I can say, is there?' She smiled. 'Now, you look as if you could do with a week's sleep yourself. Why don't you go and have a long, hot bath, while I get Mrs Welsh to cook some bacon and eggs? Everything's upstairs, just as you left it. We've all the time in the world to talk, later.'

He threw her a grateful look. 'Thank you.' He stood up, a little unsteadily. As he reached the door his father cleared his throat and Richard stopped, looking at him.

'I was just wondering – talking of time – how long will you be with us?' Robert asked the question with some difficulty. Allie held her breath.

78

Richard stood for a long moment as if lost in thought, his gaze distant. 'I'm home for good,' he said at last, his voice expressionless. 'I'm not going back. Not ever.'

As he closed the door quietly he left behind him a silence that was at the same time relieved and oddly anxious.

In a matter of days it was almost as if Richard had never been away. His mental and physical state improved rapidly; the nervous twitching of his fingers grew less and Mrs Welsh's cooking soon began to put flesh back onto his bones and to ease the fine-drawn, painful look that had shocked them all in that first moment of homecoming. Yet there could be no denying that, despite his physical recovery, this Richard was a very different one from the boy who had gone to war the year before. For the first few days he spoke very little of his experiences; then, slowly, he relaxed and was able to talk, though often, in mid-sentence, that disturbing, distant look would come into his eyes and he would stop speaking and sit almost as if listening to a sound he alone could hear. He spoke mostly, and with warm affection, of his comrades-in-arms, of their bravery and their humour, of their courage in the face of appalling conditions and in opposition to an enemy far better armed and organized than themselves. Vividly he described street fighting, air raids, ambushes, acts of desperation and of gallantry – but always, Allie noticed, as an observer rather than as a participant. He hardly ever recounted his own experiences but almost always those of someone else – and that someone usually the same person. Allie wondered, rather guiltily, if she were the only one who grew just a little tired of hearing Tom Robinson's praise so heartfeltly sung. Richard was bitter about the German involvement in Spain and, more savage still, about those on both sides of the struggle, whatever their political beliefs or nationality, whose vicious brutality bred atrocity from atrocity and threatened to bleed an already suffering people to death.

Allie was appalled at the inference of this. 'Reprisals? You mean – the Republicans? But, Richard . . .'

Richard leaned wearily back in his chair and closed his eyes. 'Don't be fooled, Pudding. They're all as bad as each other, when it comes down to it. Fascist or Republican, with a gun in his hand and hate twisting his guts, there isn't a jot of difference, one from the other. Men might start off fighting for an ideal, and the ideal might be worth fighting for – it might even be essential to fight for it. But there's one thing I've discovered, and I guess I can't be the first to find it out: in taking up arms it's only a strong man that can be sure he isn't destroying something within himself. His humanity, his conscience – I don't know. Is anything worth that? When brother murders brother and father, son – what's left in the end, whatever the rights and reasons in the beginning? Hitler's Nazis bomb Guernica, Stalin's Communists slaughter friend and foe alike if it serves their bloody political ends, Spaniard kills Spaniard – and I'm not talking of battles and brave deeds, mind, but of the simple, cold-blooded murder of men, women and children – and sows the seeds of a hatred that could last for ever. And for what?'

'But – it can't be for nothing? I mean, you can't be saying that the Republicans shouldn't be fighting?'

The tired eyes fluttered open. 'Oh, of course not. I'm sorry, love. I'm tired. I don't know what I am saying. I only know that I've seen a kind of insanity at work, and the insidious thing is that we accept such things because they're there, because they have always been there, and we shake our heads and tut-tut and then go off and kill a few more. There are things being done – unspeakable things – and things being accepted by so-called civilized human beings that make me wonder if the world hasn't gone mad.'

'What do you mean?' Her voice was faint.

He made a small, defeated gesture. 'I'm sorry. I didn't mean to upset you.'

'Tell me what you mean,' she said, stubbornly.

He hesitated for a second before speaking. 'I met a young German. A captured pilot. One of the few we actually managed to shoot down. I was detailed to guard him for a few days. We talked. He might have been any one of those lads we met in Germany a few years ago. His name was Günter. He was a nice boy. He had a mother he adored, a father he respected, two pretty sisters and a young brother still at school. He wasn't much older than you. He had a dog he called Wolf. He carried a picture of it. He showed me: a boy and his dog, walking in the Black Forest.' Richard fell silent, fingering his mouth in that newly acquired, nervous habit, his eyes distant. Allie waited. 'He liked England, he told me. Used to spend his summer holidays here. We laughed, thinking of you and me in Germany, and him here. He was a good, upright, well-educated young German. He believed fervently and implicitly in God, in the Fatherland, in his Führer, in law and order and in the inferiority – no, the sub-humanity – of Jews, gypsies, Communists, Slavs – of anyone, in fact, not fortunate enough to be of his own race or convictions. He believed that they should be exterminated as one might exterminate rats or mice, or worked, as any other animal might be worked, beneath the whip and halter until their useful life was finished . . .'

Allie shook her head in half-disbelief. 'Oh, Richard—'

He turned savagely on her. '*He believed it*! And he believed that we would join them. A war between Germany and England, he said, was simply not possible. His father had said so – how could he be wrong? We are the same, he said. The same roots, the same needs. We should combine to cleanse the world of the vermin that infest it.'

'What did you say?'

'What do you think I said? And he laughed. Said that, whatever happened, we wouldn't stop them. England, he said, would sit beyond her sheltering ditch and watch her cousin Germany take Europe by the throat and shake some order into it.'

'And will we?' Her voice was barely audible.

'Who knows? We haven't exactly covered ourselves in glory so far, have we? What did we do about Abyssinia? The Rhineland? Why should anyone expect us to do anything about anything else?'

'Well, now you're saying we should fight? A moment ago I thought you were saying that we shouldn't? You can't say we're wrong if we do and we're wrong if we don't!'

He sighed, and rubbed his mouth with the back of his hand. In the garden outside a wren trilled suddenly, a lovely glissando of notes that rippled through the still June air, bright as sunshine.

'What happened to him? The young German?' asked Allie.

'They took him out and shot him; we couldn't cart prisoners around with us. They didn't blindfold him. He cried for his mother.'

Allie drew a sharp, flinching breath.

'Oh, God, I'm sorry, Pudding. I didn't mean to talk about it. Not like that. Come on, why don't you thrash me at tennis again? I'll have to do something to improve my game. They won't have me back at Cambridge if I can't beat my baby sister at tennis . . .'

Such outbursts were, in fact, rare. It was obvious that Richard wanted to put the past year behind him once and for all, and his family were more than ready to assist him. His disenchantment was clear; what was less clear was the reason for the haunting shadow that hovered behind it, the beginning of something, Allie was not the only one to think, more threatening than natural revulsion at the atrocities of war.

A month after Richard's return, Allie, still at first under protest, started her job with Sir Brian Hinton. She began determined to hate it, obstinately prepared to make such a nuisance of herself that the end of her month's probationary period would see the termination of her employment. To her own surprise, no such thing happened. Against her own inclinations, she enjoyed the work and found Sir Brian a charming and agreeable man.

Her duties were not at first arduous – she answered the telephone, ushered Sir Brian's visitors from the plush waiting room to his even plusher office, and made copious cups of tea. Her employer, however, was quick to discover that her pleasant personality and excellent command of the German language – an accomplishment that he himself had never been able to acquire – made her popular with the wine-growers and merchants that he entertained, and before long she found herself, to her own mild surprise and pleasure, sitting in on meetings and discussions as a translator. Her contact with Celia was minimal – a fact for which she was profoundly thankful – and, as she settled into the routine of working she discovered, too, that the morning and evening trips with her father in the car – for he dropped her off in New Bond Street, where Sir Brian's office was situated, and picked her up in the evening on the way back – served, despite her initial resistance, to ease at least a little the strain between them. If they did not recapture the openly affectionate special relationship they had shared for years, their casual conversations as Robert manoeuvred the big Bentley through London's traffic and out into the rolling green Kentish countryside were part of a kind of truce upon which, Robert for one hoped, they might build. He watched his daughter closely, still hurt and puzzled at the change in her, yet relieved to see that her initial rebellious opposition to the position with Sir Brian seemed to have died. Working, she did not see so much of Ray Cheshire and the others – did not have the time nor, apparently, the inclination – and for a while, with Richard home and recovering and Libby utterly absorbed in her Edward, life ran smoothly for the Jordans.

In August Tom Robinson came to Ashdown to stay, a reluctant invalid who accepted Myra's cool ministrations with the kind of malicious grace that, Robert was amused to note, she more often used herself on others. Both he and Richard had been accepted back at Cambridge – news that came on the same day that Libby and Edward finally announced the date of their wedding, in the summer of the following year. At the end of September Myra decided to hold a small celebration dinner in honour of her daughter's official engagement. It was Libby's idea that Celia should be invited.

'. . . after all, it was through her that I met Edward. And I do feel rather badly that I haven't seen much of her lately. Besides,' she flashed a smile in Tom's direction, 'it'll even up the numbers.'

'Don't worry on my account.'

'I wouldn't dream of it. But Mother does like things nice and tidy.'

It was unseasonably cold and a fire was burning in the hearth. Robert was stacking a log carefully upon it, his back to the room. He straightened slowly. 'That's a good idea, Libby. Of course Celia must come.'

Without a word, Allie turned to the window. A drift of fine rain misted the countryside beneath low, oppressive clouds. In the sombre light the drenched woodlands and fields looked desolate. 'I think I'll go for a walk,' she said abruptly and caught, as she turned, Tom's eyes upon her, pale and unreadable.

He was in the hall when she returned an hour or so later, leaning casually against the newel post, his damaged shoulder resting against the banisters. Had it been anyone else she might have suspected that he was waiting for her.

'Did you have a good walk?' he asked, pleasantly.

'Yes – thank you,' she added as an ungracious afterthought as she squeezed past him into the small lobby behind the stairs where the outdoor clothes were hung. Bending, she tugged off her wellington boots and threw them into the cupboard. She could feel his light speculative gaze upon her and it irritated her unreasonably. Apart from the contact that good manners required, she had hardly spoken to Tom Robinson during the time he had been recuperating at Ashdown. Nothing that Richard could say would change her opinion of him, nor temper her deep-felt hostility. She could not forgive him for what she still saw as his part in Richard's going to Spain, and was haunted by the conviction that, though Tom himself had been physically wounded, the damage that, through him, had been inflicted upon her brother was far greater, if less obvious. With her back still turned to him, in pointed silence she hung her dripping mackintosh and hat in the cupboard, hoping fervently that he would take the hint and leave her alone. When she turned, however, he had not moved and she was still trapped in the confined space between the cupboard and the stairs.

'Funny sort of a day for a walk?' His smile was uncharacteristically tentative.

'I like walking in the rain.'

'Just you and the ducks.'

As an attempt at jocularity it did not impress her. She did not laugh. 'Yes.' There was no way to push past him without being obviously rude. She waited in unhelpful silence for him to step aside.

He did not seem in the least put out. 'Whatever happened,' he asked gently, 'to the girl I left behind me?'

'I don't know what you mean.' The words were barely polite.

'I'm sure that I remember being righteously lectured on the unromantic necessity of fighting Fascism in my own backyard?'

She said nothing.

'What happened?' he asked, quietly. 'Where did all that fervour go?'

'Nothing happened. Absolutely nothing.' She found his probing intolerable. Faint colour rose in her face.

'Well, something's changed,' he said, mildly.

'Yes. I have.' She snapped the words. 'I've grown up. There's no law against that, is there?'

'I guess not. It happens to most of us, sooner or later.' He could not keep the note of irony from his voice. His straight mouth twitched in a way that Allie misinterpreted entirely; the colour in her cheeks burned stronger. 'Are you telling me,' he continued before she could speak, still not moving, a faint furrow between his dark brows, 'that your concern for . . .' he paused, and this time the faint smile was unmistakably sardonic '. . . the downtrodden workers was just a schoolgirl enthusiasm?'

Mind your own bloody business. The words were on her

85

tongue; years of well-mannered restraint curbed them. She spoke coolly: 'Something like that, yes.'

His expression was totally unreadable. 'Well, well. There's a pity. Another illusion shattered.'

That, she felt, called for no reply at all. Somewhere in the house, upstairs, a gramophone was playing – a bright, syncopated dance tune that was absolutely at odds with the dreary darkness of the afternoon. Libby's happy voice, singing, floated down the stairwell to them.

'Excuse me, I—' She made to brush past him at the very moment that he pushed himself away from the post. As she cannoned awkwardly into him, she could not miss the flash of pain in his face.

'I'm sorry.' Her face flamed again. Embarrassment and irritation made her temper rise.

'It's all right. It was my fault.'

Forced to civility, she asked, 'How is it? Your shoulder?'

'Coming along. The doc says it'll be some time before I'm one hundred per cent fit, though. I'll have to give up playing soldiers for a while.'

This time, shaken for a moment from her own preoccupation, Allie did not miss the faint, self-deprecating sarcasm in the words.

'Will you be well enough to go up with Richard when the term starts?'

'Of course.' At last the cool dislike in her voice seemed to have piqued him a little. The dark head tilted. 'Don't worry. You'll be rid of me soon.'

'I'm sure I didn't mean—' She stopped. He had understood exactly what she had meant, and they both knew it. 'You'll be a hero, I expect,' she found herself saying, in tart defiance of rising discomfiture. 'Will you enjoy that, do you think?'

His good shoulder lifted in a caustically impatient shrug. He was watching her intently, his head on one side, his eyes suddenly hard. 'My old mum,' he said at last, softly, 'is a great believer in platitudes. You know the sort of thing – "A trouble shared is a trouble halved" – that sort of rubbish. Pretty stupid, eh?'

'I – can't say I've ever thought about it.' She started up the stairs, not looking at him, determinedly hearing the acid tone of the words rather than the possible meaning behind them. What could Tom Robinson possibly know of her troubles? And why should he care?

'By the way . . .'

She looked down at him. 'What?' The word made no pretence at grace.

His smile was tranquil. 'That friend of Libby's – Celia? – she won't be coming on Saturday. She's – otherwise engaged. Libby rang her.'

'That's a pity.' Her voice was expressionless.

'Yes. That's what I thought.' Still smiling, he turned and left her, poised upon the stairs, an uncertain frown upon her face as she watched him go.

'Celia, please, don't do this to me. To us. We all want you to come. Libby's really terribly disappointed. And we haven't seen each other for so long . . .'

Celia's grip on the telephone tightened until her fingers ached.

'Celia?' Robert's voice, faint upon a bad line, was pleading. 'Please come.'

'I told you. Told Libby. I'm busy on Saturday.' The sound of his voice, even distorted as it was, wrought havoc upon her hard-fought-for resolution. She must not give in. 'Robert, you know we have to stop. It can't go on. It isn't fair – to us or to anyone. Seeing each other like that can only make things worse . . .'

There was a long silence.

'Celia . . .' said Robert at last, gently.

She knew she had lost.

'All right. I'll come.'

Celia's conviction that her capitulation had been a mistake was reinforced the moment she rolled her small car to a halt in front of Ashdown and saw him standing in the open doorway beside Myra, his handsome face alight at the sight of her. For weeks she had battled with herself, fought to acquire strength enough for both of them since he, so strong in most things, seemed unable or unwilling to muster the fortitude to do what she knew for all their sakes must be done. Now, in the moment that it took for their hands to touch and for his warm mouth fleetingly to brush her cheek, she was lost again, and did not know, in her anguished confusion, if she loved or hated him for it.

Throughout the evening she found herself playing her part in the celebrations – toasting the happy couple, kissing Libby, agreeing with apparent pleasure to attend her friend as maid of honour. But as the wine flowed and the talk and the laughter grew louder she found herself – her real self – withdrawing into a shell behind emptily smiling eyes, lips that laughed and mouthed clever, irrelevant words, a body that moved perfectly naturally but which might have belonged to someone else. The small, vulnerable being that was Celia Hinton huddled alone, watching them all with an awareness of guilt and a hateful, urgent envy that poisoned happiness and made life seem a miserable charade. Yet the sound of Robert's voice, the sight of him across the table kept her captive as surely as a pin through the body of a butterfly, and she knew as she watched him that her battle, for the moment at least, was lost. If he had asked for her blood she would have opened her veins, there and then.

Richard was speaking to her. She smiled vaguely and nodded at what she hoped was an appropriate time. She was genuinely glad to see that the strain had gone from Richard's face in the weeks since his sudden homecoming. Her eyes flicked from him to his injured friend, who was sitting in silence next to him. Now there, she considered, was a strange and disconcerting young man. He was watching her with an interest she found faintly discomfiting.

'Are you looking forward to going back to Cambridge?' she asked, across Richard.

Tom nodded, smiling a little.

'Won't you find it a little tame after . . .' she paused, aware of possible tactlessness '. . . the past year?'

'I wouldn't be surprised.' His attractive voice always surprised her. 'Let's just say it's a chance to get my breath back before the next lot starts.'

It took a moment for the meaning of the words to sink in. 'The next? You mean – you think there's going to be a war? In Europe?'

'I'm absolutely certain of it.' Quiet had fallen around the table, and his clear voice fell into the silence like a blade. Richard began to fidget with his knife, his eyes downcast.

Libby jumped to her feet. 'Oh, fiddle to that, Tom Robinson! Of *course* there isn't going to be a war! Now, come on everyone, into the drawing room. We're going to play charades. Bring your glasses with you. Isn't there some more wine, Daddy?'

Celia held up her hand. 'Not for me, truly. I'm driving, remember. In fact, I really should think about starting back soon—'

'Oh, Cele, what nonsense! The fun hasn't started yet! Besides – why think about going home? Why not stay the night, like you always used—'

Celia interrupted her, talking just a shade too fast. 'I can't. I promised Mummy faithfully I'd be there first thing tomorrow. We've guests coming, and you know how flustered she gets. I really mustn't be late.'

Libby slipped around the table to hug her affectionately. 'Another hour? Please? It is supposed to be my party . . .' As she spoke, prettily pouting, she looked exactly what she was – a beguilingly charming, spoiled child with neither an uncharitable bone in her body nor a serious thought in her lovely, self-centred head. 'I've been so looking forward to it!'

Celia smiled, trapped. 'An hour then. But then I really must go.' She avoided Robert's eyes, was unaware of Allie's.

Libby caught her hand. 'Right. Come on – charades. And Celia shall start . . .'

Allie sat for a moment longer than the rest as the company, laughing, obediently followed the other two girls to the drawing room. She had watched her father and Celia all night and for her life had been unable to detect anything in the least lover-like between them. On the contrary, if anything it had seemed to her that there was an unusual restraint between them, unmistakable even if apparent only to the eyes of an astute observer. Without volition, the wish became father to the thought. For a moment, with youth's arrogance, she allowed herself to consider forgiving her father for that betrayal that had poisoned her feelings for him over these past months. She had long ago decided that the whole awful affair was Celia's fault – it had to be . . . And if her father had seen the error of his ways . . .

The wine she had drunk had blurred the edges of her mind. If it were over, then yes, she would forgive him, and the world of safety, of sanity, of childhood would be restored. It did not occur to her that her father's greatest crime had been to allow her to glimpse in him the frail and fallible human being beneath the shining armour in which, all her life, she had clothed him, and that the knowledge that she had gained of him in that glimpse would never now change. As she sat at the empty dinner table and listened to the shrieks of hilarity from across the hall, she vowed with a faintly agreeable feeling of self-righteousness that, since her father now regretted his fall from grace, she would forgive him. The utter relief that thought brought with it surprised her; she had not herself realized how desperately and for how long she had been looking for a way to reconciliation.

'Allie? Everyone's waiting.' As if summoned by her thoughts, her father stood by the door, a look of enquiry on his face.

'Coming.' Allie drained her wine and, for the first time in months, gave him an unforced smile. Everything was going to be all right . . .

# CHAPTER SIX

It was sheer, miserable chance that took Allie to the garden behind her father's office the following Wednesday lunchtime. During the morning she had realized that she had left her handbag in her father's car. It was a bright and beautiful day, golden with sunshine, and the thought of a stroll through the pleasantly bustling West End streets was inviting. Allie was still enough of a country girl to enjoy the atmosphere of London. She found the incessant noise and movement exciting, loved to feel a part of it. She did not bother to telephone her father to say that she was coming – if she missed him then she would simply wait till the evening to retrieve her bag. It was the sunshine that tempted her out; the reclamation of the bag simply directed her footsteps.

Her father's office, in a quiet street at the back of Portland Place, was within easy walking distance of New Bond Street, and the route took in some of London's busiest and most fashionable shopping thoroughfares. She sauntered through the enjoyably warm day, stopping occasionally to gaze at elegantly dressed shop windows displaying the latest styles and fashions. She herself tended towards tailored clothes, but she loved the currently popular softly feminine look, though she knew that it did not suit her as it did her sister. In vain, she had tried to sweep her heavy, waving hair to the top of her head to accommodate one of Libby's attractive, doll-sized hats, only to have the whole creation slide and tumble down the moment she moved her head. She grinned now at the thought, and the smile stayed on her face as she strolled through Oxford Street in the brilliant sunshine.

When she reached her destination, it was an impulse that took her down a side street towards the back entrance of the building in which her father's office was situated. She remembered that behind the building was one of those tiny, gardened squares that add such charm to some parts of London – great trees with the first tints of autumn touching their leaves, shaded walks and neat lawns. There was a little pond where small children gathered to feed the ducks while, outside this tiny oasis of green, beyond fretted iron railings and clipped hedges, the London traffic roared on. Allie slowed her steps on the gravelled path, wandering, hands in pockets, smiling at the pram-pushing nannies, the dog-walkers, the shouting children. Beneath the trees were seats which accommodated old men and women who sat and watched as the world strolled past them, nannies who gossiped as their charges romped noisily around them, lovers who saw no one and nothing but each other.

One such pair particularly drew her eyes; half-hidden by a screen of still-blooming roses they were so intent upon their own words, their own tight-clasped hands that they were totally unaware of the tall, slim figure who stopped at the sight of them as if she had been struck. Allie saw Celia bow her dark red head, watched sickly as her father reached a hand to the girl's smooth cheek, tilting her head, forcing her to look at him, the gesture so loving that it made the contrasting revulsion that rose in the watching girl the more unbearably bitter.

Blindly she turned, hunched against a pain that was almost physical, hating them both with a strength that was like sickness. Then fury rose. She stumbled, almost stopped. She would confront them. She would march up to them, now, and show them up for what they were – a pair of lying, deceitful hypocrites who had forfeited any right to consideration or care. With fierce pleasure she hugged to herself for a moment the thought of their punishment, of the look on their faces when they saw her . . . The world about her blurred unexpectedly, and she only just prevented herself from knuckling her eyes like a child. Words of desperate protest rose in her mind. Then a sudden, harsh calm steadied her trembling hands and she lifted her head defiantly. To confront the two of them would be to demean herself. Let them play their stupid, destructive games, but let them beware – for unknown to them, the rules had changed and fresh hazards added to the play. Without looking at them again, she turned and walked perfectly steadily back through the wrought-iron gate and out onto the street.

Behind the screen of dying, sweet-smelling roses, the tears that Allie had not been close enough to see slid unchecked down Celia's face. 'You have to let me go. Don't you see it? You *have* to.' The words were desperate.

'I know. But I can't.'

'You love Myra . . .'

'Yes.'

'Truly love her . . .'

'Yes. But I love you too.'

'I *know* that! But don't you see – the whole thing's impossible? The world simply doesn't work that way. Don't you see what you're doing to me? I have no one to love but you. I have nothing when I leave you, nowhere to go, no one to turn to, no peace. I'm haunted by the thought that you must hate me when you're with her—'

'No!'

She closed her eyes for a moment, her hands fast in his. 'One day you might.' She tilted her head tiredly and the sun sheened her wet face. When she spoke again her voice was a little calmer. 'You know, and I know, that there can be nothing but pain for us. And the possibility of pain for others. Snatched moments, guilt, fear, frustration, shame. Yes. Shame. What basis is that for anything? Sooner or later we will grow to hate each other. I know it. If you didn't love Myra, if you were unhappy with her, if you wanted to leave her, you know that I would do anything, go anywhere, face anyone to be with you and damn the consequences. It isn't that I care what people might say, might think of me. You know that. I care about you. And I care – I have to care – about myself. Send me away, Robert. Please. Send me away.'

He watched her, mutely, the strength of his hands numbing hers painfully. At last she bowed her head to those clasped hands, resting her cheek on them. 'Oh, what a mess. What a dreary, horrible mess.'

The little MG buzzed like a clockwork toy along lanes tunnelled by the interlaced branches of beech trees glimmering with the red-gold light of autumn. In the woodlands on either side of the road, squirrels scampered through the crisp carpet of leaves, alarmed by the bright and noisy intruder.

'We thought you'd given up on us, old girl.' Ray rammed his hand on the horn before taking a tight corner on the wrong side of the road.

'I've been busy, that's all.' Allie, beside him, lurched against him, laughing loudly as the car swung and straightened. He grinned and laid a long arm across her shoulders. The narrow road twisted left and then right. One-handed, he took the bends with no lessening of his speed. The dappled sunlight sped across them.

'Got any plans for tonight?'

She shook her head, her headscarf flapping in the wind.

'There's a party down at Dora's. Her people are away. Should be quite a do. Coming? All the old gang'll be there – whoops!' Horn blaring, another car approached and passed them, swerving out of their way and almost mounting the grass verge as it did so. 'Silly ass. Some people shouldn't be allowed on the roads. So – what do you think about tonight? Coming?'

'Love to.'

'What about your pa? Sure he won't object?'

That afternoon, just before she had telephoned Ray and suggested that he might take her for a spin, her mother and father had set out for a walk by the river. Allie had watched her father open the garden gate and usher Myra through it, had seen her mother's smile of thanks, and had turned away as her father had bent and dropped a light kiss on the top of his wife's fair head. The picture was with her still.

94

'He won't object,' she said grimly, 'because he won't get the chance. I shan't tell him.'

That party was the first of many. In convoy, the cars roared through the country lanes or along the main road into London, their rowdy occupants almost senseless with hilarity, the bottles passed from mouth to mouth, the kissing and cuddling by no means confined to the back seats. At home, as winter drew on, Allie was bright, brittle and absolutely unforthcoming. In company with Ray Cheshire and his friends, she was always the first to start dancing and the last to stop, the instigator of some of their wilder scrapes, and the one most ready to defy good sense in the sacred cause of having a good time.

She developed a talent for deceit that surprised herself. She lied straightfaced to her parents about where she went and how and with whom she spent her time. In the cause of further freedom, she invented a fictitious girlfriend who lived across the Thames, in Essex, and who, fortuitously, did not possess a telephone. The journey from Essex to Kent being almost impossible for a lone girl at night, visits to this 'friend' necessitated staying away all night – and so, the bitter deceptions grew. She discovered very quickly that drink smoothed the road that led from misery to mindless frivolity and, too, made less distasteful Ray's persistent physical advances. Her reaction to these when sober had her half-convinced that she was, indeed, as she had feared – frigid – and the thought added another layer of unhappiness to the underlying core of her frenetic gaiety. Ray, however, did not seem to notice, indeed appeared well satisfied with their awkward love-play, and so she counterfeited excitement and pleasure to match his own and drank to hide the sham from herself.

Christmas passed, and her nineteenth birthday approached. At Ashdown, preparations for Libby's wedding were beginning and were partly responsible for the fact that fewer questions were asked of Allie than might have been. She had been at work now for six months –

sometimes, in her more honest moments, she thought that the two or three days a week she spent working for Sir Brian Hinton were the only times of sanity in her life. Determined at first to dislike him for his daughter's sake, she had to admit to herself that she had grown rather fond of Sir Brian, and he of her. He was a bluff, kindly man for whom the cherished business of selecting and buying the finest wines in Europe was an overwhelming passion rather than a way of earning a living. Allie enjoyed the work, enjoyed the responsibility, found on those days that she helped Sir Brian perhaps the only opportunity she had for being herself, with no need for deception or bravado.

At home, as the new year moved through bleak winter to the soft birth of spring, her parents, with shaken heads, tended to attribute her changed attitudes to a new-found independence in a world that was becoming noticeably more perilous with each passing week. The news from Europe was like a menacing, if still distant, roll of thunder on a summer's day. Refugees from Hitler's Germany – mostly but by no means all Jewish – brought with them stories and warnings that most people preferred not to believe or heed. In March, the Home Secretary appealed for a million men and women to volunteer to train in civil defence in case of war: less than half that number responded to the call. Allie, in common with a lot of other people, stubbornly ignored those things that she did not wish to see, and drank, danced and flirted her way into her twentieth year, telling herself defiantly that she did not give a damn for anything. She was determined to live for the day and for herself; yet, despite the diversions provided by her wild young friends, and despite her own efforts to convince herself otherwise, by the time the cold March weather was fighting the last rearguard action against the strengthening sun of spring, Allie was battling boredom.

She was bored with dancing, bored with parties, bored with herself, bored, above all, with Ray. Over the past few weeks his attentions had become more urgent, and irritatingly persistent. The – to Allie – ludicrous gropings and squirmings in his small car or in dark corners at parties were more demanding, his reluctant acceptance of her refusals more petulant. He would not, she knew, be put off for much longer. In fairness, and knowing of the casual liaisons in the group around them, Allie knew that his assumption that, sooner or later, she would give herself to him was not unreasonable, but knowing that she had not the slightest intention of doing so, she began to toy with the idea of breaking off the relationship altogether. One Friday night she found herself physically fighting him off, slapping his face in a quick flash of temper, which she regretted the moment it had flared and died. He had refused, sullenly, to accept her apologies and roared off in a tantrum that had almost sent the MG straight into the big oak that stood at the curve of Ashdown's drive. By the following afternoon she had not heard from him and was uncertain what to do about it. To ring and abjectly apologize for her struggle last night would be to infer that on the next occasion she would behave differently. And that she had no intention of doing. Perhaps, in the long run, it was best to leave things as they were. It had had to come, sooner or later . . .

She wandered into the drawing room. The house was very quiet. Her father was in Manchester visiting a small subsidiary of Jordan Industries that made electric motors. Allie's mouth drew down, bitterly humorous – it had been quite by accident that Sir Brian had innocently mentioned that Celia was spending the weekend with a friend in Lancashire. Libby was staying for a few days with Edward and his family. Richard was home, accompanied inevitably by Tom, on a flying visit to attend the wedding of a Cambridge friend.

She stood by the window, looking into the garden. There had been a late, surprising fall of snow. It lay across the countryside in a glittering mantle beneath a rose-hued sky. The low, blood-red sun drew elongated, pencilled shadows across the iced-cake smoothness of the lawns. For a fleeting moment Allie saw three laughing children, herself the smallest, racing to be the first to plant their footsteps upon that enticing virgin surface, heard the shouts, felt the sting of a snowball, the tingle of fingers in soggy, snow-sodden woollen gloves. They had built a snowman one year, she remembered, a champion of a snowman with eyes and nose and a wide, stick mouth. They had filched one of her father's best hats to put on his head and she herself had sacrificed a favourite bright red scarf. The snowman had stood there for days, the best in the neighbourhood, the very picture of what a snowman should be.

Abruptly she turned from the window. On a nearby table was a silver tray on which stood a decanter of Madeira and several glasses. Almost without thought she reached for it. She did not hear the door open. Tom's voice almost made her drop the glass before it reached her lips.

'Bit early for that, isn't it?' He stood by the door. In the months since he had returned from Spain, he had regained his health entirely. Again, now, he stood in that oddly arrogant manner that had so infuriated Myra at the garden party, hands in pockets, head tilted. The light eyes which, from a distance, gave the impression of being almost entirely colourless were on the drink in Allie's hand, and his thin face was unsmiling.

Very deliberately she tilted the glass and drank. Then she eyed him with undisguised dislike. 'It would be almost as bad a display of manners as yours for me to tell you to mind your own business,' she said coolly. 'So I won't. You can take it as read.'

That brought a smile, if a faint one. 'You're right, of course. Most ungentlemanly of me to comment upon the drinking habits of a – young lady.' The pause was just long enough to be mildly insulting. He grinned.

'I thought we agreed, on another occasion, that you were no gentleman?' Angrily she tossed back the rest of the drink.

He watched her in apparent admiration. 'You're sinking that like an expert. Do you really need it that badly?'

'I don't *need* it at all!' She was really angry now. How dare this outsider, this interloper, try to tell her what she should or should not do in her own house? She poured another large drink.

'I say – steady on.' His face was suddenly serious and the flippancy had gone from his voice. 'Allie, do you think you should?'

'What I should or shouldn't do has absolutely nothing to do with you!' Recklessly she tossed the drink back. She could feel the effect of the alcohol, drunk too fast, spreading in her veins. The knowledge that she was acting very badly fuelled the flame of her anger. When she reached for the decanter again, she crashed it against one of the glasses, which spun across the table and splintered on the floor. 'Dammit!' she said, viciously.

Tom Robinson stepped forward and, before she realized his intention, took the decanter from her. 'Come on now, Allie, I really don't think—'

She was shaking with rage. 'I don't give a damn what you think. How dare you! Give that back to me! Give it back!' She reached for the decanter.

He stepped back, avoiding her hand. 'Allie . . .'

'Would someone kindly tell me,' the voice from the open doorway was icy, 'what in heaven's name is going on here?'

There was a moment's utter silence. It was Tom who broke it, his voice easy and apologetic. 'I do apologize, Mrs Jordan. My fault, I'm afraid. We were larking about. I'm sorry about the broken glass. I'll replace it, of course.' They all knew that in the shattered glass that covered the floor lay the best part of a week's meagre allowance for Tom.

Myra's eyes were on her daughter. 'That won't be necessary. I heard quite enough to determine with whom the responsibility lies for this – fracas. Would you leave us please?'

He hesitated, then put the decanter carefully on the table. 'Mrs Jordan—'

'Please. Leave us.'

'Why don't you just go?' Allie's face was very white. In Tom's attempt to defend her, she saw the worst humiliation of all.

He shrugged, and with no further word walked past Myra and out into the hall. Once there he stopped, unashamedly eavesdropping.

'What exactly is the meaning of this?'

He heard the chink of glass as Allie collected shards from the floor. 'I'm sorry, Mother. We were just arguing, that's all. I can't stand that man. You don't like him yourself, you know you don't.'

The listener in the hall reflected wryly on the old adage that eavesdroppers rarely heard good of themselves.

'I'm not referring to your stupid, childish quarrelling. I'm talking about this.' There came a sharp, musical sound as if Myra had flicked a finger at the decanter.

Silence.

'Well? Do you think it . . . appropriate to be drinking at this time of day? Truly, Allie, I don't know what's come over you lately. I'm coming to believe that we simply can't trust you at all! What your father would think of such behaviour I just cannot think!'

Allie uttered one short, sharp bark of laughter.

'That is quite enough, Alexandra. Give me the decanter. Thank you. Now, see to this mess. I'm displeased and disappointed in you. I shall certainly speak to your father when he comes home.' Myra's voice was cold. As she came out of the room carrying the decanter, Tom stepped swiftly into the morning room. A moment later he heard the tinkle of the bell as Allie lifted the telephone and jiggled the bar impatiently, heard the harsh ring of rage in her voice as she asked the operator for the number.

'Hello, Ray? It's me. Allie.' Her voice softened: 'Yes, I know. Look, Ray – I'm really sorry about last night . . .'

She hated it. Hated it.

She lay, afterwards, looking up at a ceiling, every line of which had been dearly familiar to her since childhood. At some time in the past it had acquired in one corner a faint brown watermark that no amount of repainting had been able to eradicate. As a child, Allie had amused herself for hours at a time on light, sleepless summer evenings making pictures from its shape – a Red Indian, complete with feathers, a fairy castle with turret. At this moment it looked exactly what it was – an unpleasant and rather ugly stain.

Beside her, Ray stirred. 'Are you . . . all right?'

'Yes.'

'Are you sure?'

She did not look at him. 'I told you. I'm fine.' She blotted from her mind the thought of the clumsily painful struggle that lovemaking had been. She was sore and uncomfortable; worse, she was filled with an unexpected, miserably empty ache that had no connection with her physical discomfort. She took a very deep breath and held it for a moment, before letting it out, long and slow. 'You're sure that – thing – worked? There won't be a baby?'

'Of course not,' Ray mumbled, reddening. 'I told you.' Then, 'What's that?' He came up on his elbow, listening, panic in his face.

'What's what?'

'A car. Oh, Christ, it isn't your parents coming back, is it?'

'No.'

'Are you sure?'

'Oh, for God's sake . . .' Allie rolled onto her stomach and rested her forehead on her clasped hands. The faint sound of the car receded. Ray laughed, nervously. Allie did not move. Hesitantly he ran his finger down her naked back to the swell of her buttocks. Infinitesimally she moved away from him. He did not notice.

'Did you like it?' His voice was tentative. 'Did you, Allie?'

For the space of a heartbeat she said nothing. Then she lifted her head and smiled brightly at him. 'Of course I did.' She knew that she sounded like an adult briskly reassuring a child; for a moment she felt truly sorry for him.

'You were . . .' he searched for the word '. . . wonderful,' he finished lamely.

'Thank you.' Her voice was expressionless. She could not

**101**

bring herself to return the compliment. She laid her chin on her tight-clasped hands. The room was very still.

'What are you thinking about?' asked Ray after a moment.

She closed her eyes. 'Nothing. Nothing at all.' In the lit darkness behind her lids, she saw her father, and Celia. Did they do this? Did they? It was horrible.

'That's not very flattering.' Ray laughed another skittering, uncertain laugh that grated her nerves.

'What? What isn't?'

'Your thinking about nothing when we've just – just . . .' Ridiculously, he could not say it and his thin, marked skin coloured.

'. . . made love. That's what they call it, Ray. Making love. Making – love.' She repeated the words slowly, thoughtfully. 'It's a stupid phrase, rather, when you come to think about it. I mean – you can't *make* love, can you? You can – fall in love. Experience love. Or lose it. Or need it. But you can't *make* it, can you?'

He turned from her, swung thin legs to the side of the bed and reached self-consciously for his trousers. 'I don't know what you're talking about.'

With the faintest of smiles, she watched his awkward efforts to dress himself without revealing his nakedness to her. 'No, I don't suppose you do.'

With his trousers on, he felt at less of a disadvantage. 'And what's more, I don't think you do either.'

'You're probably right.' She rolled onto her back, making no attempt to cover herself.

In the act of tucking his long-tailed shirt into his trousers, he paused for a moment, looking at her, chewing his lower lip. Then he cleared his throat. 'You'd better get dressed, hadn't you? Your parents are sure to be home soon.'

'I suppose so.' She did not move.

'Allie?'

'Oh, all right.' She grinned abruptly. 'Keep your trousers on.'

Encouraged by the apparent sudden lightening of her

102

mood, he leaned across her. 'That's just what I'm having difficulty in doing with you lying there like that! Honestly, Al, I just never know what to make of you! You're up and down like a yo-yo!'

She pushed him away, sitting up and drawing her knees to her small breasts. 'What a beastly unflattering way to put it!' she said mildly, resting a smooth brown arm on her knees and ducking her head, her heavy hair swinging forward across her face. 'Can you imagine Clark Gable telling a girl that? You're supposed to say that the intriguing swing of my feminine moods has you enslaved – or something.'

'I would if I'd thought of it. Now for heaven's sake, get something on before your parents get back.'

She climbed into slacks and sweater, fluffed out her hair with her fingers. As she walked past him, Ray caught her elbow with urgent fingers and swung her to face him. 'Allie?'

'Mm?'

'We will – you will see me again, won't you? I mean – we will do this again, won't we?'

Allie looked at him with clear, empty eyes. If at first you don't succeed, said a mocking voice in her head, try, try, try again.

'Certainly we will,' she said.

It was as if she had become an entirely different person, a stranger with a familiar face and a body from which her mind was utterly divorced. She no longer knew herself, no longer knew what she wanted nor where she was going. It was as if, finally, her life had been turned upside down with no hope of salvage. Treasures had proved worthless, anchoring lines had broken, and there was nothing to fill the void. Divine retribution had not been visited upon her for the breaking of what was perhaps the greatest taboo of her sex and class. Nothing had happened whatsoever. The squandering of her virginity had been an act of unhappy bravado, of miserable spite against her father, against the whole, hateful world. Yet even that gesture had somehow

103

proved empty, and the experience totally disappointing. She remembered whispered, intense conversations at school, recalled with a pang of almost nostalgic regret the innocent conviction that this must undoubtedly be the most important, the most wonderful experience of a woman's life, and wondered with bitter wryness that reality could prove so different.

She and Ray did not make love often – for she was adamant in her refusal of his urgings that they should take advantage of the local fields and woodlands and the rug he always carried, in hope, in his car. Privately she regarded the act as faintly absurd, an undignified and ungraceful exercise which, though no longer painful, brought her little real physical pleasure. She utterly refused to indulge in it anywhere but in a comfortable bed and with no chance of being interrupted. Ray, while making no secret of his disappointment, nevertheless gave in on this point with remarkable grace, and in doing so inspired in her a kind of exasperated affection that prevented her, as she otherwise might have done, from breaking off the relationship. She knew that she was using him – was at times faintly ashamed of the fact – but the new, harder Allie recognized quite clearly that she too was being used, for all Ray's sometimes desperate attempts to dress up his adolescent lust in veils of clumsy romance. Perhaps, she reflected, that was the answer; perhaps there was no such thing as love. Perhaps there was simply mutual, selfish need, a kind of greed that demanded all and gave nothing, and the devil take the hindmost?

'Do you believe in love?' she asked Ray one Sunday afternoon as they lay side by side upon her narrow bed while windblown early summer rain beat against the window.

He turned on his side, propped his head on his hand, regarding her with puzzled eyes. 'Well, of course I do. What a silly question.'

'Is it?' The big house was utterly silent around them. Myra and Libby were away for the weekend visiting relations – a chore that Allie, despite her mother's tight-lipped disapprobation, had cried off – and Robert, unable to accompany his wife and daughter because of business commitments on the Saturday, had gone off to the golf club for the afternoon. Mrs Welsh always spent Sunday afternoons in the village with her sister. 'Is it?' asked Allie again, moodily.

'You know it is. How can you not believe in love? It's like saying you don't believe in – in air, or water . . .'

'How very poetic.' She lifted provoking eyebrows.

'Don't be clever.'

She ran a thoughtful finger along the line of his mouth. 'Do you love me?' she asked, slyly.

'Yes.' He flushed a little and avoided her eyes. 'Of course I do.'

'Of course you do.' Her smile was pensive. 'What would you do to prove it? Kill dragons? Take poison? Climb Everest?'

'Daft thing.' He laughed awkwardly.

'Why do people love people, do you think? Or, rather – why do they think they do? Pretend they do?'

He flicked his head in a quick, impatient gesture. 'For heaven's sake, Al, this is our first afternoon together in a fortnight and you go all philosophical on me! I don't know. How should I know?'

She lay in silence for a moment, then said, 'I should like a drink,' and, as his eyes went to the glass of water on the bedside table, 'a real drink, ninny. Gin. Or whisky. Yes, whisky.'

'Well, I—'

'Be a darling. It's downstairs. In the cabinet in the drawing room. Bring it up here, hm?'

'Do you think we should?'

She giggled, genuinely amused. 'Do you think we should be lying here together stark naked? Oh, for goodness' sake!' – this as he reached for his trousers. 'There's no one to see! Just go and get the whisky and the glasses, there's a dear.'

When he had returned and poured each of them a generous drink, they sipped in silence for a while, sitting at opposite ends of the bed, watching each other. 'Feels wonderfully – licentious – doesn't it?' Allie asked, relishing the word. 'Though, to complete the picture, I suppose this should really be a sleazy Paris attic?'

His free hand crept to her bare foot. 'I like it here, thanks.'

She held up the glass, squinting at the world through its amber depths. 'I went to Paris on a school trip a couple of years ago. I was very impressed – thought it the most romantic place I'd ever seen. Not that I'd seen much at the time. Not that I've seen much now, I suppose. It'd be lovely to spend a few months travelling around Europe, wouldn't it? Not that it'd be much fun at the moment.' She slipped off at an unexpected tangent. 'What do you think is going to happen? In Europe, I mean? With that rat Hitler, and Mussolini and the rest?'

The stroking hand stilled for a second. 'You're a great one for changing the subject, aren't you?' Ray's voice was faintly irritated.

'Yes.' There was a brief silence. 'Well?'

'Well, I don't know. I don't suppose anyone knows. Actually, I don't think anything's going to happen. Allie?' His hand crept up her leg. She shifted a little. 'Allie, we haven't seen each other like this for simply ages . . .'

The rain drove again in a great gust against the house. The light was dim, water-filtered; shadows gathered in the quiet room about them, investing their surroundings with an aura of attractive unreality. Very deliberately Allie poured herself another large whisky and drank it at one gulp, grimacing a little, half-laughing as she did so. Then she slid down onto the bed, spread-eagled, naked, her arms lying loosely on the pillow above her head. She could hear Ray's breathing, heavy and irregular as he watched her. Lazily she drew up her knees and closed her eyes, waiting.

It was the first time that she had felt anything, the first time that she had received any inkling of the pleasure that might be taken from the coupling of their bodies. It stirred and glowed, faintly, tantalizingly, somewhere deep within her and then, before she could do more than sense its existence, Ray's inexperienced passion spent itself and he rolled away from her, panting. She turned on her side, drawing up her knees, trying desperately and in vain to recall that small, glimmering light of revelation that had warmed her a moment and then died as if it had never been.

'Allie—' They both froze at the sound of a car on the wet drive.

'Bloody hell!' Allie landed upright on her feet by the bed. 'That's Dad! Quick – get yourself dressed and get downstairs. It'll take him a couple of minutes to garage the car. Hurry! Damn and blast it, what's he doing home so early?' She was scrambling into her underclothes, reaching for her skirt and blouse. 'Keep him talking. Tell him I've gone to the loo or something. Come *on*, Ray!'

Frantically Ray threw on his clothes, tugged at his socks, smoothed his hair with his hands.

'Hurry!' Allie was balanced on one leg, wrestling with a stocking that had acquired malicious life of its own.

'I can't find my other shoe. Dammit, where's the thing gone?'

She dropped to her knees and fished under the bed. 'Here. Now, be *quick*!'

'I'm trying.' He started for the door.

'Do your shoe up, stupid, or you'll break your neck. And here' – as Ray straightened she thrust the whisky bottle at him. 'Take this with you. Put it back where you got it before Dad misses it—'

They both heard the sound of the garage doors. Footsteps crunched on the gravel, hurrying through the rain. Ray flew along the landing, almost threw himself down the stairs and was caught in mid-flight by the opening of the front door. He stood, frozen, halfway down the stairs, one hand on the banisters, the other clutching the bottle of whisky, his presence of mind, never his outstanding asset, deserting him entirely. Every line of him, from his open mouth to his ludicrous, statue-like stance, shrieked guilt. Robert stopped in the doorway, shaking the rain from his coat, looking up, his perception a split second behind the more immediate senses of sight and speech.

'Why, Ray, what on earth—' His voice died as Allie swung around the corner and started precipitately down the stairs, then stopped dead at the sight of the tableau beneath her. Despite her attempts to tidy it, her brown hair was dishevelled and she was still struggling into her cardigan. She looked at her father in a long moment of silence, then, very composedly, she finished putting on her cardigan and walked quietly down the wide stairs, passing Ray who still stood as if struck agonizedly dumb.

'Hello, Dad. What are you doing back so early? We were just going out.' As if it were the most natural thing in the world, she had gently extracted the whisky bottle from Ray's numbed fingers and then finished her descent into the hall. 'Come on, Ray, we'll be late.'

She almost got away with it. Her father watched, wordless, as she deposited the bottle on the hall table and reached composedly for her mackintosh, which was thrown over a chair nearby. Scarlet-faced Ray stumbled down the last few stairs and, woodenly, helped her into it. Her hand was almost on the doorlatch before her father spoke.

'Just one moment, young lady.' He imbued each word with a kind of violence that made Ray physically flinch.

Allie stilled but did not turn. Ray glanced over his shoulder at the older man like a hunted animal, ugly colour still staining his face.

'I think it not unreasonable to ask for an explanation?' Robert's eyes, blazing with growing anger, moved from one to the other.

Allie opened the door. 'Not now, Dad. Later. I'll explain later. When I get back. This has nothing to do with Ray.'

'Hasn't it, by God? Well, young lady, I'm afraid I beg to differ! I think it has everything to do with Ray. Well, young man?'

'Mr Jordan, I—'

'Leave it, Ray, I said. It has nothing to do with you. It's between my father and myself. I'll talk to him later. Now – are you coming?'

'You're going nowhere – nowhere, do you hear? – until I have been given some explanation as to what's been going on behind my back in my own house! I come home to find you upstairs, in an empty house, alone with – this—' he jerked a contemptuous head in Ray's direction '—and a whisky bottle – and you think you can just walk away? Oh, no—'

'Oh, yes,' she snapped. 'That's exactly what I think. It's exactly what I'm going to do! Any explanation that's due can wait for privacy. I'm not standing here being bawled at in front of Ray—'

'I would have thought that under the circumstances that's entirely appropriate, since I have every intention of . . . bawling, as you so elegantly put it, at him too!'

She lifted her head and looked at him with an expression that for all his justifiable rage struck him to the soul. 'Be careful,' she said.

He stared at her. She turned, and stepped into the rain. 'Come on, Ray.'

Ray was looking in distress at Robert. 'Mr Jordan – I'm sorry – I—'

'Ray!'

'— it isn't what you think. Honestly it isn't.' The words were miserably unconvincing.

'Is that so?'

'Ray, for God's sake, if you're coming, come. Or I'll go without you.' The cool, wet air had hit Allie hard after the whisky she had drunk. As she marched towards the MG the world tilted a little, queasily. 'Ray!' She waited a moment. 'I mean it! I'll go without you!' She could see the keys hanging on the dashboard. She had only the vaguest notion of how to drive the thing, culled from just two hilariously half-hearted driving lessons on this very drive. She opened the driver's door.

Ray took a step towards Robert. 'Please, Mr Jordan, listen to me. Don't be mad with Allie, please don't—' He turned in astonishment as the car engine roared into life. 'Allie!' He rushed through the open door. 'Allie! Don't be an idiot! Come back—'

With an over-revved snarl the small, bright car leapt past him, spraying wet gravel, and took the first curve of the drive with two wheels on the grass. It narrowly missed the huge oak and shot towards the open gates.

'Allie!'

Her drink-bemused mind a suddenly terrified blank, Allie hauled on the steering wheel. The car skidded, tyres shrieking, the front wing clipped the heavy iron gates hard and the vehicle shot out into the lane, missing by a hair's-breadth the small figure who had been cycling past, head down against the rain. Allie had a brief, horrifying glimpse of a lifted, shocked little face, saw the child wobble and fall inches from the car wheels, before the MG skidded sideways and ran with a bone-cracking thump into a tree by the side of the road.

'Oh, my God! Allie!'

Robert and Ray were sprinting down the drive. The little girl, thankfully unhurt so far as Robert could see, had scrambled to her feet, sobbing, and was trying to haul her bicycle upright.

'See to the child,' Robert shouted, and rushed to where Allie was slumped over the car's steering wheel, her face bloody. As her father wrenched open the car door, she lifted her head, her face distraught.

'Did I hit her?'

'No. Allie—'

'Thank God. Oh, thank God . . .' She lifted a hand to her tousled hair, apparently unaware of the blood that streaked from her gashed lip. 'Thank God,' she said again.

'Don't move.'

'I'm all right.' She was fighting tears.

'You're bleeding. I'll get an ambulance—'

'No! I'm all right,' she said again. 'I hit my mouth, that's all. Nothing else hurts.' Very slowly she swung her legs out of the car and stood up shakily.

'Steady.' Worriedly, her father lent her his arm, handed her a handkerchief to staunch the blood from her mouth.

'I could have killed her,' she said, her trembling voice very low. 'I could have *killed* her!'

110

The little girl, still sniffing, was crossing the road towards them, Ray's arm awkwardly about her. Allie dropped to her knees, took the child's hand into her own. 'I'm sorry. I'm so sorry.'

The girl sniffed again, mournfully. 'My bike's broke.'

'We'll buy you another. I promise. The best one we can find.' The child brightened considerably. 'But are you absolutely certain that you aren't hurt?'

The wet head nodded.

'Allie,' Robert said, 'for heaven's sake, you need to see a doctor. Get inside out of this rain . . .'

Allie shook her head. 'I keep telling you: I'm all right.' She was shaking like a leaf. With a determined effort, she calmed herself, addressed herself again to the little girl. 'What's your name?'

'Annie. Annie Beston.'

'And where do you live?'

'Allie!'

Allie ignored her father's plea, and knelt in the rain beside the child she knew she might have killed.

The girl nodded a small head in the direction of the village. 'Next to the church.'

'Would you like my father to drive you home in his car?'

Wet eyes glistened. 'Cor! Yes, please!'

'He'll explain to your parents that what happened wasn't your fault. And give them some money to buy a new bicycle.' She glanced at her father. He nodded. 'Will that be all right?' she asked gently.

The child nodded. Ray stood awkwardly, watching. Allie's trembling had become so violent that she could no longer hide or control it. Tears of shock slid unnoticed down her face. Very unsteadily she stood up, did not take her father's proffered hand. She turned to Ray, gestured at the car. 'I'm sorry. I'll pay for the damage, of course . . .'

Robert had had enough. 'Allie, I insist that you get in out of this rain. Don't you know that the shock could kill you? You're soaked to the skin. Go and get changed. Bathe your mouth. I'll see to things here.'

She hesitated, then on a long, shaking breath nodded. Before she turned away, she laid a wet, trembling hand on the child's head for a moment, as if to reassure herself, then turned and plodded away from them across the road and up the drive towards Ashdown.

Two hours later, with young Annie safely delivered to her parents, the car towed to a garage for repair and Ray, to his relief, stowed unceremoniously into the local taxi and sent homeward, she faced her father knowing that the time for evasion was long past.

'I know,' she said, dully, 'about you and Celia. I know. Didn't you guess? Sometimes I couldn't believe that you didn't know – couldn't feel – the awful things that were going on inside me . . .'

It caught him unprepared: whatever he had expected, it had not been this. She saw it in the sudden hunch of his shoulders, the look on his face. She almost felt sorry for him. There was a long silence. In the darkening room the heavy curtains stirred in the draught.

'How long . . .' Robert spoke with some difficulty '. . . how long have you known?'

She was thankful at least that he had not tried to deny it. 'Since Libby's twenty-first. I was in the conservatory, trying to get away from Arthur Millson . . .' It seemed a century ago. 'When you came in, I thought it was him, and I hid. By the time I realized – it was too late . . .' Her voice faded. Her mouth was sore and swollen, her lower lip cut. She felt miserably weak and shaken, could not eradicate from her mind the small, white face of the child that she might have killed.

Her father stood, thinking back, then he turned his head, the movement one of sharp pain. 'Oh, my poor girl. My poor Allie.'

She pressed her damaged lips together and kept her head averted. The intricate pattern of the lace tablecloth on the small table next to her chair repeated itself like an endless silken spider's web across the polished wood. She lifted a

112

finger and traced it, thread by thread. There was dried blood on the back of her hand. She heard her father move, heard the unsteady chink of glass on glass.

'Here. Drink this. It'll make you feel better.' She saw his hand, and the white edge of his cuff, the cufflink shimmering dull gold against the dark stuff of his jacket as he put a large brandy glass on the table beside her. The liquid glinted, dark in the gathering shadows.

'I don't want it.' It was pure perversity. She did want it. Badly.

'Please, darling, drink it.' The hand took the glass and pressed it into hers. She lifted it and sipped. The spirit burned her cut lip and brought tears to her eyes. She blinked.

'I saw you again. A few months ago . . . just after Libby's dinner party last year. In the park behind your office. You were taking a bit of a risk there, weren't you?' Her young voice was harsh.

'God almighty.' There was raw pain in the words. 'Of all the times – Allie, Celia was trying to break it off that day, trying to make me send her away.' There was a long, aching silence. 'I wouldn't. I couldn't.'

'I don't believe you.'

'It's true. Why would I lie?'

She lifted her shoulders. 'To protect her. To protect your—' Try as she might she could not bring herself to say the word that was in her mind.

'Allie. Oh, Allie . . .'

Suddenly and uncontrollably her broken lips began to tremble and scalding tears ran down her face. 'I hate you both!' It was the anguished cry of a child.

He made a move towards her, his hand outstretched, but stopped the instant he saw her flinch from it. 'Will you let me explain, try to explain?'

She shrugged.

In silence he walked to the window. The rain had stopped. In the evening garden, a blackbird sang, suddenly and piercingly sweet.

'God knows that I didn't want to fall in love with Celia, nor she with me. I truly believe that it's brought neither of us anything but pain. It was something that happened, despite us both. I love – have always loved – your mother – oh, yes, Allie, I do.' This in reply to the violent negative movement of the brown head. 'I love her deeply. And Celia knows it.'

'Then you don't love Celia?'

'Yes, I do.'

'You can't love two people at once! You can't!'

He turned and looked at her, levelly. 'If that were true, life would be a lot easier, my dear, believe me. Who can ration love? Measure it, drop by drop, this for you and this for me, this for her and that for him? Who can say – you love this one, you may not love that one? It isn't like that, my darling. Believe me. Does loving Richard prevent your loving Libby? Of course not. Do you love one friend to the exclusion of another? Of course not—'

'But that's different!'

'How can you believe that? How can you believe that, of all the people in the world, you are destined to love only one? And why must it be that such a love is looked on as wicked, unholy? Why must you convince yourself that my loving Celia necessarily diminishes my love for your mother?'

'Because,' she said, very clearly, a year's suffering behind her, 'you don't lie to and cheat Celia. You lie to and cheat Mother.'

The words, as she had intended, hit him hard and hurtfully. He sat down, very suddenly, in the armchair by the window and bowed his face to his hands.

'It's *wrong*,' she said remorselessly. 'You know it. You both must know it, however prettily you try to dress it up. Justify it. How could you? How could you do it?'

He did not reply. In the quiet she could hear his breathing. She stood up. 'I'm going to bed.'

That brought his head up sharply. 'No. Wait. We can't leave it like this.'

114

'How else can we leave it?'

His silence was a bottomless well of pain-filled indecision. He ran a distracted hand through his dark hair. 'Allie.' The word was an appeal. Her clenched expression rejected it entirely. At last he stood up, and when he spoke his voice was remarkably collected. 'You're right, of course. You and Celia both. We have to finish it.'

'Now.'

'Darling . . .'

'Now.'

'Yes. All right. I'll telephone her.'

'Tell her why.'

His face was shocked. 'Is that necessary?'

'Tell her! I want her to know!' The pent-up misery of months needed to inflict pain. 'I want her to know. If you don't tell her, I will.'

He lifted helpless hands. 'All right.'

'Promise.'

'I promise.'

She preceded him into the hall and began to mount the stairs in silence, but stopped as he called her name. He was standing beneath her, looking up, one hand on the telephone. 'Allie – have you mentioned – this – to anyone?'

She shook her head. 'No. Not a soul.'

'Thank you,' he said.

Her composure deserted her. She turned and fled from him, tears streaming down her face. As she opened the bedroom door to the shaming sight of her own rumpled bed, she heard his voice, very calm, as he asked for the Hintons' number.

# CHAPTER SEVEN

It fell to Allie to tell first her father and then the rest of the family of Celia Hinton's sudden decision to accept an offer of employment from a friend of her father's who lived in New York. She told Robert as he drove her home. He did not speak for a long while. As the big car nosed its way through the city traffic, she stole a look at him. His face was like stone.

'For good?' he asked at last.

'Sir Brian says no, but Celia says yes.'

He turned his head sharply. 'You spoke to her?'

'Of course not. Sir Brian told me. You haven't heard from her?'

He shook his head. There was another long silence. They rolled to a smooth halt at a red traffic light. 'It's for the best,' he said, and despite herself the sadness in his voice turned in his daughter like a knife. For the past few days, to her own surprise, she had found it progressively harder to sustain her righteous anger at her father and Celia. The wound that had festered for so long, in being laid open, was healing itself. Celia's going was a strangely painful balm; though for herself she felt nothing but relief, she knew, though she fought the knowledge, how hard it must be for her father. And for Celia.

Libby did not take the news so calmly.

'What? Next week? But she can't – she *can't*! It's only three weeks to the wedding. What can she be thinking of? She's to be the other maid of honour – it'll be totally wrong without her! Oh, she wouldn't be so beastly! There's some mistake. I've *planned* it all – she knows I have – three pairs of bridesmaids and two maids of honour. Without Celia, Allie's odd . . .'

'Thank you,' Allie said mildly.

'But what's got *into* her, for heaven's sake? Has she gone crazy? She's never mentioned anything like this to me.' Libby jumped up. 'I'm going to speak to her. There's got to be some mistake. I just don't believe it . . .' She rushed into the hall, still talking.

'I must say it seems a little extraordinary.' Myra had been reading. She marked her place with a long, slender finger and looked up. 'A little sudden?'

'Apparently the job depends upon her getting to New York as soon as possible. She sails from Southampton next week. The *Mauritania*, I think.' Allie avoided her father's eyes. In the hall, Libby's voice lifted, arguing excitably.

'But, Cele, it's absolutely *odious* of you to leave me in the lurch like this – oh, I know it isn't you I'm marrying, but – yes, I know but, well – couldn't it wait? It's only three weeks – the dresses are made and everything and – oh, Celia, it just won't be the same without you – what? – well, yes, I can see that, I suppose, but – oh, I just *knew* that something would happen to spoil it all – well, of *course* it will . . .' She sounded on the verge of stormy tears.

'Does Elizabeth never think of anything but her own convenience?' asked her father, an unusual edge of irritation to his voice.

'Rarely, dear.' Peaceably, Myra went back to her book.

A few moments later, a downcast Libby rejoined them. 'It's no good. She says she can't possibly put it off. She's written me a letter, explaining and apologizing. It's in the post. Oh, damn!' She threw herself with disconsolate grace into an armchair. 'I can't think of anyone that her dress will fit. She's so slim—'

'Oh, honestly, Libby!'

Libby took no heed of her sister's involuntary exclamation. She brightened a little. 'One thing though. It'll be very exciting seeing her off.'

Robert frowned. 'Seeing her off?'

'Well, of course. I said we'd all go – well, of course we must.'

The silence that greeted this attracted Myra's attention as the words had not. 'What was that, dear?'

117

'I told Celia we'd all put in an appearance to see her off. From Southampton. I mean – we can't let her go away for ever, just like that, without giving her a send-off, can we? It'd be too bad. If Daddy can't get the day off, then we three can go by train—'

'I almost certainly won't be able to get away,' her father interrupted brusquely.

She looked at him in surprise. 'But I haven't told you which day it is yet.'

He hesitated. 'You said next week. I can't possibly manage any day next week.'

'Well, never mind. We'll go by train. It'll be splendid fun.'

'I don't expect I'll be able to make it either,' mumbled Allie. She had wandered to the shelf where the wireless stood and was twiddling the knobs, her back to the room. Atmospherics sang and whistled almost drowning the sound of a dance band. 'I'll be working, I expect.'

'Oh, of course not, you goose. Sir Brian's closing the office for the day – he and Lady Margery are going to Southampton as well. So there you are. What do you think of the idea, Mother?'

'It sounds splendid.' The radio blared suddenly. 'For goodness' sake, Allie, what are you doing with that thing? I can't hear myself think.'

'Sorry.' Allie lowered the volume. 'It's Jack Hylton. I wanted particularly to listen . . .' She adjusted the signal, and faintly a metallically light voice echoed in the room:

> . . . *that bears a lipstick's traces,*
> *An airline ticket to romantic places* . . .

'I'm not sure that I should forgive her, mind.' Libby lifted her silk-sheathed legs and draped them across the arm of her chair. 'It really is too inconsiderate of her.'

> . . . *And still my heart has wings,*
> *These foolish things remind me of you* . . .

'If the job depended on her getting there . . .'

Libby pulled a face. 'Well – couldn't she – fly or something? People do, don't they?' She waved an exasperated hand.

'Oh, don't be daft.' Allie was still fiddling with the knobs of the wireless.

*. . . tinkling piano in the next apartment,*
*Those stumbling words . . .*

'Well, I still think it beastly that she won't be at my wedding.'

'My dear girl, there'll be so many people around that I doubt if you'd notice if your father and I weren't there,' Myra said drily.

Libby giggled, pleased. 'You may be right at that.'

*. . . A fairground's painted swings,*
*These foolish things . . .*

'Do we have to put up with that racket, Allie?' Robert's voice was tight.

'I'm listening to it.' Stubbornly Allie ignored the strain that only she heard in his voice. 'I've been waiting all evening.'

'So that's settled then.' Libby was brisk. 'Mother and Allie and I will go and see Celia off. For all that she doesn't really deserve it. I must admit that I've always rather fancied standing on the dockside waving a damp hanky.'

Allie was singing with the radio, her eyes half-closed.

*The winds of March that made my heart a dancer . . .*

'Is that all right then, Al?'

'What?'

'You'll come with us. To say goodbye to Celia.'

'I – no, I don't think so.'

'Why ever not?' It was Myra, meticulously drawn eyebrows arched in surprise.

'She – well, she won't want me there, will she?' floundered Allie. She could not look at her father.

'But of course she will. She's always been very attached to you. And I daresay that Sir Brian would be pleased if you made the effort, too.'

Trapped, Allie could do nothing but surrender. 'All right. If you like.'

*Oh, how the ghost of you clings . . .*

119

With an abruptness that made Allie jump and raised Myra's head in slight surprise, Robert stood up: 'I have to have a word with Browning before he leaves. I'm not happy with the way the soft fruit's coming along.' He strode to the door. In the garden he stood for a moment on the marble terrace breathing in the fragrance of fresh-cut grass and early summer roses. Behind him he could still hear the disembodied, taunting voice.

*These foolish things remind me of you.*

Two days before Celia Hinton left for the United States, Allie saw Ray Cheshire for the last time. It was an unhappy meeting, and Allie knew within minutes what the outcome would be. They met, by arrangement, at the tennis club on a bright, cool summer's evening, and their conversation was held against a background of calls and laughter, and the sound of racquet striking ball. Ray had just come off court. He leaned against the bar, his damp hair plastered darkly against his narrow skull, his long, white-flannel-clad legs crossed, one hand fidgeting with the white pullover he had slung across his shoulders when he had finished playing. As Allie joined him, she saw the nervous jumping of the pulse at the base of his throat, revealed by the open collar of his white tennis shirt.

'Hello.'

'Hello yourself.' The forced jocularity fell absolutely flat. 'Drink?'

'Thank you. A lemonade, please.'

He called the barman and ordered her drink. As he handed it to her she saw that his hand was shaking slightly.

'Shall we sit down?'

'Why not? It doesn't cost any more.' He laughed, too loudly. Allie sighed.

They did not touch as they walked out onto the verandah of the clubhouse and found themselves a table in a secluded corner which was formed by a trellis curtained with virginia creeper. Neither, Allie noticed, was there any physical contact as he made a great show of pulling out a chair for her and settling her comfortably. She sat with her elbows on the table, nursing the tall, coldly misted glass, staring out through the screening leaves to the sunlit tennis courts beyond.

'How—' he cleared his throat, tried again, 'how did it go? With the kid's parents, I mean?'

'Better than I deserved. They were very good about it. A damn sight better than I would have been in the circumstances.' Allie's expression was grim. The thought of what she had so nearly done still sickened her. She sat for a moment in silence, then lifted her head. 'How's the car?'

'Oh, fine. Going to be as good as new. I must say that it was jolly decent of your pa to get it all in hand so quickly for me – in the circumstances,' he said, stumbling a little, 'and footing the bill, too . . . Frightfully decent of him . . .'

'. . . in the circumstances,' Allie repeated, drily, and for the first time looked straight at him.

His thin face burned brick red. 'I – well, yes.' He was fidgeting with his hands, one bony finger picking at the nail of another. With an obvious physical effort he moved his hands apart and laid them flat on the table, one each side of his beer glass.

Allie waited, running her tongue compulsively back and forth over her still very painful damaged lip.

'Allie—' he said, and stopped. She raised her brows. He said nothing, clearly embarrassed and struggling for words.

'Perhaps I'd better warn you that Dad and I didn't tell the exact truth about what happened,' Allie said after a moment. 'It seemed—' she shrugged '—advisable to keep some of it quiet. Mother thinks that you were giving me a driving lesson when I had the accident. Dad called you an "irresponsible young puppy". He was very good, actually. Lied as if he'd been doing it all his life.' Her marked mouth drew down at the private irony of that. 'He didn't think it was necessary to tell her that he'd all but found us in bed together.' She paused. 'Frightfully decent of him, eh?' she added quietly. 'Under the circumstances?'

Ray's face was very red. 'Allie, you aren't making this any easier.'

121

'Aren't making what any easier?' She sipped her lemonade.

'Oh, for God's sake – you must see – well, we can't go on seeing each other now, can we?' He was in an agony of embarrassment. Furtively he passed the back of his hand across his damp forehead. 'I mean – your father – well, damn it, Allie, how could I face him – knowing – knowing that he knows that?'

'All ashore that's going ashore. All ashore, please.'

'That's us,' said Libby, brightly and unnecessarily.

The flower-filled cabin buzzed and hummed with talk and laughter.

'. . . Darling! Actually to *live* in New York. How absolutely divine! I'm *mad* with jealousy . . .'

'. . . if you want to get into a gas mask, I told the silly little man, then you'll have to catch me before I go to the hairdresser's, not after . . .'

'. . . what's got into the gel I can't imagine. New York indeed! And at a week's notice! I don't know what the young women of today are coming to, that I don't . . .'

'. . . all over bar the shouting, if you ask me, old man. Franco's as good as taken Bilbao. Beginning of the end . . .'

Allie pulled her mother's sleeve. 'Time to go.'

'Yes, dear. But we haven't had a chance to say goodbye properly yet.' Myra put her tall champagne glass on a nearby table. 'Let's say our farewells and leave Celia to her family.'

Reluctantly the girl allowed herself to be towed through the elegant throng to where Celia, pale and composed, stood by the door. The slim, neatly suited figure looked poised and calm. Allie hung back. It was the first time the two girls had come face to face since Allie had told her father that she knew of his liaison.

'I wish you the very best of luck, my dear.' Myra kissed the pearly cheek warmly. 'I must say that I think you're very brave indeed. It's a great pity that Robert couldn't be

here. He wanted to, I know, but pressure of work . . .
Anyway, he sends his love . . .'

Over Myra's shoulder, green eyes met blue. Celia held
Allie's look steadily.

'Good luck.' Allie felt gawky and a little stupid as she
hung back, unwilling even to offer a hand.

'Thank you.' Celia's smile was fleeting.

'Cele, you're an absolute beast, and I'm never going to
forgive you!' Libby, unknowing, eased the moment as she
burst from the crowd and flung her arms about her friend.
'Never, so there! Well, not unless you promise faithfully to
write every single week. And let me and Edward come and
stay with you for our hols next year.'

'Of course.' Celia's arms tightened around Libby and at
last her eyes left Allie's. 'Of course you must.'

'Good luck, darling. Oh, the best of good luck.' Libby's
voice was muffled against Celia's shoulder.

'All ashore . . .'

'We must go.'

'Thank you for coming. Thank you all for coming.' The
tremor in Celia's husky voice was all but lost in the noise as
the huge liner readied herself for departure. Allie steeled
herself against it.

Half an hour later, they stood on the dockside, the great
vessel rearing above them, a streamlined monster decked in
flags, bunting and streamers. A few yards away a brass band
played, its sound almost lost in the hubbub of last-minute
goodbyes and cheers. As the ship's siren shrieked, another
billow of streamers was tossed from the deck rails – a
shifting, fragile, multicoloured web that for a last few
moments tenuously linked the travellers on board with
those they were leaving behind; then the dark stretch of
water between dockside and ship slowly widened and the
great liner, siren still sounding, made for the open sea,
leaving in her wake a swell of oily water upon which floated,
sodden and pathetic, the debris of celebration.

It was full dark before the train neared London. Myra
and her daughters had a First Class compartment to them-

selves. During the journey their conversation had petered out, and they travelled for the most part in silence. Myra and Allie were reading. Libby, one elbow on the table, chin on hand, was staring moodily into the night, watching the occasional lights which flashed past as the express sped on.

'Damned stupid I call it, going away like that.' She broke a long silence, speaking as much to herself as to her mother and sister.

'I do wish you'd watch your language, dear. It really isn't very becoming to swear.'

Allie said nothing.

Libby shifted her stance restlessly. 'Jolly good job I've found someone that the maid of honour's dress fits.'

This was news to Allie. 'You have?'

'Yes. Jesse Warrington.'

'But – I thought you didn't like Jesse Warrington?'

'I don't very much. But she's the only one the right size.'

Her sister's silence said more than words.

'Well, I couldn't have you standing there all on your own, you great clumsy lummox, could I?' Libby snapped defiantly, half-turning. 'You're supposed to look after the little ones. You're more likely to fall flat on your face. I wanted two maids of honour, and two I shall have!' Angrily she turned back to the window. But not before Allie had seen the sheen of tears on her cheeks.

The morning of Libby's marriage to Edward Maybury dawned, as if to order, fresh and sunlit with a lucently cloudless sky. Ashdown was pandemonium, filled – or so it seemed to Robert Jordan – with nervously giggling, scampering small girls in pastel-coloured frills and flounces, and their equally nervous if less disruptive elders who spent a great deal of time adjusting their own and each other's dresses, hair, flowers and stocking seams. In the midst of this chaos, Libby, to everyone's surprise, was the still eye of the storm. Serenely beautiful in her sweeping ivory satin, a small, pearl-covered Juliet cap anchoring the yards of delicate lace that clouded her slim shoulders and swept to the floor behind her, she was utterly composed, utterly happy. This was her day, her perfect day. Her amazing, unruffled calm held through the trying morning as the constantly ringing doorbell and telephone heralded telegrams, flowers, last-minute presents and endless numbers of unsolicited well-wishers. At two o'clock the procession of shining, flower- and ribbon-decked limousines began to wind its way down the drive, and Libby stood with her father at the drawing-room window watching the rest of the family and their guests leave, organized with smooth efficiency by Myra.

'Uncle Bertie, you're in the first car with Richard and Aunt Liz and the others. Sarah, do stand still, child, your ribbons are getting all tangled. Jesse, you'll go with these three in the next car and Allie's in the one behind with the rest of the little ones. Allie, do keep your eye on young Dora – if she loses any more petals from her basket, she'll have none at all to scatter when the time comes. Wait just a moment, darling, your headdress is just a little – there, that's better. Off you go . . .' From apparent chaos, order emerged and the sleek black cars, glittering in the sun, rolled slowly one after the other down to the gate and out onto the road.

'Right.' Myra came, smiling, into the drawing room. 'It's my turn to be off now, my dears. I'll see you at the church.' She paused before her daughter, an extra brilliance in her sapphire eyes. 'You look wonderful, darling. Simply beautiful.' She leaned and, delicately so as not to disarrange the careful toilette, kissed Libby's cheek. 'I wish you all the happiness in the world.' Briskly then she walked to the mirror, adjusted her rakish, wide-brimmed hat to a jaunty angle, straightened the jacket of her pearl-grey suit whose pale tartan lining matched exactly her soft silk blouse, then with another quick, determined smile she left them and, a moment later, Robert and Libby were alone in the unnaturally quiet house.

'Nervous?' asked Robert softly.

'A bit, I suppose. But I'm truly too happy to care.'

'Your Edward is a very lucky young man indeed.'

'My Edward is the dearest, kindest and most wonderful man in the world.'

They smiled at each other.

'You really love him, don't you?'

'More than I can say.'

He opened his arms to her then and, laughing, she went to him, resting her head lightly on his shoulder, the drifting lace of her veil enveloping them both. Very gently he rocked her, in these last moments that she would ever be entirely his.

'Time to go,' she whispered at last and, stepping away from him, lifted her arms and drew the misty veil over her face.

Outside the church Allie waited, one gloved hand firmly grasping Dora's restive paw, the other holding her own rose-decked and ribboned basket of petals. The church path, leading from the tiled lichgate, was gold-dappled with sunshine that showered through the sheltering trees like new-minted coins. She saw the last car draw up at the gate, caught glimpses through the yew hedge of the glimmering satin of her sister's dress and the black and grey of her father's morning suit. At the gate stood a small cluster of well-wishers from the village who 'ohh-ed' and clapped and called greetings as the bride and her father passed smiling through them. From within the ancient church, the rolling organ-sound died when, as if by magic, the news of the bride's arrival was telegraphed to the organist. As Libby and her father joined the bridesmaids at the church door, there was a flurry of skirt- and veil-straightening, last-minute exhortations and stern warnings, and the little procession – its head the erect and lovely figure of the young bride, its body a pretty pastel spectrum of peach and apricot hues – entered the striking chill of the old church and made its way to the bright, flower-decked altar to the strains of Mendelssohn's 'Wedding March'.

There was one moment during her sister's wedding that Allie never forgot: as the ceremony neared its end, a shaft of sunshine, piercingly bright, and made into solid gold by the motes of dust that danced within it, fell through a small window high in the ancient walls and struck directly upon the couple as they stood at the altar exchanging rings that glinted in the light. It was as if some pagan deity blessed the union with gifts of promise. Edward looked proud and happy beside his beautiful bride and there was not a soul in the church who could help but be moved by Libby's brilliant smile as her new husband lifted her veil and gently kissed her.

Outside, with the bells pealing and the restraints of church lifted from half a dozen over-excited, self-important little girls, Allie had her hands full while the photographer tediously grouped and regrouped the principals and the guests, disappearing beneath his enveloping black shroud and then popping back, hair awry, like some eccentric jack-in-the-box. It was not until after they had arrived at the White Hart Hotel, where the reception and wedding breakfast was to be held, that Allie found a quiet moment to extend her own good wishes to her sister.

'I hope you'll always be as happy as you are today.' She kissed her warmly.

'I will be, Allie darling. What else could I be? And thank you – for your help, for everything. Young Dora would probably have dismantled the church stone by stone if you hadn't been there!'

Allie laughed. Around them, morning-suited men and elegantly dressed women enjoyed the White Hart's excellent sherry and caught up on family gossip, the Jordans grouped at one end of the panelled room, the Mayburys at the other. Libby rolled her eyes.

'We'd better get circulating, darling. They look like armies drawn up for battle. Let's hope the champers brings them together!'

It did. By the time the meal was over and the tables had been cleared and pushed back to the sides of the ballroom to make space for an afternoon's dancing, the most rigidly proper members of the two families were unbending a little.

Allie found the afternoon flying past her in a whirl of faces to which she could rarely put names and a babble of half-remembered conversations.

'. . . living in London, I understand? Near one of the parks, isn't it?'

'Yes. A lovely little flat, in Rampton Court. Edward's parents gave it to them as a wedding present . . .'

'Later, of course, we'll move to the country . . .' this from Libby herself who, glass in hand, had appeared at her sister's shoulder '. . . and have *hundreds* of children . . .' She drifted away on the laughter that produced.

'. . . a honeymoon in Paris. How romantic . . .'

'Allie, Libby's asking for you – it's time for her to change. They'll have to leave very soon or they'll miss their train.'

Upstairs, in the room set aside for the purpose, Allie helped her sister out of the exquisite wedding dress and laid out the wide-shouldered, tailored travelling suit of navy blue trimmed with white. White shoes, hat and bag completed the chic ensemble.

With the only sign of strained nerves that she had, to her credit, shown all day, Libby, bending to pull on the high-heeled white shoes, asked irritably, 'Why does Aunt Alice have to be such a pain?'

Allie was carefully folding the shining yards of wedding dress. 'Aunt Alice? What's she done?'

'She's spent the entire day – the *entire* day – talking about some speech that Lady Reading made on the wireless yesterday. Some nonsense about women's voluntary services for something or other. Civil defence or ARP or washing up or something. I don't know. I don't want to know. Not on my wedding day, *ad nauseam*. She's been damned well *recruiting* out there! On my wedding day!'

Allie laughed. 'If anyone's asking for volunteers, Aunt Alice will volunteer, you can depend on it. If the devil himself asked for volunteers Aunt Alice wouldn't be able to resist rolling up her sleeves and falling in line.'

'She'd probably find Mother there ahead of her.' The two girls exploded into laughter.

Allie smoothed the ivory satin and laid the dress in its box. 'Doesn't it seem a shame that you'll only wear this once? It's so very beautiful . . .'

'I shall keep it for ever,' Libby said, 'and I shall wear it for Edward on our golden wedding anniversary. See if I don't.'

The send-off, from the steps of the hotel, was riotous. The hired car that was to take them to the station had been festooned in streamers and balloons. A dustbin-load of tins and old boots and shoes had been attached to the back. The air as the young couple fled, laughing, down the steps to the car was a blizzard of confetti and rice. As amidst cheers and a great deal of champagne-induced last-minute advice to Edward the car pulled away and turned the corner, Allie slipped back into the almost-empty ballroom and dropped into a chair by a table that stood close to the little stage upon which a five-piece band still manfully played.

'You look as if you've had a hard day?'

She looked up. The smiling young man who stood above her looked vaguely familiar. 'Yes I have, to tell the truth. I didn't realize that being a bridesmaid would turn out to be such hard work!' She searched her memory, but could not even begin to place him. He was tall, with brownish-fair hair and an unremarkable but pleasant face to which a small blond moustache added character. His eyes were that mixture of brown and green called hazel and very clear and kindly.

He divined the reason for her confusion at once. 'Peter Wickham,' he said.

'Oh, of course . . .' She extended her hand. 'We met at Libby's twenty-first. I never ever thanked you for rescuing me from the awful Arthur.'

'Is that what I did?'

She nodded, her smile a little less ready. Of all things, today, she did not want to be reminded of that other celebration. Yet, perversely, she found herself saying, 'You came with Celia Hinton, didn't you?'

'That's right. Celia and I are old friends – practically grew up together in fact. Our parents have been chums from way back – Edward's too.'

'Why, of course, Edward was with you that night, wasn't he? Well – how does it feel to be responsible for all this?'

'I wouldn't put it that strongly.' When he smiled his eyes crinkled engagingly. 'From the look of those two, that marriage was made in heaven. If I hadn't been instrumental in bringing them together, something or someone else would have. May I join you?' He drew out a chair and stood looking at her in polite enquiry.

'Oh, of course. I'm sorry.'

He sat down, indicated the band with a nod of his head. 'They're jolly good, aren't they?'

'Yes, they are.' The room was filling now as people drifted back from the send-off, and two or three couples were dancing. There was a short, slightly uncomfortable silence.

'Do you—'

'Have you—' They both spoke at once, stopped, laughed.

'After you,' Allie said. 'I think you beat me by half a syllable.'

'I was just going to ask if you'd heard from Celia lately?'

She might have expected it, but she had not. She felt her face stiffen. Peter was watching the band, his hand tapping out the rhythm on the table top.

'I – well, yes. Libby has, that is. And Sir Brian. I get the news from them. Celia sent Libby and Edward a rather splendid modern silver fruit bowl for a wedding present. It's a lovely thing.' She thought that he must hear the desperate distaste that she could not keep from her voice, but it seemed that he did not.

'l had a letter. She seems to be making a go of it, doesn't she? But then, I can't imagine old Celia not getting what she wants in the end, can you?'

Her tongue finally gave out on her. She looked at him in silence, her face wooden. He turned, smiling in question, waiting for a response.

'I'm sorry? I didn't catch what you said.'

'I said – oh, never mind. It doesn't matter. I say, I've just remembered – you work for Sir Brian, don't you?'

'Yes, I do. Full time now that Celia's gone.'

'Do you like it?'

'Yes. Very much.'

'The business must be a bit dicey, I should think, with all the trouble in Europe?'

She nodded. 'It's all right at the moment, but if anything should happen . . .'

He was sober for a moment. 'It's a damn shame. The business means a lot to the old man, doesn't it?'

'You know him well?'

'I should say so.' He grinned, boyishly. 'He's my godfather. I'll never forget the day he caught Celia and me in his cellar at the vintage port. We must have been about eight at the time. I couldn't sit down for a week!'

She laughed, briefly.

Head on one side, he extended a square, rather bony hand. 'Would you like to dance?'

Relief that the awkward subject was past overcame her tiredness. 'I'd love to.'

He was, as she remembered, an extremely good dancer. His hands were cool, his smile pleasant and he smelled, faintly and agreeably, of soap and hair cream. As before, he did not attempt to make forced conversation, but their silence was natural and completely unstrained. By the time they returned to the table several dances later, Allie was surprised to realize that an easy mood of friendliness had grown between them. Pots of tea and small plates of biscuits, cakes and sweetmeats had been placed on the tables.

'Marzipan! Lovely! I adore marzipan . . .'

He watched with some amusement as she poked with almost childlike pleasure among the marzipan fruits. 'Aren't they pretty? Almost too good to eat. Look at these.' She lifted on a long, narrow palm two minutely perfect, rosy apples complete with stems and leaves and held them out to him. 'Would you like one?'

He laughed as he took one. 'There's progress for you.'

'What is?'

'The modern Eve. She has two apples – one to offer and one to keep.'

'Very sensible.' She nibbled at a marzipan leaf, smiling mischievously. 'Actually, I think someone made a bad mistake with that particular story,' she added.

'Oh?'

'Well, isn't it supposed to illustrate Adam's rectitude and poor Eve's female weakness?'

'I suppose it is, yes.'

'Well, perhaps it does that. But if you ask me, it makes Adam look a terrible nincompoop on the way, doesn't it? I mean – compare their two excuses . . .' Enjoying herself, she rested her chin on her hand and waited a moment before continuing. 'Eve, all wide eyes and fluttering lashes – I'm sure she'd have found out how to do that by then – says, "Lord, I truly can't imagine how it happened; you see, this magical, fascinating, terrifying serpent slithered from his lair and hid in Your garden to tempt me" – while all Adam could manage was "It wasn't my fault, Lord. *She* made me do it." If you're going to tell a story, I always say, then at least make it a good one!'

'If I were the Lord, I know which story I'd have believed.'

'And if I were, I know which one I'd have enjoyed most.'

He threw back his head and shouted with laughter. Pleased with her success Allie popped the sweet into her mouth and chewed it, grinning.

They danced again, several times, and in between they chatted like old friends. Peter's parents, Allie discovered, had recently moved to the nearby village of Watersfield; Peter, who worked for a merchant bank, lived in rooms in London during the week but would be spending most weekends in Kent.

'Do you play tennis?' Allie asked.

'Yes, I do, actually.'

'Marvellous. I'll get Daddy to put you up for the club if

you'd like. We could have a few games – that is, if you'd like to, of course?' She was suddenly acutely embarrassed. In the short time they had spent together, a kind of camaraderie had grown between them that had nothing whatever in common with the wary, sharply flirtatious contests that Allie had grown used to with most of the boys she knew. Peter was friendly, intelligent and good company. Physically, he did not particularly attract her. Only as she spoke had she realized the interpretation that might be put on her impulsive and, she supposed, rather forward suggestion. Young ladies simply did not make such advances at first meeting. She blushed furiously. 'I didn't mean—' she stammered.

'That would be really marvellous. And very kind. Thank you. I don't know this area very well – most of my friends are in London. Or getting married,' he added with his engaging smile. 'The tennis club would be super. And while we're on the subject, you don't know of a decent local stables, do you?'

Relieved that the difficult moment was past, she nodded. 'The one on Brent Hill's best. Mrs Matthews. I learned there when I was little.'

'Splendid.' He looked up sharply, then smiling he pushed his chair back and stood up, looking over Allie's head. Allie turned to find her mother standing behind her.

'Allie, darling, it's nearly time to go. A few people are coming back to the house . . .' Myra paused, smiling at Peter, waiting.

'Oh – Mother, this is Peter Wickham, remember? Edward's friend. He was at Libby's twenty-first.'

'Ah, of course. Forgive me, Mr Wickham.' Myra extended a white-gloved hand. 'Would you care to come back to Ashdown for a drink?'

'Thank you, Mrs Jordan, but I'm afraid I can't. I've already made arrangements for the evening.'

'What a pity. Never mind. Another time, perhaps? Allie?' Myra looked expectantly at her daughter.

'Coming, Mother.' Allie, too, extended her hand to Peter

Wickham. 'It's been really nice meeting you again,' she said candidly.

'The pleasure's mine. And I'll take you up on the tennis club, if I might?'

'Of course. I'll speak to Daddy. If you'd like to ring in a week or so we can make some arrangements.'

'Splendid. Thank you. —Oh – wait a sec,' he called her back as she turned to go. 'You've forgotten something.' He reached into the depleted bowl of sweets and extracted the last, tiny apple. She held out her hand and he dropped it into her palm. 'First prize in the story-telling contest,' he said solemnly.

On the way across the dance floor, their heels clicking sharply upon the highly polished boards, mother eyed daughter a little slyly. 'Mr Wickham seems an extremely nice young man.'

'Yes, he is.'

'Will we be seeing him again, do you think?'

Half-irritated, Allie glanced at her. 'Mother, honestly—' She caught, in time, the twinkle of good-tempered fun in her mother's eye. She laughed. 'I wouldn't be at all surprised.'

# CHAPTER EIGHT

It afterwards seemed to Allie that her sister's wedding was the last event in their lives to be untouched by the possibility – or rather the probability – of a coming war. She knew of course, as did everyone, that the signs had been there long before, yet always she had managed to convince herself that such a thing could not happen. Now, as controversy raged through the country over Hitler's threat to Czechoslovakia, she found herself, like so many others, scanning the papers for news and opinion, listening with unaccustomed regularity to the BBC's six o'clock news bulletins, and – again in common with most of Britain – torn between the desire to see her country do the honourable thing and champion a small, helpless nation against the brutal predacity of her Nazi neighbour and terror at the thought of what such a course of action might entail.

She listened with trepidation to the gloomily confident predictions of what modern warfare would bring: mass air attacks on civilian centres, the possibility – some said the certainty – that in the first weeks of a conflict up to 100,000 tons of bombs could be dropped on London alone, with an estimated fifty casualties to each ton of bombs – this last terrifying figure was widely believed despite the fact that neither casualty rates from the Great War nor, more recently, from Spain bore them out. That there would be no possible way to stop wave after wave of enemy bombers from pounding Britain's cities to rubble was a widely held belief. 'The bombers will always get through' was a phrase that quickly filtered through from the enclaves of Whitehall to the civilian population. There were many to wonder that the world could have come again to such a knife-edge of peril just twenty years after the savage conflict that most supposed to have at last taught the futility of war. During that September of 1938, Allie saw trenches dug in Hyde Park, collected her gas mask from the village hall, joined, with her mother, Lady Reading's new organization for women, known as the Women's Voluntary Service (WVS) and heartily detested the anguished, eldritch wail of the air-raid sirens that were tested not just in London but all over the country. Visiting the small local school with her mother to help in the distribution of Mickey Mouse and Donald Duck gas masks, she heard a group of little girls in the playground, skipping and singing cheerfully:

> *. . . Underneath the spreading chestnut tree,*
> *Neville Chamberlain said to me,*
> *'If you want to get your gas mask free,*
> *Join the blinkin' ARP' . . .*

and reflected that any future historian who took children's doggerel for reported fact might wrongly assume that any of the population that declined to join the civil defence services would be left to fend for themselves in a gas attack.

Then at Munich, as the tense month drew to its close, a kind of peace was dearly bought and the conscience of a nation twitched a little, blinked and – for a while at least – went thankfully back to sleep. Allie was more than ready to accept Mr Chamberlain's piece of paper at face value. She was nearly twenty years old and the sun was still shining. In Celia's absence and with her own self-destructive attempts to punish her father ended, she was beginning to find herself again. And though, in the distance, she could not but be aware that the dogs of war still howled threateningly, she closed her ears to the sound and convinced herself that the crisis was over and that, under the circumstances, to live for the moment was the sanest, perhaps the only, thing to do.

She saw Peter Wickham several times during that hot August and September. They played tennis together, swam once or twice in his parents' open-air swimming pool, met for drinks in the village pub. They also, apparently accidentally, bumped into each other from time to time at Libby's and Edward's flat in London. By the fourth time,

Allie had her doubts as to the nature of these supposedly chance meetings and was beginning strongly to suspect collusion between her mother and her sister, both of whom were delighted at this friendship between Allie and a 'nice young man'.

One Friday evening early in October, she dropped in to Rampton Court at her sister's request to return a book to find that Peter was there and had been invited to supper. She did not, truthfully, put up too much resistance to the idea of making it a foursome, and the evening passed pleasantly light-heartedly. The evening before, Libby and Edward had been to the Adelphi theatre to see, for the third time, Ivor Novello's popular musical play *The Dancing Years*. Edward proclaimed dolefully that he felt personally responsible for the play's enormous financial success.

'I mean – three times! And even that isn't enough for her!' He held his head in mock despair. 'She wants to see it again at Christmas!'

'But it's such a *marvellous* thing, darling, you know it is! You love it just as much as I do. Don't be such an old meany. Peter, aren't I right?'

'I'm sure you are. But I'm not taking sides between husband and wife. Besides, I haven't seen it, so I can't judge.'

'What!' Libby raised scandalized hands. 'Never seen it? Where have you been? Allie, tell the man . . .'

Allie, grinning and off her guard, fell straight into the trap. 'It's no good looking at me. I haven't seen it either.' Too late she stopped, eyeing her sister in sudden suspicion.

Libby, a small, artful smile on her pretty face, folded her hands in her lap and looked with wide blue eyes from one to the other.

Peter's hazel eyes crinkled. 'Would you like to see it?' he asked Allie.

'Well, I – oh, no – I mean yes, of course, I would but – oh, honestly, Libby, you're the living limit! Fancy—'

Peter interrupted her. 'No, please, I mean it. Would you?'

'I – yes, as a matter of fact I would.'

'That's settled then. I'll get the tickets, and perhaps we could dine afterwards?'

Libby smiled a beatifically self-satisfied smile, ignoring the swift scowl her sister sent in her direction. 'There. Isn't that nice? Now, come along children. Supper's getting cold.'

As they stood in the hall later, donning their coats and hats and saying their goodbyes – Peter was going home to Kent and had offered Allie a lift to Ashdown – Allie, in picking up her gloves from the white, glass-topped hall table, knocked a buff-coloured booklet to the floor. She picked it up and frowned at it, distaste clear on her face.

'You got one too.'

'Didn't everyone?' Libby flipped it from her fingers and tossed it back onto the table. 'What a load of tommyrot. I have no interest whatsoever in protecting my home from non-existent air raids. Damn 'em.' She shrugged. 'If Adolf comes, he comes. I'm not making up bloody sandbags for anyone. Just think what it would do to my fingernails!'

Allie laughed, then, on the landing outside the door, paused. 'Oh, that reminds me though. Mother sent a message. She's ordered some heavy black sateen from Mr Eldan, the draper. She said to tell you that she'd got enough for you too. She was sure you wouldn't think of it.'

Libby looked at her in comic and deliberate incomprehension. 'My dear, I wouldn't be seen *dead* in black sateen.'

'Don't be an idiot! Blackout curtains! Just in case, Mother says.' Allie started down the wide marble staircase that led to the handsome lobby. Peter followed.

Libby hung over the polished wooden banisters above them, her laughter echoing up the elegant stairwell. 'I'll get them lined in rose pink at Harrods! Black would play hell with my decor!'

In Peter's car, Allie brought up the subject of what she saw as her sister's none-too-subtle blackmail.

'You really don't have to take me to the theatre, you know. I shall quite understand. It was outrageous of Libby – she really can be a pain sometimes.'

'I think she's charming. I like her a lot. And very much want to take you to the theatre, if you'd like to come. It's terribly remiss of us both not to have seen something that every other inhabitant of the south of England seems to have seen at least twice!'

She laughed. 'All right then, if you put it like that. Thank you. I'd love to.'

'That's settled, then. Oh, and there was something else I thought might be fun . . .' The car swung around Piccadilly Circus with its multicoloured display of lit and moving advertisements.

'What's that?'

'Do I remember your saying that you ride? I was wondering if we might take a couple of hacks on Sunday and you could show me some of the local countryside before the weather closes in on us for the winter?'

Allie shifted a little uncomfortably. He glanced at her in the lurid light, his eyebrows raised.

She hesitated, absurdly tempted to lie, then said in a rush: 'Actually, I'm not very good at horses. Not very British of me, I know, but there you are. I never was very keen, and then a few years back I fell off and I've been terrified of the brutes ever since. My only personalized method of transport is a bicycle. It may be slow, and not look so good, but at least it can't kick you.'

His shout of laughter surprised her into a smile. 'But what a perfectly splendid idea!'

'What is?'

'Bicycles! If you're game, that is? We could take a picnic. My God, I haven't been out for the day on a bike for years! What do you think?'

She was infected by his enthusiasm. 'Wonderful. Have you got a bike?'

'I should say so. Buried somewhere or other. Dad'll know where. You?'

'Of course. It used to be Libby's. She gave it to me for my thirteenth birthday. I used to polish it religiously every Saturday morning. It's a BSA with a big basket on the front.'

'Splendid! And mine's got a saddlebag, so we can certainly carry a picnic between us. Lemonade and hard-boiled eggs.' He grinned across at her like a boy. 'What do you say?'

'Leave out the hard-boiled eggs and you're on. If the weather's good enough, we could go down to the Medway – picnic by the river. Richard and I often used to go there when we were children. It isn't very far.'

'You've got a date.'

The car chugged across London Bridge, the Thames flowing far below, darkly silent, the lights of London glimmering in ribbons along the river's banks. Five minutes later, driving through the featureless suburbs, Allie was asleep, a faint, happy smile on her lips.

Sunday morning was cool and bright. Great banks of cotton-wool cloud piled in the blue sky, gilded and fired by the rays of the south-slanting autumn sun. The reds and golds of the woodlands burned in the clear air as Allie and Peter rode their old bicycles at an easy pace down almost deserted, leaf-carpeted lanes. Allie, dressed comfortably in an old white shirt-blouse and a washed-out blue cotton skirt, her brown legs bare, her white tennis socks and plimsoles already scuffed with oil from the freshly lubricated chain of the BSA, directed the expedition, the experience of a long childhood in the area fitting her for her role as guide.

They rode down narrow lanes and unpaved farm tracks, missing the main roads wherever possible. Peter sang silly songs, recalled from his days as a Boy Scout and swung his feet up onto the handlebars, showing off and nearly making Allie fall from her machine with laughter. Before long, the woodlands gave way to rolling farmland. Red and russet apples still clustered opon sturdy orchard trees that marched in line across short, lush green grass that was sometimes grazed by docile sheep. The hop gardens were deserted now, the empty wires singing in the wind, the cheerful, noisy pickers gone back to their city streets for another year. The stripped bines were coiled in clumps at the foot of the poles, the ridged and furrowed soil trampled almost flat. Allie found a bine run wild in a hedge among the bright autumn berries and old man's beard. She picked a green, flaky hop and crushed it in her fingers, the sulphurous yellow pollen blackening her skin.

'Smell.' She held out her hand to Peter.

He steadied himself with one foot on the road and obediently sniffed. 'It's very distinctive.'

'It's one of my favourite smells in the world. Whenever we could, Richard and I used to sneak off and come to the hop gardens when the pickers were here. We used to pick sometimes with a gypsy family over Wateringbury way. Mother nearly had a fit when she found out.'

'I'll bet she did!'

They coasted downhill, laughing, to the closed level-crossing gates at the bottom, where they waited for the passing of the small local steam train on the single track railway that served the valley. Beyond, two fields away, the river Medway ran between green, tree-shaded banks, sparkling in the sunlight. Allie waved as the little train passed and a group of children in the end carriage waved enthusiastically back. She turned to find Peter watching her, smiling. She pulled a self-deprecating face: 'I never can resist waving to trains.'

The level-crossing gates were cranked squeakily open: they bumped across the railway lines and onto the road. Allie lifted a hand and pointed. 'There – do you see the bridge? It's lovely – medieval, I think, used by packhorses hundreds of years ago. There's a footpath on the other side that follows the river for – oh, miles. There's a gate we can get the bikes through. I thought we'd picnic up there, do you see? Where the little hill slopes down to the river. You can see for miles from up there. Richard and I used to come here a lot.'

They rode to the bridge, exchanging greetings with an elderly man who was walking his dog, and watched for a moment a group of small children who were throwing twigs into the water on one side of the bridge then rushing, shrieking, to the other side to watch them as they sailed slowly from the darkness out into the sunlit stream.

'Poohsticks,' said Peter, smiling, and Allie laughed delightedly.

'Fancy your knowing that.'

'I may have been a city boy, but I'll have you know I had a very good taste in literature.'

They wheeled the bikes through the gate and set off, pushing the machines, along the river. The sun was high now and very hot. Allie, her mouth dry, thought with happy anticipation of Mrs Welsh's home-made lemonade that she carried in her basket. They had walked for perhaps a mile when she stopped, pointing.

'There. That's the place, up there under the big oak tree. We can leave the bikes here. Beat you up there—' She grabbed the bag that rested in the basket and let her bicycle drop onto the grass, where it lay, back wheel spinning. Without waiting for Peter, she set off, scrambling, up the hillside. Brambles scratched her legs, the sun was hot on her face. When she reached the picnic place she set the bag she carried on the ground and then threw herself thankfully onto the cool grass beneath the tree. Utterly relaxed, her heart pumping, her legs throbbing with unaccustomed effort, she lay on her back letting the breeze cool her burning face and dry her sweat-dampened hair. Above her the flame-tinged leaves of the oak tree were a fretwork against a cobalt sky that seemed limitless as eternity. She closed her eyes. When she opened them again, a strangely disproportioned, elongated figure loomed above her; Peter's skin, like her own, was sun-flushed and bright with the exertion of climbing the hill. He was looking down at her with a small half-smile on his lips.

'You look like a little girl.'

Suddenly self-conscious, she sat up, pulling her skirt smoothly over her knees. In the tree above them, a blackbird, alarmed by the movement, skittered, chirping a sharp alarm through the branches.

After they had eaten, they sat looking across the valley

and talking in a companionable, desultory fashion, Peter lying on his side, his head propped on his hand, a long piece of feathered grass stuck between his lips, Allie sitting with her knees crooked, her arms resting upon them, her eyes focused on the green, autumn-softened distances. After a while an easy silence fell between them. Far above, a small aeroplane droned, glinting like a silver dragonfly in the sun. The train that had passed them at the level-crossing chuffed its steady way back up the valley, from this height and distance like a toy that journeyed across a patchwork quilt, the steam from its funnel unfurled behind it like a banner in the still air. Endless recollections of this childhood hillside flooded Allie, fragmented impressions of another time – truly, she thought, another life. She saw Richard up this very tree, grinning like the Cheshire cat, saw two small, muddy children down there by the river bank, jam-jars in hand, fishing for tiddlers . . .

'There's another.'

'Another what?' She jumped at Peter's voice.

'Another plane. Up there. See?' Peter was shading his eyes. 'I wonder . . .'

'What?'

'I wonder if they can see us.'

'Lord, I hope not!' The words were suddenly, absurdly sharp. She watched silently as the small plane dipped and flew from sight behind the hill. Suddenly and from nowhere she heard Richard's voice, quietly grim, as he spoke of bombings and strafings, and the mischievous, grinning Cheshire cat of her earlier imaginings was overlaid by the recollection of her brother's face as it had looked when he had come back from Spain – thin, shadowed, indefinably damaged. Her mind flinched from the memory.

'What do you think it will be like if war comes?' she found herself asking, her softly sombre voice all but lost in the still heat of the afternoon.

There was a long silence. Peter sat up. 'Who knows?' His eyes were thoughtful. 'We can't know, can we? If it comes it'll be like no other war's ever been, that's for sure. I suppose, like anything else, we must simply face it if it happens. And pray that it doesn't.'

She plucked at the grass by her green-stained plimsole. 'I suppose so.'

Something struck her arm, and as she looked up an acorn bounced away into the grass. Peter was grinning at her.

'Come on, sobersides. Cheer up. Hitler isn't at Dover yet. Any more of that lemonade left?'

They rested for another hour before starting for home. Allie lay back and closed her eyes, and to her own surprise found herself drifting into the half-dream of a doze. She was wakened by an insect crawling on her face. Sleepily she brushed it away, but immediately it was back. She opened her eyes. Peter waved a long piece of grass at her.

'Time to go, sleepyhead.'

'I didn't go to sleep.'

'Not much you didn't.'

'I just had my eyes closed.'

'Ah. I see. And do you always snore when your eyes are closed?'

'I was *not*—' She stopped, laughing.

'It's half past three.'

She lay quite still for a moment, looking up at him with sleepy eyes. Silhouetted against the sky, his face was dark, his expression indecipherable. For a moment she thought he might be about to kiss her, wondered in an oddly detached way what it would be like if he did. She waited.

'Beat you to the bikes,' he said and was up and running, galloping down the hill before she had scrambled to her feet.

They rode home, tired, in the light of a sun that set redly into a bank of heavy cloud. Allie filled her bicycle basket with twigs from the hedgerows, laden with berries and golden leaves. In the smudged shadows of evening, they stopped, side by side, at the entrance to Ashdown's drive.

'It's been lovely,' Allie said.

'Yes, it has. Thank you.'

They smiled at each other.

144

'I'll telephone you, to let you know about the theatre tickets. I'm not sure when, though – we're pretty busy at the bank at the moment, and the tickets may not be easy to come by.'

'Oh – that's all right. Whenever you like.'

''Bye then.'

'Goodbye.' There was a faint, nebulous feeling of sadness in her as she watched him cheerfully mount the old bike and pedal away into the shadows of the tree-lined lane. This carefree, sunlit day had been, unexpectedly, like a moment stolen back from a happy childhood. Now, with dark clouds piling in the sky, it was over. She doubted there could be many more like it. Sighing, she trudged up the gravel drive, pushing her bicycle.

It was many weeks before she heard from Peter again. At first she was a little disappointed, then philosophical; after all, their day together, while marvellously enjoyable, could hardly have been termed romantic. One evening a couple of weeks before Christmas, when her mother called her to the telephone, the last voice she expected to hear was his.

'Allie? I've got them at last. The tickets. Managed to buy them from a friend.'

It took a moment for his voice to register. 'The—? Oh – Peter?'

'The very same. Look, I'm sorry I haven't been in touch. There's been a bit of a crisis at the bank – I've been in Holland for the past two or three weeks. How are you?'

'Fine, thanks.'

'The tickets are for Friday evening. I know it's short notice – will it be OK?'

'Friday? Oh, yes – that'll be lovely.'

'I'll meet you in the Strand, outside the theatre – say, about six? And I thought perhaps dinner afterwards?'

'Sounds marvellous.'

'My thanks for our day in the country.'

'Oh, you don't have to—'

'I don't have to. I want to. See you on Friday. 'Bye.'

145

She replaced the receiver and looked up to find her mother's smiling eyes upon her. 'Was that Peter Wickham?'

'Yes, it was. He wants to take me to the theatre on Friday night. *The Dancing Years*. I know it's the night of the St John's meeting but—'

'Don't worry. I'll make your apologies.' Myra's smile widened. 'The Ambulance Brigade will just have to find another "casualty" to practise on. What will you wear?'

'Well – I hadn't thought about it.'

'Your green silk, I think,' her mother said positively. 'It's very becoming.'

Allie nodded, a small curl of excitement suddenly moving inside her, taking her a little by surprise. The theatre and dinner. And Peter was really very nice. Not Clark Gable or Humphrey Bogart, perhaps, but – nice.

Had she known it, the very same words were in Myra's mind as she watched her younger daughter with a fondness that was tinged strongly with relief that the strange, difficult times seemed at last to be over. Her prayers, it appeared, had been answered. Peter Wickham was really an awfully nice young man.


'You'll be at Libby's and Edward's Christmas Eve party, won't you?' Peter's small Ford chugged steadily through the night-time streets towards the country.

Allie, in the passenger seat, her head tilted back and eyes closed, was humming a lovely, lilting waltz tune under her breath. At his question, she turned her head and looked at him, a little sleepily. 'Yes, I will. I like things that are organized on the spur of the moment. I thought it was a super idea.'

'The spur of the moment?'

She grinned. 'Two weeks is the spur of the moment when it comes to my sister and parties, believe me. She usually spends *months* planning them!'

He nodded, smiling, keeping his eyes on the road ahead. The headlights flickered on hedges and walls, occasionally firing the feral gleam of a cat's eyes. Allie studied his profile. 'Thank you, Peter, for a really lovely evening. I don't ever remember enjoying myself so much.' She tilted her head back again, sang softly, '"I will give you the starlight . . ."' – oh, wasn't it all just splendid? So bright, and beautiful, and romantic and – sad.'

He laughed softly. 'I'm glad you enjoyed it.'

'Oh I did! I'd like to see it again tomorrow! And the next day, just for luck. I thought Ivor Novello was wonderful . . .' She hummed again, happily, her strong profile outlined against the flicker of the street lamps: straight nose, obstinate chin, smoothly waving hair. She giggled suddenly, like a child.

'What are you laughing at?'

'I just remembered the expression on that waiter's face when I helped myself to what was left of your peach Melba. I got the distinct impression that he thought one shouldn't do such things at the Savoy.'

'You can do what you like as long as you do it with style.'

She tilted her head. 'Mm. I rather like that. And the peach Melba was much too good to waste.'

He smiled.

'I've never been to the Savoy before. Wasn't it frightfully extravagant of you?'

'It was to make up for leaving it so long.'

For a moment she was silent, thinking back to the brilliance and glitter, the expensive scintillation of precious stones, the sheen of silk, satin and fur. 'All that wealth concentrated in one place,' she mused, more seriously. 'I must say—' She stopped, aware of the gracelessness of implied criticism in what she had been about to say.

'What?' He looked at her, quickly and curiously, before concentrating his attention on the road again.

'Oh – nothing.'

'Tell me.'

She hesitated. 'Well – I went to a meeting the other day. In my lunch hour. Ernest Bevin was speaking—'

'Bevin?' His voice was astonished. 'What on earth were you doing at one of his meetings?'

'Listening. It was a protest rally against unemployment. It just occurred to me that if half of what was hanging round some of those elegant necks in the Savoy tonight was invested in modernizing our industries – oh, cripes, hark at me. I sound like the worst kind of know-nothing bluestocking. I know it isn't really that simple.'

'Socialist politics? From a Jordan? Good Lord, girl, whatever next?' His voice was at the same time amused and genuinely interested. 'You're full of surprises.'

'I was at one time. Interested in politics, I mean, not full of surprises. But – well – life got a bit complicated and I sort of' she gestured, ruefully, 'gave up for a while. But lately – well, we can't ignore what's going on right under our noses, can we? Even if we want to?'

'Some of us can.'

'I can't. I wish I could, I really do. I wish I could be like Libby and simply enjoy life as it comes. But—' She stopped.

'But?'

'Oh, it's stupid. There's nothing I can do about it. It isn't my business. But I just can't help but feel that what's going on – what's been going on for generations – is *wrong*. It isn't right that we have everything and others have nothing. That I can walk into a nice, cosy job with Sir Brian while a skilled man with a wife and family to support walks the streets looking for work . . .'

'I doubt that Sir Brian would appreciate a Clydeside shipbuilder entertaining his clients.' There was a thread of amusement in his voice.

She fell silent. Sensing her exasperation at his facetiousness, he asked gently, 'So what would you do about it?'

She resisted answering for a moment, then pulled a face in the darkness. 'That's just it. I haven't the slightest idea. I listen to Bevin talking about the iniquities of the 1927 Trades Disputes Act and I want to be out there marching in the streets for the right to picket. I listen to Daddy and his reasoned views on individual liberty and private enterprise, and I find myself agreeing with him. Perhaps there isn't any answer.'

Peter glanced at her. 'Does that worry you?'

'Yes, it does.'

They drove in silence for a moment. 'Well, at least you care. That's more than can be said for most people. If enough people care enough, then perhaps something will change.'

Allie made an inelegant noise, and he grinned.

'What awakened your interest again?' he asked, curiosity in his voice.

It took her by surprise. 'Oh – something that one of Richard's friends said to me. Made me think, I suppose.' The recollection of that light voice – 'Where did all that fervour go?' – still, oddly, brought a faint lift of mortification. She pushed the thought away and another, rather more alarming, took its place. 'You won't mention any of this to Mother or Libby, will you?' she asked in sudden anxiety. 'About my going to the meeting, or – well – anything?'

He laughed. 'A secret vice?'

'Not exactly. It just isn't something that they understand. Or approve of,' she added honestly.

'I won't mention it, I promise.'

As they drove from the lit suburbs into the country, the quiet darkness of the small car produced a kind of warmly companionable intimacy that needed no words. There was little traffic on the roads, and as they sped through the empty lanes, it seemed to Allie that they might have been the only people awake in the world. She found herself oddly regretful when, in the car's sweeping headlights, she recognized the walls of the churchyard and the lichgate, and knew that they were nearly home. As they swung into the drive, she saw that lights still shone from the windows of Ashdown.

'Would you like to come in for a nightcap? Mother and Daddy are still up, and I'm sure they'd be glad to see you.'

'I won't, thank you. Another time, perhaps.'

She groped on the dark floor for her handbag. When she straightened, it was to find that he had half-turned, to rest

149

his arm along the back of the seat behind her. She stiffened a little. She could hardly see him in the darkness. He might have been a perfect stranger. She felt a sudden jolt of physical excitement that astonished her.

'Thank you again,' she said, in a voice that sounded peculiar in her own ears.

He leaned towards her and, very gently, his mouth brushed her cheek. 'I'll see you at the party on Christmas Eve.' His hand moved to the door handle and the door clicked open.

'I – yes, of course.' She scrambled inelegantly from the car. Her face was burning. She slammed the car door and watched as the headlights swung in a tight circle, then moved off down the drive, flickering like summer lightning in the trees.

The front door opened and Robert stood silhouetted in the light. 'That you, Allie?'

'Yes.'

'Did you have a good time?'

She refused to try to analyse the disturbing emotion that still seemed to be lodged somewhere beneath her rib cage. 'Yes, thank you. Lovely.'

In the car that ran quietly along the deserted village street, Peter Wickham smiled quietly to himself and hummed softly, '"I can give you the starlight . . ."'

On Christmas Eve, Allie went straight from work to her sister's flat. Sir Brian had finished early that day, and Allie found herself with the best part of the afternoon free. As she hurried through the bitterly cold, festive streets she felt the stirrings of a pleasant anticipation. In the small case she carried was a new dress, long and elegant, of printed pale blue silk with a dark blue bolero to cover her bare shoulders. It had been an extravagant buy only made possible by a loan from her mother; the dark blue satin shoes and tiny silver evening bag that were to complete the ensemble were her mother's, too.

The flat in Rampton Court looked the very spirit of

Christmas from the holly wreath on the door to the enormous, elegantly decorated tree in the big living room.

'Allie, darling.' Libby, wrapped in a soft, pearl-grey housecoat with wide lapels and a tightly belted waist greeted her sister with an enthusiastic kiss. 'I thought you'd never get here. Do come and tell me if the beastly table looks all right. I don't know whether to use the red candles or the white . . .'

Behind her, Allie caught sight of a small, plump maid in neat black and white uniform, hurrying through the kitchen door. She raised questioning eyebrows.

'Oh, she's from the caterers, darling. You surely didn't expect me to do the lot myself?' Libby cast appalled eyes to heaven, laughing. 'Believe me, it's absolutely *exhausted* me doing the Christmas tree, never mind about anything else! Now – what do you think?' She indicated the large oval table upon which rested an enormous cooked turkey, a ham the size of a hatbox and a great piece of roast beef. There were dishes of salad and of small, cold new potatoes. In the centre of this feast, an elaborate decoration of holly, laurel, tinsel and candles was in a state of disarray. Deftly, still talking, Libby rearranged it, removing the tall white candles and replacing them with red. 'How's that?'

'Perfect. It's all perfect. Where on earth did you get new potatoes at this time of the year?'

Libby tapped the side of her nose with a beautifully manicured finger. 'You can get anything if you can pay for it, my love. Mind you—' she let out a small shriek of laughter '—Edward is going to have a *fit* when he realizes how much this shindig is costing! I've mortgaged next month's housekeeping right up to the hilt! We'll just have to eat out for a month! Right – well, I think that's it. Now, go and pop your dress on a hanger in the spare room and then we can have a small noggin together before you jump into the bath. Do you know—' she added, her fair head on one side, a smile on her face '—I do believe that this is the best Christmas Eve I ever remember. You really should get married, you know, Allie.' Her face was mischievous. 'I do most thoroughly recommend it— What in hell's name's that?'

Allie flinched.

'They're tryin' out them air-raid sirens agin, ma'am,' said the little maid, self-importantly, from the kitchen door. 'The man on the BBC said they was goin' to.'

'What a bloody silly time to choose,' Libby muttered, then with a visible effort smiled, and gave her sister a little push. 'Off you go, then back here for drinkies and a natter before the fun starts.'

Oddly enough, though she watched for him, Allie did not see Peter Wickham arrive. The first she knew of his presence was a light hand on her arm and a quiet voice in her ear. 'Come on now, own up. It was you, wasn't it?'

She jumped, then grinned at him. 'Oh, it's you. Hello. What are you talking about?'

'The other day at the Ritz. Don't disappoint me – I was sure you must have had a hand in it? Knowing your guilty secret, and all . . .' Two days before, a hundred hungry, workless men had invaded the Grill Room of the Ritz Hotel, seating themselves at tables that had been laid for dinner and refusing to leave. The scenes that had followed had not been pleasant, but a point had been made and a few consciences stirred.

'It was a damned good idea. If I'd been there I'd have joined them.'

He leaned over to her and, perfectly naturally, dropped a kiss on her cheek. 'That's what I like to hear. You look lovely. Happy Christmas.'

Ridiculously, she blushed.

'And to you.'

'Allie, be a dear and give me a hand for a minute – oh, hello, Peter. Happy Christmas.' Libby planted a distracted kiss on Peter's cheek, leaving a bright smudge of lipstick. 'That ridiculous girl they've landed me with doesn't know her canapés from her cocktail sticks. It's murder in the kitchen – Richard, you horror, you're late!' This called to their brother as he pushed his way through the throng towards them followed by a smaller, slighter figure the sight of whom caused a twinge of irritation in Allie. 'And Tom. How nice to see you. Do come, Allie . . .' Libby plunged off in the direction of the kitchen.

Allie kissed her brother hastily, acknowledged Tom, shrugged, helplessly and apologetically, at Peter. 'I'll see you later.'

She spent ten frantic minutes in the kitchen helping the flustered waitress, smiling to herself in exasperation as she realized that her sister had disappeared back into the gay and glittering maelstrom of the big living room. As she laid the last of the canapés on a tray and, with an encouraging smile, sent the girl off with it, Libby reappeared at the door clutching two virulently pink cocktails.

'My God.' Allie eyed them warily. 'What's that?'

'Pink Lady, my angel. Edward's speciality. Here.' Libby handed her a glass and toasted her with her own. 'Thanks. Happy Christmas. By the way,' Libby picked up a tiny smoked salmon sandwich and nibbled at it, her eyes innocent on Allie's face, 'I forgot to ask. Did you enjoy yourself the other evening?'

Two could play the game of innocence. 'The other evening?'

Libby laughed, and, characteristically and easily, surrendered. 'Beast. The theatre of course. With Peter.'

'Yes, I did. Very much.'

'Where did you go afterwards?'

'The Savoy.'

Libby rolled impressed eyes. 'Did you indeed?'

Allie smiled.

'Peter,' her sister said solemnly, sipping her drink, 'is really a very nice man. Don't you think?'

Allie was aware, not for the first time, of none-too-subtle manipulation. 'There's a strange thing. That's exactly what Mother keeps telling me.'

Her sister's quick smile was an acknowledgement.

Irritation stirred. 'You've talked about it?' Allie asked sharply. 'About me?'

Libby waved an airy hand. 'I wouldn't put it quite like that . . .'

'How would you put it?'

'Now, don't get all aerated. Of course we've – mentioned it. We've been worried about you. I mean – it's all very well to have growing pains, but you must admit that you took it a bit far, one way and another. Mother – and I – are just glad that you've met someone like Peter. Someone . . .'

'Nice. And suitable.'

'Exactly.'

'And you're not above giving this nice, suitable young man a push in my direction?'

'Well, Mother thought – a little encouragement . . .'

'Like getting me to drop in when you knew he'd be here? Like practically forcing him to take me out?'

'Oh, don't be so stuffy, darling! Goodness, you can't say you didn't need someone to take a hand. You weren't doing very well on your own, were you? Whatever you saw in that odious Ray whatever-his-name-was I'll never know . . .'

Allie remained silent.

'Now, you're not to be ridiculous about this,' continued Libby, a little nervously. 'Nobody's made you, or anyone else do anything they didn't want to. We've just – well, tried to make it a little easier, that's all. Now please, don't stand there like a thunder cloud,' she added irritably. 'You do remind me most dreadfully of Celia sometimes, you know.'

'What?'

'Stubborn as mules, the pair of you.'

'Thanks a lot.'

'Alexandra Jordan,' said her sister on a short, sharp intake of breath, 'if you don't stop being so damned prickly, I'm going to tip what's left of this drink right over your very becoming and I'm certain very expensive hairdo. I swear I will.'

Allie held on to her indignation for a moment longer then, relaxing, pulled a wry face. 'Sorry.'

'You don't really mind, do you? That Mother and I have been playing cupid just the teeniest bit?'

Allie laughed. 'I suppose not. But just stop it now, will you? Let matters take their course. Peter and I are good friends.' She ignored Libby's derisive snort. 'I don't want to spoil that. I don't think of him in . . .' she hesitated '. . . that way at all.' As she said it, she was aware of a confusion within herself. The words were at the same time true, and yet an evasion of truth. She knew beyond doubt that she could never explain that to Libby, could hardly in fact explain it to herself.

'Well.' Libby smiled, knowingly. 'We'll just wait and see, shall we?'

'As long,' Allie said repressively, 'as that's all you do, I'll have no complaints.'

The conversation and its inferences returned to her, on and off, throughout the evening. For all her quite honest righteous indignation at Libby's interference, she had in truth to admit that part of her did not object too strongly. The old Allie was reasserting herself; the thought of pleasing everyone, of making up in some measure for her awful behaviour of the previous couple of years was more than appealing. And if, in pleasing others, she did not entirely displease herself – then so much the better. She found herself watching Peter Wickham as he moved about the room, his pleasant face animated, his smooth fair head bent attentively to his companions. She noticed that he listened rather more often than he spoke, that the intelligent eyes fixed steadily on the face of a speaker, that he had a habit that she had not noticed before of running his thumbnail reflectively back and forth across his small moustache as he listened. Once, lifting his head and catching her eyes upon him, he smiled. She smiled back.

'Hello there.'

She almost jumped out of her skin at the unexpected voice. Tom Robinson stood beside her, nursing a half-empty tankard of beer.

'Hello.'

He put his head on one side and contemplated her seriously, a spark of intemperate mirth in his eyes. 'Don't tell me, let me guess.'

'Guess what?'

'Which particular Miss Jordan do we have with us tonight? The Red Crusader?' He pursed his lips, shook his head. 'The Bright Young Thing? Mm. Maybe. But I suspect not . . .' He laughed at her quick, irritated movement.

'Do you do it deliberately?' she asked.

'What?'

'Aggravate the life out of people.'

'Do I?'

'Yes.'

'Better than boring them to death. Like you, Pollyanna, I like life to be interesting.' His pale, intolerant eyes were very bright and lit with a sardonic gleam of mischief. She suddenly suspected that he had drunk considerably more than his clear speech and steady gait betrayed.

'Let's start again,' he said, obligingly. 'Merry Christmas.'

'And to you,' she said shortly. She saw Peter moving towards her through the crowd. Libby called to Edward who was by the gramophone. The unmistakable sound of Tommy Dorsey's trombone swung some couples immediately onto their feet. She tapped her foot.

'You like to dance?' Tom asked.

'Yes, I do. Don't you?'

He shook his head, leaned against the wall behind him.

'Allie? Am I interrupting?'

She turned to Peter as to a rescuer. 'Of course not.'

'Would you like to dance?'

'I'd love to.'

Peter turned politely to Tom. 'If you wouldn't mind, of course?'

Tom regarded him for a moment with lucid, caustic eyes. Then he made a sardonic, sweeping gesture of acquiescence with his left hand and sipped his beer.

Allie avoided him for the rest of the evening – something which, in truth, was not difficult to do since he made no attempt to approach her again. She danced until her feet ached, talked – or rather shouted – until she was hoarse, and at last escaped to a quiet corner where she could kick her shoes off for a moment and rest. It was midnight, and as the Christmas bells pealed joyfully out across the roofs and spires of London, people began to drift away. The air was thick with cigarette smoke. Allie moved to a small open window and stood looking down into the cold, windy street, the sound of the bells coming clearly to her over the noise behind her.

'Good night, Kate, Bob – yes, and the same to you. Merry Christmas, darlings, and a Happy New Year. See you at the Thompsons' next week . . .'

The front door closed at last. A couple of people that Allie did not know were in earnest conversation in the corner of the room. Libby crossed the almost empty, littered living room.

'Well, that's that. How did it go, do you think?'

'Marvellously.' Allie looked around. Over the repetitious scratching of the gramophone needle she could hear raised, familiar voices. 'Where is everyone?'

Libby lifted the needle from the gramophone. 'In the dining room,' she said equably, 'putting the world to rights. I was just about to suggest that we go and explain to them, nicely, that this is Rampton Court, not a bear garden.'

Allie followed her sister to the open door of the dining room. They reached it in time to hear Tom say, pleasantly, 'Perhaps you don't agree that Chamberlain sold the Czechs down the river to save his own skin?' He was leaning against the table, legs crossed, watching Peter. 'Or perhaps you don't accept that appeasement in the face of monstrous provocation is simple, gutless cowardice?'

'Tom—' began Richard.

'I'm not saying he was right. I'm saying he was faced with an impossible situation.'

'Tell the Czechs that. Or the Jews who fear for their children. Ask them their opinion of an impossible situation.' The soft words were vitriolic, the voice still nervelessly pleasant.

'You cannot launch a nation into total war without due consideration of the consequences.' Peter's voice was low.

Tom's sudden grin was wolfish. 'Adolf's certainly a clever little bastard, isn't he? He knows the English character to the core.' He stabbed a long finger into the air. 'While we were duly considering consequences he's taken half of Europe—'

'That's an exaggeration.'

'—and the more we let him get away with, the more certain he becomes that he can take the other half. You can't appease a power-crazed lunatic—'

'That's enough.' Unexpectedly, Libby marched firmly into the charged air, one small hand uplifted, looked from face to face. 'That – is – quite – enough.'

Richard shrugged an apology to his sister and took Tom's arm. With a movement that verged on violence, Tom shook it free. 'I'm sorry,' he said to Libby, the disciplined evenness of his tone at odds with the savagely bright eyes. 'My fault entirely. I apologize.'

To Allie's surprise Libby smiled in a manner that was almost provocative. 'You'll have to pay a forfeit for your disgraceful manners.'

He stood away from the table, head tilted a little, watching her.

'I'm not having my party finish like this. Richard, be a dear. Put the Dorsey on again. Mr Robinson is going to dance with me.' She extended a small, imperious hand. With good grace and an abrasive half-smile Tom took it. Allie watched in astonishment as Libby, glancing over her shoulder, led him like a tethered lamb into the other room.

'Well, I'll be damned,' Allie said mildly. 'That sister of mine could wind the devil himself round her little finger if she tried, I'm sure of it.'

'Must run in the family.' Peter held out his hand. 'Dance with me?'

She moved easily into his arms. From the other room came the sound of laughter. He held her, very gently, close to him, her head on his shoulder. Dreamily she moved with him, her senses lulled. When he stopped dancing and lifted her chin with his finger, she did not resist. While they were

158

dancing, he had guided her beneath an enormous bunch of mistletoe that hung above their heads, turning gently in the warm currents of air. He looked down at her, smiling, his eyes serious. She experienced a flash of unnerving revulsion as she remembered Ray's fervid, wet kisses. She stiffened. He hesitated for a second, then bent his mouth to hers. His lips were pleasantly cool and firm, his moustache soft. He held her hard against him, wrapped firmly in his arms.

She liked it. She liked it very much. The happy realization bloomed in her like a flower. Tentatively she lifted a hand, felt his hair, smooth and soft beneath her fingers.

When, finally, they drew apart it was to discover a slight figure lounging in the doorway, a faint, amused approval on his face.

'A very merry Christmas to you both,' said Tom Robinson, gently.

Peter kissed her again, in the porch of Ashdown when he took her home. The lights strung on the tree on the lawn danced in the cold wind, throwing multicoloured, impish shadows across the house and garden. They stood in the deeper darkness of the doorway.

'Would you like to come in?'

'Not tonight. I really have to go. Mother will have me up at the crack of dawn to go to church, and we've a houseful of relations . . .'

She shivered as the wind swirled into their sheltered corner.

He tightened his arms a little. 'You must go in, out of the cold. When can I see you again?'

Her heart was beating very fast. 'I – whenever you like.'

'The weekend? Saturday? Would you like to go dancing?'

'Yes, I would.'

'I'll pick you up about eight.' He bent to her swiftly and kissed her again. 'Now off you go. You're freezing.'

She let herself quietly into the house, stood for a moment listening to the sound of his car receding into the distance, then sped upstairs. In her bedroom, in the dark, she stood for a long time looking out into the Christmas night. The black mass of the hill across the river lifted densely against a stormy sky. The bedroom was very cold. She wrapped her arms about herself, hugging herself against the chill.

Peter. Kind, strong, dependable Peter. Everyone liked him. Everyone approved of him. And so they should. He was a dear. And she had liked his kisses. She really had.

The warm glow of pleasure died. Clambering over the far rim of her consciousness came a black spider of a thought that she had been trying in vain to keep at bay.

Nice Peter. Pleasantly conventional Peter who, she was sure, would have strongly held views on the way that nice girls did and did not behave. Peter who, one day, if her family's and – if she were honest – her own hopes and expectations came to anything, might ask her to marry him.

She would have to tell him. Have to. Before things went too far. Even if it meant, as it well might, losing him before he ever became hers.

She thought of Libby and Edward, of their obvious happiness, of the tempting cradle of happy stability such a marriage would offer.

She would have to tell him.

From across the river, the church clock struck the brief hour, the sound almost lost in the rising wind.

# CHAPTER NINE

Through a crisp and frosty January they saw each other each weekend and, occasionally, at lunchtime during the week. For her twentieth birthday, in the middle of February, Peter took her, again, to the theatre and on to the Savoy for dinner, where he presented her with a small box of marzipan apples that delighted her more than anything else could have. With no declarations or dramas, it became understood, between them and to outsiders, that they were, to use a marvellously old-fashioned phrase that Allie rather liked, a courting couple. But though their personal lives were calm and happy, it was becoming increasingly impossible to ignore the dire signs of coming conflict in the world at large.

'You'll be called up, won't you,' asked Allie, as they walked one lunchtime in Regent's Park, 'if there is a war?' On the twenty-third of January a booklet had been issued entitled *The National Service Handbook* – a scheme, as Neville Chamberlain had sombrely described it, 'to make us ready for war'. In it was clearly outlined the service that the young men of the country would be called upon to fulfil.

'I'd join before they called me up,' he said simply.

She looked at him in blank astonishment. 'But – I thought you didn't agree with the idea of a war?'

'My darling, no one in his right mind would agree with the idea of a war. No one could actually *want* a war. But if it comes then I shall fight with the next man.'

'But – everything will be ruined, won't it?' Her voice was desolate.

They had stopped walking. People hurried past them, intent about their own affairs. The first miraculous and fragile signs of new growth were all about them; the brave, tender spears that would become spring's flowers stood staunchly in the cold wind, last year's dead leaves skittering across newly green grass.

'There's absolutely no point in worrying about it. Face it if it comes. Until then, be happy.' He bent to kiss her. She closed her eyes and tipped back her head, waiting, like a child, for the touch of his lips. He hesitated, his mouth a breath from hers, watching her with faintly troubled eyes.

Her eyes blinked open. 'What is it? What's the matter?'

'Nothing.' He kissed her, swiftly, took her hand. 'Come on. If we hurry we've time to walk around the zoo.'

As the weather improved he began to teach her to drive. He was a good teacher, patient and good-tempered, and she, to her own surprise, proved an apt pupil. Her initial nervousness conquered, she discovered that she really liked driving, and they spent long days, as the warmth of spring softened the air and dressed the countryside in drifts of pink and white blossom, motoring to the sea or into the country, lunching in small country pubs, exploring churches and stately homes. Their happy affection for each other grew day by day – they liked the same things, shared a slightly off-beat sense of humour. Allie's family, watching, drew a collective, silent sigh of relief. Allie herself stubbornly put off telling Peter what she knew one day would have to be told.

Later, she always told herself, later. Not now. Don't spoil it now.

Then, one day, they bumped into Ray Cheshire and a girl that Allie did not know at a dance held for charity at a big house near the village. She made the necessary introductions distantly, and was furious when, with a spectacular lack of perception, Ray asked her to dance.

'Quite like old times, eh?' he grinned, blithely obtuse, as he whirled her onto the floor.

'No,' she snapped. 'It isn't.'

Her tone brought him down to earth. 'Oh, come on, old girl. Don't be like that.'

'What I am or am not like has absolutely nothing to do

162

with you,' she retorted, adding with unnecessary cruelty, 'it never did.'

They finished the dance in silence.

The encounter frightened Allie. Naïvely, until that moment, it had not occurred to her that there might have been gossip about her and Ray. The thought appalled her. Supposing someone said something to Peter? Supposing – awful thought – that someone already had? The fear lodged in the recesses of her mind and would not be shaken free.

She had to tell him herself.

But still she did not.

By April, people were not speaking of *if* war came but *when*. Anderson shelters were buried in backyards and gardens, blackout curtains measured and made. Full-scale rehearsals were held of the evacuation of schoolchildren from possibly threatened areas. Even the coloured picture cards given free with packets of cigarettes, featured with more prudence than optimism a series called 'Air Raid Precautions'.

Myra dealt with Ashdown's windows early and with her usual efficiency. Even Hitler was not going to catch Myra Jordan unprepared. Especially Hitler. One April night Allie and her father were sent into the garden to detect any crack of light that might show through the screened windows.

'The conservatory glass will have to be wired,' said Allie.

'Great God.' Robert's voice was strained as he stared at the black bulk of the house. 'Who'd have believed that we'd come to this again?'

Allie had no answer for that. In times past, she would have touched him, comforted him. But, despite the easing of their relationship, those days were long gone. She stood rigid, a foot from him, looking at the house. 'There's a crack at the side of the bathroom window,' she said bleakly, and turned to leave him.

'Allie—' He put out a hand, caught her arm.

She waited.

'Allie, please. Aren't we friends again?'

163

'Of course we are.' She heard the attenuated lightness of her own voice and flinched from it.

He let go of her arm and stepped back.

'I'm trying,' she said, tightly. 'Truly, I'm trying.' And she fled from him.


Late that spring and into the summer there was what Libby aptly described as a 'positive epidemic' of weddings. As the likelihood of war increased, many young people decided that there was no time for niceties, and hurried marriages became the order of the day. After being a bridesmaid twice in one week – once to a cousin and once to a schoolfriend – Allie found herself the butt of some gentle but none the less meaningful teasing from her sister. She and Peter were visiting Rampton Court for dinner, and she was helping Libby to lay the table. Libby hummed melodically an old music-hall tune and, recognizing it, Allie flushed.

*Why am I always the bridesmaid,*
*Never the blushing bride . . .*

'Shut up, Lib.'

*Ding, dong, wedding bells . . .*

'I warn you.' Allie glanced fiercely over her shoulder to where Peter and Edward sat by the window in the last peach glow of the setting sun. 'I'll crown you if you don't shut up!'

*. . . only ring for other gels . . .*

Allie advanced on her sister threateningly. Libby giggled. 'Now, come on, don't tell me you haven't named the day? You aren't planning on running away together and doing us out of all the fun, are you?'

'Don't be ridiculous. We haven't even mentioned marriage.'

Libby's eyebrows climbed almost into her shining hair. 'Well, pardon my cheek, but isn't it about time you did? You'll look a pair of idiots if Adolf catches up with you before you get spliced!'

The thought had not escaped Allie. Peter had not once mentioned marriage – an omission that, under normal circumstances after only a few months' courtship, might be

164

perfectly reasonable: but the circumstances were far from normal. More and more she was coming to wonder. To worry.

That night, as they travelled home, she was very quiet. As the car rolled to a halt outside the house, Peter turned and surveyed her in silence in the darkness, one arm on the steering wheel, the other hooked over the back of the seat. She did not look at him.

'Allie? Is something wrong?'

She nodded, briefly. 'Yes.'

'Something you want to talk about?'

'Yes.'

'Do you want to go inside?'

She shook her head.

Silence stretched between them.

'Allie?'

'I don't know – how to say it. Where to start.' She had taken a handkerchief from her pocket and was pulling it nervously between her fingers, her head ducked.

He smiled a little. 'Just say it straight out, love, and we'll take it from there. It can't be all that bad?'

'It is.'

He waited.

'I suppose that—' She stopped, cleared her throat, started again. 'I suppose you would expect the girl you marry to be a virgin?' The words were too aggressively blunt. She wished them unsaid the moment they were out. 'Oh, damn and blast it,' she whispered, miserably, and covered her face with her hands.

There was a long, lacerating silence.

'Say something,' she said. '*Something.*'

He had not moved.

She felt the hot sting of tears rising behind her eyes. She chewed her lip. She would not cry. Would not.

'Are you – trying to tell me that you're not?' His voice was quiet, and careful.

'Yes.'

He said nothing.

165

'You knew, didn't you?' she asked drearily. 'Knew, or guessed.'

That snapped his head up. 'Dear God, no! It never entered my head! Why should it? Allie . . .'

She flinched from the pain and disbelief in the words.

He caught his breath, made an obvious attempt to control himself. His hands, upon the steering wheel, clenched and unclenched a couple of times, spasmodically, and was still.

Allie began to speak in a low, brittle voice, her head bent, her eyes on the faint white flicker of the twisting hand-kerchief in her lap. 'I'm not going to make excuses or pretend that it wasn't my fault. It was. Utterly. I wasn't forced. I wasn't – drunk or anything. No one took advantage of me. And it was more than once.' Once started she found to her horror that she could not stop. 'If anything, it was more my fault than his. I led him on. I instigated it. I was – angry—' she had put a hand to her mouth, as if physically to hold back the words '—with – everything.' The tears were brimming now and she knew she could not hold them. 'I've no excuse. None.'

'Angry? You were angry?' His voice was desperately puzzled and sharp with hurt. 'What kind of reason is that to – to sleep with someone?'

'I can't explain it. It's all too involved. For others, as well as myself. I can't tell you any more.' Her head was high, her cheeks wet; her quarrel with her father and with Celia was her own, and theirs. She would not, could not, share it. 'I'm sorry to have hurt you – disappointed you – so. It was the last thing that I wanted. But I had to tell you. I couldn't bear—' She hiccoughed a small sob. 'I thought you had guessed.'

'That's the second time you've said that. Whatever made you think such a thing?'

She turned to face him at last. Light fell across her face, glinting on her tears, casting austere shadows about her mouth. 'Isn't that why you haven't asked me to marry you?'

The silence was stunned. He stared at her. 'No, Allie,' he said softly at last, 'that isn't the reason I haven't asked you to marry me. It doesn't even come near it. It's very simple really. You don't love me.' He touched her wet cheek with a gentle finger. 'It's no good my trying to pretend to myself. You – don't – love me.' His voice was very calm; only the faintest, tremulous edge betrayed him.

She gasped. 'I? *I* don't love *you*? How can you say that? Why do you think that I told you about – about this?'

'Because you think you love me.'

She bit her lip in anguished perplexity.

'You want to love me,' he said gently. 'Possibly, even, in a way do love me. But not enough, and not in the right way. No matter how hard you try. Wanting to love isn't the same as loving.'

'I don't know what you're talking about.' She turned away from him and stared into the darkness.

'No.' The word was a breath, scarcely audible.

She could not bear the silence. 'You're wrong.'

'I don't think so.'

'You are!'

He did not reply.

'You're just saying it – thinking it – because of what I just told you.'

He sighed, shook his head. 'That has nothing to do with it.'

'You mean – you don't mind?'

'I didn't say that. Yes, I mind. Terribly.'

She laid her head back, closed her eyes. 'Do you hate me?' Her voice was hoarse, clenched against tears.

For an awful moment she thought that the sound that he made presaged tears. The light sheened in her swinging hair as she moved her head sharply to look at him. The glimmer of his smile in the gloom took her aback. 'Oh, Allie, you're still such a child. Of course I don't hate you. How could I?'

'Very easily I should think.' Glumly she started to fiddle with the handkerchief again. 'And I'm not a child,' she added as a miserable afterthought. Her head thumped. She wanted simply to open the car door and walk away. To be alone. To be quiet. She did not move.

167

He reached for her hand, held it still, his own grip warm and comforting. She sniffed disconsolately. 'Why did you say I don't love you?'

'Because it's true.'

'*It isn't.*'

He sat in silence. Her voice echoed mockingly in her own ears. 'It isn't,' she repeated, and knew, at last, the truth. 'Why do I always make such a mess of everything?' she asked bleakly into the darkness and, as he reached for her, turned her face into the sympathetic warmth of his shoulder. The material of his overcoat was rough on her cheek, waking sudden memories of a long-past occasion when her father had carried a sleepy seven-year-old from the car into the house after a birthday trip to the zoo. She drew away from Peter sharply, releasing a long, shaky breath.

He waited for a moment, then when she did not speak, said softly, 'Come on now. We've both had enough for one night. Indoors with you. I'll telephone tomorrow.'

She nodded, climbed tiredly from the car and walked to the front door before turning into his arms. He held her quietly to him. 'Get a good night's sleep. We'll talk tomorrow.'

'Promise?'

'Promise.'

She leaned to him. 'I'm sorry. I'm so sorry.'

His arm tightened about her. With his free hand he took the key from her cold fingers and opened the door. She stepped away from him and into the dimly lit hall.

'Allie?'

She turned.

'Did you love him very much? The man you made love with?'

She ducked her head, knowing that this would be the most hurtful of all, yet knowing too that she owed it to them both not to lie. 'I didn't love him at all. I don't think I even liked him.'

He watched her for a moment, an unguarded line of

baffled pain drawn between his brows. Then it was gone. 'I'll ring you tomorrow.'

She walked slowly to the stairs, leaned for the moment against the newel post, her hand rubbing unconsciously the smooth-domed carved acorn that crowned it, her eyes empty. She felt battered. Stunned.

'You don't love me,' he had said. And she, in good faith, had denied it fervently.

But standing here in the quiet house, the silence of sleeping darkness beating in her ears, she had to face the dismaying truth.

She had to face the fact that he was right.

# CHAPTER TEN

The summer was glorious. It was as if nature, trying to tempt mankind from the path of destruction, as attempting to balance his blindly perilous appetite for power with a tender strength of her own. As Europe waited in nerve-racking suspense for that inevitable spark that would fire the tinder of war, the sun shone with a special warmth and the days were long and balmy. Many who remembered the summer of 1914 shook their heads at the mirror-image of young people strolling hand in hand in the sunshine while around them the rising winds of international conflict whispered and scurried like the stinking breath of death.

For Allie, as for most of the population, these were strange months, a time tinged with disbelief, with an air of play-acting. She watched the preparations for war, listened to official warnings and instructions. Petrol would be rationed immediately if hostilities broke out. Places of entertainment would be closed. Rail services would be disrupted . . . the list was endless, and simply added, so far as she was concerned, to the air of unreality. She simply could not – would not – believe that the unthinkable could actually happen. She saw newspaper advertisements assuring prospective holidaymakers that bookings cancelled because of a national emergency would not have to be paid for. She helped her mother organize groups of small, bewildered children in practice evacuation, took part in civil defence exercises and mock air raids, yet all with a mild sense of absurdity. She could never get used to carrying her gas mask around with her – she found it not only irritatingly inconvenient but strangely embarrassing, as if she were an adult joining in some childish game. The stories of dance halls and picture palaces refusing admittance to people not in possession of one of these monstrous appliances struck her as the final lunacy.

Far more real to her – at least until that day in August when she, together with the rest of the world, learned of the Soviet Union's non-aggression pact with Hitler and realized at last that war must be inevitable – was the almost impossible task of repairing the fragile web of her relationship with Peter Wickham. For, as the outside world slipped towards disaster, so her own efforts to ignore the truth that Peter had shown her came to nothing. His clear perception, ironically, had all but destroyed something which her own desperate honesty had not. She was truly fond of him, but she could not deny that she did not love him. And that fact, now acknowledged, stood between them like a wall which neither Peter's understanding nor her own goodwill could breach.

In other circumstances, time might have nurtured love from a caring and true friendship, but time was the one thing that they did not have, and as the long hot days followed one upon another, they found themselves slipping from each other as surely as their world was slipping towards war. Though they still met, their time together was spent usually in the company of others and almost always in an atmosphere of bright and artificial gaiety that deceived neither of them. As time went by, she found herself going to absurd lengths to avoid his close company.

Libby watched it happen with exasperated disbelief. Her sister, she decided, together with most of the rest of the world, had taken leave of her senses. Peter Wickham was a nice-looking, charming, well-connected young man of whom the whole world approved. Additionally he was kind, generous and, handled right, would make a most amenable husband. What else could Allie possibly want? It really was too bad of her to go her own unpredictable way once again with no thought for the efforts that others had expended on her behalf. She needed, Libby thought, a good shake – as did those ridiculous warmongers who were wishing the world into disaster. That the present crisis could conceivably end in war was a possibility that she absolutely refused to take seriously – an attitude that was still resolutely unshaken the day when she opened her front door to the summons of the bell and stood, stock still and staring, at the slim figure who stood, smiling, on the doormat.

'*Celia*! Why, what on earth?' Her shriek echoed down the marble staircase. 'Well, I just don't *believe* it! Why didn't you let me know?'

Celia, still smiling, shrugged. She was thinner than ever and looked older. Her tailored suit was severe, her red hair short. 'I didn't let anyone know. I didn't want any arguments. I just came. Are you going to let me in, or do I have to drink gin and tonic on the landing?'

Libby stepped back, talking excitedly. 'How long have you got? Are you back on holiday or for good? Oh, Cele, how marvellous to see you!' Impulsively she flung her arms around her friend's neck and kissed her.

Celia advanced into the apartment, her appreciative glance taking in the art deco decor and furniture, the white rugs and bright, modern pictures. 'Ver-ry nice.'

Libby grinned. 'What else did you expect, darling? Now – tell me what you're doing here – how long you've got?'

Celia, in the act of pulling off her navy blue gloves, turned. 'Your guess is as good as mine, love. I'm home for the duration. My New York friends think I should be certified. They're probably right.'

'The duration?' Libby's fine brows drew down and her mouth tightened. 'The duration of what?'

The other girl cocked her head, an expression of wryly affectionate amusement on her face. 'Now come on, Lib, it can't have escaped even you in your ivory tower that there's going to be a war?'

Libby turned away. 'Oh, for heaven's sake, not you too! Don't be ridiculous. There isn't going to be a war. Mr Chamberlain said so. Even Hitler said so.'

'That was a year ago, love.' Celia's green eyes were sympathetic. 'Don't you read the newspapers?'

'No, I don't. And it strikes me that the world might be a

172

bloody sight easier place to live in if no one else did either!'
Libby snapped, her colour high.

Celia eyed her for a moment, reflectively. 'You think we
can let Poland go the same way as Czechoslovakia?'

'I don't know. I don't care. It isn't anything to do with
me.'

'Nothing to – Libby, if we don't stop them now, there's
no knowing what might happen—'

'Shut up, Cele. I tell you, I don't want to hear.'

'—the Russians have let us down—'

'Celia Hinton, pleased as I am to see you, you can stop
right there or go and find your next gin and tonic elsewhere.
I mean it. I tell you I don't want to hear. There's not going
to be a war, and there's an end to it. I've got something far
more interesting to talk about. My baby sister is acting the
absolute fool again and you've simply *got* to help me make
her see sense . . .'

On the first day of September 1939 a news bulletin put out
by the BBC at ten-thirty in the morning told a waiting
British public that the dictator had invaded Poland. The
blow was not unexpected; the day before, the British government had issued orders for the beginning of the
evacuation of children from threatened areas, and – even
more significant to a nation whose defenders, traditionally,
had been her seafarers – the Fleet had been mobilized.

It was Friday. Allie had gone to work through a sombre
city, and by mid-afternoon the tension was so high that all
business dealings had virtually come to a halt. Sir Brian, his
worst fears realized and his cherished company likely to be
one of the first casualties of war, philosophically suggested
that she might as well take the rest of the day off. As she was
putting on her jacket, the telephone rang.

'Allie? It's Peter.'

'Hello.'

A small silence. 'Well. Looks as if this is it.'

'Yes.'

'I wondered – are you by any chance free this afternoon?'

'Yes, as a matter of fact I am. Sir Brian's just given me the rest of the afternoon off. Libby and Edward are coming down to Ashdown for the weekend, and I've made arrangements to travel down with them.'

'I'd – like to see you. Any chance?'

Her hesitation was only momentary. 'Yes, of course.'

'Regent's Park? Usual place?'

'Fine. I'll be there in half an hour.'

He was waiting for her, his jacket off and slung over one shoulder, the ends of his tie hanging from the pocket. Their feet raised dust from the sun-dried park walks. Allie took off her own jacket and hung it over her arm. They walked in silence for a time until Allie said quietly, 'If it comes to it – will you join up?'

'Of course.'

'Which service?' It was absurd, this conversation. They were talking as if they were discussing the weather. She wanted to pinch herself.

'I thought the army.' He shrugged at her swift glance of surprise. 'Oh, for myself it'd be the RAF if they'd have me. But – well – the old regiment and all that. Dad's dead set on the Guards. I don't like to disappoint him. I don't suppose I'd make a very good flyer, anyway. I've got a rotten sense of direction.'

Her smile was strained.

'It'll probably be all over before I ever get to fire a gun in anger.'

'Probably.'

Their feet brushed through short, tinder-dry grass.

'Let's sit for a minute.'

They sat down in the shade of a tree, the rush of the traffic coming to them from a distance across the park. Somewhere in the noise, the sound of a newsboy's call echoed. Barrage balloons, like giant, lazy silver fish, floated above them, shining in the sunlight, mutely peaceful reminders of the terror of Guernica. Not far from Allie, a young couple lay in each other's arms, oblivious of the world around them. She averted her eyes, picked a blade of grass, shredded it. 'As I came past the Albion Hotel – you know, the big one on the corner by the office? – there were a whole lot of stretchers being unloaded from a lorry. Metal ones. Khaki-coloured—' She stopped, tore again nervously at the grass.

He studied her, his face sombre. 'I hope you didn't mind my asking to see you?'

'Mind? Of course not, don't be silly.'

'I wanted to tell you something.'

She waited.

'I'll never forget you. Never.'

Unexpected tears burned. She blinked. 'How silly. Of course you won't. I shan't give you the chance.'

He grinned, suddenly and infectiously, his hazel eyes crinkling. 'I wish that were a promise. But I know it isn't.'

She opened her mouth, hesitated, shut it again.

'Would you mind if I wrote to you?' he asked.

'I'd love it. Write to home. Mother will forward the letters.' She caught his brief, questioning look, laughed a little. 'You needn't think you're the only one who'll be in uniform. Times have changed, my lad. The ladies get to march to war, too, nowadays. Hadn't you heard?'

'It's odd.' He spoke thoughtfully. 'It hadn't really occurred to me.'

'You know me. Accident prone. Leave me to keep the home fires burning and I'd burn the damned house down.'

He smiled again. 'What will you join?'

'Anything that'll have me,' she responded promptly, 'anything that doesn't want me to knit socks or iron battle-dresses, that is. I thought the WAAF. With my colouring I'd look an absolute sight in khaki . . .'

An hour later he left her outside Rampton Court. 'Give my love to Libby and Edward.'

'I will.' People hurried around them. Sunlight dappled the glinting pavement. On the other side of the road, a party of soldiers was sandbagging a gun emplacement at the edge of the park. The sight shook Allie, suddenly and unexpectedly, from that daze of unreality that had dogged her for weeks. She felt for the first time a sickening rise of fear.

175

Peter took her hand. 'Take care. Take very great care.'

She blinked. 'I will.' Perfectly naturally, she moved into his arms, resting her head on his shoulder. 'And you, Peter. Be careful.'

'Of course.'

'I'm frightened.'

'So am I,' he said, gently. 'So, I guess, is half the world . . .'

'Nothing will ever be the same again, will it? Whatever happens, however it all turns out?'

He did not reply, but held her to him for a moment before, without attempting to kiss her and with no goodbye, he turned and strode into the hurrying crowds.

## PART THREE

## AUTUMN 1940

## CHAPTER ELEVEN

The grim and unequal battle that would ensure or dash any hope of Britain's survival as a free nation alone in an enslaved Europe took place in the late summer and lovely early autumn of 1940. Contrary to most people's fearful expectations, it was fought not on the beleaguered nation's beaches, nor through the streets of her towns and cities, but in the lovely summer skies above the peaceful countryside of southern England. While the fertile green fields of Kent and Sussex basked in endless days of sunshine, while fruit swelled and ripened, as it always had, on the orchard trees, while men, women and children tended their ordinary lives in circumstances extraordinary enough to try the courage of heroes, above them in the crystal, light-washed air the tiny machines of two air forces engaged in a deadly struggle.

After the first anti-climactic, uneasily quiet wartime months of feint and skirmish, which had done little but wear down the nerves and then create a perilous complacency, the sudden revving of the engines of war, the rhythmic tread of marching feet, the howl of a Messerschmitt's screaming dive heralded ruin for western Europe – a ruin effected in a few short, stunning months. Before primrose and coltsfoot had faded from the Kentish hedgerows, Denmark and Norway had fallen; by the time the woodland floor was showing its carpet of bluebells, Holland and Belgium had been lost. In the British Parliament, a new Prime Minister, Winston Churchill, had in absolute honesty promised his people blood, toil, tears and sweat, while in threatened France, the battlefield of a generation before, the Nazi war machine hammered on. Step by grim step, the French and their British allies were forced back to that seawater ditch that stood between them and relative safety, the narrow barrier that had for so long been Britain's last line of defence against invasion and that now threatened to be the very trap into which the whole of the British Expeditionary Force, together with the imperilled French army, must surely fall. By the end of May 1940, with the advancing German forces already at Abbeville, a stone's toss from the English Channel, and the Allies penned helplessly within a ring of armour, the inevitable end seemed close.

Like her battered army, Britain herself faced an enemy whose successful impetus continued to carry all before it. An enemy whose only error was one of judgement. It was perfectly reasonable to suppose that a savagely mauled nation – especially one whose reputation for good sense perhaps obscured other, more dashing characteristics – would, as others had done, take the realistic course and surrender. By the time that such practical thinking on the part of the German High Command had proved a misconception, the evacuation of Dunkirk had begun. In the first three days of June, a trapped and exhausted army was snatched from the beaches of northern France by as motley a flotilla of craft as could ever before have put to sea. Half-dead on their feet, wounded, weary, hungry men were ferried home in their thousands by hundreds of small boats, some of which had until the year before been the playthings of a traditionally seafaring nation. And as the soldiers splashed through the surf and scrambled aboard with nothing more than the dirty clothes in which they stood, the boats and crowded beaches were bombed and strafed mercilessly by a Luftwaffe that seemed to the exposed and furiously helpless men to receive little or no opposition in the air.

Across the Channel, on the hastily constructed airfields of southern England, young men – most of whom until a few short months before had never faced a harsher challenge than the opposition's fastest bowler or toughest fullback – scrambled their Spitfires and Hurricanes into the air to face wave after wave of enemy fighters in a desperate attempt to give cover to the vulnerable, fleeing forces. Many of their planes, outgunned and outmanoeuvred by a more experienced enemy, were shot to pieces by the Luftwaffe squadrons, and the young flyers, after bailing out, slogged along refugee-choked roads to the evacuation beaches and embarked for England where, a matter of hours after being shot down, they became airborne again and headed out over the littered waters of the Channel. Perhaps understandably in the circumstances, not all the 'brown jobs' in the long, weary columns who had waited in some cases for days for their turn to embark took kindly to the apparent queue-jumping of a fresh-faced young man in flying jacket and provocatively jaunty silk scarf. The RAF had not yet earned its colours, especially in the jaundiced eyes of the hard-pressed army, and the harsh words of these battle-weary men on the Dunkirk beaches were not the only criticism it found itself facing.

But the weeks after the evacuation were to change that once and for all. By the end of July the men of Britain's youngest service were being given more than ample chance to prove themselves, and beyond any reasonable hope or expectation, they rose to the challenge magnificently. Meanwhile, beneath vapour trails and a hail of shrapnel, Britain prepared for what was regarded as inevitable invasion and south-eastern England became an armed camp.

Allie Jordan, stationed at Hawkinge Aerodrome, just a couple of miles north of Folkestone on the south coast, found herself, to her own surprise, in the front line of this new war. Her fluent German had earned her a place with a special group of the Women's Auxiliary Air Force stationed at Hawkinge, operating a 'listening post' that used short-wave radio to eavesdrop on transmissions both by Luftwaffe units and by the German E-boats that infested the Channel. In the weeks following Dunkirk, she and her companions worked long hours in far from comfortable conditions and under considerable strain. She survived air attacks and brass-button parades, discovered in about equal part the anguish and the camàraderie of war, found herself to possess, to her own surprise, reserves of stubborn courage that served her well in these strangest of circumstances. When the listening post was moved from the airfield itself to rather more comfortable – and safer – quarters in a secluded house that had been requisitioned just outside the village, she and her fellow-eavesdroppers were grateful, though the hours were still long and the strain extreme. After a twelve-hour stint, Allie was not alone in finding it a positive effort not to think and speak in German.

'I'm beginning to damn well *dream* in it,' she complained, half-laughing, to the girl with whom she shared a room and whose intemperate good nature and utter refusal to take anything seriously were, she sometimes felt, the only sane things in a crazy world.

Sergeant Sue Miller grinned unsympathetically. She was a tiny Cockney girl with a halo of bright blonde hair and the widest and most innocent blue eyes Allie had ever seen. She also had, as Allie was to discover, the vocabulary of a docker and a blithe capacity for mischief that would leave a monkey standing. 'Don't tell 'em that in the village. Old Tom at the Blue Boar'll have you with his pitchfork for a fifth columnist soon as look at you!'

The coast of southern England sprouted dragon's teeth of barbed wire and solid, iron-bound cement. Pill boxes defended road and railway. Signs were taken down – and Sue was not the only one to find that, however potentially effective this particular measure might be in confounding an invading army, it certainly was a spectacular success when it came to confusing the natives.

'I'd like to punch Herr flamin' Hitler right on his stupid, ugly little nose, that I would. Him an' his bloody invasion. Ruined my twenty-four-hour pass, that's what . . .'

Allie looked up from her book, laughing. 'What happened?'

'Sailed through the bloody station, didn't I? Well, how the hell was I supposed to know where I was? By the time I found out, an' waited best part of three hours for a train back, I'd lost my date to a *Wren*!' Characteristically Sue threw back her fair head and giggled. 'Serves him right. I hope he drowns. Never cared much for sailors meself . . .'

During July the Luftwaffe launched a series of venomous attacks on British shipping in the Channel and on the coastal towns. Standing on the chalk downs above the camouflaged airfield one early July day, Allie watched a flight of German bombers attack a British convoy as it steamed past Folkestone, saw the Hurricanes of Hawkinge's 79 Squadron lift one after the other from the ground and bank out over the light-spangled water to defend the ships. The night before, in the Lion, she and Sue had been talking and laughing with those same men. She watched the battle, riveted despite herself. The very atmosphere shook. Plumes of white water rose around the embattled convoy. Smoke poured darkly from a crippled ship, a shifting veil for the flame at its heart, and the quicksilver surface of the sea was foul with spilled and burning oil. The bombers had done their job. They lifted and banked for home. Their fighter escort had turned like eager hounds upon the little attacking Hurricanes and, looking like children's toys, the planes chased each other over the lucent sky in a lunatic, life-and-death game of tag. The howl and whine of their engines, the flat chatter of their machine-guns came clearly to Allie's ears above the melodious larksong and the lazy hum of the bees that bumbled about the clover at her feet. She watched two of the planes swooping and diving upon each other, each trying to gain the advantage. One climbed, blindingly, into the sun, dived, and a machine-gun ripped once, twice, and then again, a long, tearing burst. One of the planes lurched sideways, smoke and flame streaming from its tail like a party banner. Then it went into a straight, spinning dive. The familiar squared-off wings and camouflage grey identified it as the enemy. Allie held her breath, watching, praying without words, her hands clenched as if frozen in death. Jump, for God's sake! Jump! But as the plane continued its manic dive, no silken parachute blossomed to hang gently in the summer air. A mile or so from where Allie stood, the machine hurtled down and hammered itself into the downs as if that had been its purpose all along, and perished in a bloom of flame.

'God almighty,' she said, helplessly. She would never get used to it.

From the village, the all-clear sounded.

This was a deliberate war of attrition, and though the enemy's immediate and obvious objectives were to destroy British shipping and coastal towns and defences, its real target was Fighter Command. Numerically the RAF was at such a crushing disadvantage that every single fighter lost weakened the force disproportionately. The Channel attacks were designed to lure Fighter Command to risk its precious planes and even more precious pilots and, in doing so, fatally flaw the island's fragile air defences and open the way to invasion. South-eastern England, shelled constantly from the occupied French coast, lay apprehensive beneath the summer sun and squinted into the glittering distances, watching for the first signs of an enemy fleet on the horizon. The fields were tilled by steel-hatted men, two to an ancient tractor, one facing forward and one back, First World War rifles in hands, eyes straining into the bright skies for the glint of a rogue raider whose engine-sound would be drowned by the tractor noise and who would swoop, strafe murderously and be gone in a moment. Nowhere was safe from such attacks – village streets, railway lines, roads, farms, lanes, footpaths were all vulnerable.

People became used to the sight of combat in the sky. They would stand and watch, calling unheard encouragement, damning the enemy. The spirit of the ordinary people whose back gardens had become so unexpectedly a battlefield was astounding. When German planes dropped copies of Hitler's so-called 'Last Appeal to Reason', begging the British people for their own sakes to defy their government and lay down their arms, the civilian population collected them and sold them to each other at threepence a time in aid of the Red Cross. In every pub in the country, the same happily hackneyed joke was told for a week: 'Hear some lazy blighter of a Jerry couldn't be bothered to undo the bundles before he dropped them. Bloody cheek. He could have killed someone . . .'

And then came August, a month of sunshine and ripening harvests, of long, hot days that, thanks to British Summer Time, faded into late-lit evenings of soft light and sprawled, elongated shadows – a month in which the RAF found itself truly fighting for its life.

The raiders raced in from the sea, hordes of them, fast and low, skimming over the chalk downs like flung spears, or droned high, out of reach of the anti-aircraft guns, bearing their deadly loads of high explosives and incendiaries. However they came, their targets were the same – the fighting airfields of south-eastern England – their aim to break Fighter Command once and for all.

Allie was walking to her billet a little way outside the village when the first major raid hit Hawkinge. From the vantage point of the village's only street – Hawkinge nestled on the slope of the downs, overlooking the spread of the airfield below – she watched in helpless horror as, amid a series of enormous explosions, the airfield seemed to disintegrate before her eyes. The drone of the high-flying Junkers that had delivered the big bombs vibrated through the concussed air. Buildings, including one of the great hangars, splintered into matchwood and were blasted to flame.

'Here, miss, quick!'

She turned. A small, bright-eyed boy, dancing with excitement, beckoned wildly.

'Grandad says to come in with us. You can't stay out here.' Numbly she followed him at a stumbling run, round the side of the cottage to where the welcome hump of an Anderson shelter huddled into the downland slope. As she scrambled into the sandbagged entrance and, blinded by the sudden darkness, dropped the few feet into the body of the shelter, she caught her leg on a sharp piece of corrugated iron, tearing her stocking and scratching her leg.

'There, Charlie,' scolded a good-humoured voice, 'I do keep telling you to bend that bit back. The young lady's hurt herself now.'

Outside, a thunderous explosion, fit to rend the world from its moorings, shook the air. The plump, homely-looking woman who had spoken did not so much as blink but knitted on. 'Get the first-aid box down, young Stan.'

'Oh, no, really. It's all right. Just a scratch.' Allie's eyes were getting used to the light. The pearl of faint daylight crept from the protected opening through which she had just come, and two candles guttered and swayed beneath the vaulted, corrugated-iron roof. The shelter had four bunks, a tier of two on each side. The boy had scrambled onto one of the top ones and sat with his legs swinging perilously close to the woman's ear as she sat knitting beneath him. A great bear of a man sat on a chair in the aisle between the bunks. Allie could not see his face clearly, but when he spoke, his voice was mild and pleasant and carried the same warm country accent as his wife's.

'Gettin' a bit warm out there, I'd say?'

As if to add point to his words, above the cacophony outside came the sudden demented whine of a dive-bombing aircraft and the tearing sound of machine-gun fire. Somewhere, just able to be heard, glass shattered.

'Wouldn't be surprised if that wasn't old Bill's greenhouse gone,' observed the woman thoughtfully.

'Aye.' In the gloom, Allie sensed rather than saw the man's slow smile. 'No great loss really, mind, Bill not being much of a gardener, like. You'd think Herr Goering'd find something better to shoot at, wouldn't you?' He pronounced the name 'Gorring', with a fine disdain for the niceties of the German language, Allie noticed. As she smiled, he turned to her. 'There'll be a cup of tea in two shakes, miss. When it quietens down a bit and I can pop in and make one.'

'Oh, please – don't bother for my sake.' Allie felt absurdly awkward. 'Thank you very much for – rescuing me,' she added. 'I don't think I'd like to be out there at the moment.'

He dismissed her thanks with a smile and a wave of his hand, then dug into the pocket of his overalls and produced a pouch of tobacco and a packet of cigarette papers. 'From the aerodrome, are you?'

'Yes.'

'Grandad, can I have another look outside?' The boy's voice was shrill with excitement. His grandfather ignored him.

'Been stationed here long?'

'A couple of months.' Allie was reticent.

'Aye.' Wisely, he asked no more questions.

'Grandad!'

'Hold your tongue, young Stan.' The voice was still mild.

'Oo-oh, but . . .' There was a lull outside. The quiet seemed unnatural. Allie perched on the lower bunk opposite the woman, who had stopped knitting for a moment and had lifted her head, listening to the silence.

The man had finished his carefully constructed cigarette. He surveyed it with satisfaction in the flickering light, pinched out the stray whiskers of tobacco from the ends and carefully stowed them back in his pouch, put the weedy, loose-packed tube between his lips with every appearance of enjoyment and lit it in an unexpected flare of flame with one of the candles. Then he extended a hand like a ham to Allie. 'Charlie Jessup,' he said. 'This is my wife Rose, and this is our son's lad, Stan.'

Allie took the glad hand of friendship. 'Allie Jordan. How do you do?'

The sharp eyes twinkled at the stripes on her arm. 'Sergeant Jordan.'

She laughed, self-consciously. 'Oh, we're all—' She stopped.

'Didn't serve in France for nothing, you know.' Charlie filled the silence easily, covering her self-conscious con-

185

fusion. 'I'd recognize a sergeant at a hundred paces. Though I can't say I remember any that looked a bit like you.'

She smiled at him gratefully, cursing her own clumsiness. Of all the idiocies in this idiotic war, it seemed that the one she could least get used to was that she must never mention her or her comrades' work, even in the most casual way. 'Careless talk costs lives' admonished a thousand posters, and she supposed it to be true, yet still the irksome need for secrecy faintly embarrassed her, as if she were a little girl caught putting on grown-up airs.

Stan had been inching along the bunk towards the doorway. Keeping one eye on his grandfather, he swung a skinny leg nonchalantly towards the stepped platform that led outside.

In no great haste, Charlie stood, reached for the leg, swung it none too gently back up onto the bunk and climbed up into the sheltered doorway himself and cautiously stuck his head out. 'It's quiet for the moment.'

'Let's see!' Stan scrambled after him.

Allie stood up. 'Perhaps I'd better . . .?'

'Nonsense, dear. The all-clear hasn't gone yet. Not that they bothered us with the warning, mind you. You'd think the blessed Jerries were invisible, wouldn't you? Anyway, Charlie's gone to make the tea. Stay and have a cup.'

'Well – thank you – I'd like that.'

For a moment she watched Rose's flying fingers, white in the gloom against the inevitable khaki wool. 'You're very clever to knit like that. And in the dark too. I never seem to have found the knack.'

'Why, bless you, it's easy as pie.' Rose held up the sleeve she was knitting for inspection. It looked long enough, Allie thought, to serve as a windsock. 'For our Alf. Stan's dad. Lost everything in France, he did.'

'Dunkirk?'

The older woman nodded.

'Was he hurt?'

'No, thank God.' Rose flashed a quick smile. 'Just mad as

186

a hornet. I wouldn't like to be the first Jerry our Alf lays his hands on.'

'A friend of mine was killed in the evacuation,' Allie found herself saying.

Rose moved her head and tutted sympathetically. Her needles clicked.

Outside, distantly, there came again the noise of a plane's engine, the faint crackle of gunfire, like the sound of flame.

'We were lucky we didn't lose all of them,' said Rose, after a moment.

'That's true.' Ray Cheshire had been one of the unlucky ones. He had died in an air attack before the boats had come. The news had saddened and badly shaken Allie, for all that she had not seen Ray since long before the war. His death had somehow seemed to cast a shadow on all those she knew, all those she loved.

The two women sat in thoughtful silence. A solitary bird sang in the garden. Then there came again an all-too-familiar sound. Stan appeared in the doorway and launched himself expertly onto the top bunk without touching the floor. His eyes were lanterns of excitement. 'Jerries!' he said. 'Dorniers. *Thousands* of them!'

Charlie manoeuvred his way carefully through the awkward, sandbagged doorway and handed down a tray of tea to Allie. 'Here they come again,' he said cheerfully.

That was the beginning. In common with most others who saw it in the shambles that followed that raid, Allie did not believe that Hawkinge could possibly be operational again in a month of long Sundays. But it was, and in twelve hours. Men toiled through the night by the light of the burning buildings to fill the craters and level off the ground, and – as from every other battered airfield in the south-east – when the sun rose, Hawkinge's fighters were already taking off again. Amid ruined barracks, hangars, workshops and stores, men and women worked cheerfully on, and a WVS canteen doled out tea and breakfast to all comers. It was a scene often to be repeated in the next few weeks as the

Luftwaffe hammered the Fighter Command stations mercilessly, in patterned attacks, in attacks of overwhelming force, in single, hit-and-run dive-bombing missions.

But they by no means had it all their own way. The squadrons of Spitfires and Hurricanes were the chastening gauntlet that the enemy attackers had to run, and just punishment was exacted. Young pilots lifted their battered planes to meet the challenge again and again, landed them with body-fabric streaming like summer bunting, wingtips gone, tailpieces lost, undercarriages locked or shot away, and were back in the air in a matter of minutes in a patched-up machine they had never laid eyes on before. During those last days of August the sky was never free of combat, of smoke smudges, of dogfights and the faint rip of gunfire. The well-tended fields of the 'garden of England' were littered with the detritus of war, becoming a giant graveyard for twisted, fire-blackened lumps of metal that bore no resemblance to the marvellous machines they had been a short time before. A stricken fighter would sometimes drop out of the air like a stone and bury itself and its pilot in a self-dug grave twenty feet deep. Then again, a pilotless plane might circle and threaten in the sky for endless minutes, lifting and dipping in its last, unguided flight before sliding to earth in an eruption of flame. But down below, obstinately, life went on. Children going to school would stand and watch the battles in the sky, howling spite and fury at a victorious Messerschmitt, screaming with delight at a Spitfire's victory roll, and always ready, with glee, to collect souvenirs – the more gruesome the better.

During the first week in September the anti-aircraft guns – known universally as the 'ack-ack' guns – were kept busy constantly as the pressure upon the airfields and their defenders mounted. Yet, life retained a kind of defiant gaiety, rooted in an absolute refusal to let Jerry have it all his own way. It was in just such a mood that Allie and Sue decided to picnic on the downs on a bright Saturday afternoon, the seventh of September.

There had been a particularly punishing attack on the airfield that morning – in fact, Hawkinge had been hit two or three times a day every day that week. This time, not only had the landing field been badly cratered again, but extensive damage had also been done to buildings, including the station headquarters: yet almost before the sound of the enemy engines had died, the repair work was once more under way. In this raid, the village, too, had been hit and several civilians killed. After she had come off duty that afternoon Allie had paid a call on the Jessups with whom she had become very friendly, and, delighted at finding them unharmed, she had found herself pressed into accepting a small pot of honey – a great prize in these days of constant shortages.

'Good Gordon Bennett!' Sue had almost drooled over the sticky pot. 'What are we goin' to do with it? It looks too good to eat.'

Allie smiled at, but did not comment upon, the pronoun. 'We could invite someone to tea?'

Sue pulled a face. 'The vicar's otherwise engaged, love. An' the King an' Queen came last week. I know – a picnic! It's been bloody years since I've been on a picnic!'

'Now?'

'When else is there?'

'I thought you might be seeing Jan this afternoon?'

Sue turned away, ducking her head. 'No.'

Jan Lenska, a Polish pilot with 79 Squadron, had pursued Sue with graceful singlemindedness from the first moment his dark eyes had lit upon her picturesque halo of hair and her forget-me-not eyes. They had both enjoyed the chase to the full, and it had been watched with good-humoured interest by half the personnel of the station.

'What is it?' asked Allie softly after a moment.

Sue shrugged. 'He took on one too many this morning. It was bound to happen. You know what they're all like, the Poles. Got their own private crusade going. He got himself shot up and bailed out down the coast a way.' Her voice was very nearly expressionless.

'Is he all right?'

The fair head lifted and shook. 'Burned. They wouldn't tell me how badly. But no one's gettin' to see him.'

For the space of a couple of heartbeats, there was silence as the eyes of the two girls met and all the ghosts of the past few months rose between them in bleak recollection of pain.

'Right,' Sue said briskly, 'that's settled. A picnic it is.'

From the heights behind the airfield on a day such as this, it was possible to look out across the Channel a couple of miles away to occupied France. The girls strolled through narrow lanes between hedgerows in which dog rose and wild hops scrambled, and then up onto the more exposed downland where plump sheep cropped contentedly. An occasional engine-sound, while not interrupting their idle talk, sometimes caused them to lift their eyes warily to the skies. They stopped once to lean on a field gate and watch, below, a battle-damaged Spitfire land on the patched and uneven field, its engine sputtering painfully, its tail almost shot away. The little plane pancaked down onto the chequered, chalky ground in a cloud of white dust, slewed sideways and slithered to an awkward stop. Moments later a jaunty hand waved from the cockpit and a figure, doll-sized from where they watched, scrambled onto the tilted wing and jumped to safety. It was not until that moment that Allie realized she had been holding her breath.

Farther up the lane, a farm cart drawn by a magnificently handsome giant of a carthorse ambled up behind them. They stepped aside to let it pass, smiling at the tin-hatted ancient who held the reins. The old man eyed with appreciation the two trim figures in Air Force blue. 'Goin' far, ladies?'

'Just to the top.'

'Do with a lift, could you?'

They hopped onto the tailgate of the cart as it passed and sat, feet swinging, as they climbed, slower than they could have walked, towards the summit. In the sunny distance the Channel glittered like a pirate's hoard of diamonds.

Allie, looking down at her dusty, swinging feet, laughed suddenly.

'What's up?'

'I was just remembering: I always swore that I'd never wear another pair of "sensible shoes" as long as I lived once I left school.' She stuck her feet out, comically, in front of her. 'Now look at me!'

Sue grinned. 'Think yourself lucky. I never *had* a pair of "sensible shoes" until I joined this lot!' The words were genuinely humorous, and did not carry the faintest trace of resentment or self-pity. Allie glanced, quickly and curiously, at the pretty profile of her companion. In a company composed almost entirely of upper- and middle-class young women whose backgrounds, like Allie's, owed much to money and to unheeded privilege, Sue Miller was the odd one out. She had lived all her life in Bethnal Green where her parents still lived, and had no pretensions to gentility whatsoever – would indeed hoot with laughter if anyone tried to credit her with any. 'Come to that,' she added now, tilting her head and watching the melodic rise of a lark, 'I only went to school one week in two when I was a nipper. Always seemed to be something more interesting to do. Me poor old mum was always copping it from the school board man.'

Allie laughed. 'You aren't serious?'

'Straight up. If it hadn't been for Miss Amelia Bertrand, bless her little cotton socks, I'd have finished up just another ignorant, runny-nosed kid scrapin' the back streets of Bethnal Green. As it was . . .' this time her tone changed just a little; there was in it the faintest, amused note of irony '. . . if it hadn't been for dear old Adolf, I suppose I'd have finished up a well-read, runny-nosed kid scrapin' the streets of Bethnal Green.'

'Who was Amelia Bertrand?'

'Teacher. Funny old codger. Took a likin' to me for some reason.' She chuckled, rolling her eyes. 'She was the only one who did. And I can't say I blame them when I come to think of it. I was a little bugger. But Miss Bertrand took me in hand. Gawd knows why. Showed me a few things I hadn't noticed before. Got me readin' poetry an' the like.' She threw back her head and crowed. 'What a laugh! Me mum thought I'd gone doo-lally . . .'

'Sorry?'

Sue screwed a graphic finger into her forehead. 'Crackers.'

'Ah. And was it from Miss Bertrand that you learned your German? It's much better than mine.'

Sue took her hat off, shook her sweat-damp curls and tilted her face, like a flower, to the sun. 'Oh, no. That was kind of an accident. Miss B got me a job – sort of assistant to an assistant nanny to a German family livin' in London. I picked up the lingo off the kids.'

Allie surveyed her in astonishment. 'Just like that?'

Her companion lifted one shoulder in a self-deprecating gesture. 'More or less. They were a lazy little pair of blighters and wouldn't learn a word of English. It was the only way I could get them to behave themselves.'

'Did you never want to take your formal education any further?' Allie was truly curious.

Sue sent her an affectionate glance. 'Allie, love, I didn't *have* any formal education. Like I said.'

'But – I thought everyone—' Allie stopped, suddenly embarrassed.

'Where you come from, love,' said Sue easily, 'but not where I come from.' She glanced mischievously at Allie's rather pink face. 'It's OK. Don't worry about it. It isn't your fault. I did all right with Miss Bertrand.'

'But, that isn't the point, is it? I mean – there must have been others who didn't?'

'True enough.'

'And it doesn't bother you?'

'Not a bit. Why should it?' Sue swung her legs for a moment, thoughtfully. 'Miss B wanted me to go in for a scholarship or some such thing – but I ask you, what good would it have done me? Can you imagine me at a posh school like the one I bet you went to? I'd have fitted like a foot into a glove. There's no magic wands in Bethnal Green – and precious few anywhere else.'

'You fit in here.'

'Ah, but that's different, isn't it? I'm not a scruffy, know-nothing kid without a decent pair of shoes now. I'm old enough and ugly enough to look after meself. I'd say I'm doing better than most, in fact – have you heard me complainin' about the outside loo? What you've never had you don't miss. An' as for fittin' in . . .' She glanced again at Allie. 'You don't have to be charitable. Don't think I don't know that there's one or two think I ought to be scrubbin' the floor rather than messin' in with them.'

Allie did not reply.

Sue grinned. 'Like I said – don't worry about it. It isn't your fault.'

They rode in silence for a moment. Allie was thoughtful. Something in the way Sue spoke had reminded her of someone; suddenly she saw in her mind's eye Tom Robinson's light, disinterested eyes, heard his distinctive, accented voice. 'My brother was at Cambridge with someone rather like you,' she found herself saying.

Sue was relaxing, eyes shut, in the sunshine. 'Pull the other one, it's got bells on.'

'No, honestly. I think he must have got a scholarship from a grammar school or something. I – actually, I never asked.'

Sue turned her head, lifted wry eyebrows. 'Sounds like a clever lad. Was he happy?'

Allie hesitated, taken by surprise. 'I – don't know.' Then she added, honestly, 'I suspect not, thinking about it.' Such a thing had never occurred to her before. The mere thought of Tom Robinson stirred that faint, uncomfortable feeling of dislike that he always inspired in her. She did not want to believe that it stemmed from the difference in their backgrounds; even less did she want to suspect that it had its roots in his unhappiness.

Sue turned her face back to the sun. 'There you are then.

It's like I said – it doesn't work. A place for everyone an' everyone in their place—'

'You don't believe that!' Allie was shocked.

The graceless merriment in the pretty face proclaimed clearly that she did not. "Course I do.'

'But Sue—'

'Gawd, girl,' Sue said with friendly acrimony, 'do belt up. Don't you know when you're gettin' your leg pulled?'

The cart tilted and turned, embarking on the final pull to the crest of the hill. Beneath them the village looked like a tumbled collection of toy houses, spilled and left by a careless child. The scar where the bomb had struck that morning stood raw against the green of growing things. The camouflage-colours of the aerodrome buildings, too, were fresh-flawed and gashed. In a field behind the village a game of cricket was in progress, the white-clad figures standing out in sharp relief against the sun-baked playing field. Allie smiled. The village team was captained by Charlie Jessup, who took the responsibility very seriously and had through the last few long summer evenings vigorously trained his stalwart men, the oldest of whom was seventy if a day, and the youngest his own grandson Stan whose enthusiastic knowledge of the game had been culled entirely from a hero-worship of Len Hutton and an assiduously collected set of cigarette cards. That the 'Hawkinge Flyers' – their scratch-team opponents from the airfield – numbered in their company a Leicestershire county player and an Oxford Blue worried Charlie not at all.

As the cart rumbled over the top of the downs, the two girls jumped from it, calling their thanks, and clambered over a stile into a field of short, springy grass. A couple of plump sheep skittered stupidly away from them and then turned back to their ceaseless cropping. Sue spread the blanket that she had been carrying on the grass and they sat down, their backs to a stone wall, looking over the green hilltops to the Channel and to France. In that warm, peaceful moment, with the loudest sounds being the wind, which even on the stillest of days blew across these uplands, and the steady, tearing, crunching sound of the cropping sheep, death and destruction and the fear of invasion seemed the fantasies of a demented mind.

'Doesn't seem possible, does it?'

Allie did not have to ask Sue to clarify the words. 'No.'

They sat in silence. A wren trilled. 'D'you think they'll come?'

Allie shrugged. 'I don't know. I suppose so, sooner or later. Have a sandwich.'

The peace of the afternoon held. The girls lay in the sweet-smelling grass, talking desultorily, watching the small downland butterflies as they flitted in the hot sun, their fragile wings gold-dusted. They were packing up the few remains of their picnic when Sue lifted her head suddenly, listening. 'What's that?'

Allie had been miles away; again and again during the pleasant afternoon she had found herself remembering the picnic above the Medway with Peter, that impossibly distant summer before the war. Last summer. It might have been a hundred years ago. She wondered if he ever remembered it, wherever he was. They had corresponded irregularly for the first few months of the war, but they had soon lost touch and now she had no idea where he might be.

'What's what?'

'Ssh. Listen.'

Now Allie heard it – or rather felt it – too. A vibration in the air. Distant. Threatening.

'Bloody hell,' said Sue very softly. She was standing, her eyes shaded, looking out to sea towards the coast of France. Allie followed her gaze. In the distance, the shimmer of the sunlit waters was challenged by a harsher glitter in the air: the flash of light on perspex windshields. Bombers. Hundreds of them, high and darkly purposeful, spreading as the girls watched into a vast armada that filled the sky with their throbbing power – and around them the cloud of smaller, swifter fighters, shepherding their charges.

Allie began shoving the last of their rubbish into the paper carrier bag in which she had carried their picnic.

Sue grabbed her arm. 'Never mind about that. Run.'

On the airfield beneath them, that command was already being obeyed. They could hear the 'Scramble' orders coming over the speakers; on the field the Merlin engines began to snarl one by one and then, in file, the toy planes taxied, turned, raced across the dusty grass and lifted into the air to meet the new menace that ploughed, steadily and high across the sky towards them.

Allie and Sue scrambled back over the stile and began to run down the lane, the steep slope giving them an impetus that threatened to send them sprawling. But they were not a quarter of a mile down the hill before they knew their flight was useless. Sue stopped, panting, by the gate where they had earlier watched the damaged Spitfire land.

'We'd do better to stay here. We can take to the ditch if we need to. We'd only be in the way down there. God almighty, I've never seen so many! There must be hundreds of them!'

The great formations of bombers droned inexorably on, while around them Spitfires and Hurricanes dived and harried and were in their turn driven off by the enemy bombers' fighter escorts. The air vibrated with the thunder of their passage. But this, the girls came slowly to realize, was no repetition of previous attacks. This time there was no break in formation as bombers peeled off to pound Hawkinge and Manston while others powered on to Biggin Hill, Hornchurch and the others. As the armoured, threatening cloud roared overhead, obscuring the sun and sending flashing shadows across the hillsides, the same stunning thought occurred simultaneously to both the watching girls, the same instant. They looked at each other, aghast.

The RAF had won a respite. Their damaged airfields were safe, for the moment at least.

The target had changed.

The bombers were heading for London.

# CHAPTER TWELVE

Celia Hinton walked with brisk energy through the busy Saturday afternoon streets, her heels clipping the warm pavements decisively, her neat, uniformed figure blending with the crowds – it was the occasional civilian suit or the pretty flash of a bright summer dress that stood out and attracted the eye. Despite the sandbagged doorways and wired and shuttered windows, the early September sunshine brightened the drab wartime streets, and Celia found herself humming beneath her breath as she walked. Shoulder bag swinging, one hand holding her peaked khaki forage cap onto her red head, she dodged across the road, edged her way across the crowded pavement and turned the corner into the board- and sandbag-protected doorway of Rampton Court.

As she approached the block, she paused and looked up at the windows of Libby's apartment. The windows were open to the warm air and even from here she could hear music. Celia smiled to herself. Knowing the decorously conservative – not to say positively stuffy – character of most of the other inhabitants of this respectable block she could not imagine that the swinging sound of an American dance band would fall upon appreciative ears. On the contrary, Celia had a strong suspicion that the capricious, company-loving Mrs Edward Maybury's only saving grace in the eyes of her long-suffering neighbours was her uniformed husband who was serving his country somewhere in the threatened East. And even that was likely in some cases to produce caustically raised eyebrows and acid references to the young wife's popularity with her husband's friends and comrades-in-arms more conveniently stationed than him. Despite her smile, Celia did not like to see Libby the centre of such gossip – even though she knew Libby did not give a fig for the opinion of what she had nicknamed 'the broomstick brigade'.

Within the building, despite the sandbags, fire buckets and wired windows, an atmosphere of tranquillity and luxurious respectability still reigned. It would take more than Hitler to change that. As Celia ran lightly up the flight of wide marble steps towards Libby's flat, the door opened to reveal two laughing young men in khaki, and Libby, lovely in a crisp dress of pink and white, her shining hair swinging to shoulder length. The dance band blared behind them, echoing up and down the stairwell.

'. . . till Tuesday, then,' Libby was saying, 'and don't forget to remind Jeff. You know what – Celia!' she finished on a dramatic little shriek. 'How lovely! I wasn't expecting you – I thought you were on duty all this weekend?'

'I swapped with Stanton. She wants next weekend. Some buddy of hers from the other side of the world has turned up. I thought I'd just drop by. Have I picked a bad moment?'

'Oh, don't be ridiculous, darling. How could it be?'

The two young officers had turned, smiling. One of them looked vaguely familiar to Celia.

'Celia Hinton, isn't it?' he asked.

'That's right.'

He extended a square, well-kept hand. 'Charles Philips. We met at the Robinson place a couple of years back. Before you went to America. Remember?'

'Oh, yes. Of course.' She took his hand, shook it briefly. 'Forgive me – I didn't recognize you in uniform.' The well-mannered pleasantries over, she made to move past him.

He grinned a little sheepishly, and did not step aside. 'It's the haircut that does it.'

Celia smiled politely. 'I expect so.'

Still he did not move. 'This is Lieutenant Bembridge. Mark Bembridge.'

'How do you do?' Celia made no attempt at warmth.

'Hello.'

There was an awkward pause. Celia said nothing.

Charles Philips glanced at her uniform and gestured at her distinctive 'French soldier's' cap. 'You're driving, then?' he asked with dogged disregard for the politely pointed expression of dismissal on Celia's face. 'The Mechanized Transport Corps is it?'

'Yes.'

'Celia was in France,' put in Libby, with an eye to mischief.

'Oh, really?' There was real warmth and interest in the young man's face.

'Yes.' Celia did not elaborate.

'Were you caught in the collapse?'

'Yes.'

'Dunkirk?'

'Bordeaux actually.'

Over the young man's shoulder, Libby's face was solemn, her eyes graceless. 'We're very proud of her,' she said soberly. 'She's quite a heroine.'

'Oh?'

Celia shook her head and smiled a little, her eyes, on Libby, exasperated and promising murder.

Libby, enjoying herself, ignored the threat. 'Valour under fire and all that . . .'

This was too much. 'Libby!'

Libby subsided, grinning.

'It must have been jolly exciting.' There was a truly wistful note in Charles Philips's voice.

Celia let out a small and admirably restrained breath. 'You could say that, I suppose.'

'Damned sight better than wiping noses and—' He remembered his company suddenly and stopped, flushing, and extemporized hastily and ruefully, '. . . making tea for the desk-bound wallahs at the War Office.'

For the first time Celia's smile was, if not exactly warm, at least a little sympathetic. But before he could take advantage of the slight thaw, she had moved determinedly past him to the door.

'Well . . .' He moved from foot to foot, then gave up and

sketched a salute that fell unhappily between jauntiness and embarrassment. 'We'd best be off. See you Tuesday, Libby. Perhaps we'll bump into each other again?' This to Celia.

'Oh, almost certainly.' It was Libby again, happily mischief-making. 'Celia's often here. Aren't you, darling?' Celia's silence apparently affected her not at all. ''Bye now, you two. Take care.'

From a safe position behind the door, while Libby cheerfully waved her guests down the stairs, Celia said, mildly, 'I'll murder you one of these days, you know that?'

'Oh, don't be a bore, darling. It was only a bit of fun.' Libby shut the door and kissed her friend's cheek warmly. 'I absolutely refuse to believe that you find the whole of the male sex as dull as you make out. Poor Lieutenant Philips was clearly stricken. I felt I just had to give the poor boy a hand. You weren't giving him much encouragement, were you? Drink?'

Celia tossed her hat and bag onto a chair. 'The man's an empty-headed nitwit from what I remember. What have you got?'

'Whisky – gin – you name it.'

'I don't know how you do it, honestly I don't. Don't you know there's a war on?'

'I do my level best not to.' It was the most sincere thing Libby had said all afternoon and they both knew it. 'Whisky? Ice?'

'Yes, please.'

Libby poured two drinks, lit a cigarette from the box on the table and blew pale smoke into the air. 'You were a bit harsh, weren't you? To the poor little lieutenant?'

Celia shrugged. 'When a man puts on a uniform, you know, it doesn't work a miracle on his brain. Far from it.' Suddenly truly irritable, she dropped into a chair and sipped her drink. 'If I don't want to know a man when he's in Civvy Street, I see no reason to change my opinion just because he's taken the King's shilling. Or half-a-crown, or whatever it is nowadays.'

Libby held up her hands in a gesture of surrender. 'All right. I'm sorry. I promise I won't sing your praises to the next man who makes sheep's eyes at you. Though, frankly, I don't think a bit of fun would do you any harm.'

'Thanks. But no thanks. What were they doing here anyway?'

'Charles was at school with Edward.' Libby lifted her eyes to heaven. '*Everyone* was at school with Edward. They just dropped by to—' she lifted her glass in a small, ironic toast '—pay their respects.'

Celia, half-smiling, shook her head. 'You're impossible.'

'The war's impossible. The world's impossible. Why should I be different?'

'Have you heard from Edward recently?'

'Mm-hm.' Libby nodded an affirmative as she sipped her drink. 'And if you ask me, he's having the time of his life. Gin fizz on the verandah and all that with the little yellow people waving an ostrich-feather fan to keep the handsome young captain cool. I just hope that one of those bored, passionate, Somerset Maugham planters' wives doesn't get her rubbery talons into him . . .'

'Libby, you really must be careful what you say. You aren't supposed to know where Edward is, let alone—'

'Oh, stuff and bloody nonsense! It's not as if there's even a proper war out there! For God's sake, don't *you* start. It's bad enough with Allie and all this childish cloak and dagger stuff. It's positively embarrassing, and I refuse to take it seriously. And,' she added, with no change in her tone, 'if you tell me again that there's a war on, then you won't get another drink all evening, and that's a promise.'

'That's enough threat to shut anyone up.'

They sipped their drinks in companionably irascible silence.

'Have you been home recently?' asked Celia at last.

'Lord, no. Are you joking? With all those damned planes dropping out of the sky? No fear. I'm not getting machine-gunned for anyone, thank you.'

'Has the village been badly hit?'

Libby waved an airy hand. 'Not so's you'd notice. The odd Messerschmitt in the churchyard, a stick or two of bombs in the village street and a blazing Spitfire or two about the place, that's all.'

'Is – are your family all right?' Celia was very intent upon the melting ice in her glass.

'They're fine. Daddy spends quite a bit of time away, making sure that our bits of the war effort are running smoothly. It's a shame about the profits tax,' Libby added, pensively. 'I guess we'd have made quite a killing if it weren't for that – all those bits of planes and guns and things we're turning out . . .' She ignored Celia's exasperated glance. 'Mother, of course, is working twenty-five hours a day with the WVS.' She grinned suddenly. 'Mother and Daddy must be the only people in the country mad enough actually to evacuate themselves *into* London! Mind you, as things turned out, it was quite a sensible move. The poor little evacuees that got moved into Ashdown got moved out again p.d.q. when the Luftwaffe took a hand. Have you been to the Kensington flat?'

Celia shook her head, still not looking up.

'It's rather nice, actually. Older than this, but comfortable. Actually belongs to Uncle Bertie, but I think he's decided he doesn't need his *pied à terre* for the duration. He ran like a rabbit the day war was declared. Suddenly developed a hankering for the hills of Wales, bless him. Poor old Ashdown's empty at the moment. Welshy's gone to her sister in Scotland, so the house had been closed up since the London kids left. Do you know, Browning's planted potatoes on the tennis court? And turned the rose gardens over to carrots and onions. The world's really gone quite mad . . .'

That lifted Celia's eye. 'Onions?' She made no attempt to disguise her interest.

Libby laughed. 'See what I mean? There was a time when a bottle of whisky could buy you a friend for life. Now it's onions. A pound of onions'll buy you anything!'

'Nothing tastes quite the same without them.' Celia lifted

her glass and studied the room through its golden depths. 'What an epitaph for the fallen French. We miss their onions.'

'Speak for yourself. It's their champagne I miss. Mind you, I rather like the new import of Free French officers. Very dashing. All right, all right.' She lifted a placatory hand as Celia glanced sharply at her. 'I'm joking. I think. There's a couple of pounds of onions in the kitchen – remind me to let you have them before you go.'

'Are you sure?'

'Of course. Mother's dropping in tomorrow. She's bound to bring some more.' Libby sipped her drink. 'You know, the WVS could have been invented especially with Mother in mind. She's evacuating people and feeding people and lecturing people on everything under the sun as if she'd been doing it all her life. Which I suppose in a way she has. And never a hair out of place, bless her.'

The ice in Celia's glass chinked. 'I like your mother.'

'Oh, so do I. Enormously.' There was the slightest edge to Libby's voice. 'I just wish that she wouldn't keep trying to get me involved, that's all—'

'But, Libby, you *are* involved!' It was an old, stale argument between them. 'How can you not be?'

'The war isn't my fault, is it? The only German I know is Uncle Otto. And he's the nicest old codger you could wish to meet. And look what we've done to him – he has to report to the police station every day or week or something to prove he isn't a spy! I tell you, the whole thing is madness. Why should I suffer? They've taken Edward from me – isn't that enough? Pardon me if I don't turn red, white and blue and charge into battle.' Libby's colour was suddenly high. 'It's idiotic, and it's boring and I *will not* talk about it.' She made an undisguised effort to gather her shredded temper and smiled brightly. 'Anyway, what with Mother organizing half of London, Allie fighting the Hun single-handed on the south coast and Richard navigating his wretched bomber, who needs me? Someone's got to keep the flag of civilized hedonism flying. One day you'll thank me, you mark my words. They'll probably give me a medal.'

Celia, defeated as always, subsided. 'I'm sure you're right.'

Libby lit another cigarette from the stub of the one she held before crushing the latter in the ashtray. 'Of course I am. Thank God my baby sister never took up this revolting habit. I don't know what I'd do without her ration. Have another drink.'

Celia surrendered her half-empty glass.

'How's that rather odd flatmate of yours?' Libby called from the other side of the room.

The heartbeat of silence would have been noticeable only to an ear more sensitive than Libby's. 'Stanton? She's fine. And she isn't odd.'

Libby grinned, coming back with the drinks. 'She's Australian, isn't she? That's odd enough for anyone.'

'Chauvinist.'

Libby shrugged, admitting the charge. 'Honestly, though, Cele, you have to admit that she can be a bit hard to take. I mean, she's got no sense of humour, no conversation, no,' she spread her hands expressively, 'no social graces.'

'She's a damn good driver.'

'So are you. It doesn't make you a bore.'

Celia flushed. 'Stanton saved my life in France—'

'—and we're all wonderfully grateful to her for that.' With unstudied affection, Libby dropped a kiss on her friend's cheek. 'I just wish that she'd smile occasionally, that's all. Or answer people when they speak to her. Now, that isn't too much to ask, is it?'

Celia did not reply. Beyond the open windows, the sun was slanting westward, drenching the air with golden light, sheening the clumsy bulk of the barrage balloons above the park until they glowed like fairies' wings. Libby wandered to the window. 'It's a lovely evening. Come and see.'

They stood together, looking out across the sunlit park at children who ran and played and shrieked as children always had. Couples, at least one of them invariably in uniform, strolled hand in hand or sat on the grass, absorbed in each other.

'Oh, Celia. I do miss Edward so dreadfully.' The quiet, desolate words hung like tears in the air between them, unexpected raindrops in the golden evening. Libby's voice, which had been crystal bright a moment before, sounded suddenly like a lost child's. Celia reached and rested a light arm across her shoulders.

'I miss him,' Libby said again on a caught breath.

'He'll be back.'

'I know. But – what about now? What about the days, the hours, the minutes we're missing *now*? We can never get them back. We don't know what they're doing to us . . .'

'There'll be other times.'

'I *know*, but – oh, damn!' The lifting wail of an air-raid siren echoed faintly across the city, then another, and another. In the park people paused for a moment, heads lifted, then turned back, and the scene continued unchanged. The clear sky was peaceful and unchallenged. 'I wish they wouldn't do that.'

'You wouldn't like it if they didn't.'

'Well – it isn't as if anything ever actually happens, is it? I expect they're raiding Biggin Hill again, or something. Not that that will stop the awful Misses Spencer next door from gathering their revolting little dogs and fleeing to the shelter till the all-clear goes. Listen.'

From somewhere close in the building there came a series of high, nerve-racking yelps that became more frantic by the second and ended in a long-drawn-out, hair-lifting yowl of protest. Somewhere a door slammed.

'I thought dogs weren't allowed in shelters?'

'Try telling the Misses that. There they go.' Libby grinned maliciously, her mood of a moment before once more submerged in self-defensive flippancy. 'Works like a charm every time. I'm thinking of seducing our warden so that I can arrange for a nice warning for my next party. Mind you, it'd almost be worth a direct hit to get rid of those damn dogs—'

'Libby!'

'You wouldn't believe the fuss the broomstick brigade made last week. It wasn't as if it were a real party.' Libby had wandered back into the room and was absently straightening ornaments, fluffing up cushions. 'Just a few friends.'

'Libby. Listen. What's that?'

'It isn't my fault if they live like bloody nuns and go to bed at eight. What's what?'

'Ssh.'

The vibrating drone was distant, felt rather than heard.

'I don't know. Trains perhaps.'

'Doesn't sound like trains to me.'

The silence was uneasy. The sound swelled.

'Damn me,' Libby said in mild surprise, 'it really is an air raid.'

Celia was leaning from the window, looking to the sky. 'God almighty,' she said.

'What is it? Cele? What is it?' Libby hung out of the other window and was struck to silence. In the park, arms were lifted, fingers pointing. People, suddenly, were running. Mothers gathered their children like hens their chicks and fled to shelter. The airborne armada came on in deadly formation.

'Where are the guns?' Celia asked of the sky. 'Where in hell's name are the guns?'

As the monstrous flight roared overhead, everything shook. An ornament slipped from a shelf and bounced, unbroken, across the floor.

Libby was wide-eyed. 'Where are they going? Where do you think they're going?'

In the east of the city, many of those who manned London's docks and the lifeline of the railway terminals would never live to answer the question. Hitler's *Blitzkrieg* on London had begun. On that golden September evening, the bombers came in waves, and along the river flames leapt in their wake, shimmering to the sky. The ground shook for miles around. Hot air blasted glass to splinters, shredding flesh from bone. Then a couple of hours later, with their task apparently accomplished, the raiders turned for home, leaving behind them a stunned population and acres of ruined docks and buildings that blazed like tar-filled torches – which, a few hours later, was exactly what they became.

As night fell, the men and women who fought to extinguish these great, flaming beacons were struck down by another ruthless onslaught, were blasted by high explosive, buried in rubble, cut to pieces by machine-gun bullets. Below ground, in inadequately prepared shelters, some of them knee- or ankle-deep in brackish water, the civilian population huddled while their homes and, in some cases, their families were wiped from the earth above them. For most Londoners, this was the longest and most awful night they had ever experienced. Until dawn the merciless pounding continued with no break, and when at last the all-clear sounded, it was above the deafening crackle of flame as firestorms whirled and eddied through the skeletons of what had been streets and houses.

Libby lifted a tousled head from the pillow. 'They've gone.'

She and Celia were in the basement shelter of Rampton Court – which, in the way of such things, was far more comfortable and better served than any public shelter. They had finally been driven down there by dog tiredness and the hope of some sleep after hours of watching the terrifyingly beautiful sight of what looked like half of London in flames. All around them people lay dozing – some of them sleeping as soundly as if they had been in their own beds upstairs – or sat huddled, murmuring to one another in subdued voices.

Celia was sitting on a cot across the narrow gangway, her stockinged feet curled up under her, smoking an unaccustomed cigarette. 'I'd better be going. They're going to need drivers.' When the night raid had started, she had tried to leave the building and make her way to her headquarters but had been turned back by a justifiably stern policeman and a warden who had threatened that, if she didn't get back into shelter, he'd bloody well carry her,

207

uniform or no. She stood now, stretching tiredly, slipped her feet into her shoes.

'I was beginning to think they'd never go,' Libby said a little shakily.

Celia held out her hand and hauled her to her feet. Libby was very pale and there were tell-tale smudges beneath her blue eyes. It had been a gruelling night.

'You OK?'

Libby nodded.

'Let's see if there's anything left out there.'

They picked their way through the stirring, recumbent bodies and walked towards the stairs.

'Thank God that's over,' a voice said quietly, from somewhere beyond the flickering lamplight.

'Over?' another repeated bleakly. 'Don't you believe it. It isn't over. It's just the start. They'll be back.'

They did come back, despite heavy losses inflicted by the RAF. Night after night for months, they came with never a break, with their incendiaries, their high explosives, their oil bombs, their terror – and after that first night their depredations were by no means confined to the East End. Londoners everywhere grew used to nights underground while above them a holocaust raged. Rescue and fire teams battled against inconceivable odds to reach people buried in the blasted remains of their homes, or to contain the firestorms that threatened to engulf their city. In the morning the shelterers would emerge rumpled, weary and apprehensive to discover that the face of their city had been ravaged yet again. Shattered gas mains and water pipes, collapsing walls, cratered roads, all became regular hazards to be overcome. A DANGER:UXB sign scrawled upon a placard would, after the first few days, draw only the most cursory of glances. If the damned bomb hadn't gone off by now it was unlikely to do so as you walked past it.

As the balmy autumn weather finally gave way to winter's wind and rain, conditions in the night-time city worsened. Shelters that had been merely uncomfortably inadequate in dry weather might become totally untenable in wet. In the crowded working-class areas of the city, where most people had no back garden in which to bury their own Anderson shelter, there simply was not enough provision of public shelters for the civilian population – so, with quiet determination, and against a government ban, the people took over the Underground stations, sleeping on platforms, in passages, on staircases. At first, conditions in these makeshift shelters were intolerable, with toilets still locked up for the night, and nowhere to sit or sleep but on the station benches or the floor. But it was better than nothing, and night after night the trek would begin – men, women and children, laden with blankets and food, would buy their penny ha'penny platform tickets and invade London's tube system, refusing to budge until the authorities had to bow to the inevitable and provide tiered bunks, primitive but usable toilets and fresh drinking water. From that moment, while above ground the fires raged from street to street, many found friendship, comfort and relative safety in the warrens of the Underground.

In the more affluent parts of the city, things tended to be, while no less dangerous, at least marginally more comfortable. Most hotels, stores and blocks of flats, like Rampton Court, were more than adequately provided with shelters, some of them positively luxurious. At the Savoy, one could dine and dance with no fear of interruption in the vast shelter beneath the hotel and then, if unwilling to face the hazard of the streets, spend the night – at a price – in a safe, well-protected bed. But not all social life allowed itself to be driven below the ground. As the population of the city – greatly swollen by the influx of service men and women, British, Commonwealth and exiles from almost every overrun country in Europe – became used to the nightly attacks, the dance bands played a little louder, the dancing couples clung a little closer, and clubs, theatres and cinemas were better patronized than ever before. Anything and everything might be counted cause for celebration in this wartime city – a posting, a promotion, a hurried wedding, the mere fact of survival. Over the soundtrack of *Gone with the Wind*, and the red RAIDERS OVERHEAD sign flashing beside the screen, could be heard the steady drone of enemy engines, the crash of gunfire, the crump of exploding bombs. More often than not, not a soul left his seat.

As the convoys in the Atlantic were attacked and the merchant ships were sunk, a shortage of food developed that few families' careful hoarding over the previous few months could withstand for long. What was the good of a ration book if there were no goods to ration? And though, on the whole, there was little grumbling from a population that, oddly and traditionally, always produced its best in times of crisis, there were some who noticed that the West End shops and restaurants seemed, miraculously, better stocked than most others, and that the magic crackle of a five-pound note – which a fair proportion of the population never got to see, let alone to handle – could produce by some alchemy goods that a moment before had been totally unobtainable.

'Same old story,' said Sue, good-naturedly when, a little sheepishly, Allie produced a precious tin of salmon for Charlie Jessup's birthday tea, 'the rich get fed and the poor get children. Don't be mingy with it, Rosie, love. Some poor blighter risked his neck for that. An' it wasn't the so-an'-so that Allie paid her thirty bob to, you can bet your boots on that.'

Charlie, smiling, passed the sandwiches. Sue, with exaggerated care, peeled open the bread and peered at the salmon. 'Funny colour, isn't it?'

'It's no different than usual.'

'Well, I wouldn't know, now, would I?' Grinning, Sue remade the sandwich and took a bite. 'I never saw it outside the tin before. Me mum couldn't afford it when it was three an' six, let alone one pound ten!'

Allie, uncertain if she were joking, glanced at her and received in return a bland smile and a wink that gave away absolutely nothing.

In the past months, the two girls had become unexpectedly firm friends. Allie had watched with a mixture of incredulity, concern and amusement Sue's endless scrapes and scandalous romances, had found herself more than once lending a helping hand when it was needed – which was, in fact, rather more often than was comfortable. Allie had lost count of the number of times she had lied straightfaced to extract her friend from one more jam, or slipped downstairs in the early hours to unlock and slide open a window and watch a slim, silk-clad regulation-breaking leg being flung across the sill as Sue, inevitably laughing, hair dishevelled and uniform rumpled, risked life, limb and liberty for a 'bit of fun' and refused to allow barbed wire, barricades or military police to stop her. Time and again, she was carpeted, and time and again her excellent, idiomatic German, undoubted intelligence and quick wits earned her a reprieve: though, to her enormous amusement, her rank of sergeant, conferred automatically with the special posting, was reduced step by step until she was the only Aircraftwoman, Second Class on the team.

'I've done you a favour,' she shrugged at Allie's consternation. 'Think about it. I'm the only one you lot can order about . . .'

Anyone less amenable to being ordered about, Allie had never met. She laughed. 'I do believe that you do it deliberately!'

Sue picked up her cap and squashed it becomingly onto her fair head. 'It's got to be some kind of record, hasn't it? I must be the only one in this army who's actually making her way *down* in the world!'

In mid-November the two of them, for the first time, got weekend passes together. They hitched a lift on an army truck, climbed into the back and bumped their slow and uncomfortable way, through driving rain that found every gap in the tarpaulin that covered them, along the pitch-dark roads towards London. They saw the blood-glow in the sky, heard the sounds of destruction long before they got there.

'God almighty,' Sue said, uncharacteristically gloomily,

'here we go again. It's a wonder there's anything left to bomb.'

Allie peered through a rent in the tarpaulin. The rain had eased. Bright fingers of light searched the sky. An ack-ack gun nearby crashed, nearly deafening her. 'I don't like the idea of your trying to get right across London in this. Stay with us. There's a shelter that isn't too uncomfortable.' She did not see her friend's half-smile in the dark. The last night Sue had been in a shelter had been spent with her parents, her two young brothers and three sisters, her grandmother and what seemed like half the population of Bethnal Green. They had spent the cold hours huddled in almost complete darkness with their feet in three inches of water, and the only light relief had been when Gran had taken it into her head to tell a joke that the younger element had no business understanding . . .

'Mother and Daddy would be pleased to have you, I know,' Allie said.

'We-ll . . .' The ack-ack gun reverberated again. The truck jolted to a sudden stop. They heard an unmistakable, screeching whistle.

'Look out, girls. This one could be ours.'

With one movement they dived for the floor. A moment later the truck rocked as the bomb went off a couple of streets away. Sirens wailed, whistles blew. Someone shouted unintelligibly. Sue lifted a dishevelled head. 'That shelter of yours sounds like a better idea by the minute.'

Robert Jordan was alone when they arrived at the flat in Kensington. Myra, he told them, was on duty with her mobile canteen.

'In this?' Allie asked, doubtfully.

Her father smiled. 'Try to stop them. They go from shelter to shelter in the bombed-out areas. People have to eat, and in the worst-hit areas they have no way to prepare the food for themselves.'

'The "Volunteer Ladies",' said Sue. 'God bless 'em.'

'She usually works at a rest centre during the day. Look-

212

ing after people who've been bombed out, getting clothing, bedding and what-not sorted out. She never stops.'

'You must be pretty busy yourself?' Allie asked, fighting for warmth.

'Fairly, yes. Jordan Industries is doing its bit. I was up in Birmingham yesterday. They've had almost as bad a pasting as we've had down here. But the factory's missed it so far. They're turning out shell cases as if they've been doing it for years.' Robert held his daughter's eyes with his own. 'And you?'

'I'm as you see. Very well.' Unbidden, the faint tension that often rose between these two hung now between them, a fragile, indestructible web of disillusion and hurt. Allie turned away from him, tossed her cap onto the table. 'Will it be all right for Sue to stay the night? It doesn't seem a good idea for her to try to get home through this.'

'Of course, she must stay. The Underground's impossible at night anyway. Shall we stay up here? I don't usually go below unless it gets really bad, at least until Myra makes it back.' Outside, the rumble of the big guns and the distant concussion of falling bombs accompanied his words.

Sue threw herself into a deep armchair and looked with frank and cheerful admiration around the elegant, cosily firelit room. 'This suits me fine. If you're going to get bombed, I say, get bombed in comfort . . .'

Much later, in the early hours of the morning, Myra let herself into the apartment and paused at the sound of laughter.

'. . . I don't believe it! What happened?'

'When the foreman saw it lying there, he said – if you'll excuse the language – "Jesus, it's a bomb!" And the shift leader said, cool as you please, "Don't tell Him, dear. Go and find the army. We've got a quota to fill," and fill it they did, bless them.'

Sue laughed again, delightedly.

'Almost the whole of the workforce are women now,' Robert went on, 'and a fine job they're doing. I have to admit that if anyone had told me a couple of years ago that we could run Jordan Industries on a war footing with mostly female labour, I simply wouldn't have believed it. But there they are, at the lathes and the benches, working like Trojans.'

'And earning a fair whack for the first time in their lives,' Sue put in, grinning. 'Has it occurred to you what you're going to do with the working girls once this lot's over and the boys come marching home again? You could have a revolution on your hands.'

Myra, standing unnoticed by the door, smiled faintly.

Robert shook his head. 'Oh, no, I don't think so. They know the agreements we have with the unions. Dilution of labour – use of non-union labour – it'll all have to stop when the emergency is over. I should think the girls will be all too pleased—'

'—to get back to the kitchen sink, eh?' teased Sue, gently. 'Well, perhaps you're right, Mr Jordan. We'll have to wait and see, won't we?' In the past couple of hours, surprisingly perhaps, Sue and Robert had struck up an immediate friendship, and the mood between them was easy.

Allie, sitting on the rug in front of the dying fire, looked up. 'Why the lathes and the benches?' she asked suddenly, almost as if the question surprised her. 'Why not the manager's desk? Why not the boardroom?'

Her father smiled. 'Because the men already in those positions are mostly – like me – too old to fight. And most of our industry comes under the "reserved occupation" category.'

'Is that the only reason?'

'Of course it isn't. It goes back to way before the war. I don't deny that women have the brains, the capability, to do those jobs – they simply don't have the experience, the know-how—'

'How will they get it if they aren't given the opportunity?' Allie leaned forward intently. 'And here's a question: why did we have to have a war to bring about this conversation?' She looked up, and stopped as she caught sight of Myra in the doorway. 'Mother!'

Myra held open her arms, smiling, and Allie ran to her and hugged her. 'We thought you weren't going to make it home tonight.'

'I had my doubts myself once or twice. Stratford and Silvertown caught it really badly.' Myra disentangled herself gently. Her dark green greatcoat was dusty and there was an uncharacteristic smear of dirt on her cheek. She walked across the room and lifted her face to her husband's kiss.

Allie said, her voice suddenly expressionless, 'Shall I make a cup of tea?'

'Aren't you going to introduce me to your friend first?'

Sue had been watching Myra, wide-eyed. She scrambled to her feet.

'Oh, I'm sorry. Sue Miller. You've heard me speak of her. Sue, this is my mother—' Allie's voice stopped abruptly as, too late, Myra pulled back the hand that she had automatically put out to Sue – blood smeared the back of it. 'Mother! You're hurt!'

'It's nothing. A scratch. Flying glass. How do you do, Sue?' Myra smiled her brilliant smile. 'I'm very pleased to meet you. And yes, please, Allie, I should like a cup of tea.'

'Let me make it,' said Sue. 'You and Allie have a lot to talk about.'

'Thank you, my dear – ah, listen. Over for the night. That's good.' In the sudden stillness the single wailing note of one all-clear siren was joined by others. 'They've packed up a bit earlier tonight.'

On her way to the door, Sue suggested, 'Perhaps the Führer's stopped their overtime payments?' and was rewarded by another smile.

'Let me come and help you,' Allie said to her mother. 'That hand needs cleaning.'

In the bathroom she bathed Myra's hand and bound it up. 'You should have gone to a first-aid post.'

'Don't be absurd, darling. They had a lot worse than this to cope with. Thank you. That's very much better. Come and talk to me while I change.'

215

In the bedroom she climbed out of her WVS uniform and wrapped a brightly coloured silk housecoat around her slim body. 'This is a luxury! I don't allow myself to wear this very often. There won't be many more where this came from for some time . . .' Vigorously she began to brush the dust from her silky hair.

Allie watched her, smiling. 'You look marvellous. Young enough to be your own daughter!'

Myra chuckled. 'Well, thank you for that. But between you, me and the gatepost, tonight I feel old enough to be my own grandmother! Oh – talking of daughters . . .' She reached into a drawer, pulled out a small silver pendant and tossed it to Allie. 'Would you be a dear and take that to Libby's with you tomorrow? I borrowed it ages ago and keep forgetting to give it back – Allie?' Almost reflexively Allie had shaken her head. 'Oh, don't say you can't go? Libby will be so disappointed. I thought you had a weekend pass?'

'I have. It's just – well – I hadn't really made up my mind whether to go to Libby's or not. I don't know that I feel much like a party.'

'Oh, I don't think it's exactly a party. Just a little get-together.' Myra had turned and was studying her younger daughter's face. Allie averted her eyes. 'Allie? What is it?'

Allie jumped up from the bed, walked to the dressing table and stood looking down, tinkering with her mother's perfume bottles. Myra watched her.

'I don't think—' Allie started, stopped, then blurted, 'I don't think that Libby should carry on the way she does. Not with Edward away and everything. It – isn't right . . .'

The silence behind her stretched to perhaps a minute. She looked round. Myra, who had been waiting for that, beckoned and patted the bed beside her. Allie crossed the room and sat down. Myra took her hand. 'Listen to me, darling. And try to understand. We can't all be the same – you know that. We all have to find our own way to cope with the things that make us unhappy. The things that frighten us.'

216

'But—'

Myra lifted a finger, stilling the interruption. 'I know that you and I – and everyone – are frightened and unhappy from time to time. Some of us don't show it. Some of us do and rely upon the comfort provided by those closest to us. But we don't – of course, we can't – all react the same way. You and Richard have both chosen to take your part in this war, and you know how proud of you both I am.' She squeezed her daughter's hand gently and Allie gave her a small smile in return. 'But Libby – poor Libby – is lost. Don't you see that? She's lost, and she's frightened, and she's desperately unhappy. In a way it's my fault—'

'No!'

'Yes. Libby was given the kind of upbringing perfectly suited to her life as I envisaged it. As she envisaged it herself. In no way did it suit her to withstand the kind of pressure she is suffering at the moment.'

'You couldn't have known there'd be a war.'

'Of course not. I'm not blaming myself. I'm simply explaining. Libby thinks that as long as she can pretend that things haven't changed, they won't—'

'But isn't that terribly childish?'

'Of course it is. You and I know it. She probably knows it herself. But for Libby it works, and that, for the moment, is all that matters to her. She doesn't mean any harm. It's just her way of surviving.'

Allie sat in silence for a moment. She recognized the truth of her mother's words; her problem lay in her secret conviction that her mother did not guess just how far Libby's obstinate rejection of reality sometimes took her.

'She'll be terribly upset if you don't go tomorrow. She arranged it specially, knowing you'd be home. Richard's driving down too, I think – he'd be disappointed if you aren't there.' Richard's bomber squadron was stationed in Suffolk. 'Don't be too hard on Libby, my dear. Let her find her own way. I'm sure she will, sooner or later. For now – please, don't disappoint her.'

Allie kissed her mother's cheek. 'All right. I'll go.'

Myra held her at arm's length for a moment, looking into the earnest young face. This was the daughter she had never understood. The difficult one. The problem. Self-deception had rarely been one of Myra's failings. The one, she mentally amended, about whom, time and time again, she had been totally wrong. 'Thank you, darling. And now –' she stood up, pulled Allie to her feet '– let's go and see if your friend's managed to make tea with the heap of dust that was all that was left in the tea caddy!'

In the morning, Allie walked Sue to the nearest tube station. 'See you Sunday night. And Sue, for heaven's sake do try to be on time.'

'Yes, ma'am.' Sue sketched a subversive salute, and Allie laughed.

'I really liked your parents,' Sue continued unexpectedly after a moment. 'They're terrific. Your dad's a real gent, isn't he? Understands things. You're very lucky.'

Allie did not answer. Sue rattled on, unnoticing. 'They're pretty brave too, you know. With their money they could be livin' anywhere in the country. Just give me dad the chance –' she laughed outright ' – he'd have run like a hare if me mum'd let him! But there you are – me mum won't leave me gran, an' me gran won't leave her cats an' her pint of mild-and-bitter down at the Dragon of a Saturday night. So that's me dad snookered.' She grinned up at Allie. 'Other people's problems, eh?' They stopped outside the entrance to the station. A news placard proclaimed 43 ENEMY DOWN. RAF 15. 'Look at that. They make it sound like a bloody cricket score. Well, here we are.' People were still emerging, clutching blankets, pillows and sleepy small children. 'Thanks for havin' me, as they say – T.T.F.N.'

Allie watched as the bright head, cap at an illegally jaunty angle, bobbed through the crowd to the barrier. She stood for a moment, turning her greatcoat collar to her ears against the bitingly cold November wind. As she did so, a movement on a bombed site across the street caught her eye. In the ragged gap between two buildings, a woman was tending a small piece of painstakingly cleared ground that

218

could only be a vegetable patch – an enterprising, lovingly cared-for fragment of sanity in the wilderness of weeds that had already overrun the fire- and blast-disfigured plot. To Allie, as she stood watching, it suddenly seemed that she was seeing, in the small, trousered and headscarfed figure who appeared equally oblivious of the passing traffic and of the towering, scarred walls above her, the personification of London under fire. Tonight the bombs would fall again. And the next night, and the next. But still the woman hoed and planted while above her in the bitter wind torn wallpaper flapped pathetically beside an exposed tiled fireplace. Strangely, it was somehow a comforting sight. Allie settled her collar high about her ears and turned for home.

# CHAPTER THIRTEEN

The dim-lit, blacked-out flat at Rampton Court was, it seemed to Allie, full of uniforms: the khaki of the Army and the ATS, the neat, dark blue of the Navy and the Wrens and, predominantly, her own Air Force blue. Half of the Armed Forces in London must be here. Where on earth did Libby get to meet them all? She stood uncertainly by the front door, searching for a familiar face. The young airman who had let her in, and whom she had not recognized, had breezily placed a glass in her hand and disappeared into the crowded drawing room. She sniffed the glass. Whisky, or something approximating it. How did Libby do it?

From the drawing room came the sound of an infectiously swinging dance band, the unmistakable sound of Tommy Dorsey. With an unpleasant jolt she remembered suddenly that other evening – Christmas Eve, 1938 – when the world had been a different place, and none of them had known what was to come. She hitched her leather bag firmly onto her shoulder, tilted her head, drank half the whisky in one gulp and battled for breath and composure as the fiery liquid went down, taking the skin off her throat as it went.

'If I didn't remember too well the consequences of saying the same thing once before,' said a pleasant voice at her elbow, 'I'd say that you knocked that back as if you needed it.'

She turned. Tom Robinson, in RAF uniform, a pair of wings above his breast pocket, smiled blandly. For the first time in her life, she was glad to see him – would indeed have been glad to see the devil himself if his face had been familiar. 'Hello.'

'Hello yourself.' His eyes flickered over her neat uniform. 'I did need it, actually.'

'Welcome to the club. Follow me. With luck we'll find

some more.' He led the way through the noisy crowd to the kitchen. 'Libby – look who I found on the front door mat.'

'*Allie*! Darling, how lovely to see you!' Libby looked spectacular in a creation of glinting silver and blue that shimmered as she moved. Allie remembered the dress from before the war, but like so many other things, she thought wryly, it had been altered, and now there was a lot less of it . . . She allowed herself to be swept into her sister's sweet-smelling embrace, survived several garbled introductions, managed not to wince as Libby informed everyone within earshot of how proud she was of her baby sister in uniform. Then she caught Tom's eyes on her and knew from the abrasive spark of laughter she detected in them that, so far as one person there was concerned, her acting ability was no better now than it had ever been.

Across the shadowed room, she caught sight of Celia Hinton's dark red head. Celia was standing a little apart from the crowd, apparently totally absorbed in the conversation of a tall, chunkily built, square-faced young woman who wore the same uniform as she did. Allie, curious, caught Libby's arm. 'Who's that with Celia Hinton?'

Libby pulled a face. 'Well might you ask. Name's Stanton. She's an Aussie. Shares a flat with Celia – you do know that the Transport Corps doesn't live in barracks and parade up and down like the rest of you?'

Allie nodded.

'Stanton and Celia live in Pimlico, or somewhere else outlandish. Can't stand her myself. She's got absolutely no style. I can't think what Celia sees in her.' There was, her sister suspected, a mild touch of pique in the words.

'Stanton? Is that her first name?'

Libby made a theatrical gesture. 'Who knows? Something Stanton, Stanton something, who cares, darling? I never much liked our antipodean friends myself. That accent! Now, be a dear and help me hand round the sandwiches . . .'

It was a full hour later that Allie cornered Libby to ask

221

about Richard. 'I thought he'd be here before me. Couldn't he get away after all?'

Her sister regarded her with provokingly blank surprise. 'Richard? Good heavens, I'd quite forgotten.'

'Forgotten what?'

'He's here. Been here for ages. Arrived with Tom—'

'What?' Allie looked around the crowded room. 'Well, where is he then?'

Libby flicked her head and her fair hair swung around her shoulders. 'He's being dreadfully tiresome . . .'

'Libby, where *is* he? I haven't seen him for weeks! Why didn't you *tell* me he was here?'

'Well, I'm trying to, aren't I, darling? You won't let me get a word in edgeways.'

Allie held her breath and her temper.

'He's getting drunk, I think,' her sister said imperturbably, 'all by himself in the bedroom. I ask you – all by himself. In the bedroom.' She emphasized the words caustically, her tone still light. 'I meant to mention it before. It slipped my mind. The wobbler's gone off, by the way, in case you didn't hear it.' She moved off into the crowd, talking over her shoulder: 'All ashore that's going ashore and all that. The shelter's thataway.' She turned her curved thumb down and jerked it at the floor before being swallowed by a newly arrived crowd of revellers who swept her to them noisily.

Allie turned away and, trying to curb her irritation, began to push her way towards the door. Music blared. Couples, unable to dance because of the crush, jigged up and down or clung to each other unashamedly in the blacked-out gloom. Faintly, above the noise, she could hear the lifting sound of the siren still wailing. She was almost at the door when Tom Robinson collided with her.

'Well, well. If it isn't everyone's favourite little sister. Come and dance.' His fingers caught her wrist and drew her firmly back towards the crowded room.

She pulled away. 'Not now, Tom. I'm looking for Richard.' Across the hallway she could see Libby's bedroom door standing a little open.

To her surprise the grip on her wrist did not slacken. 'But I insist.'

'Tom—' Really angry, she tried to disengage her wrist, glaring up into his face. The long fingers tightened. At the same time, both remembered. Tom smiled, only half apologetically.

'We do seem to make a habit of things, don't we?'

She did not reply as she waited for him to release her. Instead, she found herself drawn gently but with constraining strength into his arms and propelled into the darkness of the room among the dancing couples. Furious now, she tried to wrench away from him. She might as well have tried to uproot a tree. Smiling, he moved, and willy-nilly she followed.

'Tom Robinson!' she hissed. 'Will you let me go! I want to find Richard—'

'But suppose, my dear,' he whispered softly into her hair, his arms like steel bands around her, 'Richard doesn't actually want to be found at the moment? Least of all by you?'

For the space of half a dozen heartbeats, she stood still, her eyes turned up to his thin face in the gloom. 'Don't be ridiculous. Why wouldn't he want to see me?'

'I'm not saying he doesn't want to see you.' His voice was enragingly patient. 'I'm simply suggesting that you might like to leave it for a while. I thought you liked to dance?' he added, raising one injured eyebrow.

'And I thought you didn't?' she snapped.

'And, as usual, we're both right.' His long mouth twitched; one very strong hand cradled her head none too gently and forced it onto his shoulder. She could feel his laughter. 'There. Isn't that nice?'

This time, in rage, she really struggled, and it took him by surprise. As she wrenched away from him, he caught her quickly by her shoulders. 'Allie—'

She glared at him, eyes blazing; she was trembling with fury. 'Let me go!'

'I'm sorry.'

223

'You're always bloody sorry. Always bloody laughing. Always know bloody well best . . .' Her voice had risen. The obvious illogicality of her own words served simply to make her angrier. People around them glanced curiously, half-smiling at what looked like a lovers' quarrel. She caught her breath, fought fiercely for self-control. He watched her with that shuttered lack of expression that she detested more than anything else about him. It showed on her face. Very slowly she felt his hands release their pressure on her shoulders. Then, unexpectedly, his eyes flicked over her head at someone pushing his way through the crowd towards them, and he smiled, wide and welcoming, turning Allie forcefully to face the newcomer – almost indeed pushing her into the stranger's arms.

'Tom! Hello – and Allie! Good Lord, it is Allie, isn't it?' The voice of the young man in army uniform was totally unfamiliar. He threw his arm about Allie and kissed her enthusiastically, pumped Tom's hand. 'Libby told me you were here.' He turned back to Allie, grinned at her confused expression. 'You've forgotten me.'

'No, I – yes, I'm sorry, I have.'

'Charles Philips. I was at Libby's and Edward's wedding. Old school pal. Aren't we all?'

'Oh – of course.' She still did not remember him from Adam.

'How's things?'

'Fine, thank you.' She could hardly hear him above the noise. From outside the building came a distant concussion. The windows rattled. Almost imperceptibly conversation in the room died and then resumed again.

Tom had gone.

Over the heads of the crowd, Allie saw him making his way purposefully to the door.

'Edward's out East somewhere I hear.'

'What?' She dragged her attention back to Charles Philips. 'Oh, sorry. Yes, I believe he is. Look, I'm sorry – would you mind awfully if . . .?'

He grinned knowingly. He had not missed Tom's rapid

escape. 'Of course. Apologies for the interruption. By all means. See you later.' He stepped aside and she pushed through the mass of bodies in Tom's wake to the door. The hall was empty, the bedroom door, open before, was now shut. She turned the handle. Nothing happened. The door was locked. She rattled it.

'Richard? Richard, are you in there?'

Silence.

'Richard!' She knocked hard on the wooden panel.

Still nothing.

She turned her back to the door and leaned on it, fighting anger. 'Tom?' She dared not raise her voice too high. To cause a scene was unthinkable. 'Will you let me in, please? I want to talk to my brother.'

In the silence which followed the words, she felt rather than heard the windows of the building rattle again.

'I say,' said a voice a little uncomfortably, 'they're getting a bit close, aren't they?'

'Don't be daft, man, they're miles off. Have another drink . . .'

From the bedroom Allie heard the sound of something falling, a sharp cry, the murmur of voices. She thumped the door, hard. 'Tom Robinson! Let me in before I kick this damned thing in!'

Moments later she heard the key turn in the lock, and the door swung open. She looked into a pair of pale, unfriendly eyes. 'By God, girl, you take a lot of telling,' said Tom, pleasantly. Over his shoulder Allie could see Richard, doubled over Libby's pretty pink vanity sink, retching miserably.

Allie hesitated.

'Why don't you go away like a good little girl and let me get him sobered up for you?' He stepped back, opened the door a little wider, his face hard. 'Unless you'd like to do it yourself, of course?'

Richard coughed chokingly, rested his head on the sink; his face held the pallor of death. 'Jesus Christ,' he said.

Allie turned and left them.

Half an hour later Libby found her in the kitchen, washing glasses. 'Allie – what on earth do you think you're doing?'

'I thought I'd give a hand clearing up. There's going to be an awful mess.'

'Well, it's awfully sweet of you, darling, but, really, there's no need. You're supposed to be enjoying yourself. Celia, darling – you tell her.'

Allie turned. Celia Hinton was standing by the door, watching her. She smiled a little. 'Hello, Allie.'

'Hello.' The two girls had not met since Celia's return from America. Looking at the other girl, Allie was struck by the severity of the lines that marked the thin face.

'Do get her away from that sink, Cele. Shan't be a mo—' Libby, in a shimmer of silver and blue, left them.

The silence was difficult. Very slowly Allie reached for a tea towel and dried her hands, not looking at Celia. The other girl opened her mouth to speak, stopped, shrugged. 'Allie?'

Allie shook her head, her eyes on the tea towel.

'You won't even speak to me?'

Allie's tongue seemed to have cleaved to the roof of her mouth.

Celia sighed. 'Don't be so angry, Allie. Don't be so sad. What happened, happened. I'm sorry. Truly sorry.'

Allie lifted her eyes. Celia shook her head.

'Oh, no. Not for loving him. I could never be sorry for that. One day you'll understand that. But I am sorry that you found out, you of all people. That we hurt you so.'

'I don't want to talk about it.'

A shadow flickered in Celia's eyes. She stepped back, her expression chilling. Allie pushed past her, walked blindly back into the drawing room and almost cannoned into the two who stood very close to each other by the door. Libby withdrew the arm that had been around Tom's waist and smiled, a little too brightly. 'Ah, there you are. Tom tells me our naughty brother's almost human again. Shall we go and tell him what we think of him?'

Allie nodded. With an easy movement Tom slid his arm about Libby's shoulders, his thin, long-fingered hand dark against the pearl of her bare shoulder. 'Come on, now. He doesn't deserve both of you. Dance with me. Let Allie read the riot act to Richard.'

A flash of pure pleasure crossed Libby's face. She tilted her head to look up at him, and her swinging hair brushed and clung to the sleeve of his uniform.

'I'd love to.' She moved close to him, swaying already to the easy tempo of the music, and slid her arms about his neck.

Allie watched, stone-faced. Very briefly, cool eyes flicked at her. 'Richard's still in the bedroom. Be careful. He isn't as sober as he seems.'

Richard was sitting on the bed, his damp head in his hands. He looked up, wincing a little, when Allie came in and smiled sheepishly. His sister closed the door softly behind her and leaned on it, watching him.

'Feeling better?'

He nodded. Flinched again. His words when he spoke were still just a little slurred. 'Sorry about that. Had a few before we came, and then the whisky . . .' He smiled lopsidedly. 'Do you think Libby makes it in the bath?'

'Probably. It certainly tastes like it.' She crossed to the bed, sat beside him. He avoided her eyes, ran his hand through the fair hair that was slick and dark with the water that Tom had used on him. 'How are you? I mean, apart from . . .' She gestured, in a general way, towards the sink and raised her eyebrows.

'Fine. Just fine.' He got up and wandered towards the window, stood with his back to her as he fiddled with the blackout curtain. Even in the dim, reddish light of the bedroom and taking into account his present state, Allie thought he looked far from fine. He was very pale, the fine bones of his face -- Myra's bones -- were knife-sharp and painful through the thin skin, and there were dark, pouched rings beneath his eyes. He moved the curtain a fraction and peered out. 'Seems to have quietened down a bit.'

Through the gap in the curtain Allie could see the pencilled sweep of searchlights. The all-clear had not gone. 'You'd better close that.'

He let the curtain drop and turned. 'Tell you what, Pudding – why don't we both get out of here? Just you and me? We could go to the Kensington flat. Talk all night. A bit of peace and quiet, just you and me. What do you say? We haven't seen each other in months.'

The use of the silly, childish nickname affected her strangely. She stood up, blinking, held out a hand. After only the tiniest hesitation, he took it, and then was hugging her very tight. He was shaking terribly. 'Let's have just one more for the road and go.'

'Why wait for another drink? Why not go now, while it's quiet? The Underground's only just round the corner.' She wanted, suddenly and desperately, to get away.

He put her from him. 'I need it,' he said simply.

She glanced at him in sharp concern.

He spread placating hands. 'To settle my stomach.'

'Well . . .'

'Come on.' He caught her hand again. 'With luck Lib'll have an extra bottle somewhere. We can take it with us.'

'I doubt she'll be happy about that.'

'No harm in trying.' He pulled her towards the door. She allowed him to tow her through it and back into the drawing room. The crowd had thinned a little.

'Richard! Where on earth have you been all night? Come and join us – have a drink . . .'

'Richard . . .' Allie tried to tug him away.

'Oh, come on, Pudding. Just a quick one.' Like magic, a glass had appeared in Richard's hand. He tossed back its contents. Laughing, a girl refilled it. It went the same way. Grinning, he held out the glass.

Allie cocked her head. 'Listen.' She could see Libby and Tom approaching them, Libby's hand possessively on the man's arm. The drone of engines drowned even the sound of the music. The chattering around them died. In the park the ack-ack guns bellowed.

'P'raps we should go down to the shelter?' asked a girl's voice, nervously.

'Mightn't be a bad idea.'

'Why not?' It was Libby's voice, pitched a little higher than normal. 'A shelter party! Might be fun at that. Let's show the broomstick brigade how to enjoy themselves! The drink's in the kitchen. Grab a glass and follow your Aunty Libby . . .'

The whine and crump of a bomb cut off her words. The windows shook in their frames and the curtains moved.

'Come on . . .'

Allie looked around for her brother.

'Where's Richard?' asked Tom urgently.

'I don't know. In the kitchen, I think.'

'Don't let—'

'Tom, come *on!*' Libby dragged at his hand. Her face was bright with colour and very beautiful. Allie found herself caught in the general surge towards the front door. More explosions shook the building. A girl squealed.

'Right, Pudding, off we go.' Richard had appeared at her side. He was laughing. The colour had returned to his face. In his hand he held a half-full bottle, and he had his greatcoat thrown around his shoulders. She allowed him to hustle her down the stairs in the wake of the others, but as she turned, with them, towards the basement steps, he caught her arm. 'This way.' He pulled her in the direction of the outside door.

'Richard, don't be silly.'

'We're going home. I told you. Just the two of us. Come on.' His voice was clear, his words unslurred, yet Allie knew with conviction that he was very drunk indeed.

She tried to hold him back. 'Later, Richard, when the raid eases. Let's go with the others.'

He shook his head. 'The station's only just round the corner,' he said, his mouth a stubborn line. 'We'll be all right down there. We can make a run for it.'

A couple, giggling, hand in hand, fled past them and

clattered towards the basement steps. Allie glanced round. They were alone. 'Richard—'

'Don't you want to come? What's the matter? Scared?' The old, childish taunt brought her head up sharply. 'Allie cat, scaredy cat . . .' sang Richard softly.

'You're drunk.'

'Sober as a lord and going home to Mother. Coming?' He made towards the door.

'Don't be stupid!' She ran after him as, bottle swinging, he ran lightly down the steps and through the narrow sandbagged gap into the street. The dusty, smoke-laden air hit him harder than he had expected, and he staggered a little before, regaining his balance, he set off at a fast lope down the road. Allie flew after him.

'Richard! Richard, you're going the wrong way!'

He did not stop, gave no indication that he had heard her. Willy-nilly she ran by his side down the deserted road, towards the corner. Whistles blew in the next street. A high-pitched whine sang savagely in the air. Ahead of them a four-storeyed building seemed slowly to inflate, its brick walls bulging, glass shattering, before the whole edifice crumbled like a house of cards in a bloom of choking dust. The blast threw Allie backwards like a rag doll, painfully against a wall, knocking the wind from her lungs. The guns in the park pounded deafeningly and shrapnel whined with menace around her head. She found herself on all fours, head hanging, eyes streaming, coughing and choking.

'Richard?' she managed at last. 'Richard, are you there? Are you all right?'

There was no reply. From a few streets away came another explosion. A fire-engine bell clanged. Not far away a gas main had caught; the flames reached, hungry and blue-tinged, to the sky.

'Richard!'

And then she heard it – a strangled, agonized sobbing, a tearing gasping for breath. Richard was crouched just a few yards from her, hunched on elbows and knees, curled in a ball, rocking back and forth. 'God! Oh God! Oh God!'

Panic-stricken, she flew to him. 'Richard, what is it? Where are you hurt?' Terrified of what she might see, she tried to straighten him up, to turn his face towards her. Rigidly he resisted her, his muscles locked like stone. Somewhere close, a man's voice shouted and she heard sharp, running footsteps.

'Richard!' her voice, even in her own ears, sounded close to hysteria.

Richard pulled away from her, hunched lower, his voice grating in his throat as in a monotone he whispered the awful litany: 'God, oh God . . .'

'Need some help?'

Allie dazedly looked up. The figure above her wore an RAF uniform. She could not see his face, silhouetted as he was against the dying light of the flares.

'It's my brother. I think he may be hurt.'

The stranger bent and slid a strong arm about Richard. 'He'll get hurt worse if we don't get him under cover. Give me a hand. We can get him back down the road a bit – there's a cellar – I was sheltering there.' The flares had died, but the beginnings of conflagration lit their way.

'My sister's flat isn't far.'

'Everything's far at the moment, I'm afraid.' The young voice was amazingly cheerful. 'I don't think he's badly hurt. Take his other arm.'

'I'm all right,' Richard mumbled.

'So am I. And we're going to stay that way.' The young man hitched a shoulder under Richard's arm. 'Right-oh. Off we go.'

Several explosions in quick succession shook the air. Somewhere close, glass shattered. 'Duck,' said their rescuer, blithely succinct. Richard was gasping for breath, clinging to the stranger like a drowning man. 'All right, old man.' The young voice was gentle. 'Here we are. Mind the rubbish. That's the stuff. We'll be OK here for a bit.'

Stumbling, Allie followed them into darkness.

'Hold on. There's a candle here somewhere. Damn thing's blown out.' There was a flare of light as a match was struck, flickered for a moment and then burned, bright and steady. The young man turned. 'Not exactly the Ritz, I'm afraid.' Allie saw a shock of hair, the quick flash of a friendly smile. Richard had turned away from the light, was leaning against a dirty wall, his shoulders hunched almost to his ears, his spread hands to his face. Allie moved carefully across the littered floor to him. The cellar had obviously been used as a shelter until a bomb had struck and destroyed the house above it. Apart from the candle burning on the shelf there were two rickety chairs and a couple of bunks, their metal webbing rusted. The place smelled horribly of damp and of cats, and the floor was strewn with unrecognizable debris.

She touched her brother's shoulder. 'Richard?'

He pulled away from her. 'I'm all right.'

'Are you sure?'

He turned to her a face sheened sickly with sweat and with tears. A small thread of blood smeared his lip. His eyes were anguished, and his trembling uncontrollable. 'I'm sure.'

She put a hand to the blood on his mouth. He jerked his head away. 'Self-inflicted wound.' The words were brutal with self-disgust. Another series of explosions shook the world outside and he flinched physically from the sound. It was only then that Allie realized that, through it all, he had kept hold of the whisky bottle. Shaking, he unscrewed it, lifted it to his lips, banging it against his teeth. Allie and the stranger watched in silence as he tilted his head and took a long swig from the bottle, the whisky running from his mouth and down the front of his uniform. Wordlessly, as he finished, he offered the bottle to Allie. She shook her head. His face like bone in the candlelight, the caverns of his eyes unfathomable, he extended it in a shaking hand to his rescuer.

'Thanks.' The word was quiet. The young man, his eyes thoughtfully on Richard, took the bottle and drank briefly. The anti-aircraft guns were pounding again, punctuated by the venomous rattle of machine-gun fire. They all heard clearly an odd, smothered explosion followed by the demented howling whine of a crippled aircraft.

'Sounds as if they got one of the bastards.' The unknown airman wiped the neck of the bottle on his sleeve, took the top from Richard's nerveless fingers.

Richard bowed his head and sank to his knees, as if his bones had suddenly ceased to support him, and buried his face in his hands, his shoulders shaking.

Allie, beside him on the filthy floor, put a helplessly protective arm about him and looked up to see, in the candlelight, a young, bright face full of sympathy.

'Bomber Command?' asked the airman. Allie could see the wings of a pilot on his own breast.

She nodded.

He moved across the cellar, hunkered down next to her, silently offered her the bottle.

This time she took it.

Never as long as she lived did Allie forget that strange, nerve-racking night spent in a cellar with Pilot Officer Buzz Webster and a Richard who seemed to have withdrawn from her into some demon-haunted world of his own. Her brother sat on a creaking bunk, rigidly upright, his hands braced on either side of him on the wooden frame, staring into the flickering shadows, silent. Outside their refuge the raiders thundered and the night burned. Allie could sense the immense physical and mental effort that Richard was expending to prevent himself from breaking down again. She herself flinched from the dreadful sounds of destruction; Richard sat as if made from stone, fighting himself.

Their companion watched them both pensively for a while. Then, after brief introductions, which Richard scarcely acknowledged, suddenly cheerful, he talked about inconsequentials until Richard, with an odd, long breath, lay back on the rusted bunk, closed his eyes and immediately went to sleep. Allie looked worriedly at the other man. He smiled, reassuringly.

'Best thing for him, don't worry.' He lifted the dead weight of Richard's legs, settled them on the bunk. Richard did not move. 'Too much whisky and too little sleep is Doc Webster's diagnosis. Something of an epidemic at the moment. It catches the best of us from time to time.'

'I – haven't thanked you properly. I don't know what I'd have done without you.'

'Think nothing of it. Rescuing maidens in distress is a Webster speciality. At least – ' he smiled engagingly and his eyes were warm ' – it could easily become one. Pure selfishness, really. Didn't fancy spending the night all alone down here. I'll let you into a secret – ' he leaned forward confidentially – 'I'm scared of spiders.' In the light of the candle, his snub nose and bright eyes could have belonged to a schoolboy engaged in a midnight prank. Allie tried to laugh with him, achieved only a strange sound somewhere between a cough and a sob. Apparently unnoticing, he turned away from her to lean over Richard and turn the collar of his coat up around the bloodless face. Allie groped for a handkerchief and surreptitiously blew her nose, managing in the darkness to dab at her eyes as well. When she spoke again, her voice was close to normal.

'You're a pilot?'

'Mm. Hurricanes. Best little fighters in the world, bless 'em.' He wandered to the bottom of the steps, peered up into the garish night. 'You?'

'Fighter Command. Hawkinge.'

'Lord above, fancy that. Good old Hawkinge. Saved my bacon many a time.' Hawkinge, so close to the Channel, was often used as an emergency landing field for crippled or damaged aircraft. 'What's the name of that pub on the hill there?'

'The Lion.'

'Right.' He laughed, a quick, infectious sound that drew an answering smile from her. 'The last time I was in there, a mate of mine – name of Lofty Stanforth – damn near drank the place dry single-handed, then took off across the airfield on my Norton. He'd never ridden a motorbike before in his life. Never saw anything so funny. Pranged it into the side of Number One hangar and finished up in the glasshouse for damaging RAF property. No one seemed to care much about my bike.' He came back to her, pulled one of the rickety chairs over beside her and sat astride it, leaning his arms on the unstable back. 'Bit of a hot spot for a girl like you?' he said softly.

'I like it. Love it. At least I feel as if I'm doing something.'

He nodded.

She shivered. In following Richard, she had left her greatcoat behind at Libby's.

'Good Lord, you've no coat. You must be frozen.' Before she could prevent him, he had jumped up and slipped his own coat from his shoulders.

'Oh, no – please – I couldn't possibly . . .'

'Don't be daft. Here. A reward for protecting me from the spiders.' He settled the coat, still warm from his body, comfortably around her shoulders.

'Thank you. That's marvellous.'

'Do you mind if I smoke?'

'Not at all.' She watched him as he drew a battered pack of Players from his pocket and extracted a cigarette, shook her head as he looked at her enquiringly. 'I don't, thank you.' The flare of the match, cupped in his hand, lit beneath a thatch of untidy hair a young face that, though unremarkable in feature, was a picture of irrepressible vitality. The wide mouth tilted at the corners as if perpetually on the verge of laughter, his bright eyes, glancing through the draught-swept flame, glimmered with some constant inner amusement. She could not help but smile back.

'Ah. That's better.' He exhaled a long, thin stream of blue smoke, which swirled and eddied in the draught. 'Now, what shall we do to pass the time?' He glanced, laughing, at Richard. 'Join the Sleeping Beauty here? Sing? Dance? Or – ' his eyes came back to her ' – get to know each other a little better?'

She watched him in stillness for a moment, smiling. 'I think I'd like that.'

They were still talking a long time later when, with daylight a faint greyness in the ash-darkened skies and with the raid at last easing in its ferocity, Richard stirred, moaned, and with some difficulty sat up. 'God almighty,' he said, and clutched his head.

Allie stopped in mid-sentence, reached to touch his hand. He lifted his head slowly. In the faint light she saw recollection seep like poison into his dulled brain. Saw him stiffen, his mouth tight.

'It's all right,' she said, softly.

Buzz Webster said nothing. Richard's eyes moved slowly from one to the other. Colour stained the bright bones of his face. The silence was awkward.

'First prize for making a damned fool of myself, eh?' Richard asked at last, with difficulty.

Buzz made an easy, deprecating gesture. 'Don't be daft, old man. Happens to the best of us from time to time.'

'Oh?' Richard's tone was defensively harsh. 'When was the last time you went into a blue funk?'

'Richard!'

Buzz smiled and shook his head. In the last few hours, Allie realized with something of a shock, she had come to like that smile very much indeed. 'You've been dreaming, old man. Touch of the shakes, if you ask me.' He shrugged happily. 'You were falling-down drunk, that's all.'

'And is that,' asked Allie with interest, her gratitude in her eyes, 'what happens to you all from time to time?'

Richard was looking at the young pilot with eyes in which embattled pride vied with bitter uncertainty. In truth, he did not know whether to believe the man's words or not – he only barely remembered the events of the night. He recalled only the old enemies, terror and despair, the oft-fought battle for sanity in a world run mad. He could not be certain that this time the battle had not been fought in public. His worst suspicions told him that it had and, looking at Allie, the humiliation of it rose, physically bitter, in his throat.

In the tired, firelit dawn the single note of the all-clear sounded. Wearily Allie stood and stretched. Buzz's coatsleeves overhung her hands by inches, the shoulders of the coat were half-way down her arms and the hem flapped at her ankles. She caught the spark of friendly laughter in his face, grimaced, put a hand to her disarrayed hair. 'I must look a terrible sight,' she said, and blushed stupidly as she said it, furious with herself, willing him to spare her the false compliment she might have been angling for.

'Like something the cat dragged in,' he agreed soberly. 'And out again, come to that.'

She gave a small, explosive shout of laughter. 'Thanks very much!'

Something in the tone of their voices roused Richard. His head still thumped horribly, but with his equilibrium somewhat restored, he looked from one to the other. 'Did I miss something?'

'No, Richard dear, of course not.' Allie's voice was suddenly, absurdly, light-hearted. She tugged on his hand, pulling him to his feet, grinning unsympathetically at his exaggerated gesture of pain. 'Serves you right. You shouldn't have drunk so much of Libby's bathtub booze. As for missing anything – well, you missed us putting the world to rights over your snores. Also, several hundred tons of high explosive . . .'

'. . . and the odd oil bomb . . .' put in Buzz.

'. . . but apart from that you haven't missed anything at all.' Allie stood on tiptoe and kissed her brother lightly on his cheek, her eyes sharp on his face in the growing light. She saw him relax, finally convinced, felt it in his body.

'Well, that's all right then. I wouldn't like to think I'd slept through anything important. I'm sorry, did she keep you awake the whole night?' he asked Buzz with sympathetic concern. 'I know what a pest she can be.'

'Not at all, old man. Haven't had so much fun since Guy Fawkes night.' In the grey dawn light Allie saw suddenly that Buzz's face was pinched with cold. She quickly slipped the heavy, warm greatcoat from her shoulders. As she helped him into it, his hand as it touched hers was like ice. The night's growth of beard was tow-coloured, like his hair. He shrugged the coat onto his shoulders and turned. They stood for a quiet moment looking at each other. He reached his cold hand to her and she took it.

'Goodbye.'

'Goodbye.' She waited.

'Perhaps we'll bump into each other again some day?'

'Perhaps.' Disappointment moved in her. She had half-expected – certainly hoped for – more.

Buzz shook Richard's hand. ''Bye, old chap. Watch that booze. You were really flying there for a while.'

'I will. Thanks for your help.'

He lifted a cheery hand, climbed the rickety steps and left them. They heard his footsteps scrunching through rubble as he walked away.

'Well,' Richard said into the silence, 'that's that then. Where to from here?'

Allie blinked, turned her eyes away from the square of strengthening daylight at the door. 'Libby's. She probably thinks we've been blown limb from limb.'

'Don't be silly.' Her brother pulled her arm through his and, a little unsteadily, started up the steps. 'The state she was in, she probably hasn't even missed us.'

It was Tom, surprisingly enough, who opened the door. He did not smile. His eyes flicked briefly from one to the other, rested upon Richard's face. 'What the hell happened to you?'

Allie, immediately irritated, opened her mouth to snap an answer, then shut it again. She was simply too tired to take on Tom Robinson at this moment. She was very aware of her dishevelled appearance and her temper seemed, from the moment that Buzz Webster had walked into the ruined street, to be getting shorter by the minute.

'My fault,' Richard said. 'I dragged Allie out to take her home. We missed the way to the station. Had to take shelter in a cellar.'

238

Tom's expressive eyebrows quirked a little. The Underground station was not fifty yards down the street.

Allie pushed past him into the hall. 'Is Libby about?'

'She's still in bed. Dead to the world, I think.' The words were utterly casual.

Allie stopped short and looked at him sharply. The apartment was absolutely quiet. When Tom had opened the door, she had assumed that several of Libby's guests, stranded by the raid, would still be there. Now, with the early morning light filtering through untidily opened curtains to shine upon the detritus of last night's party, it became perfectly obvious that everyone else had either left or was still sleeping off over-indulgence in the shelter below.

And Libby was in bed.

Tom watched her, his face expressionless, obviously about to offer neither comment nor explanation. The night's growth of dark beard on his face emphasized the hard line of his mouth.

Allie took a deep breath. Ridiculously, in the face of the man's apparently nerveless composure, she felt a surge of embarrassment.

Richard seemingly noticed nothing. If the possible significance of Tom's words had reached him, he ignored it. 'Any hot water? I feel filthy. I'd give my eye teeth for a bath.'

Tom shook his head. 'They got a gas main. There's cold, though. I've got a kettle on if you want a wash and shave?'

'Thanks.' Richard rasped a hand over his chin. 'That'd certainly help. Mind if I bag the bathroom first?' he asked Allie.

'Go ahead.' She knew how short the words sounded.

As Richard passed him, Tom put a quick hand on his arm. 'You OK?'

Richard avoided the other man's eyes. 'Sure.'

Tom withdrew his hand. 'The water's in the kitchen. Put the kettle back on when you've finished, would you?' Once again Allie was struck by the easy, proprietary way the

239

words were spoken. She noticed now, through the open doorway of the drawing room, that the room had been half-tidied. Glasses were stacked together on a tray on the big coffee table, ashtrays emptied into a waste-paper basket that stood in the middle of the floor. As Richard left them, Tom, without a word to or a glance at Allie, went back into the room and bent to stack more glasses on the tray.

Allie followed him, closed the door behind her, stood watching, fighting anger. 'Why didn't you tell me? About Richard?' She found it an effort to keep her voice low and even; illogically she wanted to scream at him.

She saw the narrow hand pause for a fraction of a second before reaching for another glass. 'Tell you? Tell you what?'

The bathroom door banged. Richard was whistling tunelessly: '*Yes, sir, that's my baby . . .*'

'Don't play games. I was out in that last night. With Richard.'

'Ah.' He straightened, empty glasses in hand, and regarded her with peaceful eyes.

'Why didn't you tell me?' she asked again. 'Or *someone*? Richard's suffering from – ' she paused as he watched her unhelpfully, long fingers clinking on the glass ' – from, I don't know – some sort of shell shock?'

'We're all,' he said softly, 'suffering from some sort of shell shock. Aren't we?'

For the first time, she remembered hearing that, a month before, Tom Robinson had been forced to bail out of a crippled Spitfire twice in one week. She steeled herself against the knowledge. 'Not like that.'

'He was bad?'

'Yes. He – I'm not sure – he sort of broke down.'

Tom nodded.

'Has he been like this long?'

He nodded again.

'How long?'

He shrugged. 'I suppose – since Spain.'

She stared at him. 'Since *Spain*? You mean that he knew – you knew – the state his nerves were in when he joined the

RAF? How could you let him? Tom – he was terrified out there. Literally petrified. He – cried.' She ground the word through gritted teeth, her brother's humiliation her own before the impassive appraisal of this outsider. 'He can't keep flying like this. He *can't*. You have to stop him.'

'I?'

'No one else could do it.'

He said nothing.

'He'll have a complete breakdown if we don't stop him. Worse. God only knows what could happen.'

'What do you suggest?'

'Go to his commanding officer. Tell him—' She knew the crass stupidity of the words as she spoke them.

Tom very carefully put down the glass he was holding. His eyes were not friendly. 'You want to destroy your brother entirely? Very well – *you* go to his CO. *You* tell him. And may God forgive you, because sure as hell Richard won't.'

'But we have to do *something*.'

'Why? Why in God's name must you always be doing something?' Because of the quietness of his voice, it took a moment for his anger to filter through. Allie blinked at the thread of violence that drew her skin to goose-bumps. 'Don't you see the damage you could do with your interfering? Why can't you leave a man alone to work out his own salvation? There is nothing that anyone can do for Richard until he *asks* – can't you see that? Until he comes to terms with himself and accepts the fact that he needs help. Do you think that'll be easy for him? Until then there is absolutely nothing that we can do that isn't likely to rebound on Richard and make things a thousand times worse. For Christ's sake, girl, you surely can understand that?' He stood, fierce and taut as a strung wire. Then, as suddenly as it had flared, his temper died. He gave a short, abrasive laugh. 'For a clever girl you can be as thick as two short planks, you know that?'

The arrogance took her breath away. 'I don't—'

'Leave him alone. Just leave him alone. Sooner or later he'll sort things out for himself. It isn't up to us.'

She looked at him for a long, quiet moment. 'I just hope you're right.'

Something flickered in the pale eyes. 'You think I don't?' He picked up the tray, balanced it on one perfectly steady hand. 'One more thing that may not have occurred to you . . .'

'What?'

'It may be that you – or I – are the last people Richard might eventually turn to. It isn't always the people that you're closest to who can help at times like that.'

'I don't give a damn who he goes to,' she snapped, 'as long as he goes to *someone*.'

'Don't bank on it.'

A door opened in the hall outside. 'Where is everyone?' Libby's voice, sleepy, a little petulant.

'Tom?' Allie's voice had changed. There was something she had to say and, stupidly, she herself had made it difficult. She had hardly, over the past few minutes, created an atmosphere in which to beg a favour.

He looked down at her questioningly. Remembering Richard and his hero-worship of the man, she swallowed her own antipathy, and her pride. 'Look after him as much as you can? Please? At least try to stop him from drinking so much? Whatever you might think, he does listen to you. Please help him, if you can . . .'

A straight furrow of anger split his forehead. 'You think you have to ask?' he said, brusquely, as Libby, her body sheathed in a nightdress of pale blue satin that emphasized its lovely lines as even nakedness could not have done, wobbled into the room and blinked at them.

'Good heavens. Allie. Where did you spring from?'

'I—'

'God, look at this mess. Tom, darling, save my life with one of those obnoxious but perfectly wonderful mixtures of yours, would you? I think I'm dying.'

Wordless, Tom left them. Libby ran distracted fingers through her hair. 'Whew. What a night!'

Allie sat down, suddenly and hard, in an armchair. 'You can say that again,' she muttered.

242

# CHAPTER FOURTEEN

During the next couple of weeks Allie became alarmed – and just a little put out – at the number of times that Pilot Officer Buzz Webster crept into her mind. Like a thread of bright laughter in the more sombre fabric of her worries about Richard and the stresses of war, the recollection of his snub-nosed face beneath the mop of tow-coloured hair came to her again and again. She discovered that she could recall each expression, every inflection of his voice. On the day that she turned in response to her name and a touch on her shoulder and found herself looking into an unmistakable pair of laughing eyes, she was in an odd way unsurprised. It was as if she had unconsciously conjured his image, warm and vital, three-dimensional before her. She was standing with Sue and a couple of pilots from 603 Squadron at the bar of the Lion. Around them chatter and laughter rose, almost deafening in the confined space. The warm air was fogged with cigarette smoke.

'Remember me?'

'Of course.' She did not try to keep the happiness from her voice. 'What are you doing here?'

'Here?' Grinning, he stabbed a finger at the spot where he stood. 'Looking for you, what else? Here – ' he waved a hand, indicating the larger area of Hawkinge in general ' – getting the kite patched up. Ran into a spot of bother. Got bounced by a couple of 109s. Poor old lady's in a bit of a mess. Looks like an all-night job.'

Her smile faded as she remembered the battered Hurricane that had limped into Hawkinge late that afternoon with its fabric streaming and half its tail shot away. 'I think I saw you come in.' The recollection of the lurching, clumsily dangerous landing that the little, battle-damaged plane had made suddenly stirred sickness in the pit of her stomach.

'Glad somebody did. Work of art, that was.' They stood, smiling, watching one another, almost oblivious of the sound, movement, laughter around them.

Sue, turning, looked from one to the other with interested, amused eyes. 'Well, well, well, Sergeant, who's your friend?'

Allie did not look at her; she was studying Buzz Webster's bright, mobile face, trying to interpret the warmth that she found there, almost afraid to admit to what she saw. 'Buzz Webster,' she said. 'You remember? I mentioned him to you.'

'So you did. Once or twice.'

'This is my friend Sue Miller,' Allie said to Buzz.

Without taking his eyes from Allie's, Buzz stuck a hand out. 'How do you do?'

Sue took it gravely. 'She's very well, thank you. At least, she was until a moment or so ago.'

He walked Allie back to the house, later, in a darkness that was like blindness and a brittle cold that was the very breath of winter. Their hands were linked together, lightly, in the most natural way. His hand was small for a man's, hard and very strong. Allie carried a small, shaded torch, shining it at their feet.

'Been a bit busy round here lately?' His voice, though quiet, echoed in the chill silence.

'Yes, it has. Watch it here, the ground's a bit rough. You've been in action?'

'Fair bit. Did I hear that someone got Helmut Wick yesterday?'

'That's right.' Wick had been the Luftwaffe's leading ace with too many kills to his credit for anyone with sense in the RAF to regret the loss of a true genius of a flyer. Allie did not mention that the pilot who had destroyed Wick's 109 had himself died just seconds later.

'How's your brother?' It was said in the same, inconsequential tone. Allie wished she could see his face.

'He's fine.' What else could she say? 'I don't see a lot of him.'

'You mustn't worry about him.' His voice was gentle. 'It's not the first time I've seen it. It's funny, but the lads who drop the bombs seem to suffer worse in a raid than the rest of us.'

'Why's that?'

She sensed his shrug in the darkness. 'I don't know. Hard to live with, p'raps – knowing what you're doing to the civilians in Berlin and Dusseldorf . . .'

'Maybe.' She left it at that.

He drew her towards him, slid her hand through the crook of his arm. 'I've flipped over this place a dozen times in the last couple of weeks. And every time I've thought of you.'

'It must be catching.' Her voice was soft.

He stopped walking, reached for the shaded light, took it from her and, turning it off, slipped it into the pocket of his flying jacket. Then he turned her gently towards him. She lifted her hands and rested them lightly on his shoulders, feeling, through the worn leather, the warmth, the reality of him. Not thinking – desperately not thinking – of the venomous airborne dogfights, the swooping flights of enemy fighters, the lunacy that reduced young men like this to charred wrecks . . . She sensed in the darkness his move towards her. She lifted her face. His lips were ice-cold, as were her own. He slipped his hands inside her coat, wrapped his arms tightly about her. She stood quite still. The touch of his mouth was beguilingly gentle, in contrast to the strength of his arms, the urgency of his slight body against hers. Somewhere within her, like the opening of a flower, she felt her own need stir and come to life, aching pleasurably, almost unbearably exciting; a feeling she had never experienced before, that indeed she had convinced herself she never would. She trembled. His lips moved, roughly tender, over her cheeks to her eyes, the tip of her cold nose, her ears. With an odd, shaky sigh, he buried his face in her hair, his breath warm on her neck. She tilted her

245

head, closed her eyes, shut her mind to everything but the feel of him. At that moment, had he willed it, she would have surrendered to this stranger any part of her body, mind or spirit that he cared to demand. His hand moved tentatively on the buttons of her uniform jacket; she shifted her body against him so that her breast, constricted beneath her shirt, lifted and pressed into his hand. His mouth opened, and this time his kiss was not gentle.

Footsteps clipped the tarmac road, accompanied by an unmistakable giggle.

'Now, you, Ben – just give over.'

'It isn't Ben!' The voice was aggrieved.

'*This* is Ben.'

Another explosive giggle.

Allie and Buzz stood quite still. The world settled around them, dark and cold. Buzz was breathing very fast. He reached for both her hands, drew them up, warm, between their bodies. 'Allie, I'm sorry. Did I . . .?'

'No.' She whispered the word quickly, not allowing him to finish.

'Well, whichever one of you *that* is,' Sue said in the darkness, 'he'd just better keep his hands to himself or he's likely to get 'em chopped clean off!' A small, dancing light moved like a will o' the wisp, erratically, towards them. Buzz drew Allie into shadows that were damply leaf-smelling and deep as black velvet. Their feet rustled in ice-dry leaves.

'What's that?' asked a man's voice, startled.

'Mice,' Sue said, imperturbably. 'Don't worry. I'll protect you.'

'Didn't sound like mice to me.' The words were a little slurred.

'Well, you'll just have to take my word, won't you?' As the three passed, their footsteps just a little unsteady, Sue's voice sang out again, full of laughter. ''Night, Allie. 'Night, Buzz.'

'Good night.' Allie smiled into the darkness. As the sound of voices and laughter receded down the lane, she turned back into Buzz's arms.

246

'I've thought about you every day,' he said, 'every single damned day.'

'And I you.'

The rough trunk of a tree was at her back. With light strength he caught her wrists, holding her captive between his body and the tree. The surge of excitement that engulfed her took her by surprise. Her heart thudded painfully in her throat beneath his cold mouth.

High above them an engine sounded, spluttered, died, and revved again. Buzz stilled. She felt the echoes of the sound in his body, throbbing with his blood. They stood stone-still for a moment, listening as the crippled aircraft circled, looking for the airfield.

'It's a Spit,' he said.

The engine coughed again, stopped for the space of a few frantic heartbeats, crackled into life once more. They waited. Allie laid her face against Buzz's, felt the tense throb of the muscles of his jaw. A few minutes later they heard the plane land, bumping and slithering on the cold ground. Allie held her breath, waiting for the crash. Nothing happened.

'He's down,' said Buzz, lightly. 'Silly bugger. Someone should have told him the pubs shut half an hour ago.'

Allie wrapped her arms tightly around his neck and buried her face in the shoulder of his flying jacket. 'Fifteen days ago I didn't know you.'

'That's right.' He held her, gently.

'And now . . .'

'Now?'

'The world's changed.'

He laid his cheek against her hair. 'You, too? I was afraid to think it.' He laughed, softly. 'If I'd known, I'd have got myself shot up earlier.'

'Don't say that! Please, don't joke about it.'

'Hey!' He moved her a little away from him, peered into her face. 'What's this?'

She shook her head.

'They won't get me, Allie Jordan,' he said, the lovely note

247

of laughter still in his voice, 'not now they won't. Don't you know only the good die young?'

She closed her eyes and leaned against him. On the nearby airfield the Spitfire's engine gave a last, coughing roar and died.

# CHAPTER FIFTEEN

'I strongly suspect,' said Sue Miller, feet swinging six inches from the floor, the winter sun, through the wire-protected window of the wireless room, blazing in the fair nimbus of her hair, '*strongly* suspect – that Sergeant Alexandra Jordan is in love at last. And about time, too.' She jumped from the desk where she had been sitting and regarded Allie with mischievous eyes.

'Don't be daft.' Allie pulled off her headset, rubbed sore ears. The girls had decorated the wireless room, a little prematurely, for Christmas, and the headset, courtesy of Sue, was wreathed in mistletoe.

'Daft, is it? Oh, no. You can't fool me, Sergeant. This is your Aunty Sue, remember? I'm the expert around here.'

'Expert in talking too much.' Allie's smile took the sting from the words.

'You should blush more often,' Sue said, unrepentantly. 'It suits you.'

Allie acknowledged the greeting of the relief operator who stood waiting to take her place, and followed Sue to the door. Sue was still talking over her shoulder. 'I must say I approve. I wasn't sure at first – he somehow didn't seem quite your type – but on closer acquaintance . . .'

'Sue, do shut up.'

'. . . I've decided that he's just right for you. You take life too seriously, you know that? Buzz is just the fella for you.'

'Well, that's very nice of you. I appreciate your approval no end. Didn't anyone ever teach you to mind your own business?'

'Nope. Anyway, this is my business. Lord, when you think about how much you know about *my* love life!' Sue rolled her eyes.

Allie sighed.

'Oh, all right. I'll stop talking.'

The girls walked out into the cold air. The weather was changing. Although for the moment the sun still shone, slate-grey clouds were piling over the landscape to the north, the downs lifting darkly against them. Allie stretched tiredly, breathing deeply the sharp, cold air.

'When are you seeing him again?' Sue, once on a subject close to her heart, could no more leave it than she could stop breathing.

Allie took an exasperated breath, which turned somehow into a snort of laughter. 'Tomorrow. Satisfied? Or would you like a written itinerary?'

Sue lifted smug eyebrows. 'No, thank you. I've got a very vivid imagination. Let's see – that's three times in ten days, isn't it?'

'Yes.'

'Not bad going.'

Allie said nothing. The cold air stung her face, refreshing and reviving her after the fuggy, smoke-filled radio room. Tomorrow. A day to live through, and a night. Twenty-four hours of ignoring the constant, gnawing anxiety, of trying not to picture Buzz up there in the perilous sky, playing the desperate game of death that he so enjoyed. The only time she did not worry was when he was with her, when she could touch him, watch him, know him whole and for the moment unthreatened. Every other minute was a quiet torment of anxiety. Yet she would not have had it any other way. Sue was right. She was in love. Head over heels. Incredibly, marvellously in love. She lived for the sight of him, the sound of his voice.

'Coming on the Norton, is he?'

Allie came back from her reverie. 'Hm?'

'Buzz. Coming on his motorbike?'

'Oh – yes.' They turned from the cold into the warmth of the requisitioned house.

'Ever been out with him on it?'

Allie shook her head.

'You should give it a try. Motorbikes are fun.'

'Like this?' Allie looked down at her tailored, skirted uniform. 'Don't be an idiot.'

Sue surveyed her with bland composure. 'It's a good job I don't take offence easily, isn't it? Listen, girl, where there's a will, there's a way. There's a girl in MT must be just about your size. And she owes me a favour or three.'

'What's that got to do with anything?' Allie was yawning, ready for bed. She had been up since four.

The other girl shook her head in comic disbelief. 'You've got to be in love. Or you couldn't be so slow on the uptake. Do the girls in Transport climb in and out of their little lorries in ladylike skirts? No. They've got nice, comfortable trousers, haven't they?'

Light dawned. 'Sue, I couldn't possibly—'

'Let's give the lad a surprise. I'll bet you'll look smashing in battle-dress.'

The big Norton, Buzz Webster's pride and joy, raced along the narrow lane, its engine reverberating thunderously. Allie, clinging like grim death behind him, consigned Sue and her bright ideas to perdition. The day was overcast, trees and hedges were skeletal in winter leaflessness, and a pall of drifting mist drenched the landscape. She was freezing cold, her back ached, the unfamiliar trousers and battle-dress jacket, for all Buzz's wholehearted and delighted approval when he had seen them, chafed her skin, and she was certain that every bone in her body had shaken loose from its neighbour. Neither was she now convinced that her impulsive suggestion as to their destination was as good an idea as it had at first seemed. The last time she had seen Ashdown had been just before the boisterous evacuees had moved out. She hated to think of the house shut up and empty. Yet when Buzz had asked her where she would like to go, she had found herself suggesting that he might like to see her old home, and his enthusiasm for the idea had done the rest. Now, though she knew the actual distance to be only a little over thirty miles, she felt, bouncing uncomfortably on the Norton's pillion, that they must have covered at least three hundred. Her only consolation was that the familiar lanes and villages they were passing meant they were almost there; the return journey, she decided grimly, she would not contemplate until it was actually upon her.

The gates of Ashdown were closed. As Buzz, at her shouted instructions, rolled the bike to a halt, she climbed stiffly from the pillion seat and opened them. The hinges creaked dismally. Flakes of red dust came off on her hand, and the wetly acrid smell put her teeth on edge. She wondered how it was that the gates had escaped being requisitioned and turned into the hardware of war. Rather to her own surprise, she discovered that she was very glad that they had, and was glad too, after all, as she paused for a moment and looked at the house, that she had come. Here were her roots. She was glad to bring her happiness home.

The drive was weed-grown and unkempt. The lawns were gone – even the front garden had been given over entirely to orderly rows of vegetables. In contrast to the weedless, neatly husbanded land, the house looked neglected. Paint peeled from the windowsills and Allie could see the untidy vestiges of last spring's birds' nests still cluttering the gutters, so that rain-dirt streaked the brickwork beneath them. Buzz wheeled the sputtering motorbike up the drive, parked it and, in the silence left by the dying engine, surveyed his surroundings.

'What a wonderful old place.'

'You like it?'

'Very much.'

'The gardens used to be lovely. Mother's pride and joy. I can quite see why she doesn't come down here much. It must break her heart.'

'Someone's certainly digging for victory.'

'Browning, our old gardener. He keeps almost the whole village in vegetables from what I hear – *and* he's a corporal in the Home Guard to boot. Damn it, this lock's stiff. Ah, there we are . . .'

The big door swung open. The house was cold, and the

252

darkness of the winter afternoon shadowed the corners and the stairs. Automatically, Allie's finger went to the light switch. As the light clicked on, Buzz's hand covered hers. 'Better not. The blackouts aren't up.' She turned the light off again and the contrasting gloom seemed deeper than ever. Buzz tossed his leather gauntlets onto the hall table, looked doubtfully down at his heavy flying boots. 'Should I take these off?'

She shook her head. 'The carpets, other than the ones they took to Kensington, are in store. We had to take them up when the evacuees were here. The floors are in a pretty bad state already – a dozen or so kids in hobnailed boots saw to that. I believe Dad's got a chitty from the War Office entitling him to have them sanded and polished for nothing when the war's over.' She grinned. 'There's something worth fighting for.'

She pushed open the dining-room door. Across the white, shapeless humps of the dust-sheeted furniture, through the french windows, the ploughed-up garden suddenly looked ridiculously incongruous. High on the hillside opposite, the tangled wreckage of a crashed plane stood out against the dark woods. Only the orchard looked the same as it ever had, and the brown glint of water in the distance. Allie remembered the garden parties that now seemed part of another life, another person; tried to remember, and amazingly could not, what it was like to live a normal, settled life with everyday problems that did not include the exigencies of war and the fear of death, for oneself and for others. She walked to the tall windows, stood for a moment pensively looking out, not at a bleakly cold afternoon and a sweep of ploughed and planted earth, but at sunshine, and a drift of rose-petals on velvet grass. She found that, from nowhere, a tune had begun in her head. She hummed it softly: '*A cigarette that bears a lipstick's traces . . .*' Why did the room remind her of that particular song? She searched her memory, but the recollection eluded her.

'I say – what a lovely room.' She went back into the hall. Buzz had pushed open the drawing-room door. Again, the furniture that was left was covered, and the walls and paintwork were finger-marked and dirty. Soot had splashed down the chimney with the rain, and flecked the floor and the fireplace; the room smelled of it. Yet the beautiful proportions, the lofty ceiling, the tall, diamond-paned windows still retained their grace.

'What's in there?' Buzz's boots clicked on the wooden floor as he walked the length of the room.

'The conservatory. I shouldn't think that—'

'Good Lord. Come and see.' Buzz's voice was amused. 'I'll bet the local constabulary doesn't know about this!'

Allie joined him at the conservatory door. As he had opened it, a wave of warm, moist air had escaped into the cold room, misting the mirror that hung on the wall. A tiny paraffin heater burned in the middle of the tiled floor, the plants – that Allie had expected to see dead, or dying, of cold and neglect – were as green, glossy and healthy as they had ever been. She looked at the little heater. 'That isn't allowed, surely?'

'You can bet your boots it isn't. But who's arguing? What a smashing little spot. Looks as if our fairy godmother got here before us.'

'It must be Browning, bless his heart. How strange to see it looking so normal – the only part of the house that hasn't changed a bit . . .' Her voice faded. Buzz had gently shut the door behind them and was standing watching her, his face for once serious. The warm and verdant smell of the conservatory engulfed them. As he stepped to her she stiffened for a moment, pulling away from him.

'Allie? What is it?'

'Nothing.' But as she lifted her face to his kiss she saw again those other lovers, felt again the physical shock experienced by that other achingly, stubbornly young Allie as she had watched. But also felt something else, something so surprising that it took a moment for her to identify it as the first, faint stirrings of an astonishing sympathy. The Allie who stood here now was herself in love. Could anything – anyone – have prevented her from falling in love with Buzz?

She doubted it. Was there anything she would not do for him? She knew there was not. But Buzz was not someone else's husband. Someone else's father. The old antagonistic hurt rose freshly, burning like acid through the softer fabric of a faint, newborn understanding. Destroying it. With a physical effort she shut out the thoughts. Shut out the memories.

Buzz kissed her, long and slowly, held her to him, rocking her gently, like a child, her head on his shoulder. Faintly, through the cold air, the sound of the church clock striking the half hour came to their ears. Allie closed her eyes.

'I'm glad I've seen you here.' His voice was soft, muffled in her thick hair. 'You belong. It's a lovely old house. A real home. I think you must have been very happy here.'

She opened her eyes. The vibrations of the chimes still hung in the air. 'Yes. I was.' And once again a treacherous stirring of loving nostalgia smoothed the raw edges of her hurt. There had been other things than that awful night, than the miseries of misunderstanding in the intervening years. She had always known it, had never been able to face the knowledge. Even now she fought it. She had not been wrong. She knew she had not been wrong. They – *they* – had been wrong. And yet – suddenly, her clearest memory was of her father's face as she had seen it last, on her weekend leave – tired, older, and with always that awful depth of sadness in his eyes when he looked at her.

She turned from Buzz to the window, stood looking through the live, patterned lacing of leaves into the garden. He came to her, and she leaned back against him, her head tipped to his shoulder – and again came that razor-sharp stab of recollection. In just that way, Celia had leaned to Robert Jordan, her face streaked with tears. Curiously, it was the first time she had remembered those tears.

'I wanted to ask you something,' Buzz said into the curve of her neck. 'Tell you something.'

'Mm?'

'Well – ask you something. If you say yes, then I'll tell you something.'

255

His unaccustomed awkwardness surprised her. She turned in his arms to look at him. There was a look of boyish uncertainty about him that made her want to hug him, hard. 'What is it?'

'Do you think – that is – any chance that you could get a few days off after Christmas? Some time in January, say?'

'I'm not sure. I might be able to. My last real leave was a good few months ago. Depends on how busy we might be, I suppose. Why?'

'I've got some leave owing. Haven't been bothering to take it. But – well – I thought – wondered – there's somewhere I'd like you to see. Someone I'd like you to meet. If you'd like to, that is. I thought it might be fun – just the two of us . . .' He hesitated, misinterpreting her silence. 'I'm sorry, perhaps it wasn't such a bright idea. I just thought—'

'Buzz, I'd love to. Love to.'

His arms tightened around her. 'Really?'

'Really. Where are we going?'

'Northamptonshire. Do you know it?'

She shook her head, her eyes on his animated face.

'Good. Then I can show it to you. A bit of it, anyway. Now, come on, show me the rest of the house. I want to see every nook and cranny. I want to know what it was like to be you, here, a long time ago. I already know what you were like.'

'Oh? What was I like?'

He contemplated her, smiling. 'A very serious little girl, all arms and legs and big blue eyes. You didn't say much, and you spent a lot of time hiding from people.'

She looked at him startled. 'How did you know that?'

'I'm not silly.' He held out his hand and she took it. He pulled her towards the door. 'Show me the house.'

She hung back, laughing. 'Hold on a minute. You said you were going to tell me something. Ask me something, you said, and then tell me something.'

He put an arm about her shoulders, guided her back into the cold drawing room. 'Ah, but I didn't say when, did I?

Northamptonshire, as I remember it, is a jolly good place for telling people things . . .'

They explored the rest of the empty house, came back into the warm conservatory to eat the sandwiches they had brought with them and to share a thermos of hot tea. Then they went out into the back garden, wandered past the soldierly ranks of winter cabbage and onions that were strewn, Allie noticed, with a weird fertilizer of shrapnel. There must an anti-aircraft battery somewhere near. In the orchard, the river-mist wreathed ghost-ribbons through the spreading bare branches of the trees. They stood by the muddy, swirling water and listened to the unmistakable sound, high and distant, of enemy bombers heading for London, heard too the heavy guns start up from the direction of the city. A little sobered, hand in hand, they walked back to the house. It was now almost full dark. With the flashlight Allie checked the doors and windows, pulled the front door firmly closed behind her and trudged down the wet drive to where Buzz awaited her. As she shut the rusted gates, she looked back at the dark mass of the house. A real home, Buzz had said. Yes, it had been that. And, please God, would be again.

With one last, long, thoughtful look, she turned to Buzz and the wretched Norton.

Libby Maybury, ensconced behind an enormous, steaming tea urn under the eagle eye of her mother, at first did not recognize the young man in army uniform who stood, smiling, waiting for her to remember him. The smooth fair hair was shorter, the moustache a little more military.

'Peter! Good heavens, how marvellous! Where did you spring from?' Her voice faltered as her eyes took in the slightly lopsided stance, the stick with which Peter Wickham propped himself up. She recovered, smiled brilliantly. 'How lovely to see you! It must be – what? – two years?'

'Something like that.' The pleasant, quiet voice was the same. 'How are you?'

Libby spread her small, well-manicured hands. 'As you see. Suffering like everyone else. My clothes are wearing out. I haven't had a decent hairdo – or a decent night's sleep, for that matter – for months, and—' Suddenly the superficial brightness faded under his quiet smile. 'Hark at me. I don't change, do I? I never could stop talking and say something straight.' She extended her hand across the littered, tea-stained table. 'It really is marvellous to see a face from the old days. You don't know how marvellous.'

The bustling station hall was full of men and women in uniform. An engine shrieked, the sound echoing through the twisted girders that perilously supported a roof half-burned away in a recent raid. A guard blew his whistle and the great locomotive began to move, belching and coughing steam, roaring its eagerness to be off, the long line of packed carriages jolting and clanking behind it. Libby put her hands over her ears and grimaced. Peter, smiling, stood back to make way for a young sailor, kitbag high on his shoulder, his hat, with its dark ribbon showing only the letters HMS, at a jaunty angle on his mop of hair.

'Cuppa tea, miss, please. An' a kiss fer luck, if there's one goin?'

'Don't be cheeky, sailor. I might be tempted to put a little extra something in your tea.'

The lad grinned acknowledgement, took his mug. A train was pulling into a platform with short, sharp chuffs that turned into a long, relieved sigh as it came to rest against the buffers. The carriage doors banged open like a volley of pistol shots and the platform became a swirling river of uniforms, kitbags, luggage.

'Batten down the hatches, here come the next lot.' Libby beckoned to Peter, shouted over the noise. 'I'm off in about twenty minutes. Can you wait?'

He smiled, nodded, toasted her with his mug of tea and limped to a nearby wooden seat onto which, very slowly and with painful care, he lowered himself, his damaged left leg sticking straight out in front of him. Libby remembered Ashdown, a tennis court, shouts, and laughter, Allie's

258

voice: 'Oh, Peter, honestly, you'll have to move faster than that!'

'Two teas and some biscuits, please, miss. One with, one without . . .'

Half an hour later they were walking through the wrecked streets, Libby sauntering, slowing her footsteps to Peter's awkward, swinging gait. She pulled off her headscarf, shook her hair free. She was wearing trousers and a man's heavy jumper that Peter recognized as Edward's, her only real concession to femininity the small, wedge-heeled shoes that picked their careful way through brickdust and rubble. Yet despite the masculine attire and the faint, dark rings beneath her eyes, she was still utterly lovely.

Not far from them, women queued patiently for water at an emergency standpipe. Every road had its raw and ragged gap, almost every house showed some sign of damage – broken windows, shattered roofs, some of which were spread with tarpaulins in an attempt to keep out the worst of the December weather.

'They've caught it badly round here ever since the start of the Blitz.' Libby skirted a bomb crater. 'It's the station, you see.'

'Couldn't the people be evacuated?'

'Most of them have been. They came back.' Libby shrugged. 'You can't blame them, I suppose. All they have is here – possessions, home, family, friends.'

'Do you work at the station every day?'

She laughed. 'Good Lord, no. Only when I can't get out of it,' she said with disarming frankness. 'My mother – you remember my mother . . .' Her tone was dry.

He nodded, smiling.

'. . . has a wonderful way with her when it comes to bulldozing people into doing things they thought they wouldn't be seen dead doing. Must be awfully good for the war effort, my mother.'

He glanced down at her. The times made it difficult to enquire after old friends. One never knew what one might hear. 'Edward?' he asked, gently.

'Abroad. Malaya, I believe. His family have connections

out there, as you know. I don't know quite what he's doing – but he knows about rubber, and the rubber supply is essential, so . . .' She paused, added on a strange little half-breath, 'I just wish it weren't so damned far away.'

They walked in silence for a while, picked their way around a roped-off street where hung a carelessly strung, lopsided notice: KEEP OUT. UXB.

'And – Allie?' His voice was still perfectly even, but it took him just a fraction of a second too long to get the name out. 'She's in the WAAFs still?'

'Yes. Down at Hawkinge.' Libby flicked him a sympathetic glance. 'You haven't seen her?'

'No.' The monosyllable gently but firmly closed the subject. He stopped for a moment, leaning on his stick. His face was suddenly pale and lines of strain showed themselves around his eyes. 'Sorry. Have to rest up for a sec.'

'Of course.'

'Caught it in Belgium,' he said, 'in the retreat. Machine-gun. They're still trying to patch it together but . . .' He shrugged, smiled wryly, and left it at that. 'In between hospital trips, I'm at the War Office, so at least I can try to convince myself I'm still doing something halfway useful.'

'Do you have to get straight back there this afternoon?'

He shook his head. 'I'm off till tonight.'

'Can you make it to Rampton Court? We could have a drink – a chat – oh, please do.' She took his free hand, held it in both of hers. 'The world's full of strangers, isn't it?' she said in an odd little voice. 'I didn't know, until I saw you standing there, how much I missed my old friends.'

In the flat, which was bright with pre-war Christmas decorations, he lowered himself with an undisguised sigh of relief into an armchair, propping his stick by his side.

Libby pulled off her jumper, tossed it onto a chair, straightened the collar of her blouse, ran her fingers through her hair, tidying it. 'Drink?'

'Well, as a matter of fact – if you wouldn't mind? – I'd really love a cup of tea. If you've got tea, that is?'

'Good Lord,' Libby threw back her head and laughed. 'Tea? Well, yes, it happens you're in luck. I managed to get hold of a quarter yesterday. Is that what you'd like? Really?'

'Please.'

They sat as winter shadows gathered around them, sipping from fine, bone-china cups of eggshell colour and fragility. Libby caught Peter's quizzical glance. 'Aunt Maude's wedding present. Supposed to be an heirloom. But needs must and all that. I broke the last of the everyday china last week and there's absolutely nothing in the shops. I refuse – absolutely refuse – to drink my tea out of that awful white stuff an inch thick and with no handles. You have to draw the line somewhere. So out came Aunt Maude's Spode. I keep meaning to poke around a couple of second-hand shops – they might have something, I suppose.'

The tea was steaming and strong, the silence companionable. After a while, they talked, desultorily, about old times and old friends, about normality – trips to the seaside, tea on the lawn. About another life. At last Peter glanced at his watch. Darkness was closing in. He stirred, reached for his stick. 'Well, I suppose I'd better—'

Libby cut his words short. She was slumped in an armchair, her head resting on her hand. The lights were not yet switched on, and as the fire was screened, the curtains had not yet been drawn. Her fair hair was a smudge in the faint light. 'They'll be here in a minute, I suppose, our little kraut chums. Damn them.' Her voice was suddenly bleakly bitter.

Peter struggled to his feet. She stood up, reached and brushed a speck of dust from his uniform jacket. 'I've always been afraid of the dark, you know that? Always. As a child I was terrified. Stupid, isn't it? Even now I'm – marginally – more afraid of the dark out there than I am of the bombs, of being alone, of what's happening to Edward, of the damned mice in the damned shelter—' She broke off with a nervous catch of her breath that was not quite laughter. 'I hate it. Hate it all. I hate the shortages, and the blackout, and the fear, and the Woolton pie. Oh, I know – no one in their right mind would admit to enjoying it – but sometimes I wonder. Have you heard them singing in the shelters night after night? Seen the queues for the clubs and dance halls?' She took a long breath and ruffled her hair with her hand. 'Christ, hark at me. If the others heard me, they'd think I'd taken leave of my senses. I'm the worst of the lot. I never stop. I can't stop. I can't bear to be alone. Because I'm so – wretchedly – terribly – afraid. Of the present. Of the future. Of the whole bloody awful mess. Why am I such a coward? Does everyone feel the same?' She was speaking rapidly, the words running into each other, her breath shallow and sharp in her throat.

Peter reached a friendly arm. She leaned tiredly against him, her head bowed. He could feel her tears. As he held her, awkwardly unbalanced, searching for words, he felt a wave of pity for this small, bright, fragile creature. 'Of course it isn't just you. We all feel the same to a greater or lesser extent. You just mustn't give in to it. Look on the bright side.' The words sounded, even in his own ears, empty of meaning. 'Sooner or later it will all be over, and Edward will come back, and everything will be the same as it was before.'

In her own unthinking misery, she did not sense the flinch of pain that crossed his face as he spoke the last words, nor feel the instinctive movement of his shattered leg. 'Perhaps,' she said.

The first distant siren sounded, a wailing banshee that immediately awoke echoes from all over the city.

'Damn and blast that thing!' Libby drew away from him, sniffing, and dashed an embarrassed hand across her face. 'Sorry about that.'

He smiled in the darkness. 'What are friends for? But, truly, I have to go now . . .'

'Of course.' She was bright again, brittle as glass. 'And I have people coming. But you will come again, won't you? I do promise faithfully not to weep all over you again.'

He kissed her cheek gently. 'Weep all you like. As I said – what are friends for?'

# CHAPTER SIXTEEN

The Christmas dance for the men and women of the RAF station at Hawkinge was held in the restaurant of a big department store in Folkestone on two consecutive evenings, it being felt unwise to offer the target of the massed personnel of the station to the possibility of enemy action in one go. Disappointingly, Buzz Webster could make neither evening, so Allie – determined not to miss the fun altogether – went with Sue and a couple of other girls.

Despite the obviously adverse circumstances, nothing could suppress the Christmas spirit. Hired buses carried them the short distance to shell-battered Folkestone. The station band gave festive and enthusiastic rendering of spot-waltzes, ladies' excuse-mes and the inevitable Paul Jones. Allie danced every dance, drank a little more than was now her custom, and was standing fanning herself vigorously with her cardboard ticket during the brief interval, looking for Sue, when an airman she knew by sight tapped her on the shoulder.

She turned, smiling.

'There's a fella outside looking for you. It is Allie Jordan, isn't it?'

Happiness lifted. Buzz. It had to be Buzz. 'Where is he?'

'Through the doors. In the foyer.' The young mechanic opened his mouth as if to add something, then thought better of it. Allie did not notice. 'Thanks a lot.' She was away, squeezing through the crowds, pushing her way to the doors, her face alight with expectation. Buzz! Trust him to – the doors swung closed behind her, shutting off sound. The air in the gaudily carpeted, rose-lit foyer was cooler. A slight figure in RAF uniform stood with his back to her. She could see his face in the tall, pink-tinted mirrors which lined the room.

Tom Robinson.

She halted, stood stock-still. He saw her in the mirror and turned. His face, that hard, impassive face, was the very picture of pain.

Allie's heart was beating, suddenly and sickly, in her throat. She could not – quite simply could not – move. Behind her, faintly, the band started up again: '*Yes, sir, that's my baby* . . .'

Tom looked at her for a fraction of a second with pale, exhausted eyes. Then he moved quickly to her.

'It's Richard,' she said.

'Yes, I'm afraid so.'

'What? Crashed? Lost?'

'No.'

'Then what? What?'

The muscles of his dark face were iron-bound and throbbing. 'A car crash. This afternoon. It's bad. Your parents and Libby are on their way to him. I offered to come to tell you. I didn't want you to hear—' He stopped.

She stared at him. 'A – a *car* crash? Oh, no.' She shook her head, dazedly, rejecting the thought, trembling with shock. 'Oh, no. That's – that's ridiculous—' She spun on him. 'Why didn't you telephone? I could have been on my way . . .'

He shook his head. 'I said it's bad, and it is. But not that bad. His life isn't in danger—'

'Then – what?' She watched him, waiting, her breath a choking constriction in her throat.

'It's his eyes.'

She made a curious, gasping sound and put a hand to her mouth.

'They're working to save the sight of one eye,' he said expressionlessly. 'The other . . .' He shook his head.

'Oh, my God.' She turned away from him and clung for a moment to the back of a chair. The doors to the dance hall swung open and a couple, hand in hand and laughing, came through them. They cast curious looks in Allie's direction as they passed, then, their voices lifting again in laughter, they clattered down the stairs and were gone.

A quiet touch on her shoulder steadied her trembling. 'I've a car outside. I can take you back to Hawkinge if you'd like. They're going to telephone. From the hospital. As soon as there's any news.'

She nodded, dazedly. 'Yes. Yes, of course.' She looked around her vaguely. 'I need my bag. In there.' She jerked her head towards the doors. 'And Sue. I'll have to tell Sue.'

'I'll come with you.'

His hand firmly under her elbow, he guided her through the streamer-tangled, boisterous crowds to where Sue, perched upon a table, was holding laughing court. Allie hardly heard Tom's brief explanation, hardly took in the concern on Sue's face. Nervelessly she took the bag that Tom proffered, allowed him to steer her back through the foyer and down the stairs into the street. Once settled in the car, however, her trembling eased a little and her mind began to function again. As they nosed their way through the dim-lit, deserted streets, she glanced at the man beside her. He was staring straight ahead, his profile shadowed. Across the water the enemy guns had started up.

'How did it happen?' she asked at last.

'Wait.' They had left the town. In the faint light from the shaded headlights a small lane wound upwards to the right. Suddenly and unexpectedly Tom swung the wheel and the car was swallowed in the hedge-shadows, nosing upwards towards the downs.

'Where are you going? *Tom!*'

'Just for a moment. There's something I have to tell you.' His voice, she had noticed before, had lost its normal, disciplined lightness. It was raw. Painful. The car rolled to a stop where the ground levelled off at the top of the hill. As the engine died, Tom turned out the lights and for a moment they sat in utter stillness looking out at the strange, darkling landscape, with the sky frost-bright above them and the firefly flicker of guns on the horizon. Tom sat quite still, staring ahead, his hands still on the steering wheel.

'What happened?' she asked, quietly.

'They'll say he was drunk.' The words were even. 'He

265

was acting drunk.' He took one hand from the wheel and rubbed his forehead with long fingers. Allie could hear his breathing, quick and shallow.

'Acting drunk? What do you mean?'

'Just that.' He paused for an interminable moment. 'Allie, I'm sorry. I have to tell you. You were right; someone has to know. Someone he can turn to. Someone he can trust.'

She was feeling sick again. 'Go on.'

'I'd been spending a few days' leave in Suffolk with Richard – staying in a pub near where he's stationed. There are a couple of girls up there . . .' He shrugged in the darkness, left the sentence unfinished. 'Richard and his crew took a hammering last night. The squadron was shot to pieces. Four planes down and a lot of the others badly damaged, including Richard's. Pretty bloody. They'd scrambled home somehow, God only knows how. The gunner died in Richard's arms, somewhere over the Channel.'

The car was deathly quiet. Allie squeezed her eyes shut for a split second.

'Anyway, this lunchtime, we really hung one on – a dozen or so of us. Except Richard.'

'But—?'

'He wasn't drinking. I noticed it particularly. You forget how well I know him. He was getting them in, paying his whack, but he wasn't drinking. He just sat there, very quietly. Too quietly.' Tom's words were still spaced and even but in his voice trembled something that crept in an awful way along Allie's nerves. 'After closing time we took a bottle up to my room. Boozed a bit, talked a bit, started up a card school. Then suddenly, for no apparent reason, Richard started to act like an absolute idiot. Horsing about. Singing silly songs. Talking too loudly. As if he were drunk.'

'But he wasn't?'

'No. I'd stake my life on it. Then the next thing I knew, he'd gone. He was calling to us from outside, in the car park. Playing the fool. Trying his keys in everyone's car. I shouted to him. He pretended not to hear me – but I noticed that he then went straight to his own car and opened the door. Then he looked up. Waved.' The guns had fallen silent. The starlit night lapped the car in peaceful waves of darkness. 'He waved,' said Tom again, with difficulty, 'stood for a minute like that, looking up at me. Then he got in his car and roared off as if all the fiends of hell were behind him.'

'What did you do?'

'I followed him. On a motorbike belonging to one of the other lads. I saw it happen. He drove into a tree. Deliberately.'

'No!'

'Yes.' His voice was harsh. He turned and grabbed her hands in a hurtful grip. 'Yes, I tell you – I saw it. It was no accident.'

'But *why*? And why pretend . . .?'

'Who the hell knows what was going on in his mind? He probably didn't know himself. Perhaps he thought it'd make it easier for everyone else – God knows . . .'

She could feel his violent trembling through his hands, and even in her own pain she could not bear the depth of his. 'It wasn't your fault.'

'Wasn't it?' He almost flung her hands from him, turned away from her. '*Wasn't it?*' Shockingly, she could hear the tears in his voice that he refused to shed. Uncalled, her own words to him about Richard rose in her mind: 'I just hope you're right,' she had said. And the odd, uncertain flicker in his eyes as he had answered: 'You think I don't?'

He had been wrong.

'You think he tried to kill himself?' The words were curiously detached.

'I don't know. I think that all he knew was that he had to stop it somehow. That he couldn't fly again. Couldn't go through it all again. And he couldn't see any way out. I should have seen. I should have stopped him.'

'It doesn't sound as if anyone could have done that.'

He bowed his head to his clenched hands on the steering wheel. Tentatively she touched his shoulder. The fierce tension of his body rejected the gesture. She took her hand away. 'Thank you for telling me.'

That surprised him. He lifted his head. 'I wasn't going to. Right to the last minute I wasn't going to. But he has to live with it. You see that, don't you? And you may be able to help.' The words were a flat admission of culpability, and they both knew it. He flicked his head in the gesture that she remembered well. The dark hair flew up and away from his forehead. 'We'd better get back to camp. There may be news.'

There was. Richard had suffered a broken leg, an arm fractured in several places and three cracked ribs. He had lost the sight of one eye, and was about to undergo an operation to save the sight of the other. His war, at last, was over.

Between that Christmas and the New Year, the City of London burned as it never had before. The intense incendiary raids of the twenty-ninth of December left the massive dome of St Paul's marooned in a sea of flame-shot smoke, making a picture that Londoners were never to forget, and only a miracle saved the great cathedral itself from destruction. The commercial area of the city had been deserted because of the holiday, and too late it was realized that threatened areas must not be left unwatched and undermanned. Through simple lack of manpower, none of the hard-won experience of the city's defenders could help London on that night, and the City was devastated. To the Jordans, however, the fiery destruction, awful as it was, was only background to a battle of their own. Richard lay quiet as death in his hospital bed, rarely moving, rarely speaking, docile and despairing. It was as though the bandages that still covered his damaged eyes were the outward sign of a total spiritual withdrawal: from the world, from life, from all who loved him. Myra spent every possible moment at his bedside, and the others came and went as and when they could. Richard thanked them for coming, politely and passively, and lay like a corpse, while in desperation they conversed around him.

'Poor young man,' said an elderly and well-intentioned nurse to Myra, within earshot of the still figure in the narrow bed. 'It takes some of them like this, when they realize they'll never fly again. Knowing that their friends are still up there, doing their bit without them. They're so dedicated, these young men of ours . . .' She did not see the painful twitch of Richard's mouth as he turned his head away.

A fortnight after the accident Richard was transferred to a hospital just outside London and it became, from a practical point of view, marginally easier for the family to reach him. But for all of them, the visits became more rather than less difficult as Richard quietly and obdurately refused to recover. Libby, for one, at last flatly refused to visit him alone, and often towed along a reluctant Peter or an, at first, even more reluctant Celia with her. Allie, burdened by the truth – which she mentioned to no one – made the trip to the hospital as often as she could, held her brother's hand and racked her brains, uselessly, for a way to help him. She of all of them knew, or guessed, the torture for Richard of being in a hospital that was almost entirely full of airmen who had received their injuries in combat, and who were remarkably cheerful. Richard was the only one not to share in the warmth and camaraderie with which these young men supported themselves and each other. On the day that, the operation having been successful, the bandages were removed from his right eye and he saw for the first time faint movement and colour, he turned his head from the light and stared at the blank wall. He was no trouble to anyone. He moved from bed to wheelchair and back again, obediently, as instructed, ignoring all friendly overtures from staff and patients alike, suffering his family's determined visits with dogged forbearance, living in solitary confinement within that very worst of prisons, his own mind.

Allie had been on duty throughout the Christmas period,

though in fact, under the circumstances, this had not been the misfortune it otherwise might have been, since with Richard still desperately ill, none of the planned family celebrations had taken place anyway. She did manage to have Christmas dinner with the Jessups, who kindly adapted their timetable to suit her, serving the precious roasted chicken at the slightly odd hour of four-thirty in the afternoon. She met the Jessups' son, Alfred, Stan's father, for the first time that day, and liked him as much as she liked the rest of his family. He was a big, slow-speaking man very like his father but with Rose's warm smile and placid temper. He had been out of work for nearly five years before the war had started, and his wife had died from tuberculosis during that time; only his parents' labour and help had kept him and his son together and in decent comfort and health. Now, however, he confided to Allie, he had high hopes that after the war, with the trade of motor mechanic that he had acquired in the army, things would be better.

Charlie Jessup shook his head. 'Don't bank on it, lad. What will have changed? We might beat the Jerries, but we'll not beat the Tories. Don't think it.'

Allie looked at him in surprise. She had never heard Charlie offer an opinion of even the faintest political nature before and had assumed that he, like so many others, held the scornful view that life was life and politics were politics and no good ever came of mixing the two. He rolled a careful, wispy cigarette, pinched off the ends of the tobacco and stowed them in his pouch, then looked up to find Allie's eyes upon him.

'Do you really think the war won't change anything?' she asked.

'The last one didn't.' Peaceably he lit the limp cigarette, half-closing his eyes against the drift of pungent smoke. 'Don't see any reason why this one should be any different, do you?'

'But we've Labour politicians in the government now. Don't you think that'll make a difference? Don't you think they'll do something?'

His eyes twinkled through the wreathing smoke. 'Oh, I daresay. They'll do something all right. They'll see which side their bread's buttered and jump on the same bandwagon as everyone else. They'd be daft not to. But they won't do a lot for the common or garden working folk, you mark my words.' And with this faintly scurrilous pronouncement, he reached for another cup of tea.

'Now, Charlie!' scolded Rose from behind her knitting. 'You just watch what you say. Allie doesn't want to listen to your nonsense.' And Allie was assaulted by the strong suspicion that Charlie's slightly cynical political views had been until now restrained in deference to her and her family connections.

Allie did contrive, after her operational Christmas, to get to London for the New Year, which she spent at Rampton Court with Libby. Buzz came up from Biggin Hill for the afternoon of New Year's Day, Libby's birthday, and elicited absolute approval from the astonished Libby.

'You wretched dark horse!' she hissed at Allie in the kitchen. 'He's adorable! And what's all this about your going off together?'

'We aren't going *off* together. We're going away for a few days. To Northamptonshire. At the beginning of February, God, Goering and the RAF willing.'

Libby curved suggestive eyebrows.

Allie blushed. 'You're impossible, you know that? It's all very proper. We're staying in a pub that I think is owned by some old friends of his.'

Her sister's smile did not change. Allie refused to be drawn further. 'And, incidentally, I've a bone to pick with you. Why didn't you warn me that Peter was coming this afternoon? It could have been embarrassing . . .'

'Peter? Embarrassing? Oh, don't be silly, darling, Peter couldn't embarrass a fly. It didn't occur to me to mention it, that's all. And since Celia insisted on bringing that awful Stanton to our little tea party – or perhaps it was she who insisted on coming, I wouldn't put it past her – I thought we needed the extra man to balance things up a bit. Peter's a dear. Here – make yourself useful, butter the bread, would you? Or, to be more exact, scrape the margarine on and off again. Ugh! Detestable stuff. I couldn't say no to Cele,' she added, after a moment. 'She's been so good, coming with me to visit Richard, and everything . . .' There was that moment's odd, awkward silence that often now seemed to follow the mention of Richard's name.

After a second, Allie asked, 'Will it be all right if I stay the night? Buzz has to get back, but I don't – not till tomorrow.'

Her sister looked at her, bread knife poised. 'You aren't going back to Kensington with Dad? He's on his own with Mother away.'

The battle had already been fought and lost. Despite her good resolutions at Ashdown, the sight of Celia and her father in the same room had reawakened old hurts, and she had found herself unable to contemplate even the thought of time alone with her father. Not yet, she told herself, not just yet. And hated herself for it. She ducked her head, brushed the hair from her eyes. 'I'd rather stay here, if you don't mind. I have to leave pretty early in the morning and the trip's easier from here.'

Libby surveyed her for a moment, frowning. 'Well of course, if you like. But—'

'The kettle's boiling,' Allie said abruptly, and applied herself single-mindedly to the sandwiches.

When they returned to the drawing room with the food, a good-tempered discussion was in progress as to the effectiveness of a Free French army that seemed more intent upon fighting within itself in the pubs and clubs of London than anything else.

'. . . the problem is that de Gaulle won't accept that anyone but he can represent Free France, and he and Churchill hate each other's guts.'

'Oh, I say, that's putting it a bit strongly, isn't it?'

'From what I've heard, it's the other French chappie that de Gaulle can't stand. The Admiral. What's his name?'

272

'Muselier,' said Robert.

'That's the one. Someone said de Gaulle's had him arrested or something.'

'God almighty, now I've heard it all. We've enough trouble fighting bloody Hitler, I'd have thought, without scrapping among ourselves.'

Buzz grinned, incapable of staying serious for any length of time, and winked at Allie as she handed him the sandwich plate. 'Well, what else would you expect from the perishing French, free or otherwise?'

Allie pulled a face at him and turned towards Celia and her flatmate who were sitting a little apart from the others. As she came within earshot of their low-voiced and forceful conversation, however, it was immediately obvious that it was both more heated and more personal than the general argument. She hesitated, unable to move away without drawing attention to herself. Stanton's square, indefinably unattractive face was dark with anger. 'I just don't see why you have to spend so much bloody time with her, that's all. This brother of hers isn't dying or anything, is he? For Christ's sake, why do you have to keep tearing off to see him with her?'

'Stanton, it isn't any of your business. You don't own me. If Libby needs me with her—' Celia's green eyes flickered as she saw Allie standing close by, and she stopped abruptly.

Allie proffered the sandwiches, awkwardly. 'There's only paste, I'm afraid.'

'No. Thanks.' The Australian girl was surly, the thanks an afterthought helped along by a furious glance from Celia. She stood up, her movements curiously jerky and violent. ''Fraid I'll have to go,' she said, shortly, to the room at large.

'Oh.' Libby was politely surprised. 'Why – well, of course, if you have to. I'll go and get your coat.'

'Coming?' The word was addressed, with an outrageous lack of manners, to the still-seated Celia.

Celia shook her head. 'No, I'm not. I'll see you later.' Despite her composure, her voice shook a little.

273

Stanton, caught by her own impulsiveness, and with Libby standing by holding her uniform greatcoat ready to slip onto her shoulders, muttered something under her breath, glanced around the room in a brief and ill-tempered farewell, and left.

Celia sighed, studiously avoided Robert's sympathetic eyes and ate her paste sandwich.

# CHAPTER SEVENTEEN

There was, at the end of January, one last long week of waiting during which Allie almost convinced herself that the precious leave was never actually going to materialize. She almost superstitiously refused to believe that it could happen until the day when, small suitcase in hand, she at last stood at war-scarred St Pancras station and watched the swarming throngs anxiously as the station clock ticked on with uncharitable precision. Even so, she missed him. The first she knew of his presence was a light arm across her shoulders and that bright, carefree smile. He kissed her, lightly and quickly.

'You are Lobby Lud and I claim my five pounds.'

'You are late. And if one of us has to stand, it's you.' As always, the very sight of him lifted her heart.

In the end, for most of the way, both of them had to stand, uncomfortably, in the packed corridor as the train crept, stopping and starting, through the chill February afternoon northwards into the flat and fertile Midlands. Allie, sensibly dressed in old slacks and jumper, finally with a shrug forgot decorum and sat on the floor, her back against the kitbag of a naval rating who sat nearby, his head on his knees, dead to the world. Buzz, in uniform still, for he had had no time to change, perched on their suitcases as their fellow-travellers pushed, jostled and stepped around them. With the dusk the blackout blinds were secured against the ghostly blue lights and the already confusingly anonymous, ill-lit stations became even harder to identify. Allie, proud of her own forethought, produced spam sandwiches and a flask of tea, which they shared with a mother and her small, fraught child. The little girl, all eyes and pigtails, pecked at the bread like a small bird and resolutely resisted her mother's efforts to make her say 'thank you nicely' to her benefactors. Eventually, in the catch-as-catch-can fracas that occurred at each stop Buzz hauled Allie into a carriage and stuffed her, breathless, into a vacated corner seat, then peered through a crack in the blinds. 'Unless I'm much mistaken, another couple of stations'll do it.'

The town of Kettering, when they alighted, was apparently lifeless and absolutely pitch dark. No traffic disturbed the quiet. A biting wind whipped around corners, skittering in rubbish and long-dead, winter-darkened leaves.

'This way.' Cheerily Buzz took her hand and led her out of the station into the ice-dark street. 'Bus station here we come.'

'Are you sure you can find it?'

'With my eyes shut. Do you doubt me, woman?'

His eyes, Allie reflected, might just as well be shut in the disorientating darkness. She slipped and stumbled beside him, her hand tightly in his, her little suitcase banging her legs, her ears and the skin of her face painfully numb with cold.

The big bus station was faintly lit. Without question she allowed him to bundle her onto a single-decker bus and subsided in an empty seat, leaning her head back and closing her eyes. She heard Buzz's cheerful voice, opened one eye as he bounced into the seat beside her. 'An hour to wait, I'm afraid,' he said with exasperating good humour, and she closed the eye again.

An hour and twenty minutes later they were at last on their way, to the accompaniment of a distant sound that Allie recognized all too well. 'Coventry catching it again by the sound of it,' said the bus conductor, conversationally, as he took Buzz's money. 'Brackworth Village? That'll be tenpence the two. Be a bit slow, I'm afraid. Daren't show a light with them buggers about up there . . .'

And it was slow. It was also cold and uncomfortable. The bus rattled and bumped like a crazy sideshow at a fair. Yet when, to a cheery goodbye from the conductor and a couple of other passengers, they alighted, Allie felt as if she were leaving home. The bus at least had held some vestige of warmth, some human comfort, whereas Brackworth appeared to be, to all intents and purposes, a deserted village with the wind scouring the one street as if intent upon destruction. Allie's bones seemed to be frozen together and her nose was running. In the distance, she could still hear that abominable sound that, against all reason, she had thought to leave behind her in London. Planes droned overhead, infinitely menacing.

'The longest mile,' Buzz said, infuriatingly unimpressed by cold, darkness or foul weather, 'is the last mile home. Or to be exact the last half mile. Chin up. Nearly there.'

They stumbled into the bar of the George and Dragon twenty minutes later, windblown, hungry and all but frozen to death. Allie let drop the heavy curtain that shielded the door, keeping the light in and the draughts out, and stared bemusedly at a roaring fire, polished wood and brass that glittered wonderfully in the light of gas mantles, and two enormous dogs that sprawled one each side of the fireplace that was almost as big as the room itself. The bar was tiny, welcoming and almost empty. As they entered, bringing with them a gust of bitter wind, the only two customers in the place and the plump, handsome woman behind the bar looked up. In a moment the woman was coming towards them, arms outstretched.

'Buzz! You made it! We thought you must have missed the train. The service gets worse every day . . .' She bustled to them, gave Buzz a smacking kiss, beamed at Allie. 'And your young lady! Oh, look at you, you poor thing. You look frozen!' Her voice rose in a controlled shriek. 'Pat? Pat – they're here! Buzz and his young lady. Put the stew back on, would you? Stew and dumplings, my loves, how does that sound?' She reverted to her normal voice without taking breath; indeed, it seemed to Allie that she had perfected the art of speaking without drawing breath. 'Come in, come in. Get yourselves sat by the fire. My, my, just look at you, Buzz Webster! I can never see you without remembering you, knee-high, scrumping my apples. George, Albert – you remember young Buzz Webster, don't you? Spent most of his time here in the village as a lad, up there with Miss Wimbush?'

George and Albert did indeed remember young Buzz Webster. Dazedly Allie smiled as her hostess, whose name, improbably, was Abigail, swept her to the fireside. The warmth and the light first dazzled and then almost stupefied her. By the time Pat, Abigail's diminutive and apparently voiceless husband, had appeared with two enormous plates of the most appetizing stew Allie had ever tasted, watched with evident satisfaction as they tucked it away and then went off in search of another plateful for Buzz, she had reached the end of her tether.

'I'm sorry – I'm just so tired – do you think I might . . .?'

'Oh, but of course, my love, you must be exhausted. Come along, and I'll show you your room. I put a brick in the bed an hour ago – it should be nice and snug by now.' To Allie's astonishment Abigail reached for and lit a candle in a small enamel candlestick that stood on a shelf by the door, smiling at her guest's undisguised surprise. 'Didn't Buzz warn you that this was the back of beyond? The electricity was just about to be laid on when Mr Hitler started his tricks; now it looks as if we're stuck for the duration – gas downstairs, candles up. It's not so bad once you get used to it. Just remember to put it out before you go to sleep. Now come along and let's get you to bed. You look dead on your feet.'

Allie sent a fleeting smile in Buzz's direction. He was watching her with that expression in his eyes that made her want to ignore onlookers and fling her arms around him, and she knew with certainty that he knew it. They looked at each other for a long moment, and even Abigail fell silent, smiling.

"Night, love,' he said. 'Sleep well.'

And in a strange bed that smelled of lavender, faint, fusty rose-petals and blowy washdays, warmed by a heated brick wrapped in a pillowcase and lulled by the wind that battered at shutters that stood like sentinels between the cosy room and the wild February night, she slept well indeed.

She awoke to a gleam of pale sunlight through the crack of the shutters, the cheep of a bird, and absolute, incredible peace. She had forgotten that such peace existed. Pre-war peace. No engines. No traffic. No sound at all except, faintly, downstairs, the rattle of crockery, a voice lifted softly in song and, beyond the window, the cheeky sparrow-cheep and the sound of leaves in a gentler wind than she remembered from the night before. She lay for a moment, unwilling to move, sunk deep in the feather mattress, warm as a newborn babe, the undisturbed bedclothes witness to a night's sleep that had been like death. Then a dog barked, a rumbling sound, low and friendly, and a voice she would have recognized anywhere said, 'Hello, old boy. Coming for a walk, eh? Coming?'

She slipped from the bed and crossed the cold room to the window. By the time she had opened it and pushed back the shutters, Buzz was on his way, swinging down the road that led between bare hedgerows that edged dark, neatly ploughed fields, with the two enormous dogs from the pub bounding at his side. He was wearing a heavy sports jacket and corduroy trousers: it was, Allie realized with a start, the first time she had seen him out of uniform. She watched as he bent, picked up a stick and hurled it, spinning, for the dogs to chase. The air that gusted into the room was fresh and invigorating; clouds scudded across the pale eggshell of the winter sky; the greens and browns of the flat, rich countryside were as much a balm as was the silence and the songs of the birds. With no more thought of sleep, she turned to the washstand and its bowl of cold water.

When Buzz came back from his walk, she was in the big kitchen, sitting at a vast, scrubbed pine table tucking into toast and – unbelievably – two new-laid eggs.

He ruffled her hair. 'Hello, sleepyhead. Thought you'd decided to take to your bed for a week!'

She gave him a toasty smile. The dogs bounded to her, sat panting one each side of her chair, tongues lolling in happy expectation of titbits.

'Now, you – Bogey! Gable! Come away from there!'

Abigail scolded from the scullery. The dogs took no notice whatsoever, but continued to watch Allie with velvet, begging eyes. There came the sound of a spoon rattling in a dish. With one concerted bound that threatened to wreck the kitchen, they were gone, following the noise. 'Thought that'd shift you,' said Abigail with wicked satisfaction, and shut the door.

Allie looked at Buzz. 'Bogey? Gable? Are those their names?'

He nodded, grinning.

'What strange . . . oh, no!'

He laughed outright. 'Oh, yes. Abbie's a great film fan. Bogart and Gable are her heroes.' He paused, touched her hair lightly. 'Who's yours?'

She turned back composedly to her eggs. 'I've always rather fancied Lawrence of Arabia myself.' She almost lost a precious spoonful of egg as he tugged her hair harder than she had expected.

Later in the morning, wrapped against the weather, they walked through the deserted lanes towards the outskirts of the village. Bogey and Gable, to their disgust and Allie's mild disappointment, had been left behind. 'We'll take them out later,' Buzz had said, positively. 'They can't come with us this morning.'

He led her now over a stile, holding her hand as she jumped down beside him, and, still hand in hand, they strolled through a small, winter-bare wood that smelled wonderfully of leaf-mould and new growth. Already a faint young haze of green foretold the spring. Something scurried almost from beneath their feet into the barbed-wire tangles of last year's brambles. They jumped a small, muddy stream, climbed the gently sloping path up to where light and the pale, bright wash of sky showed open land ahead.

'Oh, Buzz – look!' Allie, careless of the muddy ground, crouched and parted the grass and eaves with her finger. The drooping, delicate flower bowed its head like a shy and graceful girl. 'A snowdrop! Isn't it beautiful?' When he did not reply she tossed the windblown hair from her eyes and looked up.

He was looking not at the flower, but at her. 'Very.'

She touched the petals gently with her fingers, then brushed the grass carefully back over it and stood up. In silence they walked through the breeze-stirred woodland until they came to another stile that took the little path away from the trees to skirt a wide field that was already misted with the tender green of winter wheat. Perched on the stile, looking across to the distant roofs of the village, an arm across Buzz's shoulders, Allie at last asked the question that had been unspoken on her tongue all morning. 'What were you going to tell me?'

'Tell you?' His eyes were innocent.

'Tell me. You said that Northamptonshire was a good place for telling people things. Well, here we are. This is Northamptonshire, isn't it?'

He looked around. 'Do you know, I do believe you're right.'

'Well?'

He shrugged. 'It isn't all *that* important. Are you sure you want to know? I mean – you aren't in a hurry, or anything?'

She took a moment to consider. 'I guess I can spare a few minutes. If you're quick.'

He leaned against the stile, his head tilted back to look at her, the keen-edged wind ruffling his mop of hair. 'I love you,' he said, 'very much indeed.'

She touched his cold face, ran a gentle finger from his cheek to the line of his mouth, traced it lightly before bending to kiss him beneath a sky that sang with light. 'You mean,' she asked, breathlessly, a long, long time later, 'that you dragged me all the way here just to tell me that?'

He pulled her down to stand beside him, wrapped his arms around her and leaned his cheek against her tangled hair. 'Mm-hmm. Pretty grim of me, eh?'

'Pretty.'

'And now, there's someone I want you to meet.' He stepped away from her, caught her hand.

She pulled back. 'Oh, no you don't. You just hang on a minute. You might not have had anything very important to tell me, but that doesn't mean that what *I've* got to say to *you* isn't important.'

He feigned happy disinterest. 'Oh? What's that?'

'I love you,' she said, 'much, much, *much* more than you love me—'

His bear hug and kiss took every ounce of breath from her body. 'Let that be a lesson to you,' he said sternly, as he released her at last, laughing. 'Never challenge a Webster!'

Like children they ran, calling and laughing, through the cold and lovely countryside. He showed her a pond, dark and dangerous-looking now, where he had swum every summer as a child. She peered into the hollowed oak where a Red Indian had camped with tomahawk and scalping knife, saw his initials carved into the wooden handrail of a small bridge beneath which the water tumbled and swirled, ice-cold and silver-dark.

'. . . But where did you actually live?'

'I thought you knew? In India.'

'India? No, I didn't know.' There was so much she didn't know. She leaned against the rail, watching him, loving him so that it almost stopped her breath.

'Well, that is, Mother and Father lived in India. Pa still does as a matter of fact. The climate didn't suit me. Nor my mother.' A faint shadow crossed his face. 'After she died, Pa decided it'd be best if I stayed in England. I was already at school here, of course – so from the time I was ten or thereabouts I spent all my hols here, with Pa's old nanny. And *that*,' he added, tugging at her hand, 'is who you're about to meet. So come *on*!'

Bendlowes Cottage was a picture, grey-stoned and ivy-grown with windows like bright, compassionate eyes and a tall chimney from which fragrant smoke drifted to smudge the sky. Allie loved it the moment she saw it. She also, from the minute they entered the cottage gate, understood why the dogs had been barred from the expedition. An enormous and beautiful Persian cat watched them with proprietorial, haughty eyes from the porch. On the small lawn another disdainfully performed her fastidious toilette with a long, pink tongue and did not spare the intruders so much as a glance. Buzz beat a familiar tattoo on the brass knocker of the front door, and the faint lift of apprehension that Allie had experienced as she walked up the path was dispelled immediately as the door opened to reveal a small woman with a cap of soft white hair and bright, clever eyes. 'Bertie,' she said, and the single word was a loving greeting. He opened his arms to her, lifted her almost off her feet, swung her round.

Bertie? Allie caught his eye over the old lady's shoulder. 'Is there anything else I don't know about you?' she asked, under cover of laughter.

Buzz set his slight burden back on her feet, left one arm about her, drew Allie to him with the other. 'Allie, this is Nan Wimbush. Nan, dear, this is Allie. She's going to marry me.'

'Goodness,' said the apparently imperturbable Nan, 'there's a brave girl. How do you do, my dear? I'm very pleased to meet you.'

Allie was having a good deal of trouble with her voice. 'I – er – how do you do?' She was staring at Buzz. 'I am?'

'Well, of course you are. Aren't you?'

'When?'

'Today? Tomorrow? Saturday? I don't mind. I'm in no particular hurry.'

Nan's bright, birdlike eyes moved from one face to the other. 'While you're making up your minds, why don't we have a nice cup of tea?' She turned and bustled away from them. Allie was still watching Buzz, her eyes wide.

'Well, what did you expect?' He kissed her softly. 'A proposal?'

'I – hadn't thought about it,' she lied, straightfaced.

'Think about it now. Will you marry me?'

'I – Buzz, can we? I mean – the war – the—'

He caught both her hands fiercely, brought them up to cup his face. 'What would you have us do, girl? Wait?' The

283

words were painfully intense, the meaning behind them hovered blackly on the boundaries of Allie's happiness.

She closed her eyes for a fraction of a second, in defence against the expression on his face. 'No,' she said.

'Right, then.' The tension was gone; he was laughing again. 'Stop arguing and come and drink your tea like a good girl.'

The couple of hours they spent in the shining little living room of Bendlowes Cottage were happy ones, spent mostly reminiscing about a childhood of which Allie could not hear enough. In this friendly, happy little house in front of a glowing fire that gave off the distinctive smell that she had noticed in the George the night before and that came, she learned, from the fuel – 'leather bits' from the local boot and shoe factory – she learned more about Buzz than she had in the less than three months that she had known him. And was greedy for more – when the time came to leave, Buzz almost had to drag her away. When they left, promising to visit again before the short leave was over, the old lady kissed them both fondly, standing at the cottage door with one of the enormous cats in her arms as she watched them down the path to the gate.

As they turned to wave, neither of them perceived the sadness in her eyes.

'Isn't she a love?' Buzz drew Allie's hand through the crook of his arm.

'Yes,' Allie said, and added as a solemn afterthought '. . . Bertie.'

He grinned widely, lifted a threatening finger. 'Enough of that, my girl. Weren't you ever taught it was cruel to mock the afflicted?'

'Yes, Bertie.'

As he swung her to him, she let out a little shriek of laughter. A passer-by glanced at them, smiling. Buzz ignored him. His kiss, started in laughter, ended fiercely. 'You will marry me? You mean it?'

'Yes.'

'When?'

'This minute.' She was perfectly serious.

He put his head on one side. 'I'm not sure I can wait that long.'

'Can't make it any sooner, I'm afraid.'

'Where shall we live?'

'In Nan's coal scuttle with the leather bits,' she said promptly.

'What a marvellous idea.' He kissed her, lifted his head. 'Seriously. There are things to arrange, aren't there? Next month?'

Next month. Thirty days. Four weeks. An uncertain eternity of danger. Somewhere in Allie's head, she seemed to hear the faint rattle of gunfire, the scream of a diving plane. She buried her face in his shoulder, shut her mind angrily to everything but immediate happiness. 'Next month.'

They took a long time to stroll back to the George and Dragon. There was so much, suddenly, to say, so much to share, and every moment was precious.

'From now on,' Allie said in a quiet moment as they retraced their steps through the wood, 'this is going to be my favourite time of year. Who needs spring?'

'The birds do, idiot. They've got a far greater sense of decorum than we have.'

Those five blissful days were for Allie both endless and ridiculously, unbelievably short. When they boarded, for the return journey, what might have been the same dim, cold, crowded, uncomfortable train that had brought them, there might have been no time between – no magical, timeless days in the Northamptonshire countryside, no walks with the dogs, no evenings spent companionably around the fire in the cosy bar of the George, no tea and scones with Nan Wimbush and her lovely cats, no nights behind cloistering shutters with a warm brick for company, Buzz the thickness of a wall away and the knowledge that it would not always be so. Yet as the train swayed and crawled gracelessly back towards the realities of life, she discovered that the memories of that time were measured not in days or hours, but in heartbeats – a thousand thousand heartbeats, and each a word, an event, a discovery. Five days could, after all, be a lifetime.

And a lifetime could be all too short.

# CHAPTER EIGHTEEN

Allie and Buzz were married at the beginning of March, with the Blitz only slightly abated and a new name – Rommel – on everyone's lips. There was little ceremony – no wedding dress, no church bells, and a tiny cake that, hidden beneath a mouthwateringly splendid cardboard facsimile of the real thing, owed rather more to Myra's ingenuity than to the confectioner's art. There was, however, a bottle of fine champagne with which to toast the health of the bride and groom, and another as a personal present to the young couple – these unheard-of luxuries being Sir Brian Hinton's contribution to the celebrations. Quite unknowingly, too, in deputing his daughter to deliver his gift to the Kensington flat the night before the wedding, Sir Brian also precipitated the private meeting between Allie and Celia that Allie had done so much, both consciously and unconsciously, to avoid.

When Allie opened the door to Celia's knock, it would have been hard to judge which of the two was the more disconcerted. Celia, a large and obviously heavy brown-paper-wrapped parcel in her arms, looked blankly at Allie, who was dressed in her father's towelling bathrobe, her just-washed hair hanging in rats' tails about her face.

'Allie – I didn't know – that is, I thought Libby said that you couldn't get away until tomorrow?'

'I couldn't. A friend of mine wangled it for me.' Allie stood uncertainly, clutching the robe to her. 'Everyone's out.' The words were unintentionally brusque.

Celia's chin lifted slightly at the tone and her mouth tightened a little. 'I wouldn't have bothered you if I'd known. I did try to ring, but the lines are down again. So I came on the offchance, to deliver this. A present from Father. He particularly wanted you to have it for tomorrow.

287

He wishes you every happiness.' Her voice was cool and controlled. She held out the parcel, added with no change of expression, 'And believe it or not, so do I.'

Allie made no move to take the parcel. After a second she stepped back, opening the door wider. 'Come in. Please . . .' she added as Celia hesitated '. . . do come in.'

Unsmiling, and with a kind of caution, Celia stepped into the hall, followed Allie into the big sitting room, watching the other girl as she shut the door firmly behind her.

Allie's heart was pounding. 'Talk to her, Allie,' Buzz had said gently, leaning on a wooden gate, his eyes on the peace of the Northamptonshire countryside, 'listen to her side. You can't spend your life hating someone for one mistake. Not you.' And, knowing him to be right, knowing it indeed before the words had been spoken, she had resolved that one day she would. But that the day would come so soon and so unexpectedly was a shock, and she was unprepared. She made a small, embarrassed gesture. 'Excuse the outfit. I just got out of the bath.' She paused. Celia, still holding the parcel, said nothing.

Allie tried again. 'Would you like a drink? Not that we have much, I'm afraid, but I daresay I might find something . . .'

Celia, after a moment's just noticeable hesitation, proffered her burden again. 'Unless I'm much mistaken in my father, the answer to that small problem is probably in here.' Her eyes were still very wary.

Tightening the belt of the too-large robe, Allie took the parcel, sat on the sofa and untied the string, winding it carefully round her fingers and tucking it in the pocket of the dressing gown. In a large cardboard box were two bottles of champagne, two bottles of wine and a bottle of French brandy.

'Goodness!'

'He raided his cellar.' Celia was still standing, her hands deep in her coat pockets, her collar turned up to her ears.

'It's – oh, it's really too good of him! Champagne! And—' She held up the bottle of brandy, looked up at the other girl. 'Will you stay and have a drink with me? To wish me luck?'

Real bafflement showed on the thin face. 'Are you sure you want me to? I'd have laid money that you'd rather have thrown me out,' Celia said bluntly.

Allie flushed and fiddled with the top of the brandy bottle. Absurdly and irritatingly she felt that familiar feeling of childhood – an anxiety to please, a fear of being in the wrong. When she spoke, she herself heard the harsh note in her too-loud voice that was the reaction to that. 'It's time we talked, isn't it?'

Celia hunched her shoulders a little, her face pensive, a small, uncertain line appearing between her fine brows. Then, as if making up her mind, she nodded abruptly, pulled her cap from her red hair and tossed it onto the table, began to undo the buttons of her greatcoat. 'All right. If you'd like. And – yes – I will have a mouthful of Father's brandy. It's cold as death out there.'

Allie found two glasses in the sideboard, poured a little brandy into each. Celia threw her coat over the back of a chair, watching the other girl's every movement, her stance still wary.

In silence Allie held out a glass. Celia took it.

'Cheers.'

'Cheers. And all the very best to you and Buzz.'

They sipped the drink. In the silence, the clock on the wall ticked, softly persistent, the only sound. A small, coal-dust fire warmed one end of the chilly room. Allie reached for the bottle, splashed a little more brandy in each of their glasses. 'Come closer to the fire. It's cold over there.'

Celia perched herself on the edge of a big armchair, nursed her glass and waited. Allie, for the life of her, could think of nothing to say. Nervously she took too large a mouthful of the brandy and almost choked. When she could be certain of her voice, she said, 'Will you thank your father for me? It was very sweet of him.'

'Of course.'

'I'll write, of course, but – he's in the country isn't he? –

one can never be really certain of the post these days – with the raids, I mean.'

Celia nodded, turned her head a little, in a listening attitude. Everything was quiet. 'Funny, isn't it? When they don't come, you almost miss them.'

'Yes.'

Silence again. Celia, with a quick movement, tossed back the last of her brandy and stood up. 'Well, I mustn't keep you. You must have heaps to do.'

'No. Don't go. I – want to talk to you.'

Celia straightened and took a long, tired breath. 'Allie, I don't see Robert any more. I haven't seen him – seen him alone, that is – for years. You know that?'

Allie nodded. 'Father told me. Tried to tell me,' she amended with painful honesty.

'So if you want more blood,' Celia's voice was flatly weary, 'more penance, then you'll have to look elsewhere. I will not be punished any more. I'll cry no more tears, make no more apologies . . .'

'No!' Allie had gone very white. Her hair, drying, fluffed around her pale face. 'No, you don't understand. I wanted—' She gestured helplessly. 'I wanted to tell you – to ask you—' She stopped again, biting her lip. Even now she found it hard to say the words. ' – if we could, well, let bygones be bygones? I'm sorry I was so childish – so hurtful – for so long. To both of you.'

Very, very slowly, Celia sat down again.

'Buzz made me see. I had to tell him. It was the first time I'd spoken about it to anyone . . .' Allie, intent upon her own words, did not notice the wry twist to the other girl's mouth at that. 'I told him – all of it.' Allie paused. Yes, all of it, from that first dreadful moment in the conservatory at Ashdown to the dreary affair with Ray Cheshire – and in speaking of it had lanced the wound. It had not really needed his gentle words to draw away the curtain of blind childhood and show her the new perspective, the clearer light of adulthood. It had been happening within her, slowly, for a long time. He had merely made her face her own reluctant understanding. 'He made me see what I was doing. I'm not a child any more. I know what it is to love someone enough to be willing to do anything for them. And I know now that you can't choose who you might love . . .'

Celia's long eyelids fluttered for a moment, veiling her eyes.

'. . . and though I can't pretend that I can forget what happened – how it happened – at least I understand it better now. And that's a start, isn't it?'

Celia laid a quick, work-hardened hand on her arm. 'I'd say so, yes. Allie, thank you for this. And thank your Buzz. He's a lovely man, isn't he?'

Allie nodded.

'And so is your father.' The tone was even. Celia watched her closely. 'You know that?'

'Yes.'

'And can you finally forgive him for being human like everyone else?'

The space of a heartbeat. 'Yes.'

Celia, for the first time, smiled her old, infectious smile. 'Shall we be devils and celebrate with a drop more of Father's tipple?'

The tension eased, they talked for a while of the inevitable things – of the shortages, of war, of the individual experiences of their services. Allie had forgotten Celia's intelligence, her dry, often self-deprecating wit. With the brandy bottle showing decided signs of wear, she came to a sudden decision and acted upon it before she could change her mind.

'Would you – do you think you could get away tomorrow? For the wedding?'

Celia lifted honestly surprised eyes. 'Would you like me to?'

'Yes, I would. We all would.' She was pleased that her voice sounded so positive.

'Then, thank you. I'd love to.'

'It's at St Saviour's. Just around the corner. At eleven, we hope, providing Buzz can make it on time. And then back here for a small reception. It won't be much, I'm afraid. Spam sandwiches and orange juice. When you think what we got through at Libby's wedding—' She stopped, remembering that Celia had not been at Libby's wedding. Remembering why. 'Would you believe it, Libby wanted to give me her wedding dress.' She laughed a little uncertainly, stuck out long legs from beneath the towelling dressing gown. 'I ask you! It was a lovely thought, but look at the difference in the size of us! It wouldn't have come to my knees!' and then her laughter died as, swirling her drink reflectively in her glass, she remembered that bright and lovely day when she had folded Libby's beautiful wedding dress back into its box – what had Libby said? – something about keeping it for ever, wearing it on her golden wedding anniversary? There was a faint, recalled smell of roses and box hedge, the sound of bells and of happy voices. For one instantly suppressed moment she experienced a pang of self-indulgent misery, of longing for something that once she might have taken for granted but now could not possibly be. She sniffed. Buzz would look pretty silly in morning dress . . .

'People think we're mad,' she said, suddenly and soberly, not looking at Celia. 'Getting married now, with things as they are. Perhaps we are. Perhaps they're right. We've both been lectured – in the nicest way, of course – by our COs. Buzz's squadron leader isn't best pleased. My request for a posting to Biggin Hill has been turned down. Mother isn't keen, I know, though, bless her, she's done her best not to show it. But Dad – well, he hasn't actually said much but . . .'

'But he thinks you're right,' Celia said. 'I know him well enough to guess that.' It was said easily and with no embarrassment. 'And, for what it's worth, so do I. Take your chances for happiness as they come, Allie. They're few and far between, and not always easy to recognize.'

Allie looked at her intently, hearing the note of pain in the words. 'And you?' she asked, suddenly and softly. 'Are you happy now?'

The question stopped Celia in her tracks. She did not reply for a moment, but stood up and moved to the dying fire, leaning both hands, spread wide, on the high mantelpiece, surveying the reflection of the room through the enormous mirror which hung above the fireplace. 'If you want the truth, I guess I haven't been happy since the day that I realized that I loved your father. Or no – perhaps that isn't fair. Perhaps it goes back even further than that. I never seemed to have found the knack – that facility that others have simply to be happy. I don't know why. Somehow, when it comes to loving, I keep making the same stupid mistake. I always fall for the wrong person. I've done it again, as you must have noticed.'

The brandy was beginning to sing a little in Allie's head. 'Noticed?'

Celia turned as if to say something, shook her head and remained silent.

'Noticed what?' Even as she said the words, Allie, remembering a strong, sulky face, an imperative voice, felt an uncomfortable understanding stir. She shook her head. She did not want to know.

Celia laughed, very softly, painfully compassionate. 'I'd better go.'

For a rebellious moment, Allie was ready to leave it at that. She had done her bit, had had her say, mended her fences. Why should she go further? She was happy; at last, she was truly happy again. Why poison that with another's pain? With Celia Hinton's pain above all?

'Stanton,' she said.

'Stanton.' The name hung in the air like a weary imprecation. 'Poor bloody, benighted Stanton.'

'How can you do it?' *After my father*. The thought took Allie by surprise. She did not voice it.

Celia shrugged. 'It's easy enough, once you start.'

'That doesn't sound much like love.'

Celia laughed a little, not unkindly. Allie's in love. She knows all about it. 'What does?' she asked.

After a small silence, Allie asked, 'Do you? Love her, I

293

mean.' The words came out awkwardly, as if even to voice the conception was difficult.

'In a way, yes. Though not as she would have me love her. Not as she loves me. I sometimes think she hates everyone but me.'

'And you?'

'I? I hate no one. I gave that up a long time ago. But then – I'm not sure that I can truly love anyone, either. I can't seem to give the things they need me to give, to take the things they need to give me.' She stood up, just a trifle unsteadily, picked up her cap and, without looking in the mirror, clapped it onto the back of her head at its familiar jaunty angle. 'Goodness, little Allie, you still have that unenviable facility for making people talk to you, don't you? I really must go. If you honestly don't mind my coming, then I'll see you tomorrow,' she grimaced, half-laughing, 'minus Stanton, don't worry – though she'll play hell for a week.' She leaned quickly to Allie, kissed her cheek lightly. 'Thank you. Oh – I almost forgot.' Turning towards the door, she stopped suddenly, fumbling with the catch of her leather bag. 'I had a little something of my own I was going to leave.' She held up a tiny package wrapped in fine and obviously much-used tissue paper. 'A totally useless present. The best kind, I always think. Don't open it until I'm gone.'

Allie went with her to the door, paused with her hand on the doorhandle. 'Celia? What will you do?'

'About Stanton? Or about myself?'

'Both.'

'Wait for a sign from heaven.' She lifted her hands, palms upward, in a comic gesture of supplication. 'And that's likely to be a long time coming, wouldn't you say? 'Bye.' With a lifted hand and no backward glance, she ran down the stairs, her footsteps echoing sharply long after she herself had disappeared from sight. Allie shut the door and listened for a moment before going back into the sitting room and, sitting on the rug in front of the almost dead fire, opening the little package that Celia had given her. It contained, with no message, a tiny and obviously expensive bottle of French perfume – a hoarded, pre-war treasure. Allie was still holding it tightly in her hand, fast asleep, her head resting on the sofa, when her mother returned an hour later.

Buzz, who as far as Allie could tell, had never managed to arrive anywhere on time in his life, was indeed, and predictably, late for the wedding, but on this occasion he had good reason, since he had been in the air over the English Channel just ninety minutes before. He arrived at the church on the Norton with his best man riding pillion to find Allie, in uniform, a small bouquet of precious fresh flowers in her hand, waiting beneath coldly leaden skies on the steps of the church with her father. He bounded up the steps, shook hands with Robert, kissed Allie. 'I was afraid you might have started without me.'

'We thought about it.' In the darkness of the church porch, Allie saw her sister signalling wildly, heard the thunder of the great church organ. 'Here.' She broke off a flower head from her bouquet and tucked it into his jacket. 'In you go. *You're* supposed to be waiting for *me*, remember?' As he turned, laughing, to leave her, she caught his hand suddenly, drew him back to her, looking into his face, seeing for the first time its pallor, the dark rings of sleeplessness beneath his eyes. 'Have you been up all night?'

'More or less. Jerry must have heard the wedding of the year was on. I told you not to announce it in the *Tatler*. He wanted to invite himself. Took some dissuading.' He looked exhausted. 'There's one or two won't be trying again,' he added. And Allie, seeing the look in his eyes, heard clearly the unspoken corollary: and one or two faces that would be missing from the mess when he got back to Biggin Hill tomorrow . . .

'Come on, Buzz, they're waiting.' The young man who was to act as best man – and who, Allie saw, looked no less tired than the groom – grabbed Buzz's arm and dragged him up the steps to the huge church door. Allie watched as both young men paused, taking off their hats, smoothing their hair – in Buzz's case totally ineffectually – tugging down their jackets before they strode into the chill gloom of the building. When she turned, she found her father's eyes on her, full of sympathy.

'Ready?' he asked briskly.

The service in the darkened church, with its boarded-up windows and its candles flickering smokily in the cold draughts, was brief, and most of the congregation, while lending one earnest ear to the proceedings, nevertheless prudently kept the other pricked for the sound of the warning sirens. However, as an unusually solemn Buzz kissed his new wife and escorted her from the church, peace still held. Allie fingered the ring that Buzz had slipped on her finger and breathed a small, superstitious prayer of thanks: it was considered the worst of bad luck for the alert to sound during a wedding. Outside, the rain that had threatened all morning had finally begun to drift in a grey mist through the dark canyons of the buildings. In a dream Allie acknowledged kisses and congratulations. A good many of their guests had snatched the time to be there and had to leave immediately, amidst a flurry of swift goodbyes and good wishes. Those that remained stood in the sheltering doorway of the church in the lull left by the hasty leave-taking.

'Wait.' Libby dodged inside the porch, reappeared triumphantly with an enormous golfing umbrella. 'There. I just *prayed* that it would rain . . .' The umbrella had been decorated with streamers and tinsel that Allie recognized from Christmases long past. Allie's and Buzz's names had been painted on it in white within an enormous silver heart, beneath which were the initials RAF surmounted by a pair of creditable if inexpertly executed wings. The happy, unexpected gesture broke the slight restraint – in wild good humour the party streamed into the wet street. Beneath the splendid umbrella, to roars of approval, Buzz kissed Allie till her breath was gone. When she finally managed to extricate herself, Allie, scarlet-faced, tossed her bouquet in the air so awkwardly that the only person anywhere near it was the best man. He caught it with aplomb, bowed to the applause and instantly proposed to Sue – whom, so far as Allie knew, he had met just five minutes before.

Sue grinned. 'I'd have thought you were living dangerously enough already without adding to the risk?'

Back at the Jordans' flat, they found that, apparently miraculously, what had looked like a rather scanty spread had turned into something close to a feast. Everyone, it seemed, had brought something to contribute. Tiny fancy cakes, squares of chocolate, tins of spam, dried egg sandwiches and – wonder of wonders – a whole cold roast chicken.

'Where on earth did that come from?'

Myra surveyed her newly married daughter, poker-faced. 'Don't ask, my dear. I'm discovering that I can be quite as devious as the next one if the occasion arises. And don't share it either—' Deftly she removed the bird from public view and tucked it into a cupboard. 'Save it for the two of you after we've gone.' The brief, twenty-four-hour honeymoon was to be spent here, at her parents' flat while they stayed with Libby at Rampton Court. 'Now, where's your father and that corkscrew? Some magician has produced another couple of bottles of wine . . .'

'Allie, darling . . .' Libby, as always at her best in a crowd, danced to her sister's side, 'come and open the presents. Buzz!' she added, calling across the room. 'Be a dear – put a record on? Let's dance.'

The small pile of presents had been stacked on the table next to the splendid-looking, camouflaged wedding cake. They had all been wrapped with a care that was touching: most in gaily coloured paper that had obviously served its purpose several times since the outbreak of war, two in wallpaper, one in painted newspaper. The presents themselves ranged from the thoughtful and practical to the ridiculous.

'A whole jar of jam! And cups, you lucky thing!' Libby gave a small shriek. 'Celia! Come and see – my sister's rich!'

She broke off, giggling, holding up a remarkably ugly plaster poodle. 'My God! Whose attic did you come out of?'

Celia, in uniform like most of the guests, joined them, smiling, but before she could speak, Buzz, surrounded by several friends, swooped on them. Above the sound of voices and laughter, a dance band played, smooth and swinging. Libby's clear voice rose: *'Ev'ry kiss, ev'ry hug seems to act just like a drug . . .'* The three girls found themselves steered to the centre of the large room, and while several young men squabbled good-naturedly over who should first dance with the other two, Buzz, very firmly, claimed his new wife for himself.

*. . . You're getting to be a habit with me . . .*

'Happy?' he asked.

'Very. You?'

He shook his head, grinned. 'What have I got to be happy about?'

She kissed him.

'Break it up, you two. You've got the rest of your lives for all that. It's my turn to dance with the bride . . .' Allie found herself whirled away in first one pair of arms and then another. She caught sight of Libby, dancing with Buzz, head thrown back in that characteristic way, laughing. Her father was, slightly bemusedly, trying to keep up with a wildly Charlestoning Sue. He caught his daughter's eye, rolled his own wryly to heaven. Allie wondered, fleetingly, if Celia had told him of their conversation of the night before. Outside, the rain still drifted from grey skies; inside, as if there were no shadows and no threats, the hilarity heightened. There was a pause for refreshment and for not very serious speechmaking; the spam and dried egg sandwiches disappeared, the cardboard cake cover – a towering, beautifully modelled replica of a wedding cake that any bride might dream of – was with great ceremony removed to reveal a small sponge cake with a 'V for Victory' sign picked out inexpertly in melted chocolate. Amidst cheers, Allie cut it. The health of the bride and groom was drunk in welfare orange juice spiced with Sir Brian's champagne, then on went the records again, up went the volume and Libby and the best man took charge of the games. Allie, standing by the door watching a scrambling and slightly dangerous game of musical chairs, found herself thinking back to the gatherings of young people at Ashdown before the war. The bittersweet recollection brought Richard to mind, not for the first time that day, and she nibbled her lip. Her brother still showed no signs of improvement. Then, inconsequentially, the thought of him brought to mind another absentee, and she found herself trying not to admit to an uncharitable relief that Tom Robinson, whom she had invited from sheer politeness, had equally politely excused himself from the festivities.

'Allie?'

She turned to find her father standing beside her.

'Could you spare me a moment?'

She had half-expected it. Nodding, she followed him into the empty kitchen. He faced her, seriously. There was a long moment's silence.

'Celia told me you spoke to her last night,' he said softly at last.

Allie nodded.

'She told me what you said.'

Allie hesitated, then she said simply, 'I'm glad.'

'You meant it? You understand now – about . . . ' he paused, 'about what happened?'

'Yes.'

It was not quite enough, and they both knew it. Silence lengthened. Then her father held out his hand. She took it. The gesture, small as it was, did more than any words to break the tension between them. Robert smiled. 'Allie—'

The door to the drawing room had burst open and there was a babble of voices and laughter in the hall.

'I'm sorry,' Allie said quietly, under cover of the noise, 'I'm really sorry.'

'So here you are! Come on – we're having a knobbly knee contest, and Libby says you must judge it. They won't start without you. Excuse us, sir,' added the young man who had caught hold of Allie's hand. 'Important business to attend to.'

Robert laughed. 'Go ahead. Don't mind me.'

Allie hung back for a moment before allowing herself to be towed from the kitchen, a moment that was long enough to read the relief and happiness in her father's face, and to know that it matched her own.

An hour or so later, the guests, called by their various duties and aware that, in the circumstances, time alone together was the most precious gift of all to the young couple, began to leave. An hour after that the last goodbyes had been said and only the Jordan family remained.

Myra, in the kitchen, was stacking away the washed-up plates and glasses, while Libby patted cushions and straightened furniture. Allie stood with her father, alone for a moment, in the hall. Wordlessly he took both her hands in his, and in silence she stood on tiptoe and kissed his cheek, affectionately and naturally for the first time in years.

'Come along then, my dears.' Myra swept into the hall, with Libby behind her. 'Let's leave the young people to themselves.' She hugged Allie, kissed her cheek. 'I do wish you every happiness, my darling. Take care of that young man in there. He may not admit it, but he's dead on his feet. Robert? Are you ready?'

'I'm ready.' Robert kissed his daughter, held her tightly to him for a moment.

'Toodle pip, love. Don't do anything I wouldn't do.' Winking, Libby followed her parents through the door and slammed it resoundingly behind her. Allie heard her laughter, dying into the quiet.

She went back into the sitting room. Buzz was sprawled on the sofa, his jacket and tie off, shirt collar open, his head tilted back against the cushions, his eyes shut. Myra was right; he looked dead on his feet. She stood quietly for a moment, watching him, until, sensing her presence, his eyes snapped open and, with a swift, easy movement, he sat up, holding out a hand to her. Smiling, she moved to him and sat down beside him, allowed him to draw her to him as he lay back again, her head tucked onto his shoulder, his arm about her. They lay so, peacefully, for a long moment, unmoving.

'It's a pity Richard couldn't make it.'

She shifted a little against him. 'Yes.'

'He's still at that nursing home?'

'Yes.'

'Bloody shame.'

She said nothing. He rubbed his cheek softly against her hair. She took his hand. It was small-boned, and calloused across the palm; his nails were neat and short. She traced the strong line around the base of his thumb with a gentle finger. 'Did anyone ever tell you that you have a perfect life-line?'

He laughed, softly, sleepily. 'A fortune-teller yet?'

She shook her head against him, curled his fingers back over the palm of his hand. Outside, the rain drifted in a grey curtain to the windows, quiet and cold. Myra, fuel shortages notwithstanding, had built up the fire before she had left. Flames licked now through the tamped coal dust and warm, bright shadows danced in the dark afternoon. Buzz's breathing was even and gentle.

'There's chicken,' she said, 'and champagne.'

He did not reply.

Very carefully she lifted her head. The hand she had been holding slid, still curled like a child's, from her lap. Buzz's head had drooped sideways, his eyes were closed, long fair lashes sweeping cheeks that seemed to Allie to be thinner than when she had first known him. New, too, was the permanent, faint furrow between his brows. She moved gently away from him. He did not move. His sleep was the sleep of exhaustion. A pulse beat regularly in the white, fine skin of his throat where his shirt collar lay open. He looked incredibly – appallingly – young.

She watched him for a long time as the afternoon slipped towards evening, taking with it their precious hours. When at last he stirred and mumbled something, the March dusk was closing in. The rain had stopped and the skies were lighter – a bad sign for London, Allie knew.

301

Buzz's eyelids lifted a little, then flicked wide open as he started awake. She saw the hand that reached automatically for flying jacket and helmet, saw too the physical effort he made to prevent himself from leaping to his feet.

'Good Lord! I must have dropped off . . .'

She nodded, smiling a little.

'What time is it?'

'Fivish.'

'*Five?* Lord, girl, why didn't you wake me?'

'You needed to sleep.' Allie stood up and walked to the window, began to fix up her mother's plywood blackout shutters. 'It's stopped raining and the clouds are much higher. I hope there isn't going to be a raid.' She felt his eyes upon her, felt too the sudden irregular beating of her heart. She fumbled with the wooden catch.

'Allie—'

'Damn the thing. How does it work?'

'Allie.'

The catch slid into place. She stood quite still for a moment, her back to him. When she turned in the darkness, he had stood up, his figure limned like a stranger's in the flickering firelight. She stood, rooted to the spot. Panic beat in her veins. In God's name, what had she done? The recollected misery of those awful struggles with Ray Cheshire froze her where she stood.

He came to her, lifted her chin with his finger, kissed her. After a moment she relaxed, tentatively lifted her hand to his hair. It was thick and springy beneath her fingers, full of life. This was no stranger. This was Buzz. Her Buzz. And she loved him. He drew her to the rug in front of the fire, pulled cushions from the sofa for her head. His hands were hard and urgent now, and her own no less so. She helped him with her clothes, baring her body to him in the firelight, to his mouth, to his small, strong fingers. And discovered at last what the act of love could mean when its root was love and its flower mutual need, mutual pleasure.

A long time later, she stirred and moved a little way away from him. 'There's chicken. And champagne.'

302

He lifted his head, loomed over her, his teeth gleaming in the glimmering darkness. 'Later, woman.'

Later, they did eat – and Allie thought she had never tasted anything so good. Wrapped in her father's dressing gown she sat curled into an armchair in front of the fire and picked at her chicken wing with greasy fingers, washing it down with champagne that sparkled on her tongue like sunlight on water.

'We'll go to France,' he said, 'when the war's over. Down to the south, to one of those little villages that look as if they've been there lying in the sun for ever. We'll take a little house and we'll stay there for weeks. We'll smell the lavender and watch the bees and drink nothing but champagne.' He was sitting on the floor at her feet, his arm across her knee. 'We'll sit in the village square and watch the world go by. We'll live on bread and cheese and pâté de foie . . .'

She licked her fingers. '. . . and cold chicken . . .'

'. . . and cold chicken, of course.' He took the plate from her, handed her her refilled glass. 'Bring it with you.'

'Bring it with me where?'

'To bed, of course. Do you think I married you to sit and watch you eat cold chicken all night?'

The bedroom was cold, the bed colder. Absurdly shy, she scrambled naked between the sheets, rubbing her goose-bumped skin and huddled, sitting with her knees drawn almost up to her chin, watching him as he undressed. She could see nothing about him that was not perfect; the curve of his back, the muscles that bunched lightly in his slight shoulders as he moved, the set of his head. She slipped a cold hand from beneath the covers and reached for her wineglass. He trapped her hand, raised it to his mouth, nibbled her fingers with sharp teeth. 'Like I said – later, woman.'

She giggled and pretended to resist him. He slipped and tumbled on top of her, knocking her flat. They wrestled, tangled in bedclothes, helpless with laughter, stopped as if frozen as the unmistakable lifting wail of a siren came to their ears.

They lay still for a moment, wrapped in each other's arms, listening.

'Should we go to the shelter?'

He brushed her tangled hair from her face with gentle fingers. 'Do you want to?'

'No.'

His warm mouth touched her forehead, her closed eyes, her lips, her throat. 'Damn 'em then. Let 'em come.'

Had anyone, Allie often found herself wondering in the ensuing weeks, ever had such a strange start to married life? She sometimes thought, remembering her joke about living in Nan Wimbush's coal scuttle with the 'leather bits', that they might have been better off doing just that. With no home of their own, their brief, snatched meetings – sometimes at Ashdown, conveniently situated between their two stations, sometimes in hotels where Buzz found the knowing looks and raised eyebrows that embarrassed the life from Allie absolutely hilarious – were more like those between illicit lovers than respectable married people. 'Speak for yourself,' said Buzz. 'Who's respectable?' And though she could not deny that the situation had about it a certain excitement, a wonderful anticipation and an air of romance, she desperately missed the small things, the everyday, ordinary happiness of a working marriage.

It showed in the things that she knew of Buzz and in the things she did not. She knew his laughter and his loving; she did not know his sock size or if he liked his eggs cooked for three minutes or four. She knew his courage and his bright, smiling eyes. She did not know his fears or his everyday moods. Their lives were lived in a fragile cage of unreality, almost of pretence; their time together was a permanent honeymoon, a lovers' tryst haunted by the brutal reality of deadly danger. She longed for the chance to know him, to hold him, still and quiet and safe from the world. She saw him sometimes strung tight as a bow, laughing, talking non-stop, shadows in his eyes. She saw him haggard from lack of sleep, anguished from the loss of a comrade, shaking after a near miss, high with excitement after a successful mission. She woke to find him sweating and tossing beside her, or standing by the bedroom window at Ashdown counting away the hours of the night to the sound of the clock's chimes, and found it hard not to compare this strange life with that they might have led in another time.

In April the Germans took Greece and the British were forced to retreat to the island of Crete. Allie remembered Crete, and was sad. She had spent a happily remembered holiday there as a child – she could imagine too well what might be in store for the lovely, peaceful island, the cradle of Western civilization, and its people now.

The bombers came again to London, and in the middle of the month the city suffered a raid as heavy as anything that had gone before. With the Registration for Employment Order coming into force, Libby, to her oft-expressed disgust, found herself reporting to her nearest Employment Exchange to be directed into work that could be properly deemed part of the war effort. To her credit – for they all guessed that, with Libby's contacts, she could well have avoided it – she accepted the new ruling remarkably philosophically and found herself working for four mornings a week in, of all things, a 'war nursery' that cared for the young children of women working in the shops and factories. Her good grace was rewarded. To her own astonishment, she discovered that she liked it, though at first wild horses would not drag the admission from her.

On Saturday the tenth of May came, unexpectedly, perhaps the worst raid of the Blitz. The bombers pounded London, Liverpool, Coventry and many other cities all night, and the fires blazed savagely. Then incredibly, there was quiet. Nights passed, turning into one week, two. Londoners were oddly jumpy; there was no relief, just tension and a worried distrust of this strange lull. What were the damned Jerries planning now? In the raid of May the tenth, Rampton Court had suffered some damage and

Libby had moved to Kensington with her parents while windows were repaired and essential services reconnected.

When Allie began to suspect, about this time, that she was pregnant, she could not say in honesty that it was entirely an accident. To be sure, they had agreed not to have children until after the war – but there had been times when they had not taken the necessary precautions, almost, she thought, as a challenge to a decision neither of them had really wanted to take. She said nothing to Buzz. She was not certain yet. She would tell him as soon as she was sure – for if she were pregnant, she knew that, within weeks, it would show in her routine monthly health checks and she would have to leave the WAAF. Almost superstitiously, she refused to think of it, to mention it. Buzz, she told herself, had enough on his mind for the moment, and anyway, the time was so early that she could be mistaken. Another month, and if it were confirmed, she would tell him. Meanwhile, ignoring backache, she worked her shifts, lived for the next time she would see Buzz, and tried, with the rest of the country's population, not to recognize the fact that all the war news appeared to be bad and getting worse, not to suspect that, unless something happened soon, while Britain was left standing alone, disaster could be imminent.

# CHAPTER NINETEEN

If Celia Hinton had been forced to prophesy the end of her bitter, fragile affair with the unstable Stanton, she might in honesty have guessed that it would finish in violence, and she would have been right. She might also have guessed that the break would come over her friendship with Libby, of whom Stanton, against all reason, was mindlessly jealous. The matter came to a head one afternoon as Celia was getting ready to visit Richard with Libby. In the ensuing, savage row, inevitably, the words that were spoken were harsh and utterly unforgivable. Worse, when the words ran out, Stanton, in an overwhelming flash of rage, struck Celia, backhanded, her knuckle catching the other girl high and painfully on the cheekbone.

Celia stared at her, trembling with rage and with revulsion. She held herself very straight and still until the other girl stepped back. Then, with neither word nor look, she stepped past her and opened the door. As she ran swiftly down the steep and narrow stairway, she heard her name called once, in a miserably fierce, anguished voice.

She did not look back.

By the time she reached Rampton Court, she had, at least partially, regained control of herself. Her face throbbed where Stanton had struck her, their angry voices still rang in her head, the words repeated again and again like those on a cracked gramophone record, but she no longer shook and the red rage of anger had left her. Workmen were resandbagging the entrance to the Court as she ran up the steps to Libby's flat and rang the doorbell. So absorbed was she in her own problems that she did not at first notice the hectic colour in Libby's face, the shine in her eyes.

'Celia!' Libby put her hands to her face. 'Oh, Lord!'

'What do you mean "Oh, Lord"? Libby, you can't have

forgotten?' Quick exasperation surged through her. 'I don't believe it!'

'Well, yes – no – that is – Celia, Edward's coming home! On leave! Two whole weeks!'

Celia stared. 'Edward? But, Libby, that's wonderful news! When?'

'Well, that's just it – now. Today, or tomorrow. I only got back from Kensington yesterday. The letter was waiting for me. Celia, darling, I'm most terribly sorry – it just drove everything clean out of my head! I can't possibly go to see Richard today. Supposing Edward came?' She paused, frowning suddenly. 'What have you done to your face?'

Celia put a quick hand to her cheek. 'Nothing. Blackout accident. Walked into a door. Of course you can't leave. But Richard's going to be disappointed if no one turns up, isn't he?'

Libby shrugged. 'To be truthful, I sometimes wonder if he cares one way or another.'

The thought of turning around and going straight back to Pimlico was not appealing. 'Nonsense, I'll go alone. It's a lovely afternoon. The trip will do me good.'

Richard sat, utterly still, thin, pale, his flawed face lifted and empty, beneath the dappled spread of the huge oak tree in the grounds of the nursing home where he had been for the past weeks. He was dressed in flannels and an open-necked shirt. A stick was propped by his side. He had a patch over his blind eye. Celia, directed to him by a nurse, paused a little way from him, studying him. She sensed that he knew she was there, but he gave no sign.

'Well, hello there.'

He moved his head. 'Celia.'

'Right first time.' She moved closer, so that he could see her clearer. 'Alone, I'm afraid. Libby couldn't make it. Edward's due home on leave.'

'That's good news.'

'Isn't it?' She sat on the bench beside him. 'I like the patch. Very dashing.'

He said nothing.

'How are you?'

'Fine.' The word was empty. 'Thank you,' he added, with an effort.

'Allie sends her love.'

'How does married life suit her? I haven't seen her for a couple of weeks.'

'She's blooming. And very happy. No one sees that much of her at the moment. She and Buzz grab every moment they can together.'

'Of course.' Something moved in the damaged face at the mention of Buzz's name and was gone. 'Funny, isn't it? Allie married, I mean? I still think of her as a little girl.'

'It strikes me,' Celia said, softly, 'that one of Allie's problems has been that everyone thinks of her as a little girl.'

'You could be right.'

The leaves of the tree rustled above them in the early summer breeze. The air was fresh and fragrant. 'It's a wonderful day.'

'Is it?' He caught himself. 'Yes, I suppose so. Sorry.'

'How's the leg?'

He nodded a little. 'Mended. It'll be as good as new soon.'

'And – your eye?'

He lifted a hand to trace the scar that ran across his forehead, and for the first time turned to face her. 'I can see, though not all that well. They say that this is probably the best I can hope for. The damage to the other eye is irreparable. I suppose I'm lucky at that.'

They sat quietly for a moment. On the grass by Richard's feet was a book. Celia bent to pick it up. 'What's this?'

'Hemingway. *A Farewell to Arms*. One of the nurses was reading it to me earlier.'

She flicked through it, found the marked page. 'Would you like me to carry on?'

'Would you?' Faint surprise tinged his voice, as if her offer were something extraordinary.

'Of course.' She ran her eye over the page. 'The beginning of the chapter?'

He nodded.

She cleared her throat and began to read in her attractive, husky voice, a little uncertainly at first but gaining in confidence as she went along: '"That fall the snow came very late. We lived in a brown wooden house in the pine trees on the side of the mountain . . ."'

He leaned back, listening. The afternoon sun danced and glittered through the leaves of the tree, shimmered on the bright windows of the nursing home in the distance, across the lawns. He touched the patch that covered his blind eye. She glanced up quickly at the movement, then read on. So quiet and still was he that once or twice she wondered if he had fallen asleep, but each time she lifted her eyes, he was watching her, his scarred face intent.

'". . . It was like saying goodbye to a statue. After a while I went out and left the hospital and walked back to the hotel in the rain."' She closed the book slowly. 'How that man can write.'

'Yes.'

The book lay in her lap. She smoothed the worn cover with her fingers. 'Richard?'

'Yes?'

'When are you going to get yourself out of here?'

Silence.

'You could, couldn't you?'

He made a small, protesting movement with his head, then said, 'Yes.'

'Then when?'

'I don't know.'

'You have to, sooner or later. You can't hide here for ever.'

'Hide? What do you mean?'

The violence of his words startled her. 'I'm sorry. That was a clumsy way to put it. But, then, it is what you're doing, isn't it? Hiding? You have to get out of here and lick it some time, don't you?'

He turned his head away. She reached a hand to him. A nurse was approaching, briskly and with purpose. 'Richard, what is it? What's the matter?'

'I—' He stopped.

'Well, well, young man, so here we are. We still aren't very sociable, are we? Time for our exercises. Off we go, the doctor's waiting . . .' The nurse smiled, brightly and impersonally from one to the other.

Richard stood up. Celia reached for his stick, but he stopped her with a gentle word. 'It's all right. I can see it.' He picked it up, hesitated. 'Celia?'

'Yes?'

'Would you come to see me again? I mean – just you? Without the others?'

Celia stood up. Her eyes were on a level with his. 'Yes, of course. I'd like to.' She took his hand, kissed his cheek lightly.

'Thank you.' He smiled very faintly, turned and limped off beside the nurse.

When Celia got back to Pimlico that evening, it was to find the door locked and bolted against her and her suitcase and bags, roughly packed, stacked on the dark landing. She did not bother even to knock. She remembered, vaguely, telling Allie that she was waiting for a sign from heaven. She shrugged ruefully: this must surely be it. Ignoring the tense, waiting silence from beyond the door, with some difficulty she manhandled her cases down the steep stairs and out onto the street.

A few days after Edward's homecoming, a happy Libby predictably insisted upon throwing a party to celebrate. Buzz, his squadron down to half-strength, and passes hard to come by, had to leave half-way through the festivities. Allie saw him to the station.

'Take care.' Always, her last words to him.

'I will. And you. See you Wednesday week, at Ashdown, all being well. I'll let you know the time. Bring your French nightie . . .'

311

She grinned and kissed him, and he was gone. She turned in the summer dusk and walked back to Rampton Court. More certain every day of her pregnancy, she still had not told him.

'Allie, there you are – Buzz gone?' Edward looked very well – suntanned, lean and handsome, his fair hair bleached almost white. Libby clung to his arm, radiant. She had not wandered more than a foot from his side since he had arrived home.

'Yes, he has. And I'm afraid I'll have to leave, too, in a couple of hours. I'm on at four – one of the lads has promised to pick me up at the corner at ten. I'll be dead if I don't get some sleep.'

'Of course. But come on into the kitchen for a minute. Celia's arrived. She was asking for you.'

Celia was sitting on the kitchen table, her legs swinging, an inelegant mug of orange juice in her hand.

'Hello.'

'Hello.' There was still just the faintest air of restraint in the word. Allie glanced around. Celia shook her head.

'No Stanton. It's over, kaput.'

'I—'

'It's all right. You can say it.'

'I'm glad.'

'So am I. I think.' Celia jumped from the table, took her mug to the sink and ran it under the tap. 'I'm staying with friends at the moment.' She wiped the mug dry and set it on the table. 'I saw Richard a couple of days ago.'

'Oh? How is he?' Allie was aware of a small prickle of guilt. She had not been to see Richard for what seemed ages.

'He's fine. Walking well, and his good eye is quite strong. They've fixed him up with an eye patch. Looks terrific. But . . .'

'But?'

Celia shrugged. 'Oh, I don't know. There's something else wrong with Richard, isn't there? Something – hidden. We all know it. As if – well, as if all the damage that's been done doesn't show. Don't you sense it?'

312

'No.' The other girl looked at her sharply, surprised. Allie flushed. 'Well, yes, I suppose so. But it's only natural, isn't it? I think he feels badly about the accident – about it being his own fault, more or less.'

'Didn't they establish that there was something faulty in the steering of the car?'

'Yes. But he'd been drinking. He still feels it was his fault.'

'Maybe that's it.' Celia did not sound convinced. A gust of laughter reached them from the drawing room. Celia stood pensively, her fingernail clicking on the table top. 'He needs to leave that nursing home.'

'We all know that. How do you make him?'

'The Richard I knew was always ready to rise to a challenge.'

Allie held her eyes steadily for a moment. 'The Richard you knew isn't the Richard in that nursing home,' she said simply.

Celia sustained the regard calmly before turning to leave the room. 'Maybe not. We'll see.'

Before she left to go back to Hawkinge that night, Allie, to her discomfort, found herself cornered by the one man she had spent the best part of the evening avoiding: Tom Robinson. He had seated himself beside her on the settee with the air of a man who had no intention of being ignored. 'I haven't had a chance to extend my good wishes.'

'Thank you.' As always, the man produced in her a feeling of uneasy dislike that made her desperately uncomfortable in his presence. 'I'm sorry you couldn't make it for the wedding.'

'I couldn't get away.' The tiniest flicker of hilarity sparked in his eyes. 'I also didn't want to spoil your mother's day.'

She could not help smiling at that.

'Have you seen Richard lately?' he asked.

'A couple of weeks ago. But Celia's seen him. She was just talking about him. Saying he has to leave that nursing home.'

'She's right.'

'Yes.' She paused. 'Tom, about the – accident. Are you still certain of what you say happened? I mean, they've said that the steering on the car was faulty—'

'On my evidence.'

'What?'

'I said that I'd driven the thing the day before and noticed that there was something wrong with the steering . . . It fitted in with the accident – no other car involved, and the car itself was too far gone to check.'

'You still think he did it deliberately.'

He did not reply.

'Has Richard said anything to you? About what happened?'

'No.' Over his shoulder she could see the girl who had come to the party with Tom glaring at them both. She was a spectacular blonde with dramatic eyes, an even more dramatic body and the sheerest stockings in the room. Libby had cast disbelieving eyes to heaven when first she had seen her. 'Where does that man *find* them?'

'I think we're being watched,' Allie said. 'Your friend isn't happy.'

He shrugged impatiently, did not even glance in the girl's direction. 'He won't talk to me. Sometimes won't even see me.'

She studied his face. She knew his concern, his genuine affection for Richard, yet, she reflected, to look at his disciplined face, at the straight, almost harsh line of his mouth, he might have been talking of something that moved him not at all. And then she remembered that same face on the night of the accident, in the car on the downs above Hawkinge, and her spurt of irritation died.

'You think he guesses that you know what happened? Knows that was why you lied about the steering?'

'Yes.'

The blonde girl was moving purposefully towards them.

'It really wasn't your fault, you know.' Allie had no idea why she said it, wished she hadn't the moment she saw the look in his eyes. 'All right. I'm sorry. You don't need me to tell you that.'

'I didn't say that.'

'You were thinking it.' The needle-sharp antagonism was there again, unbidden, between them.

'Tom, baby, if you don't come and dance with me then I swear that I'll seduce the first man who will. And I've had some offers.'

'Wait a minute, Bet.' His tone was brusque. Allie, embarrassed, did not look at the other girl. Astonishingly, however, she did not seem to take any offence. She was obviously, Allie found herself thinking caustically, used to her escort's lack of manners. She leaned over him, wound a long, bare arm about his neck.

'No,' she said, simply.

He had to laugh. 'I'm busy.'

'Come and be busier.'

'Don't mind me,' Allie said tartly, and was treated to one of those infuriating, amused smiles. 'I was just going anyway.'

The girl's eyes surveyed her, taking in her uniform, their expression all bland and provoking innocence. 'Oh, I say – I'll bet you're one of those clever little things that drives a truck or something, and fiddles around with gaskets and things?'

'No, I'm not.'

'Oh,' she pouted, playing at disappointment. She looked at Tom. 'What does she do?' she asked, as if Allie were not there, and Allie could cheerfully have strangled her.

'A damn sight more than you do.' Tom slapped her bottom. She caught his hand and tried to pull him to his feet. He gave in.

'OK, OK.' He turned to Allie. 'You'll excuse us?'

She could not resist it; her eyes travelled slowly from the statuesque Bet to his impassive face. 'You've managed to get over your aversion to dancing then?'

'It took some doing,' he said soberly, and left her.

'They got the jolly old *Bismarck* then.' A young man that

she remembered as Geoffrey something had obviously been waiting his moment. He bounced onto the settee beside her.

'What?' Her eyes were on a bent, dark head, a lifted, lovely face. Oh yes, Tom Robinson had certainly got over his aversion to dancing . . . 'Er – oh, yes.'

'Jolly good news, what?'

'I suppose so.' She wrenched her attention to the young man, found herself adding unkindly, 'Didn't bring back the jolly old *Hood* though, did it?' She had found the celebrations at the sinking of the German battleship oddly distasteful. But then, she thought, revenge could hardly be called a tasteful thing under any circumstances. Geoffrey Something was still talking. Suddenly she could not bring herself even to listen. She wanted Buzz. She wanted Buzz at Ashdown, alone, and peace in which to love him. She wanted no one and nothing but Buzz. And there was more than a week to wait.

Abruptly she stood up. 'I'm sorry, I have to go.' She had caught him in the middle of a sentence. He gaped. She softened the blow. 'Duty calls.'

'Ah. Of course.'

She pushed her way through the crowds to find Edward and Libby to say goodbye. She did not take leave of anyone else. Minutes later, she was in the dark, cool street, strolling slowly towards her rendezvous with the truck that was to carry her back to Hawkinge, her footsteps echoing eerily, her thoughts on a June night and Ashdown and Buzz. She felt the faint, taut, painful swelling of her breasts as they rubbed against her shirt. She was certain now. The time had come. This time she would tell him.

Ashdown, in the long, soft shadows of evening, looked less neglected than she knew it would in the full light of day. She walked up the drive, her footsteps crunching on the gravel, her eyes dazzled by the gleaming, gold sword-strokes of sunshine that cut through the trees as she moved. As she approached the house, disappointment moved in her. The Norton was not there. Buzz had not

316

arrived yet. She smiled to herself ruefully. He'd be late for his own – she stopped the unguarded thought almost before it could form. Bad luck, even to think it.

She let herself into the house. Dust motes swirled, the sun lay in silent pools of light upon the scratched and unpolished wooden floor. She went into the kitchen, dumped the carrier bag she had brought with her onto the kitchen table: bread, cheese and a precious bottle of beer for Buzz. She was hoping there might be something fresh and edible in the garden. No use hoping that Buzz would think to bring anything . . . Her feet ached. She kicked off her shoes, padded from room to room in her stockinged feet, checking the house, drawing back curtains. In her own bedroom, she stood for a long time looking out towards the river. The garden looked like a small-holding. She rubbed the dirty window to clear the haze. The top of the church spire was caught in the last fiery rays of the sunset, its weathercock lit to gold. The sky was a painter's palette of delicate colour, the pinks and saffrons and golds of a fairytale. She glanced at her watch, and realized with a jolt that it was far later than she had thought. Summer Time she could cope with – Double Summer Time, which added two hours of daylight to an already long day, threw her completely.

Where was Buzz?

She tried to ignore the chill stirrings of anxiety. There could be any number of perfectly reasonable explanations. She wandered back down the stairs, stood in the hall looking at the big black telephone. He had never rung her here. He probably did not even know the number. She reached for the receiver, picked it up, put it down again with a clatter that reverberated through the empty house. There could be no point in ringing Biggin Hill now. He must be on his way. He must be.

In a kitchen that darkened moment by moment as the wash of lovely colour drained from the sky, she prepared the meal, such as it was, and carried it into the conservatory, which had become their favourite place in the old house, her ears all the time alert in the singing silence for the sound of the Norton's engine.

Nothing.

She sat in an armchair by the window in the dust-sheeted drawing room watching the empty drive. She would not believe, could not believe, that anything bad had happened. She would have known if it had. She would.

In gathering darkness that brought with it the chill of night, she watched. The clock in the church tower struck the hour and the half hour. Eleven. Half past. Twelve.

He wasn't coming.

Of course he was coming.

Something had happened.

Nothing could have happened. She would have known. Surely – she would have known?

She woke, stiff, sore and deadly cold with the dawn and the senseless chatter of the dawn chorus. Leadenly she packed the food back into the carrier bag. He must have sent a message to Hawkinge that had arrived after she left. It would be waiting for her. It might be any number of things – a change of duty, a sudden scramble, even, possibly, being unable to find half a gallon of black-market petrol.

In the hall she stood for a long time looking at the telephone. Once she reached her hand to it, but pulled it back as if the instrument had been red hot. She trudged out into the early brilliance of a June morning that stung her eyes almost to tears.

There was, indeed, a message awaiting her at Hawkinge. It was given to her, gently, by a commanding officer who had seen too many such messages.

Late the previous afternoon, Pilot Officer Albert Webster's Hurricane had been one of three pounced upon by a formation of Messerschmitts over the Channel not far from Folkestone. One of the British planes had gone down immediately. P/O Webster had claimed an enemy aircraft, sending it into the sea in flames before turning to flee for home. Too late. Caught in a murderous crossfire the

Hurricane had been almost shot to pieces. Buzz had tried to control the crippled plane, tried to bring it back, as he had done so often before, to Hawkinge. In doing so he had left it too late to bale out. He had still been at the controls when the little plane had buried itself in the hillside not a mile from the airfield.

Tearless, Allie stared out of the window at the ranks of small fighters lined up across the grass, and remembered, apparently inconsequentially, the wonderful sunset of the evening before.

# CHAPTER TWENTY

Allie had never believed of herself that she could resent another's happiness, let alone a person's very existence – but in the weeks that followed Buzz's death, she found herself, in unguarded moments, doing just that. A young man walking in a street, a serviceman standing at a bar or waiting at a bus stop could bring the involuntary thought: why should you be alive, when he is dead? It was not that she could not accept the fact of his death – on the contrary, this she did so immediately that it was as if, all along, she had been prepared for it, which perhaps was the case. Her reaction was sheer, helplessly desolate resentment of a world that could live on without him apparently unchanged while her own existence had, at a stroke, been emptied of meaning. Her pregnancy, strangely, was no consolation. She felt miserably ill for much of the time, suspected from very early on that all was not well and could not bring herself to care very much.

In July, when she left the WAAF, just a month after Buzz's death, the German attack on the Soviet Union made Britain realize with relief that at last she was no longer the sole target for the bombers of the Luftwaffe. Allie moved into Ashdown on her own, over her family's horrified protests. She needed desperately to be alone for a while, to come to terms with her loss in her own way. Unexpectedly, she found an ally in her father, who, though worried at the thought of her being alone, nevertheless understood her need, and it was his persuasion that finally stilled the protests of the others. She thanked him with as much warmth as she could muster, and left for Kent with an overwhelming sense of relief at getting away from the constant, sympathetic attention of friends and family.

In the warm summer weather she wandered around the

transformed gardens, sat on the banks of the river, watched away the hours from the windows of the house. Her only occasional companion was old Browning the gardener, and to him she was grateful for his absorption in his own tasks, which made for little general discussion other than the state of the weather and of the crop and no personal conversation at all. Browning, a veteran of the first war, had his own crusade to conduct, and this he did with a fierce pre-occupation that precluded almost everything else. Since Ashdown's lovely grounds had become a casualty of the war effort, he was determined that the sacrifice should not be in vain. He tended his vegetables as if they were his own personal secret weapon against Hitler – indeed Allie, watching with affection his bent back and dirt-grimed, meticulous old hands, suspected that was exactly how he viewed them.

She meanwhile, painfully and compulsively, spent her hours with her pathetically small store of memories – sorting, inspecting, hoarding them, protecting them from out-siders as a miser might his gold. She and Buzz had had such a very short time together. Had she tried, she could have numbered their meetings – perhaps a dozen before their marriage, less than that since. Sometimes she could see him, hear him, whole and laughing by her side, as clearly as if he were truly there – at others she was terrified she might lose him, forget the sound of his voice, the turn of his head, the touch of his hand.

It was Sue Miller, visiting her in the middle of a hot August who realized just how badly Allie was neglecting her own health – and Sue, typically, who decided, willy-nilly, to do something about it. She turned up again a few days later with Rose Jessup in tow. Rose had a small suitcase in her hand and an expression of good-natured determination on her face. She looked at Allie's thin, colourless face and shook her head, tutting.

'Well, now, my love. What's this? We can't have you making yourself ill, you know.'

'I'm all right. Honestly I am.'

321

'That's as may be, my dear. But just look at you – when did you last eat a proper meal?'

Allie shrugged and cast an exasperated look at Sue, who met it blandly unrepentant, unimpressed by the promise of retribution it held.

'A couple of days in bed's what you need, and someone to make sure you eat. I'll stay a day or so, and get you on your feet again . . .' Rose bustled out of the room and into the kitchen, still talking.

'I'm not *off* my feet!' Allie hissed to Sue.

'You will be soon. And so you should be. You look bloody terrible,' Sue said candidly. 'Making yourself ill won't bring Buzz back.'

Allie turned away. 'You think I don't know that?'

Sue regarded her with bright, sympathetic eyes. 'Hey – noticed anything?' she asked, after a moment.

'What?'

Sue extended her arm. Allie stared and, despite herself, laughed. 'Good Lord! A corporal? What did you do?'

'God knows. I must be slipping. I've been posted, too.'

'Where to?' Allie was surprised at the sudden sinking of her heart. She had hardly realized how fond she had grown of this flighty, happy-go-lucky girl.

'Hornchurch. Not too far. Don't worry, girl, you won't get rid of me that easy.'

Allie laughed.

Sue took her hand. 'Take care, Allie dear. Of yourself and of Junior there.'

Very gently Allie withdrew her hand, shook her head, said nothing.

'Allie? What is it?'

The other girl hesitated for a moment, then shrugged. 'The doctor isn't very happy with me. He wanted me to go into hospital for a rest and some tests . . .'

'Wanted? You mean you didn't go?'

'No.'

'But why ever not?'

'I – don't know really. I just couldn't bear the thought.

All those people. All the fuss.' She lifted blue, empty eyes. 'Don't say anything to anyone, Sue. I haven't mentioned it.'

'But—' Sue subsided, watching her worriedly. 'Don't you want the baby?' she asked at last, quietly.

'I don't know,' Allie said again, painfully and honestly. 'Truly I don't know. I don't understand it myself. I can't seem to think of it. Believe in it. Perhaps it's because I didn't tell Buzz. Because he didn't know.' She shrugged, sadly and helplessly. 'I don't know. I just can't seem to care.'

Sue took her hand again. 'You'll feel differently in a month or so. It's the shock. You'll get over it.'

Allie smiled reassuringly. 'Of course I will.'

Three weeks later she miscarried. At the time, she was neither surprised nor particularly sorry. As she had said to Sue, the child had never assumed any real identity for her. She was sad, certainly, but this sorrow was the faintest shadow compared to her pain at the loss of Buzz. Her tears had all been shed; there were few left for the scrap of humanity that had been destined never to see the light of day. It was, she discovered, almost a relief in a way. A final ending. And, strangely, as she recovered her physical strength, she recovered too a kind of equilibrium that had eluded her in the months before.

She lay in bed in her room at Ashdown listening to Rose's soft country accents and feeling, almost in spite of herself, a returning interest in life, an awareness of a future of which, until now, she had been unable to think. She was alive. The world had not stopped with Buzz's death. She could face that now. She found herself, at last, talking of him, laughing at recollected idiocies, weeping on occasion, but less often and less bitterly than before. Rose, seated by the bed, her hands always busy with her knitting, wisely listened and encouraged her charge to talk, knowing the balm of shared sorrow. And as autumn crept to the window in reds and golds and the smell of woodsmoke, Allie discovered at last that the keen edge of her pain had dulled, that sometimes an hour might pass when she thought of something other than Buzz and of the child who had not lived.

She talked to Rose of her childhood, of life at Ashdown before the war. Rose loved the house, treated it with a kind of reverence, polished it and cleaned it with pleasure until it lost its look of neglect and regained its old splendour. Charlie and Stan, she assured Allie when she asked a little worriedly, were more than capable of looking after themselves for a while longer. In her turn, Rose spoke to Allie of a country childhood of fifty years before, of her courtship and marriage, of the hard times and the happy times, of the difficulties of bringing up a family in times of depression. As they had grown, her children had been forced to leave the village for lack of work. Only Alfred, Stan's father, had stayed on the land – two other sons had emigrated to Canada, a daughter was living in Manchester, married to a mill worker, another had died of diphtheria in childhood. Allie found herself questioning eagerly, truly interested, anxious to learn. Nothing could be further removed from her own secure and happy childhood than Rose's tale of gruelling hard work for a pittance, of children sharing a pair of shoes, of washing taken in to make ends meet and of sons driven from home in a hopeless search for work. A month before Stan's mother had died from tuberculosis, the family had been turned out of their tied cottage, and Rose had had to take work as a cleaner to help feed the extra mouths. Allie was astonished at her uncomplicatedly philosophical acceptance of her lot – until now, indeed, had never suspected that the small, kindly woman's life had been so hard. Again she was struck forcibly by the injustices of a system that perpetuated a divided society, that rewarded wealth and punished penury, and she told Rose as much.

'Why, bless you,' Rose looked at her in honest astonishment, 'you sound just like my Charlie, that you do. But it's always been so. 'Tis the way of things.'

* * *

Two of Allie's first visitors were, surprisingly, Richard and Celia. Allie was lying comfortably on the sofa in the drawing room, a rug across her knees. Watching her visitors, she did not miss Celia's hand laid lightly on her brother's arm, nor Richard's quiet smile, his new air of confidence. After an hour or so, Browning arrived, pedalling laboriously up the drive on his old pushbike, and Richard left to speak to him. The silence, when he had gone, was constrained. Allie sat, hands folded quietly in her lap, waiting. For the first time, it occurred to her that, while she had been hiding here, the world had moved on without her.

'You and Richard?' she asked at last, bluntly, unable to conceal the distaste that she felt.

Celia's face coloured a little. She held Allie's gaze. 'I know what it must seem like – what you must think . . .'

Allie waited.

'Allie – if you really hate the idea . . .'

'Of course I hate the idea!' The words burst from her without volition. She bit her lip. 'Richard is my brother. My father's son,' she said after a moment, more calmly.

'He's also a man who needs help.'

'We can help him.'

'No. You can't.' Celia's voice was quiet. 'I don't know why, but you can't. I got him out of that hospital. I've got him walking and talking like a living man again, instead of some kind of zombie. Allie, he needs me . . .'

Allie said nothing.

'And I need him.' It was said simply, a kind of plea. Allie found suddenly that she could not look into the green eyes.

'I would have thought that you'd had enough of our family.' A strange, harsh sympathy threaded the words.

Celia looked down at her clenched hands. 'If you really can't stand the idea of Richard and me – if you really hate it – ' she lifted her head ' – then I'll finish it. That's what I came to say. I won't fight you.'

Allie stared.

'I mean it.'

In the kitchen Rose was singing, softly. A door banged.

'What does my father think?'

She saw the effort the other girl made not to flinch from the blunt question. 'I don't know.' Celia touched a nervous finger to her mouth. 'I don't know,' she repeated, and Allie, watching, saw a familiar pain.

'You still love him,' she said quietly.

The other girl closed her eyes for a long second. 'You must have discovered by now that loving isn't something you can just stop doing. Yes. I still love him.' She leaned forward, her face intent. 'But Allie, believe me, that has nothing to do with me and Richard. I swear it. I love him. For himself. I want to help him, make him happy. And it's working, Allie – look at him – you can surely see it?' From beyond the door came the sound of men's voices, Richard's quick laugh. Celia's voice had in it an edge of desperation. 'Allie, I told you I won't fight you over this. I can't. I need—' She stopped.

'My approval?' The words were faint and disbelieving.

'Your understanding at least.'

Allie looked at her for a long time, and something in that austere, unhappy face reached into that last dark corner of her being where a child still huddled, hurt and resentful. 'I understand,' she said, and to her own astonishment it was true. The child had grown up at last.


Her father came alone to see her, Myra having promised to travel down a day later and stay for a few days. They did not speak of Celia, except indirectly, in relation to Richard, and Allie was astonished at the ease with which they discussed the subject. Celia and Richard had set the date for their wedding. It was to be a quiet affair, with only the family invited. Yet even as they spoke of it, she was aware that this was not the only thing on her father's mind. But when he spoke of the other reason for his visit she found herself totally unprepared.

'Me?' she said, looked at him blankly. 'Join the business?'

Robert was standing in front of the fire, feet astride,

hands behind his back, as she had seen him so often in the past. The weather had turned, suddenly, and a gale-force wind lashed around the house and tossed in the trees, whirling the stripped leaves into the air. 'Why not?' His tired, handsome face was serious. 'You were the one who asked "Why not the manager's desk?", remember? Well – here's your chance. Sam Welton had a heart attack last week. He won't work again. I need someone to take his place. Someone I can rely on. Someone I can trust. I can't think of anyone I'd rather have.'

'But Richard . . .?'

'It's out of the question,' he said quietly. 'Richard knows it. I spoke to him of the idea of bringing you in and he approves wholeheartedly. Some time later perhaps we can find him a place in the London office – but there's no way he could do Sam's job.'

'But you think I could?' The faint stirrings of excitement that accompanied the words surprised her. She had not until now given a thought to the future, would have said just a short time before that she had none.

'I'm certain that you could.'

She was thoughtfully silent for a moment. 'Sam Welton. He was industrial relations, wasn't he?'

'That's right. And damn good he was. It won't be easy to fill his shoes, believe me. This couldn't have come at a worse time. There's trouble stirring in a couple of the plants. I don't want it to take hold. I need help. Intelligent help. You're good with people. They talk to you. More important, you listen.'

She tapped her teeth reflectively with her fingernail. 'You're talking of the whole of Jordan Industries? Men, women?'

'Yes.'

'Do you think the men would accept me?'

'That would be up to you, wouldn't it? You might have a few problems to start with. Would you let that stop you? Allie, I think you'd enjoy it. I think – even more important – that you'd be good at it. The government are keen to encourage women to step into this kind of job. There's a training scheme . . .'

She frowned. 'You aren't just being kind? Finding me something to do?'

His laughter was genuine. 'My darling, if it were as simple as that, your mother would have been down here long ago with a nice green uniform for you. No. It's something I've been considering for some time. Sam's illness has just precipitated it, that's all.' He came to her, sat beside her. 'I'm not offering a sinecure. It'll be damned hard work. Will you have a go?'

The astonishing feeling of excitement was growing, minute by minute. 'How long do I have to think about it?'

'A couple of days.'

She nodded. 'And, Daddy?'

'Mm?'

'If I took it – would I be an independent agent? Make my own decisions? Or would I have to keep running to you?'

He grinned like a boy. 'Allie darling, you're going to have your work cut out to stop *me* from running to *you*!'


Allie started work at Jordan Industries in December of that year. Six months a widow, her grief had blunted though it had not died, and here she knew was a perfect chance for her to begin a new life, to take responsibility for her own future. Yet even for Allie herself this momentous change in her life was overshadowed by outside events – for this was the month of Pearl Harbor, of a vicious and unprovoked attack upon a neutral nation that was to change the course and conduct of the war and send the waves of battle lapping other shores as the conflict grew to encompass the East.

A couple of days after America's entry into the war, the British battleship *Prince of Wales* and the battlecruiser *Repulse* were sunk off the coast of Malaya by Japanese aircraft. On Christmas Day Hong Kong fell, and within days Singapore was under siege by the victorious Japanese. Most of Burma was gone; the battle for the Philippines was all but lost. In wickedly cold weather made more brutal by a desperate fuel shortage, Britons watched in dismay as the eastern reaches of Empire fell, piece by piece, beneath the merciless blade of Japanese domination. The Jordans were by no means exempted from the national misery. In the middle of February 1942, Singapore fell, and upwards of 85,000 British soldiers surrendered to the savage mercies of an untender enemy. Many simply disappeared without trace. Among these last was Captain Edward Maybury, Libby's husband.

## PART FOUR

*MARCH 1943*

# CHAPTER TWENTY-ONE

The winter, Allie thought with sudden and uncharacteristic pessimism, like the interminable, dreary war, was going to go on for ever. The mild, wet, weeping day held no apparent promise of spring, the London street that she surveyed through the wire-reinforced window of her father's office was shabbily cheerless beneath skies bruised darkly purple by heavy clouds. Across the road the inevitable ruin, fire-scarred and irredeemably ugly, reached skeletal fingers of brickwork and plaster, casualty of a tip-and-run raid. Had there really been a time, she found herself wondering, when London's streets had been whole and unscarred?

Behind her the voice of her cousin George, aggrieved and unpleasant, the words clipped in that pseudo-military way that always irritated her – unreasonably, she knew – rattled inexorably on. Where, asked Allie grimly of the leaden skies, are the air-raid sirens now that I need them? She had never found her cousin anything but pompous, self-opinionated and generally disagreeable. He in his turn, she knew, viewed her with an uncompromising and, she readily admitted, probably justifiable dislike and disapproval that had taken root on the day almost twenty years before when – dared by Richard – she had presented him in the garden at Ashdown with a paper bag of toads, which he detested. That enmity had lain dormant until the day that, to his open dismay, she had joined Jordan Industries, which he considered, Allie was sure, to be his own personal domain.

'. . . the worst kind of sabotage! Shop steward? The man should be in jail! If you remember, Uncle Robert, I tried – God knows I tried – a couple of years ago to—'

'Yes, George, I do remember.' Allie allowed herself a small smile at the tone of her father's voice, which clearly indicated that he also remembered the strikes and near-chaos that had attended his nephew's efforts. Un-surprisingly, the inference went clean over George's smooth fair head; he barely paused for breath.

'The man's a rabble-rouser of the worst order. A ruffian. I can quite see why Allie has difficulty in handling him.'

Allie, her back still to the room, took a long, exasperated breath and hung on to the shreds of her temper.

'She—' George corrected himself stiffly, 'we – should never have given way over the Smithson compensation claim—'

That was too much. 'Good grief, George,' she said wearily, over her shoulder. 'Smithson lost the best part of his right hand through—'

'—his own negligence,' snapped her cousin.

'—through an inadequately guarded cutter.'

'The settlement was too high.'

Allie turned back to the window. 'It would have been higher still if MacKenzie had taken it up.'

'Exactly.' George, to his credit, did his best to keep the satisfaction from his voice. 'MacKenzie again. It's as I said – the man's a saboteur. A Communist agitator. And now this latest . . .'

Robert had looked up sharply. 'A Communist? But – surely – haven't the Communists changed their tune now that Russia is under attack? I understood that Communist trade unionists were now doing their damndest to work for full production and avoid industrial action?'

'That's right. They are.' Allie rubbed at the misted window. 'But MacKenzie isn't that kind of Communist. He's a Trotskyist.'

'Ah,' said Robert.

George snorted. 'What the devil difference does it make

332

what kind of a damned Red he is? He's a disruptive influence and has caused us nothing but trouble.'

Allie cast a look at her father; he voiced her thoughts for her: 'A very great deal of difference, I should have thought,' he said patiently. 'I don't pretend to know the finer points of doctrine – I leave that to Allie – but even I know that Trotsky's followers are not run-of-the-mill Communists. You can't bag them all together like same-sized marbles. Allie?' He looked questioningly at his daughter.

In her year with Jordan Industries, Allie's interest in the politics of her fellow-workers had deepened and strengthened, her earlier instinctive but sometimes ill-reasoned ideals now tempered by practical knowledge and experience. And while her own political leanings were by no means extreme, her father knew she would have been at pains to discover the driving force behind the man with whom, as George had pointed out, she found herself so often at odds.

She nodded. 'The differences are pretty basic, actually. The Trotskyists believe in world-wide, armed revolution. A kind of constant international class warfare if you like, irrespective of national allegiances. They think that all wars between nations are wars of capital, and that workers should refuse to fight in them. According to Trotsky, the only true war is between the ruling and the working classes – in other words, I'd guess that he'd say that a German factory worker and a factory worker on Merseyside would have more in common with each other than with – as he would put it – their imperialist bosses.' She grinned, a little lopsidedly. 'That, unfortunately, is us, believe it or not. There's a good deal of conflict at the moment between the Trots and the Communist Party because the Communists, with Russia under attack and bleeding to death at Stalingrad, have suddenly changed their minds about this particular war and have decided that the workers after all should put their backs into turning out as many tanks, guns and planes as it takes to get Hitler off Stalin's back, apparently regardless of conditions or complaints.' She pulled a wry face. 'When we, in desperation and fear of invasion, put forward the same proposition a couple of years ago, of course they called it exploitation of the workers . . .'

'I still say,' said George, conveying with irritating clarity that he had not attended a word she had said, 'that it doesn't matter what shade of damned Communist he is. He's a menace. He forced us to spend a small fortune on a deep shelter when the one we had supplied was perfectly adequate . . .'

'I never saw you use it.' Allie's voice was brusque, her colour high. 'The Coventry workers are as much in the front line as any soldier in this war, George. They're entitled to protection.'

'Nobody would dispute that. But there's another thing: having acquired this shelter, how does MacKenzie use it? He treats it as his own personal property – a combination of office and soapbox. He turns every enemy attack into a union meeting. Takes every opportunity to preach sedition—'

'Is that true?' Robert asked Allie sharply.

She shrugged. 'Yes.'

George was in full swing now, and not to be stopped. 'He refuses point blank to co-operate with the Joint Production Committee – calls it an "imperialist tool". More of his damned jargon. The man needs to be shown who's master—'

'George, he knows who's master.' Allie had snapped the words before she could prevent herself. 'How could he not? The problem is that he doesn't *like* who's master . . .' And neither do I, said the unspoken words, doing nothing to lessen the hostile atmosphere in the darkening room. 'I'm not defending the man. I'm saying that you handle him badly. He isn't always wrong.'

Robert looked from his daughter to his nephew, sighing, and remained silent.

George, with real dignity, smoothed his already smooth hair and picked up his black Homburg. 'Clearly, Allie, we are never going to agree about this – as, I am forced to say, we do not agree about most things. There is absolutely no doubt in my mind that Alistair MacKenzie should be dismissed from the company's service. And I can only suggest that it would be more fitting for you to consider the well-being of Jordan Industries and of your country before any other – misjudged – allegiances you may have acquired.'

'For God's sake, George, that's what I *am* doing! The Coventry works'll collapse into bloody chaos if you try to sack him, can't you see that? The workers simply won't let him go.'

The pained look on her cousin's face at her unladylike language caught her suddenly and unexpectedly between a furious need to throw the ink pot at his pompous head and an equally strong desire to burst out laughing. She subsided. 'I'm sorry, George, I really am. But you're *wrong* about this, and I'm not going to let you do it. I know MacKenzie's a thorn in your side – how the dickens do you think I feel about him? But you have to accept the fact that he has the support – the admiration even – of his workmates.' She ignored the smothered, derisive sound that George made. 'In 1940, when Coventry was blitzed and half the workforce lost their homes and some of them their families, who helped them? Who set up the relief fund? Who administered it? You? Me? The local authority?' She waited.

George cleared his throat. 'I'm not denying that the man—'

'No. MacKenzie did. In all that shambles *he* organized food, shelter, welfare – his mates don't forget that. Nor have they forgot that he was campaigning against long exhausting shifts well before it became fashionable to call them counter-productive. George, why do you think MacKenzie survived your attempt to have him put in prison under good old Regulation 18B? Because his mates wouldn't have it, that's why. And they won't let him go now.'

George could not keep silent. 'Exactly. Anarchy! I will not be dictated to by a bunch of louts. If we lose the right to manage our own affairs, we lose everything. MacKenzie's a rabble-rouser . . .'

'Agreed. He's also an extremely clever young man.'

George looked at her coolly for a long, silent moment. 'Yes,' he said at last, quietly, but with significant emphasis. 'He is. Sometimes I think you forget that.'

She bit her lip, fighting rising anger again. 'I can handle him.'

'I hope so. I truly hope so.' His point made, George made as if to leave. 'The committee meets next Thursday. I trust you'll be there?'

Allie nodded.

'Perhaps by then Mr MacKenzie will be in a more amenable frame of mind. Though I am bound to say that I doubt it. As far as I'm concerned the JPC is a thoroughgoing waste of everyone's time . . .'

'A point of view that you share with friend MacKenzie,' Allie could not resist pointing out, sweet reason in her voice. 'Could that be why the Coventry shop is the only place that the system isn't working relatively well?'

George turned to the door without answering. 'I have to go. I'm meeting Benson at the club in half an hour. Goodbye, Uncle Robert. Allie, I'll see you on Thursday.'

Allie silently pulled a satisfyingly childish face at his impeccable, departing back. Robert saw his nephew to the door, closed it quietly behind him and stood wordless, surveying his daughter, who had turned back to the window. She ignored the silence for as long as she could, then turned to face him, lifting helpless, apologetic hands, her face a picture of exasperation. 'I'm sorry,' she said with little trace of repentance in her voice. 'I really thought that meeting him here might help.' She smiled half-heartedly. 'I should have known better.'

Robert walked to a heavy mahogany cabinet that housed several display shelves of cut glasses. The shelves designed to hold bottles were empty but for one half-full bottle of whisky. 'Drink?'

'No, thanks. You have one though.' Allie wandered to

her father's desk, perched upon it, one wedge-heeled foot swinging, her fingers drumming the polished wood.

Robert splashed a careful amount into the bottom of a glass. 'With the world in the state it is,' he said ruefully, 'you'd think that I wouldn't greatly care that this is the last of the malt.'

Allie smiled. 'Libby's got some. God knows where from. But it's the real stuff. I'll smile nicely at her for you if you want.'

'Please.' Robert swirled the drink, lifted it, savouring the bouquet before he drank. 'How is she?'

'She's OK. Same as ever. Except – ' she paused ' – well, you know, she really hates the Japanese. Far more than the Germans. She thinks they may be mistreating Edward. The stories you hear . . .'

Robert took a precious mouthful of Scotch, held it for a moment on his tongue, his face thoughtful. 'You know that Edward almost certainly must be dead?' he asked at last, quietly. 'It's been more than a year with no word.'

'Yes. I do know. But Libby simply won't have it. She's absolutely convinced herself that he's still alive. That he'll come back.'

'Yes. Well . . .' Sad shadows flickered in her father's face. 'There's little we can do to help her yet. She has to come to terms with it in her own time. Now – what about your problems? Is MacKenzie really as bad as he sounds?'

'Worse!' She pulled a ferociously glum face. 'He's an absolute pain. But then,' she added uncharitably, 'so's George. The two of them are at each other's throats the whole time.' She slipped from the desk, pulled up a chair and sat in it, her elbows on the desk, a heavy wave of brown hair shadowing a face that had thinned and strengthened to a striking degree in the past year. 'It's like mediating between Custer and the Indians. And just guess who keeps getting the tomahawk in her scalp? You know what my first priority was when I took this job? To get management and workers talking to each other reasonably, instead of fighting like cats and dogs over every little problem. In every other machine shop and factory in Jordan Industries, we've more or less done it – oh, I'm not saying we have no problems; when was the engineering industry ever without problems? – but by and large, Jordan's is establishing a damned good industrial relations record. It helps that we're small, of course, and that quite a few of our workers have been with us for a long time. The Production Committees are working well, the welfare officers – though I don't deny they're still rather resented as busybodies by some of the workforce – are doing a good job. Except at Coventry. And there, thanks about equally to George and to Mr Bloody-Minded MacKenzie, we've got a permanent war on our hands that'd take the Eighth Army, Monty and all, to sort out.'

'What's MacKenzie actually like? What's his background?'

Allie thought for a moment. 'He gives the impression of having drunk in militant trade unionism with his mother's milk. He's from Clydeside. As a boy he was involved with the apprentices' strikes of '37, I think . . .'

'Ah.' Robert's face dropped.

'Exactly. I strongly suspect that he came south and joined us specifically to organize the Coventry shop – though he'd deny it, of course. He's an extremely intelligent and rather terrifying young man who can run rings round George – and more often than not,' she added honestly, 'round me too.' She leaned her chin upon her hand. 'I truly don't understand why so much of politics has to be so extreme. With George on one side and MacKenzie on the other, how's anything ever going to get done? George would preserve the status quo while the ship sinks under him and the water laps his ears—'

'And MacKenzie?'

'I told you. He's a Trotskyist. A revolutionary. But, to his credit, he has stuck to a road that's been hard sometimes, what with the Communists blowing hot and cold. His view is the same as it has always been. His allegiance is not to the Party, nor to Russia, nor to us, but to his class, his fellow-workers. As far as he's concerned, he's

338

fighting the same battle now as was fought – and lost – through the Twenties and the Thirties, and that will be fought again when this little spot of international unpleasantness is over. You have to give the man his due: it hasn't always been an easy stand to take. He sees not a war for national survival but an opportunity offered by full employment – even a shortage of workers in some areas – to improve the lot of his people beyond the point where any gains that are made can be easily taken from them the minute the war stops. As happened in 1918. To be honest, I believe that, if MacKenzie ever found himself faced with a Fascist regime, he'd fight them with the same dedication.' She leaned back a little tiredly, shook her hair out and ran her fingers through it. 'How does it feel to be the lesser of two evils?'

'A Fascist regime would stand him up against a wall and shoot him.'

'True. But then, so would Cousin George if he could.' She grinned, briefly. 'Me too, sometimes.'

Her father was watching her, curiosity in his face. 'Yet I get the feeling that you aren't entirely unsympathetic to this young man?'

She considered that for a moment. 'MacKenzie? No. He's a fanatic, and I very much dislike fanatics. He's cold and calculating, and I honestly don't think I've found the tiniest human failing to recommend him. But I think he has something of a case, yes. You know as well as I do what happened after the last war: Thanks, lads, and back on the dole. A world fit for heroes, indeed! And you also know that a lot of industrialists took a very foolish public stand not so very long before this war broke out: anti-socialist, anti-union, pro-Fascist, even. And people don't forget just because someone's bombing them; well – not people like MacKenzie, anyway.'

'He really sees things that black and white?'

'He really does.' She stood up. 'Alistair MacKenzie is so far to the left that he thinks the Beveridge Plan's a right-wing ploy.' She laughed again. 'And to show you what I'm up against, George thinks it's a left-wing takeover and swears he'll never pay another penny of tax if it's adopted!'

'And you? What do you think?'

'About Beveridge?' Allie, thoughtful, picked up a pair of neatly darned gloves and a rather battered leather handbag. 'I think it would be a start. An essential start. And I think Churchill's being rather short-sighted in not seeing the enthusiasm of ordinary people for the proposals. They'll remember it later, I think – his lukewarm attitude – after the war, when we go back to proper elections.'

'You surely don't agree with the people who say that Labour would win?'

She shrugged. 'Who knows? Stranger things have happened. All right – people now are simply concerned with winning the war, understandably. But later? I don't think that even Beveridge himself realized the popular support his plan would get. It's significant – well, I think so, anyway.' She dropped a quick kiss on his cheek. 'I'll see you next week. I'll be in Coventry from Tuesday to Friday – you can contact me there if you need me.'

'Fine.' He walked her to the door, but before he opened it, he took her hand in his. 'Allie – you're all right? All this isn't too much for you?'

She smiled, shook her head. 'I love it. Most of it, anyway.'

'Give or take MacKenzie?'

'To be truthful – give or take George.' She raised rueful eyebrows. 'I have to keep reminding myself that we're on the same side!' She kissed him again lightly. 'Give my love to Mother – tell her I'll see her next weekend.'

The rain hung like a sodden curtain across the darkening streets. She hesitated on the kerb, contemplating the possibility of finding a taxi, but in a moment, more or less philosophically, turned up her collar against the weather and set off for the nearest Underground station. With the arrival of the well-paid, open-handed GI in war-deprived London, an empty taxi-cab – together with most other luxuries – had become a thing of fond memories. Strap-hanging in the noisy tube train, she ran over the recent meeting in her mind, the recollection of her cousin's neatly handsome features and crisp, over-confident voice goading her, as always, to that ready antagonism that is strongest between people of blood relationship and totally opposite interests and temperament. She sighed, and changed hands. The train rattled, swaying, through the dark tunnels, and then stopped, the dim lights flickering.

"Ere we go again,' said someone.

Allie leaned, swinging slightly, stiff-armed, on the strap, musing. It would not be so bad, she felt, if she had not been so absolutely certain that George's refusal to take her, her ideas or her abilities seriously stemmed not so much from that childhood bag of toads as from the simple – and irrel-evant – fact that she was a woman. To George, the advent of a female into his working life, into the sacred world of boardrooms and business meetings, had been nothing less than an outrage. He had managed bravely to come to terms with women on the engineering shop floor, with women operating London's ack-ack guns, indeed with women tak-ing over all manner of heavy and unpleasant jobs and doing them well. But war or no war, there were, in George's opinion, standards to be maintained, and a woman in man-agement was, in his often-expressed view, taking things too far. That this was one of the few opinions that he shared with the odious MacKenzie made Allie's life no easier, and while she appreciated the irony of that, it did not exactly amuse her.

In one of her first battles with George – over his arbitrary sacking of any woman worker who smoked, wore trousers or used strong language – MacKenzie had refused, laconically, to back her up. He had even, Allie was certain, extracted a good deal of enjoyment from the sight of two Jordans battling in public over an issue he clearly and contemptuously considered beneath him. She wondered what his attitude would be now that those same women had been accepted into a union that, up to a couple of months before, had resolutely refused to have them.

Oddly, it had been that fight – which she had resoundingly won – that had given Allie her first faint insight into MacKenzie's own uncompromising attitudes. He knew from bitter experience that the egalitarian camaraderie of war would not last any longer than it took for the ink to dry on the documents of peace. He knew that hard-won advantages – full employment, steady wages, reasonable conditions – could disappear overnight and, in a bright new world, unemployment, homelessness and hardship be the lot not just of the workers who had stayed in the factories, but of the homecoming men who had been expected to offer even more than their labour to ensure their country's victory. And he would allow nothing to stand in the way of consolidating those victories that a hard-pressed, understaffed industry had to concede in order to keep the war machine rolling.

To Allie, very often, the man's inflexible refusal to take into account what seemed to her to be the realities of the situation – young men like Buzz grounded for want of aircraft while men like MacKenzie fought a wage claim; the Eighth Army, gallant, dogged, victorious, desperately in need of tanks, guns and ammunition; the need to defend a democratic way of life, however imperfect, from the grasping claws of Fascism – was abhorrent. Yet when she heard open preaching against the acceptance of women into a trade union, when she heard of a woman doing a man's job for half the wage, or of a woman refused training for fear her skill might compete with a man's, she felt a stirring of fellow-feeling for MacKenzie's single-mindedness. She accepted that most women would not wish to stay at work once the war was over. But what of those who did? What of the widows, mothers, daughters, whose men had been killed and who would be denied the right to earn a decent living for themselves? What of those who did not want to give up the independence, the prospect of self-determination that their work had, for the first time, given them?

What, indeed, of herself? Could she face the thought of anything less challenging than her present employment? How many others felt the same way? And what could they do about it when the future of their jobs was protected neither by employer nor by union?

The train jerked forward, surprising her out of her reverie. She was astonished to find that her eyelids had drooped and she had almost been asleep on her feet. A soldier sitting not far from her, his kitbag between his knees, grinned sympathetically.

'Here you are, love. I'm getting out at the next stop.'

Gratefully she subsided into the warm seat. Three more stops and she'd be there. And Libby's flat, thank the Lord, was only a step from the station. It amused her to discover that she still thought of the home that she had shared with her sister for more than a year as 'Libby's flat'.

The train clanked to a halt again, hummed agitatedly, pulled off once more.

'Blessed thing,' grumbled the woman next to Allie.

'Air raid up top, I expect,' another voice said.

'We're in the best place, then.'

'Don't you bank on that. You hear what happened over at Bethnal Green the other day?'

Allie made a conscious effort to stop listening. She could not stand to hear yet another version of the persistent rumour of a terrible accident on the staircase of an East End station during the panic of a tip-and-run raid. Some reports said that two hundred people had died, trampled and crushed as shelterers had fled into the station just as the packed trains had disgorged their rush-hour crowds. She found the thought particularly appalling and – in common with many other Londoners – she found it haunted her every time she put her foot on a steep and crowded Underground stairway. The incident had not been reported in the newspapers, but by word of mouth the story had spread like wildfire across the city, too obstinately often repeated to be ignored or dismissed.

"Undreds of 'em, I 'eard,' an old lady was saying, with a certain relish, 'most of 'em women and little 'uns . . .'

Allie concentrated firmly upon a poster admonishing her to look for the squanderbug in her purse, a reproof, she felt wryly, that might have had more impact had she a purse to look in. Her old one had finally fallen to pieces a couple of weeks before and she had so far been unable to find a new one to buy. Presumably the squanderbugs had got them all . . .

When, wet and tired, she finally reached the flat at Rampton Court, she found Libby dressed for the theatre. The Luftwaffe's latest spate of raids, roof-high and in small formations to evade the city's defensive radar screen, and nicknamed 'scalded cat raids', had not ruffled London's theatre-goers but had simply dictated an earlier start.

'How do I look?' Libby twirled on tiptoe.

'Wonderful.' Allie paused at the drawing-room door. 'Isn't that one of the dresses you had for your honeymoon? It looks different.'

'Well, of course, darling. I cut the sleeves back – so – and took a panel from the overskirt to make the bolero—' Libby stopped, shrugged light-heartedly at the expression on her sister's face. 'Oh, all right – *I* didn't actually *do* it – not with my own fair hands, so to speak – but I had the ideas, and Mavis, bless her heart, did her bit with the old needle and cotton.' She twirled again, delightedly. 'Wizard, isn't it?'

Allie smiled. 'If I had your talent for getting other people to work for me, I wouldn't have half the problems I've got. Do you want my job?'

Libby threw up her hands in a not altogether frivolous pantomime of horror. 'Good God, no! At least I can order my little devils about and they do as they're told. Most of the time, anyway. They're positively *petrified* of me.'

'I'll bet.' Allie divested herself of wet coat and shoes.

'By the way, I've borrowed your bag – the gold one – you don't mind, do you?'

Allie shook her head, padded into the drawing room. 'Have a good time.'

344

'Right – off I go – oh!' almost at the front door Libby turned. 'I nearly forgot. Guess who rang this afternoon?'

Allie waited to be told.

'Tom. Tom Robinson, remember? Haven't heard from him in an age. He's been in Wales, or somewhere equally wet and dreary. He's at a loose end tonight – wanted to know if he could pop over – he'd hoped to go to Richard and Celia, but they're out of town.'

Allie stared at her with sinking heart. 'What did you say?'

'Why, I said yes, of course.'

'But, Libby, you aren't going to *be* here.'

'Well, I know that, don't I? But you are – you aren't doing anything, are you? I won't be late. You only have to keep him occupied until I get back.'

'But I—'

'It'll be very entertaining. I intend to pin him down and make him tell me all the scandalous things he's done. Richard's been telling tales.'

'Libby, I was going to have a bath and go to bed. I'm worn out.'

'Oh, for heaven's sake, darling – it's hardly worth having a bath nowadays, what with a few inches of water and the likelihood you might have to dive for cover. Bloody Jerries. I'd quite got used to the quiet. Look – just look after Tom until I get back, there's a dear. Oh – and don't let him drink all my Scotch.' She flitted to the door.

'Libby!'

''Bye, darling. See you later.'

Damn and blast it! Allie stared at the closed door. Damn and bloody blast it; first her cousin George, and now this. Her one quiet, much-anticipated evening to herself ruined. Disgruntled, she stumped into the drawing room, tossed her bag onto a chair, helped herself in righteous wrath to a generous shot of Libby's Scotch and slumped onto the sofa, swinging her feet up. One high-priced, queued-for stocking was thoroughly laddered. Well, that was about par for today's course. She sipped the drink, set the glass down on the floor beside her, tilted her tired head back and closed her eyes. Tom Robinson. Of all people. Difficult, contentious, *clever* Tom Robinson. She had not seen him to talk to for nearly two years. She did not want to see him now. In fact – next to cousin George and Mr Trotsky MacKenzie, she could not think of anyone she wanted to see less. She could not remember a single moment in his company when he had made her feel anything but gauche and ill-at-ease. Well, it wasn't her arrangement. She had decided two fraught days ago that this evening was to be her own – bath, bed and Tolstoy. And by hook or by crook, that was what she would do, Tom Robinson or no. If he came, he would be welcome to the whole of Libby's precious store of Scotch. To himself. And by himself.

She took a long, deep breath, trying to relax, the tension in her neck and along her spine making every movement an effort. She was tired. The world was tired. She closed her eyes.

She started awake in chill darkness. The fire had died to barely glowing ash, the blackout curtains had not been fixed. She felt terrible: cold, stiff and uncomfortable. Muttering, she swung her feet to the floor and buried her face in her spread hands, squeezing shut her aching eyes. Then she stilled, her attention caught by a noise in the hall. She lifted her head, listening, her heart beating a little faster – surely not Libby home already? She couldn't have slept that long?

'Anyone home?' A man's voice, light, distinctive.

Tom Robinson evidently had a key.

'In here. Don't switch the light on yet. The blackout isn't up.' Swearing under her breath she stumbled to the window, stubbing her toe on the substantial coffee table. With the heavy curtains drawn, the darkness was like pitch. 'Do you know where the light switch is?'

'Yes.'

Of course he did. As the dim light clicked on, she blinked, suddenly aware of her dishevelled appearance. Her hair was a bird's nest, her clothes rumpled.

Tom, in uniform, stood in the doorway, smiling collectedly.

'I'm sorry, did I startle you? Libby told me she might not be here, so when no one answered the door, I thought I might as well use the key.' He tossed the key he held onto the coffee table.

'I – I was asleep.'

He grinned sympathetically. He looked neat and spruce and very wide awake indeed. She felt a mess and her head ached. 'May I get you something?'

He hesitated. 'Well – I'd love a cup of tea, if it's not too much trouble – but . . .'

'A cup of tea.' She made a determined effort to collect her scattered wits. 'Yes. I think I can just about manage that.' She padded past him on her stockinged feet, stoically ignoring the amusement in his eyes. In the kitchen she put up the blackout shutter, turned on the light and put the kettle on to boil before glancing in the small mirror which Libby had hung on a cupboard door. God – even in this dim light she looked awful. She ran her fingers through her hair, stuck her tongue out at her reflection.

From the doorway, Tom cleared his throat politely. 'May I help?'

She spun round, red-faced. His expression was grave, his eyes lit with enjoyment. 'I—' Surprising herself, she dissolved into sudden laughter. 'I'm sorry. I feel absolutely *awful*!' She rubbed her hand over her eyes, still giggling. 'Look at the state of me.'

'You look fine to me.'

She shook her head, her laughter subsiding, suspecting mockery.

'Tell you what—' He advanced into the kitchen. 'You go and wake yourself up. I make a fair cup of tea. It's about the only thing I can do.'

In her bedroom she pulled off her rumpled skirt and blouse and put on smart slacks and a warm pullover. Running a comb through her hair, she glanced in the mirror. Her face was very pale and there were shadows beneath her eyes. Quickly she reached for powder and rouge, added a touch of lipstick. There. The thought flitted through her mind that Tom might reasonably suppose these efforts to be for his benefit. She shrugged. Perhaps they were. The fact that she did not always like him very much did not entirely counteract a perversely feminine desire to impress him. She pulled a face at her reflection. Some hopes.

Tom was waiting in the drawing room, smoking a cigarette, two strong and steaming cups of tea on the table. He had coaxed the fire to life again and the room was already warmer. The first thing Allie did was almost to kick over the glass of whisky she had left on the floor by the sofa. That was a good start. With as much aplomb as she could muster, she picked it up and put it on the table. Tom – well-mannered – refrained from comment.

They talked, over their tea, of generalities: of the on-the-whole satisfactory progress of the war, of mutual friends, of Allie's family. Then, without knowing quite how the change of subject came about, Allie found herself talking about her work and he surprised her by listening attentively, questioning and commenting with every appearance of genuine interest. She paused at last, embarrassed to realize that she had been monopolizing the conversation with her own affairs for quite some time. 'I'm sorry. You can't possibly be interested in all this.'

He shook his head, smiling. 'Don't be silly. I'm fascinated. And impressed.'

More pleased than she cared to admit, she settled herself more comfortably on the sofa, tucking her feet under her. 'Well, now it's your turn. What's your news? Libby said you'd been stationed in Wales?'

He leaned back. 'That's right. Training schoolboys to be fighter pilots.'

'Training?' She could not quite keep the surprise out of her voice.

He nodded. 'Quite. Not exactly my cup of tea. But I'm operational again as from now. I made such a nuisance of myself that they've kicked me upstairs and back into action.'

'Kicked you upstairs?'

'Given me a squadron.' His face was impassive.

'But Tom – that's marvellous. Congratulations!'

He shook his head.

'You aren't pleased?'

'Not exactly. I tried to get out of it, but had it made clear that, if I didn't behave myself and do as I was told, I didn't get back into the game. So here I am, Squadron Leader Thomas Robinson. Comic, isn't it?'

'Comic? That's an odd word to use.'

He smiled humourlessly. 'Is it?'

'I think so.' Illogically a laughing ghost rose suddenly between them. 'A good squadron leader can mean a lot to his men.'

He extinguished his cigarette. 'I said they'd made me a squadron leader,' he said gently. 'I didn't say they'd made me a good one.'

The silence was undisguisedly awkward. Allie found that she was fiddling with her wedding ring. It took a physical effort to still her hands and fold them quietly in her lap. 'So,' she said at last, over-brightly, 'where are you stationed?'

His pause was fractional. 'Biggin Hill.'

She flinched. 'And you can't wait to get back into the fray?'

'Something like that.'

'Buzz – ' she cleared her throat ' – Buzz was the same. I could never understand it. Even at the worst times, a day or two away and he was pining.' Silence settled around them. She gazed unhappily into the fire, then lifted her head suddenly and looked at him intently. 'Tom, what is it? I never knew. What's up there for you but fear, and possible death? Why haven't you stayed safely in Wales? Why?' She knew the questions to be painfully personal, saw it in the flicker of his dark lashes, the set of his mouth. For a moment she thought he would not answer, or would turn from the difficult moment with banter. He stood up and walked to the fireplace, stood for a moment frowning into the flames before he turned to face her.

'What's up there? Fear, yes. Unimaginable fear. Possible

349

death – that too. But – a kind of exhilaration. The wildest excitement you can imagine. A challenge. The game of death. Freedom.' He turned back to the fire, his voice low. 'The wildest excitement that you can imagine,' he repeated. 'The plain truth is that I enjoy it. Love it. The risks. The fear, even. The power of life and death – kill or be killed . . .' He turned, caught the look on her face before she could disguise it. His expression changed, the lucent eyes suddenly hard and flat as stone. 'You see what I mean? Hardly the feelings of an officer and a gentleman, would you say?' He reached into his pocket for his cigarettes. 'But then, we both know, don't we, that I'm no gentleman, however many shiny buttons they give me, so I guess it's all right. Don't worry, Allie, I'm sure Buzz's motives were far more admirable.'

She stared at him, shocked by the unnecessary cruelty of that, all her antipathy for the man flooding back. He watched her coolly, the familiar, mocking, shuttered look on his face.

'Little girls shouldn't ask questions they don't want answered,' he said at last, lightly.

She flushed angrily. 'And little boys shouldn't play games that kill people. Whatever the excuse.' The words were out before thought, harsh with disgust.

He regarded her expressionlessly for a long moment. 'I know,' he said and tossed his cigarette into the fire, reaching for his hat which lay on a chair. 'Tell Libby I'll ring next time I'm in town.'

Taken by surprise, she watched him to the door. 'Tom. Don't go.'

He paused. Turned.

'Libby'll kill me if you don't wait.'

He leaned on the door jamb. 'Allie, my love, you've always had a devastating talent for making a man feel wanted.'

It came to her then that his gesture had been more for effect than anything else. He had had no intention of leaving. It was a small and dismal victory, but better than nothing. She made a sharp, exasperated gesture. 'Oh, come and sit down for heaven's sake. Here – ' she slammed the half-full glass of whisky on the table ' – have some of that.'

Dark eyebrows lifted. 'Yes, ma'am.'

To give herself something to do, she got up and with quick, angry movements poured herself a small drink. Tom, glass in hand, had perched on the arm of a chair and was watching her pensively.

'Why,' she asked of the silence, 'do we always finish up damned well fighting?'

'Because you can't stand me,' he said readily.

The words, catching her with a mouthful of whisky, nearly choked her. 'I—'

'You never could,' Tom continued placidly. 'I've always lived in hopes, but . . .' He shook his head slowly, in mock sadness.

She regarded him with the open dislike she had been indignantly about to deny. 'You never take anything seriously, do you?'

'I wouldn't say that.'

She leaned forward. 'Then explain. What makes you think I can't stand you?'

He slid with grace from the arm into the chair, the glass clasped before him, his thin fingers laced around it. When he spoke, it was not apparently in direct answer to her words. 'Do you know what your family used to do to me?' His voice was pleasantly conversational.

She looked at him blankly. 'Do to you?'

'The Jordans – truly – should be pickled in aspic for future generations to study. They have every one of the classic English middle-class defence mechanisms, which come into play the minute an outsider hoves into view. Particularly an outsider that brings with him, perhaps, the faint breath of danger. Of change. Then watch the game begin. The perfect manners. The utter confidence of the godly. The damningly faint interest in anything outside the charmed circle. The conviction of right. The assumption that we all get only what we deserve – oh, a good one that,

351

and worth instilling into others, since it effectively deters them from expecting more. The brick wall between you and anything or anyone who doesn't quite fit into the mould—'

'That isn't fair!'

'Of course it isn't,' he agreed equably. 'It's a gross over-simplification. But have you ever tried to look at yourselves from the outside? I did – because I was very politely never given the opportunity to do anything else. Did it never occur to you that you made me feel totally excluded – an outsider? That you looked down on me not because of who I was but because of what I was?'

'You're wrong,' she said flatly, but somewhere, doubt nibbled.

'It's been known. But I don't think so. I'm not suggesting that you did it deliberately. It's inbred. As automatic as breathing. The right accent, the right name, the right schools . . .'

She shook her head.

'Has Richard ever told you how we met?'

'No.'

'He found me in his room. Accused me of being a thief.'

'Surely not?' Allie could not keep the shock from her voice.

'My room was next to his. I'd made a mistake – it was my first day, and one door looked much like another . . .'

'But it isn't like Richard to—'

'—jump to such conclusions? Allie, Allie, you aren't listening. Don't you see? If my accent had been Winchester or Wellington, the thought wouldn't have crossed his mind. But there I was: badly dressed, badly spoken and defensive. Of course I must have been a thief.'

'What happened?'

'I laid him out. When he came to, I offered to lay him out again. It was the beginning of a beautiful friendship.'

She had to laugh. 'He thinks the world of you.'

A faint colour rose in Tom's face. He tilted the glass in his hand, watched the movement of the liquid with apparent absorption.

'You don't still blame yourself? For – what happened to Richard?'

He did not reply.

'You mustn't, you know. It wasn't your fault.'

'You didn't always think that.'

It was her turn to colour. 'It wasn't your fault that Richard is easily influenced.'

'It was my fault that I influenced him. I'll say one thing, though: it taught me something.' He lay back, tilting his head against the back of the chair and closing his eyes. The faint light gleamed on sharp-cut bone.

'Not to take the responsibility for other people?' she hazarded.

'Something like that, yes.'

'You don't like responsibility.'

'No.'

'Isn't that a bit . . .' she shrugged, half-smiling '. . . irresponsible?'

'Of course it is. My only saving grace is that I take full responsibility for my own actions. Which is more than you can say for most people.'

'That's not a very – friendly – philosophy.'

'It's not a very friendly world.'

She watched him curiously. He opened one eye. 'Is the catechism over?'

She shook her head. He closed the eye again. His dark skin was smooth and clear, his long mouth twitched into a faint smile.

'So – I think that what you are saying is that in fact *you* didn't like *us*,' Allie said, 'and – you think that's why I don't like you?'

'Complicated, but yes. Something like that.'

'But still you used to come.'

'Yes.'

'Why?'

Silence fell. He opened his eyes. 'The truth?'

'The truth.'

'It was – a sort of fascination. A love-hate thing. I

needed you.' It was said simply, with no apparent emotion. 'Though I didn't realize it myself then, and probably wouldn't have admitted it if I had. In a strange way, through Richard, I *was* a part of you. Even though you didn't want me.' There was no self-pity in the words. 'There were things that only you – the Jordans, I mean – could teach me. And you did teach me a lot.'

'None of it good from the sound of it,' she said, softly.

He shrugged. 'It was hardly your fault that I fell between two stools and finished up believing very little and belonging nowhere.' He laughed at the expression on her face. 'Don't look so stricken. It isn't painful. On the contrary.'

'It seems so to me.'

'Well, of course it does. You want to belong. Need to belong. I don't. There's nothing I want to belong to.'

'Not to anything? Or – anyone?'

His gaze was reflective. For some reason it made her uncomfortable. 'I don't understand what you mean about not believing in anything,' she said hastily. 'You certainly did once.'

'Did I?'

'Well, of course you did. You went and fought in Spain.'

'Ah.' His eyes were half-closed, his face deadly serious. 'And knowing myself as I know myself now – who knows why I did that? And dragged Richard with me to – ' a clear spasm of pain crossed his face ' – to deathless glory.' He sat up, leaned forward, rolling the almost empty glass between his hands. 'I guess it was Spain that was the real end for me. In Spain I discovered something that I had suspected all along – that no ideal can survive the human failings of its followers. Religions, political ideologies – they're all infinitely corruptible – all, in the end, prospective instruments of oppression.'

'You're preaching anarchy.'

He made a brief gesture of irritation. 'I'm not preaching anything. Preaching infers an attempt to convert. I'm not trying to convert you. I am – God knows why – attempting to answer your questions and in my own feeble way to explain myself. I would never try to convert anyone. I don't care what others think or believe. I don't expect them to care what I think or believe.'

'And does that work?'

'For me, yes.'

She considered. 'It wouldn't for me.'

'Well, of course it wouldn't. Why should you expect it to?' A slow, attractive smile lit the thin face. 'Let's have another drink.'

She rested her chin on her hand and watched him pour the drinks, aware, suddenly, that she was enjoying herself. She laughed. 'Do you remember the time you caught me at Daddy's Madeira?'

'I do.'

'That was when I told you you weren't a gentleman.'

'That's right.'

'I was a pain.'

'You were unhappy.'

She lifted surprised eyes. 'You knew that?'

'Let me hazard a guess.' He sat beside her, proffering her drink, smiling still, and she was struck, forcefully and unexpectedly, by the capricious attraction of the man. What did the old nursery rhyme say? 'When he was good he was very very good, and when he was bad he was . . .'

'I would guess that you'd discovered what was going on between your father and Celia.'

She sat like a statue. '*You knew?*'

He nodded.

'But – how?'

'You'd have to be blind and deaf not to.'

'I don't think Libby and Richard ever knew.'

'I'm sure they didn't. But in a way – they were blind and deaf.'

'And – Mother?' How often had she wondered that?

'I don't know. I sometimes thought she must suspect something.' He paused, added quietly, 'It really knocked you for six, didn't it?'

She looked at the glass in her hand, nodded slightly.

'Poor little Allie.' His voice was very soft.

'I – it was pretty awful for a while. Like – I don't know – like not being me. I didn't think I'd ever forgive them.' She smiled, a little wanly. 'What a cheek children have got. It's funny, isn't it – Celia finishing up with Richard? I wasn't happy about it at first. But she's been so very good for him. I think she really loves him.'

'And you don't hate her any more?'

She shook her head.

He had moved closer to her and was studying her face with a single-minded attention that suddenly brought blood to her cheeks. For a moment she had the absurd idea that he was going to kiss her – and, as the thought occurred, she knew that she wanted him to, very much indeed.

'Allie?' He reached for her hand. His touch shocked her, oddly. Her heart thumped irregularly. In heaven's name, what was she doing? This was Tom Robinson. Exasperating, overbearing, by all accounts womanizing – her mind paused uncomfortably upon that thought – Tom Robinson –

'Yes?'

'I wanted to ask you . . .' His voice was warm, a little uncertain.

'What?' Then, too late, she saw the graceless gleam in his eyes, the familiar, mocking line of his mouth.

He grinned heartlessly, kissed lightly the hand he held. 'You've managed a whole half-hour without metaphorically scratching my eyes out. You wouldn't like to let me know what I've been doing right, would you – for future reference so to speak.'

She snatched her hand away. 'You!'

The front door slammed. 'Where is everybody?' Libby's voice.

'In here.' Allie stood up, her movements wooden, the fury of self-induced embarrassment in her face.

Tom, the laughter gone, caught her hand. 'Allie—'

She pulled away from him. 'You've had your fun. I hope you enjoyed it. I'm going to bed.'

He opened his mouth, closed it without speaking, shrugged. 'As you like.'

'Hello there.' Libby appeared in the doorway, Peter Wickham leaning on his stick behind her. 'Tom, you naughty thing, where have you been hiding? We haven't seen you in *ages*. Allie – be a darling and get us a drink?'

Tom stood up easily. 'I'll do it. Allie was just about to go to bed.'

She glared at him, seething, and received his most charming smile in return. Trapped, as he had known she would be, by her own stubbornness, with ill grace she said her goodnights.

Peter kissed her gently on the cheek. 'I hear you're having trouble with MacKenzie again?'

'Nothing I can't handle.' She hoped that no one else recognized that there was rather more bravado than conviction in the words. She did not look at Tom.

'You're doing a marvellous job. Your father must be proud of you.'

'We're all proud of her.' Libby kissed her lightly. 'But she's wearing herself out. You're right, darling – off you go and get a good night's sleep.' Feeling like a child packed off to bed at an adults' party, Allie caught sight, over Libby's slim shoulder, of a derisive spark of laughter in a pair of pale eyes.

It was later, lying in bed and staring into darkness in an infuriating state of sleeplessness, that an uncharitably satisfying thought occurred to her. Tom Robinson, for all his self-assurance, his apparent disdain for the world, its works and its opinions, had a chip on his shoulder a mile wide.

But somehow, even the malicious gratification that she derived from the realization that he too was human, and vulnerable, no matter how he might try to hide it, in no way compensated for the disturbing discovery she had made about herself that evening.

# CHAPTER TWENTY-TWO

'I'll no' be a part of a face-saving exercise to cover up management's exploitation of the workers. Neither am I about to let George Jordan get away with cutting my members' wages. That's flat, Miss Jordan, an' there's no' a damn thing you can do about it.'

Allie, very, very carefully, placed the pencil she had been fingering down at right angles to her blotter. 'Mr MacKenzie.' Her voice – astoundingly – was perfectly calm. 'In the first place, the Joint Production Committee is not a face-saving exercise, as you call it. I must say that I find it both disappointing and absurd that, after all these months, you still refuse to see the value of co-operation – *co-operation*, Mr MacKenzie,' she emphasized the word, 'between workers and management. It cannot have escaped you that in many engineering shops, it is, in fact, the management who have refused to set up a committee?'

'Aye. When they've discovered that the workers won't stand for a gaffer's committee. As we won't, Miss Jordan.'

She ignored the terse interjection. 'Both the government and the unions are supporting the scheme. If you continue to refuse to co-operate, then I'm afraid I shall have no alternative but to ask your men to elect someone else who will. In the second place,' she continued evenly, giving him no time to interrupt, 'the new bonus scheme is not a cut in wages. It is simply a restructuring of the present, somewhat complicated system of—'

'Hah!' The exclamation was a compound of disbelief and contempt. 'An' do ye no' think we've heard that before? Go back and do your homework, Miss Jordan. Ask your precious cousin why he's pushing this new scheme so hard.'

Allie looked at him in silence for a moment. Alistair MacKenzie was a young man of medium height and build, with a thatch of fine, sandy hair and a closed, clever face. The sharp blue eyes within their fringe of pale lashes seemed to Allie to be lit with a permanent hostility that she found both exasperating and wearying, and his readiness to take – or give – offence was in every quick movement, every lift of his head. It made matters considerably worse that she often found it difficult to follow his quick-fire speech with its strong Glaswegian accent – an accent that she had tried, unsuccessfully, to convince herself did not become more marked and difficult when he addressed her. She looked now into the bright, intolerant eyes and a little of her confidence deserted her as an uncomfortable suspicion wormed through her mind. Cousin George most certainly had been extremely eager to see the new bonus scheme put into effect, and despite good intentions, she had not had time since he had dropped the idea on her to give it anything but the most cursory attention. Discretion being the better part of valour, she changed the subject. 'One more thing,' she said and paused, marshalling careful words. She would not give him the satisfaction of detecting overt disagreement between herself and George. 'Mr Jordan has asked me to mention the matter of the union meetings you hold in the new shelter each time there is an air raid. He finds it – inappropriate.'

'Oh, aye. You'd rather the men played cards and lost their wages, would you?'

'Mr MacKenzie, you aren't listening to me. I said that Mr Jordan asked me to bring the matter up. And I have. For myself,' she sat back in her chair, watching him thoughtfully, 'I see no reason why you should not use the time for union business. On two conditions. One – that you don't then take up unnecessary working hours as well. Two – that nobody is forced to attend a meeting against his will. Apart from that . . .' She smiled, trying to soften the man, to bring out at least some faintly human response. He regarded her with stony suspicion. 'Apart from that, I would simply ask you to be a little circumspect. Mr Jordan, as you know, has very strong convictions.'

359

He stood up. 'As have we all, Miss Jordan. I'll bid you good day.'

He was half-way to the door before she could bring her flaring anger under control. 'Mr MacKenzie!'

The man stopped, turned.

'My name – as I believe you well know – is not Miss Jordan. It's Webster. Mrs Webster. I would ask you please to accord me the courtesy of remembering that in future.'

'Aye. I'll do that, Miss – Mrs Webster.' He shut the door behind him very quietly.

She sat absolutely still, her hands fisted on the desk before her. Odious man. Pigheaded, unpleasant, odious man! But she had not liked the look in his eyes when he spoke of the bonus scheme. There was only one person to speak to about that . . .

She stared at her cousin's handsome face – a face that at the moment was undeniably a little pinker than usual. George passed a suspiciously nervous hand over his slick hair.

'Are you – trying to tell me –' she could hardly keep from shrieking the words ' – that MacKenzie's *right?*'

'For goodness' sake, Allie, you're making too much of this—'

'*Is he?*'

He hesitated. 'It depends which way you look at it. For some men, yes, the new bonus scheme may not – work quite as well as for others.'

She battled for composure. 'You told me – assured me – that no one would be the worse off through the new scheme, that indeed most – *most* – workers would benefit. Are you now telling me that this isn't the case?'

'I – didn't have all the figures when we spoke before.'

'Good God, George, you're supposed to be running this bloody place! And you're trying to tell me that you didn't know it would work to the disadvantage of the mèn?'

He did not reply.

'You've put me – us – in an impossible position. You're a fool, George, you know that? A bloody fool!'

360

He sat up at that. 'Oh, I say, that's a bit thick. There's no need to be offensive, surely? I'm just trying to do my best for the company. This scheme would have worked – the men would have accepted it if that meddling good-for-nothing hadn't—'

'—seen right through you. As he always does.' Allie let out a slow breath. 'When are you going to wake up, George? When are you going to realize that times are changing – have to change? You aren't dealing with a bunch of illiterate, unquestioning, desperate men who are dependent on your bounty for their living.'

'And I suppose that pleases you.' His voice was waspish.

'Indeed it does. I see nothing ennobling in humiliation. Nor yet in – ' she paused ' – financial sleight-of-hand. The new bonus scheme is out, George. O–U–T. *Out*.' She stood up, reached for her bag.

'I think that's for me to decide,' he said, stiffly. 'As you so rightly pointed out, it is I who run this works.'

She stabbed a finger, her patience exhausted. 'Try it. Just try it. I'll go over your head. I'll go *under* it. I'll explain to our working committee how you tried to diddle them.'

He flushed. 'Honestly, Allie, I don't know what's got into you. I don't think sometimes you know yourself which side you're on.'

She was at the door. Opened it. 'I'm on the side of reason, George.' Her smile held very little humour. 'The losing side.' She shut the door a lot harder than MacKenzie had shut hers.

A couple of hours later, as she sat on a dirty and crowded station platform, she was still seething. No doubt by the time she got to London, George – pompously outraged – would have been on the telephone to her father to complain of her handling of the affair of the bonus scheme. She sighed. She supposed that, in a way, she really had not done very well. She shouldn't have lost her temper . . .

Pale April sunshine gleamed through a hole in the dirty, bomb-damaged roof. At least spring had arrived at last. She had hardly noticed it in the city – had been surprised the previous weekend on a visit to the Jessups in Kent, by the carpets of bluebells, the pleasant warmth of the sun. The countryside had looked lovely, the green fields and flowered woodlands seeming even more beautiful in contrast to the sadness of the occasion. Charlie Jessup was dying. Several operations had sapped the old man's strength and failed to arrest the cancerous growth that was killing him. Allie and Sue had gone together to visit him, knowing from Rose that it would be the last time they would see their old friend. He'd been weak but still in full command of his senses. He'd grinned wickedly to hear of Allie's problems. 'That's what you get, my girl, for meddling in a man's world.'

'Charlie Jessup!' Rose had been scandalized.

Allie had laughed. 'A man's world? Maybe. But not for much longer, Charlie. Things are changing . . .'

'Not fast enough for you, though, eh?' He had laughed, lost his breath, coughed agonizingly. 'Just remember, girl,' he'd wheezed at last, lying against the pillow, grey with pain, still smiling, his eyes twinkling, 'one swallow don't make a summer . . .'

She sighed now a little dispiritedly. Change. She had told George that times were changing. But were they, really? Or was it simply the exigencies of war that gave the appearance of change? Would the world just slip back into its bad old ways when peace came again? Would anyone care? And what could anyone – least of all Allie Webster – do about it?

A train whistle shrieked and an engine, trailing its snaking tail of crowded coaches, shunted into a platform. She glanced at her watch. The connection to London was late. Again. Her mind wandered back to the weekend. It had been good to see Sue again. There was someone who had not changed – laughing, restless, reckless, seemingly irresponsible. Yet even she had allowed Allie a glimpse of a more sober side to her character. She had been light-heartedly recounting her latest adventure with one of her apparent army of admirers: '. . . and, damn me, there was poor Johnny still waiting on the blessed corner! I'd forgotten all about him!'

'Poor man! Sue, you're impossible! When are you going to settle down?'

The laughter had gone from the blue eyes. 'While this stinkin' war's on, never,' she had said, flatly and unexpectedly. 'We don't all have your guts, you know, love.'

'Guts?'

'What else do you think it was that gave you those months with Buzz? I couldn't do it.'

'But—'

'But nothing. The minute I feel my temperature rising I run a mile.'

'You mean – you think you can actually stop yourself from – from loving someone? From – ' her own problem in mind, Allie had struggled for the right word, 'well, from – wanting them?'

'Of course you damn well can. Take my word for it.' Sue had grinned mischievously. 'You just have to work at it a bit. With a bit of help from a friend . . .'

A plume of steam in the distance signalled the approach of the London train. People reached for luggage, moved to the edge of the platform expectantly. A slightly built young man in RAF uniform almost tripped over Allie's feet, apologized with a smile. She smiled back, stood up, swung her battered bag onto her shoulder. He had reminded her – as everything lately seemed to remind her – not of Buzz, but of Tom Robinson. His face, enigmatic, mocking, infuriating, was as clear in her mind as if he had been sitting beside her. She wished she could subscribe to Sue's belief that a violent attraction such as had so unexpectedly materialized from apparent antagonism that night in the flat could be easily dismissed. It's easy enough, she found herself thinking now, to run away – as long as your desires turn up in a box, neatly ribboned and labelled, so you know what to run from . . .

Libby, as blithely blind as ever she had been, had invited Squadron Leader Tom Robinson to dinner tonight.

* * *

He was, beneath a veneer of good manners, in the worst mood she had ever known him to be. Even Libby noticed it.

'Really, Tom, you are being most terribly tiresome. We haven't seen you for weeks, and here you are like a bear with a sore head! It isn't very entertaining of you.' Her voice was light but, as so often lately, there were lines of strain around her eyes.

'I'm sorry.' Tom looked tired. And more: there was a kind of tension in him that bespoke an obstinately held control over intolerably stretched nerves. Allie picked at her unappetizing meal. The evening had turned out, if possible, to be even worse than she had expected. She had hardly been able to bring herself to look at him, while for his part it seemed to her that she might just as well not have been in the room.

'So I should hope,' Libby said, not in the least mollified. 'I can't offer you coffee, I'm afraid, and I strongly suspect that the brandy isn't brandy, but it's drinkable . . .'

Tom stood up. 'I'm sorry. I can't stay. I have to be back for a briefing tonight. There's a truck coming through in half an hour. I've arranged a pick-up.' He bent to kiss Libby's cheek. 'Thank you for the meal. I know how hard it is.' The light eyes flicked to Allie. His face was impassive. 'Good night.'

She nodded.

'I'll see myself out.'

As the front door closed behind him, Libby pulled a face. 'My God. The day the war gets to Tom Robinson we're really in trouble.'

Allie ran her finger round the rim of her empty water glass. 'I don't think it's the war. It's this squadron leader thing. He hates it. The responsibility.'

'Could be.' Her sister regarded her for a moment. 'And what in hell's name's wrong with you?' she enquired pleasantly. 'You hardly said a word all evening.'

'I'm tired.'

'We're all tired. Toss you for the washing up.'

'With your double-headed penny?'

'Of course. What else?'

'Heads,' Allie said.

A fortnight later, having survived all the hazards that the Germans had provided for her, Myra slipped on a flight of steps and broke her ankle. Predictably, she did not make a good patient, and equally predictably, since she absolutely refused to give up her own personal crusade against Hitler, both Allie and Libby found themselves, despite their own commitments, unceremoniously roped in to substitute for her. So it was that in a London cheered enormously by Allied victories in North Africa, Allie found herself serving tea, sorting clothes and handing out advice as if she had nothing else to do with her spare time – which, in fact, she had to admit was precisely the case. There was, however, one very great advantage to the situation; her mother's car, because of her WVS work, was plentifully supplied with petrol, and on some occasions – when she was able by a slight stretching of credibility to combine her own work for Jordan Industries with deliveries, collections or other errands for the Voluntary Service – she experienced the almost forgotten luxury of driving along roads almost empty but for public-service vehicles and army convoys, instead of fighting for a seat on an overcrowded and uncomfortable train.

One Sunday afternoon she was packing her small case for just such a trip when the telephone rang.

'Hello, Pudding? Richard. Got a small favour to ask.'

'Of course. What is it?'

'Mother tells me you're motoring down Tonbridge way later on this afternoon?'

'That's right. I've a meeting tomorrow.'

'Do me a favour, love, and drop a couple of hangovers off at Biggin Hill on the way? We've had Tom and one of his mates up here for the weekend. They really hung one on last night – a bit fragile today. I thought – well, door to door's one up on hitching a ride in a jeep.'

'Well – I—'

'Come on, Pud. Robbie's got to be back by nine, and you must be going right past the place?'

He was right. She could invent no reasonable excuse. She had not seen Tom in more than a month; the prudent half of her did not want to see him now. 'Of course. Can they be ready in half an hour?'

She heard the smile in her brother's voice. 'As ready as they'll ever be.'

Half an hour later, she saw what he meant. Tom, though as always impeccably neat and tidy, still somehow managed to look as if he had been up all night every night for a week, and his young friend, Flight Lieutenant Robbie Gower, winced each time he moved his tousled fair head.

'Off you go.' Celia, her hand as always lightly upon her husband's arm, smiled at them both, cheerfully unsympathetic. 'I'm sure Allie will avoid the potholes if you ask her very nicely.' She looked well and happy, her red hair grown longer and softer, her smile ready. Allie, acknowledging the near-miracle she had worked upon Richard, no longer felt any resentment towards her. It seemed to her sometimes that the events, so long ago at peacetime Ashdown, that had come between them were part of another lifetime. She and Celia were, if not actually bosom friends, at least much more than the wary antagonists they had been a couple of years before.

Robbie, two buttons of his uniform jacket undone and his tie slightly askew, brightened up considerably at the sight of Allie. 'I say! Are you our chauffeur? Jolly sight better-looking than the old man's, I must say – ' he blushed a little ' – if you don't mind my saying so?' He looked a boy, fresh-faced and fair.

She smiled. 'I don't mind. In you get.'

With an eager agility that belied the fragile pallor of his fair skin and the bruises of over-indulgence beneath his eyes, he scrambled into the front passenger seat. Allie, her smile still commendably in place, looked at Tom. He was spruce and composed, and only his eyes and the line of his mouth betrayed him. She had not realized until that moment how very much she had wanted to see him.

366

'You're sure we aren't taking you out of your way?'

'Of course not. I'm going right past the door.'

'You don't have to go right to the camp – you can drop us off outside the village, if you'd prefer. Rob's family have a cottage there – we use it when we're off duty.'

'Fine.' She watched him as he opened the back door of the little Austin and slid into the back seat, then turned to kiss Richard goodbye. He smiled at the soft touch of her lips. 'Take care.'

'I will.'

Robbie, his state of health apparently miraculously improved by female company, talked almost non-stop. Boyish and ebullient, he told her his life history and that of his family, discussed flying tactics and the finer points of the Austin with about equal enthusiasm and demanded nothing but the odd, smiling word in return. Released from the necessity of real comment, even, unkindly perhaps, the necessity of listening, Allie studied Tom in the driving mirror. He sat very still, his head turned to the window, taking no part in the conversation, apparently absorbed in the panorama of London's wrecked streets. After a while she saw his eyelids droop, his head loll, watched as he snapped awake, a spasm of irritation on his face. Three times it happened before, finally, he gave in, settled himself against the leather upholstery, and slept, the sharp-boned face relaxed at last.

She waited a good ten minutes before asking, quietly and abruptly, 'You know Tom well?'

Robbie, caught almost in mid-sentence, looked a little surprised. 'Pretty well, yes.'

'You're in his squadron?'

He shook his head.

'You're just – friends?'

His boy's face lit. 'I should say so. You know – I reckon Tom to be the finest flyer I've ever known. Or ever likely to for that matter.'

'You know the men of his squadron?' She knew it was unforgivable to quiz him so; knew it and did not care.

'Most of them, yes.'

'Do they find him as – easy to get along with, would you say?' She kept her voice light.

He paused, caught. 'I – er—'

'Most of them call me the "Flying Razor Blade". Behind my back, of course.' The voice from the back seat was mild. 'Does that answer your question?'

She felt the warmth of embarrassment rise in her face. She did not answer, concentrated on the road ahead. Robbie cleared his throat and held his tongue for a full three minutes before starting again. When Allie brought herself to glance in the mirror, Tom, apparently, was fast asleep once more.

It was gone seven o'clock and they were nearing their destination when they found themselves tailing an army convoy. Ten frustrating minutes later, with no warning, two Junkers found them.

The first Allie knew of the attack was the quick lift of Tom's head, his hand hard on her shoulder. 'Stop the car!'

A second after he had detected it, she too heard the high-pitched scream of a dive-bombing plane.

'Into the ditch!'

She flung open the car door and took a flying leap into the ditch by the side of the road. From the camouflaged lorries and trucks uniformed men tumbled, swearing and shouting, diving for cover. Someone yelled unintelligible orders. A machine-gun ripped, tearing the air, and the wild shock waves of an explosion laid Allie bruisingly flat as the enemy aircraft roared overhead, low enough for the pilot to be seen clearly in his perspex cockpit. Bullets ricocheted, screaming.

'Keep down!' Tom yelled in her ear, entirely unnecessarily, and laid an arm like a steel bar across her shoulders.

The crack of rifle fire echoed up and down the country road.

'Look out! 'Ere comes the other bugger!'

Allie felt the pressure of Tom's arm ease as he lifted his head to look for the threat.

'Get yer 'ead down, Brylcreme, or it'll get shot off,' said a voice, not without some grim enjoyment. It was a byword in the other services that flyers hated to be on the receiving end of an air attack.

Allie, from the corner of her eye, saw Tom's quick grin, then he was on top of her, his body shielding hers as the second raider howled in, spitting death. Somewhere not far away someone screamed horribly. Unable to move, her cheek pressed painfully into the coarse grass and stony mud in the bottom of the ditch, she squeezed her eyes shut.

Another explosion, and another. Someone was swearing, very inventively, in a steady monotone. Orders were shouted, there were more rifle shots, and again the bedlam of a machine-gun. Her face hurt badly and she could hardly breathe. She found herself thinking that, for a man as slight as he was, Tom seemed to weigh a ton. As slight as he was; in her mind's eye she saw suddenly the breadth and length of his exposed back. Oh God – please God – she struggled to free herself.

'Keep still, dammit!'

Another run and it was over. 'The Seventh Cavalry's arrived,' commented a soldier, laconically, one sardonic eye on Tom's uniform, 'an' not before time, as per.'

The Junkers had lifted and turned, pursued by a small formation of Hurricanes. As they watched, in the distance the little fighters overhauled their slower prey and streaked into the attack. Tom meticulously brushed himself down. Allie, not to be outdone in coolness, glanced down ready to do the same.

'Lord!' she said, appalled. Her pale green dress was filthy, her stockings torn, and one shoe was gone.

A little way along the road, brusque orders were given and a sagging, bloody bundle was lifted from the ditch. The lane was cratered in both directions. Figures rose sheepishly from the hedge-sheltered ditches on either side of the road. Allie watched in awful fascination a blood-soaked apparition that rose and staggered just yards from her. 'Bastards!' it said. 'Bastards! Bastards!' She turned away.

'Back in the car,' Tom said gently, proffering her missing shoe. 'The army's got everything under control. We're just in the way.'

'Pretty decent bit of flying that.' Robbie was leaning against the Austin's bonnet. He looked very pale indeed; Allie wondered if he had been sick. 'Our boys got one of them though, did you see?'

'Excuse me, miss.' Allie turned to find a young army officer at her elbow. 'Are you all right?'

She nodded. 'Yes, thank you.' She was astonished at the normality of her voice.

'How long before we can move on, Captain?'

The young man turned at Tom's question, shrugged. 'Half an hour or so, I'd guess. Give or take a few minutes. We've some holes to fill in first.'

It was, in the event, closer to an hour and a half. Robbie, now recovered, fumed.

'Don't be daft, man.' Tom, apparently relaxed, leaned back, his eyes closed. 'There's nothing you can do about it.'

'Damn it – I'm due back at nine. I could have bloody walked it in the time—'

'This way, miss.' A lanky private had appeared by the driver's window. 'We've patched it up OK. Captain says, would you like to go ahead?'

'Thanks.' Allie nosed the little car past the camouflaged lorries, aware of the interested stares of their occupants. 'I'll drop you at the gates of the camp if you like,' she said, soothingly, to Robbie, who sat bolt upright beside her. 'We'll get you there in time, don't worry.'

'That'd be jolly decent of you. Thanks.'

She dropped him at the gate. 'Where to now?'

Tom had moved into the vacated front seat. 'Well, I was going to offer to walk from here – the cottage isn't far – but I'd guess that you'd like to tidy yourself up and perhaps change before you go on?'

'I would, rather.'

'Straight ahead, then, and the lane on the left. The cottage is about a mile on.'

They drove in silence until, on Tom's instructions, she pulled up outside a small house set back behind a high hedge. The June evening had cooled considerably, though thanks to the government's manipulation of the clocks, the sun had not yet set. A light, chill breeze whispered through the stirring, shaded woodland on the rise of land beyond the cottage. Tom let them both in, pointed her in the direction of a latched door, handed her her small suitcase. 'Bedroom's in there. There's a small sink. I think you'll find everything you need. I can offer you NAAFI beer or burnt acorn coffee. Any preference?'

'The coffee, please.'

He grinned. 'You may live to regret that. Ready in five minutes.'

Which was more than she was. Finally, in despair, she gave up the unequal struggle with a face that still bore unmistakable signs of its unexpected confrontation with a ditch bottom, and joined him in the small sitting room that overlooked the garden. It was shadowed and dappled with late-evening sunshine. Tom had taken off his jacket, loosened his tie and shirt collar and was sitting in a deep, comfortable armchair, a glass of beer in one hand, the other perfectly still on the arm of his chair. She stood for a moment watching the profile that was etched sharply against the dying light. Sensing her presence, he turned and, ignoring her quick gesture of protest, stood up politely. She moved to the chair opposite his and sat down, her scratched cheek turned away from him. Self-consciously she smoothed the material of her skirt, cursing the necessity of travelling with only one pair of stockings. Her business-like white shirt and plain dark skirt – intended for wear at the meeting the next day – felt both unflattering and out of place. He sat down again, smiling.

'Your coffee . . .'

She sipped, and almost choked. He laughed aloud. 'Don't say I didn't warn you. God only knows where Robbie found it. It's foul. Here – ' he held out a glass ' – the beer's marginally better.'

It was. She sipped it, thankfully.

'Face hurt much?'

She shrugged. 'A bit.'

He watched her, smiling, then unexpectedly lifted his glass to her. 'Congratulations.' His voice was quiet.

'On?'

'Bravery under fire.'

'I was scared stiff actually,' she said honestly. 'I just didn't have time to show it.'

'I guess many a hero's said the same.'

She shook her head, smiling. In the distance they heard the low drone of a large formation of aircraft. Tom turned his head, listening. 'Ours,' he said. 'Lancasters from the sound of it.'

'Do you think it's working? Bombing the German cities, I mean?'

He shrugged. 'Who knows?'

It was becoming darker by the minute. She glanced around the room. 'This place belongs to Robbie's family?'

'That's right. It's jolly convenient. We use it sort of unofficially, if we want a bit of peace and quiet. I spend quite a bit of time here.'

'May I ask you something?'

'Of course.'

'Isn't Robbie a little – well, young for you? A little – inexperienced?'

Real amusement rang in his laughter. 'Afraid I'm leading the poor little lamb astray? Don't you believe it. No one's too young in this man's army. Robbie's all right. And, let's say, he makes an undemanding drinking companion . . .'

'He thinks you like him.'

'I do.'

'—and hero-worship is hard to resist?' The moment she had spoken she thought the words were too harsh. 'I'm sorry,' she said, quickly.

He regarded her pensively. 'Has anyone ever told you that you say sorry far too often?'

'No.'

'Well, somebody's telling you now,' he said pleasantly.

They sat in not unfriendly silence. The sun had gone now, leaving a rosy light in the sky and a faint sheen of gold in the lace of the tree tops.

'You're very quiet?'

She stirred, spoke her thoughts candidly, her brow furrowed. 'I was just thinking. About this afternoon. It only just seems to be sinking in. We could have been killed, couldn't we?'

'Yes. Takes a bit of getting used to, doesn't it?' A match flared in the gathering darkness. She looked at him in the flickering light, astonished to discover that every line of his face, every movement of his spare body was familiar to her. Had he really been in her mind and memory that much?

'I ought to go,' she said.

'Oh, stay a while. You've been through a tough time this afternoon. In fact – it occurred to me – ' he leaned forward, cigarette glowing ' – there's no reason why I shouldn't go back to camp for the night. I'm on duty at six anyway. You could stay here in peace – get a good night's sleep—'

'Oh, I couldn't possibly put you out so . . .'

'Nonsense. You aren't trying to say that you'd rather drive on?'

'Well – no – but—'

'It's settled, then.'

'You're sure?' She could not keep the relief from her voice. She knew that she would not now have reached Tonbridge in daylight, and the thought of hotel-hunting in the blackout did not appeal at all.

'I'm sure.'

She relaxed, leaning back in her chair, sipping her beer. In the peace of the evening, the events of the afternoon seemed all at once like events from a nightmare. Without volition she found herself recalling the indescribable noise, the terror. A bloodstained figure loomed, staggering – 'Bastards! Bastards!' She shuddered.

'Are you all right?' His voice was quiet.

'Yes. Fine.' But she was not. Her sudden and unexpected loss of nerve was in her trembling voice. She clenched her hands hard. Stupid!

There was a movement in the dimness and he was beside her, perched on the arm of her chair, her shaking hands grasped hard in his. 'Don't worry, it's a natural reaction. Don't think about it. It's over. We're all right. Nothing happened.'

She remembered the sodden bundle that had been lifted from the ditch. A man is dead. Nothing happened? Oh, God, the world really has gone mad. She ducked her head, tears stinging. Tom lived through this or something like it almost every day of his life. As had Buzz. And Buzz had died. She bowed her wet cheek to the warm hands that held hers, felt his sudden stillness at the intimacy of the gesture. For the space of a dozen heartbeats they sat so. Then she lifted her head. 'I'm sorry.' She could hardly see him in the darkness.

A long finger brushed her sore face, smudging the tears. 'I thought I told you,' Tom said pensively, 'to stop saying sorry?' His face was not a hand's breadth from hers. She sat quite still, head tilted back, waiting, sensing his hard-held control, willing it to break. He hesitated, obviously expecting her to move away.

'Tom?' She did not care that her voice begged, would, she knew, have begged had he demanded it.

He kissed her then, softly and carefully, as gently as if she had been an unpredictable child, easily frightened. In two long years no one had touched her so. A surge of physical excitement flooded her, painfully urgent. She lifted a hand, pulled his mouth hard against hers and then, feeling his faint, surprised resistance, with a subtlety she had not known she possessed, released him, her fingers light on the nape of his neck, her lips soft. This time it was he who, suddenly and fiercely, pulled her to him. Moments later he let her go and stood up, abruptly. She sat, touching with her tongue that place on her lip where his teeth had bruised her, and waited. She heard him move across the room, heard the

374

swish of the long curtains. Then a small, shaded light clicked on. He stood in the shadows, watching her, his straight, dark hair untidy across his forehead.

A long moment passed in perfect stillness.

'I think I'd better go,' he said, carefully.

'No.' Her voice was clear and perfectly steady.

'Allie . . .'

'You don't have to.' She had never dreamed that she could want anything as much as she wanted his touch at that moment. 'Stay.' She lifted her chin, her cheeks burning. 'Please?'

'Allie – you don't mean that . . .' He moved towards her, stopped, more uncertain in his movements than she had ever seen him. 'You've had a bad fright. You don't know what you're saying—'

'I know perfectly well what I'm saying. I'm – asking you – ' she almost lost her breath to that, had to make a physical effort to control her voice ' – not to go. I mean it, Tom.' She was trembling. Would he never move? Don't make me ask again. Please don't.

The distant sound of a plane buzzed in the silence.

She stood up but would not – could not – move towards him. He was frowning, studying her. 'You really mean it.'

'Yes.' She saw the flicker in his eyes, knew the mounting excitement that matched her own. Yet still he did not move.

'No,' he said.

She flinched as if he had slapped her.

He flicked his hair from his eyes, not looking at her.

'Why not?'

He did not answer.

'Tom, why not?'

'Because – because the time isn't right – the reasons aren't right—' There was an edge of desperation in the words.

'How do you know that? How can you know it?'

He spread his hands into the distance between them. 'Allie, try to understand. I can't commit myself. My life is not my own—'

'I'm not asking for your life. I'm not asking for a commitment. I'm asking you to stay with me. Tonight.'

He looked at her, long and steady. Shook his head. 'You won't understand, will you? I can't.'

'Won't, you mean.' Bitter with mortification and disappointment, she turned from him. 'What's so different between me and my sister?'

'God almighty!' He stared at her, and then as the sense of the words reached him, in two steps he had reached her, catching her upper arm with hard fingers and swinging her to face him, taking easy refuge in anger. 'What in hell's name's that supposed to mean?'

The fury in his face, the pain of his fingers, brought the relief of rage. She shook herself free, violently. 'Do you want it in words of one syllable?'

He stared. Then, 'Christ,' he said, bitterly, 'what do you think I am?'

'I saw you myself, there in the flat, that morning after the party. You have a key – what do you expect me to think?' She was aware of a kind of miserable relief at having spoken the words at last, careless for the moment of his white-faced anger.

He stepped away from her. 'Do you really need me to tell you that your sister was so dead drunk that night that she couldn't stand up?' he asked at last, his voice stone-cold, the words clipped. 'Or are you now going to suspect that that's the way I like my women?'

She bit her lip.

'There was no one else there to look after her, if you remember. Her brother and sister had troubles of their own.'

It had the undeniable ring of truth. She took a breath. 'I'm—'

'Say it,' he said, very hard.

'—sorry.'

'I should bloody well think so. As for the key—'

'It doesn't matter.'

'As for the key, she lent it to Richard, years ago, and he

passed it on to me. I had meant to return it. I have now done so. Christ, Allie – do you really know me as little as that?'

The words, an open if unconscious plea, took her by surprise. She blinked, saw again the bleak exhaustion in his eyes, the spare tension of a body under too much strain. In that moment, suddenly and irrationally, she would have given her life to comfort him. She clasped her hands, forcing herself to calm. Now. Now, or the chance would slip from her for ever; she would never be able to bring herself to this again.

'Tom.'

He lifted pale, impassive eyes.

'Answer me just one question. Honestly.'

He waited.

'Do you really want to go?'

He turned away. 'God almighty.'

'Do you?'

'No.'

'Then stay. You don't have to give me anything you don't want to give. I'm not asking for tomorrow or the next day. I don't need declarations of undying love. I want you. Now. And I think you want me.' She moved to him, stood without touching him, looking into the tired face that was almost on a level with her own. 'Don't you?'

'You know I do.'

'Then why go?'

'Because I'm afraid.'

'Of what?'

'Of – hurting you.'

'I'm not a baby.'

His face softened at last. 'You think I don't know that? That I haven't known it for longer than you have?'

'Well, then . . .'

'It isn't just that—'

'—I know.' She lifted a hand and with her finger traced the line of his mouth, seeing the shock of excitement in him at her touch, knowing his iron control almost gone. 'Listen to me, please. You're free. And always will be. I wouldn't try to tie you down. I won't become a responsibility. I promise.' She moved closer to him, slipped her arms about his neck. 'We're here. We're alive. Now's what counts. Let tomorrow take care of itself.'

She remembered those words, that she knew to be lies, in the brightness of morning when she woke to find him gone with neither word nor sign of what the night might have meant – remembered them, the price she had willingly paid, and wept.

# CHAPTER TWENTY-THREE

Allie and Tom saw each other only four times in the two months that followed before, with very little warning, Tom's squadron was posted to Sicily with the invading Allies. They spent his short leave together in a London agog with news of the German defeats in the Soviet Union and amid open talk of an Allied invasion of the mainland of Europe. Their relationship, to Allie's relief, had gone strangely unmarked by friends and family, largely because both of them wished it so, and for those few days they took a room in a small and rather dingy hotel in a tree-lined avenue near Kew Gardens. To Libby, Allie conveyed the impression that her absence was due to business, and her sister, absorbed as always in her own affairs, did not question her.

Allie, in the days, sometimes weeks, that intervened between her meetings with Tom, had had time now to come to terms with her feelings for him. To her own astonishment she discovered them to be steady and intense. Love. An emotion she had foolishly believed she would never feel again after Buzz. After the first week she had stopped trying to analyse the whys and wherefores of her emotions. It had happened – that was enough. It was as though, through the years, the glimpses she had had of that other Tom, the Tom she knew she now loved, had served to lead the way through a maze of misapprehension to understanding, for now, slowly, she was coming to understand him, to know the stiff pride and irritating arrogance that was his defence against a world he felt always to be hostile, the fear of failure that drove him relentlessly to excellence, the weakness that preserved his strength for himself alone and shied from taking responsibility for others. She knew he cared for her; how much, or how little, she did not know. Despite her own strong feelings, she demanded nothing of him that he was not ready unthinkingly to give; she had promised this difficult man that he would be free, and she was determined to keep that promise – knowing anyway that the surest way to lose him would be to break it. In many ways she knew him to be right: Tom would never give up operational flying, and with the war moving into a new and obviously offensive phase, this was no time to insist on life-long commitments, even had he been the man to make them. Physically their relationship was better than any she had known, even with Buzz. His lovemaking was the most exciting thing she had ever experienced, and if it bore the unmistakable assurance of long practice, she did not care; while he was there, loving her, laughing with her, quarrelling with her, infuriating her, she knew herself happy again. She did not ask for more. And neither did she give away all her own secrets.

They spent their four precious days in summer London like tourists – walking hand in hand along the paths of Kew Gardens; sitting beneath the trees and watching the river and its life beneath its safety net of barrage balloons; dodging taxi-cabs around a boarded-up Eros in Piccadilly Circus; dancing until the small hours to an American dance band on a postage-stamp floor while, outside, the sirens wailed; making love at any hour of the day or night that they found themselves in their dim little room with its narrow, creaking bed. She was surprised by his passion – he, who always seemed so collected, so utterly self-possessed, used her sometimes with a kind of fury that, afterwards, tempted her to tears for him. But most of the time their lovemaking was just that – a physical manifestation of emotion made more poignant by the imminence of separation. Inevitably, the last hours came and they found themselves wandering in silence along the Embankment watching the quiet, dirty waters of the Thames as they swirled against the piers of Westminster Bridge.

Allie looked down at their linked hands. 'You will write?'

'Of course.'

'And you will – take care?'

He smiled.

'I hate goodbyes.'

'Me too.'

'Let's not say it.'

'All right.'

They stopped. A flock of pigeons strutted up to their feet, grumbling throatily as they pecked. 'Even the pigeons are getting thin,' Allie said. She looked out across the river. 'Funny, isn't it – you and me, here. Who'd have thought it a year ago?'

'I would.' His voice was serious: 'I always knew you harboured a secret passion.'

'I didn't!' She looked up in time to see his laughter. 'Oh, you!' She leaned against him, her chin resting on his shoulder. 'As a matter of fact, I used to think you insufferable. Still do, sometimes.'

'What happened?' She detected, beneath the lightness of his tone, real interest.

'I found you were human after all. Who could resist that? You?'

'Me?'

'Oh, come on.' She lifted her head to look at him. 'You had no time for me at all. You thought me a – a plain, sanctimonious little—' She stopped.

'—pain in the arse?' He supplied obligingly.

'Something like that.'

He cocked his head. 'For your information,' he said, the old, abrasively mocking expression on his face completely belying the words, 'I always did harbour a secret passion.'

'Liar.'

He grinned. They walked to the river wall, leaned over it to look down into the water.

'You aren't sorry?' she asked, after a moment.

'Good God, no.' There was no denying his sincerity this time. He reached a finger, lifted her chin and kissed her, very softly. 'That night? At the cottage?'

'Yes?'

'I know what it took. Don't ever believe I don't.'

She blinked.

'Thank you,' he said, very quietly, the words almost lost in the roar of traffic. 'For that and for everything. I would never have had the guts.'

She could not for a moment speak.

'Now,' he kissed her, lightly, 'I have to go. And since we aren't going to say goodbye then I guess we'll just have to say – what?'

'See you soon?' Her voice was not quite as steady as she had hoped.

'Right. See you soon.' He looked at her, smiling, for a long moment before turning away.

'Tom?'

He turned back.

She looked at him helplessly, words locked in her throat, knowing that what she had not told him before she could not possibly tell him now. 'Take care,' she said.

'I will.' He stepped back from her, his hand lifted, then in two steps had turned and walked swiftly away.

She watched him, unblinking, until he dodged across the wide busy road and was lost to sight.

Charlie Jessup died a few days later. On the morning of the day of his funeral, Allie and Sue walked up the lane to the downs and leaned by the stile where they had seen, nearly three years before, the first formations of enemy bombers heading for London. Hawkinge, with its memories, was spread, patched and battle-scarred beneath them.

Sue tilted her cap to the back of her head. 'Poor old Charlie.'

Allie nodded.

'Still – in the end – I guess it was for the best. He could have died a lot harder, in the circumstances.'

They stood pensively, their eyes on the grey, distant Channel. 'Well,' Sue said at last, more cheerfully, 'looks like we've got them on the run, eh? Russia – Africa – Italy—'

'Yes.'

'Soon be over now.'

Allie turned her eyes from the dark, gleaming water. 'Do you think so? I can't see them giving in without a fight.'

The other girl shrugged. 'Maybe. I reckon myself it's all over bar the shouting. In Europe, anyway. Which reminds me – any news of your sister's husband?'

Allie shook her head.

'Reckon he's a gonner?'

'Yes. Almost certainly.'

Silence.

Sue tried again. 'How's the job?'

'OK.'

Sue turned her head, eyes narrowed against a sudden gleam of sunshine. 'Allie? Are you all right? I mean – I know you're upset about Charlie, but we've known it was coming a long time . . .'

'I'm pregnant.' It was the first time she had actually spoken the words. They sounded even worse than she expected. Nausea stirred.

'Good God!'

Allie smiled crookedly. 'Sorry. I just had to tell someone.'

Sue was still staring at her as if she had been an apparition. 'But – Allie – who? I mean—'

Allie did not reply. 'I don't know what to do,' she said, after a moment.

'How far gone are you?'

'A couple of months.' She knew to the day. The night at the cottage had been the only time they had taken no precautions.

'Does – the father – know?'

'No.'

'But – you'll tell him?'

'No.'

'But, Allie—' Sue stopped.

'No.'

In the quiet a lark rose, singing.

Sue sat, suddenly and hard, upon the crosspiece of the stile. 'Does anyone else know?'

'No one.'

'And are you absolutely certain? About the pregnancy, I mean?'

'Absolutely.'

Sue picked a dandelion clock, twisted it in her fingers and watched the delicate seed-heads float away. 'Allie – if you want – I could get an address . . .'

Allie stood quite still. She had known all along, in her heart, that this was her reason for telling Sue. Had known, and had hated herself for it.

'A girl at Hornchurch got herself into trouble. She – got out of it.' Sue was still apparently intent upon the dandelion. 'I could get the address from her. She owes me a favour.'

'I don't know.'

The fair head jerked back. 'You can't be thinking of *having* it?'

Tom's child, and hers. Buzz's child had died. Her fault? She did not know. Had never known. She said nothing.

'Allie, love, look at me.' Sue jumped up and caught her arm. 'If you aren't going to tell the guy, aren't going to marry him?' She paused, enquiringly. Allie shook her head. '— then how can you *think* of having it? What about your family? Your job? Your – your bloody *life*? The brave new world isn't quite with us yet, you know.'

'I just don't know if I can kill it, that's all.' The ugly words were harsh.

'You'll have to. For your own sake.'

Allie shook her head slowly. 'No. Not for my sake. For his.'

'The father's?'

'Yes. He wouldn't want it. If I do it, I'll do it for him.'

'Christ.' Sue looked at her in a kind of despairing wonder. 'You love him.'

'Yes.'

Sue let out a small, explosive breath, shaking her head. 'An' I thought I was supposed to be the daft one.' She slipped an arm through Allie's and they turned to start

384

walking back down the lane. 'Come on, mustn't keep poor old Charlie waiting.'

They walked in silence, as the sun came and went through scudding cloud, dappling the countryside with fleeing shadows. As they approached the Jessups' house, where neighbours gathered at the gate, Allie stopped for a moment, grasping Sue's arm. 'Sue?'

'Mm?'

'How long would it take – to get that address?'

The suburban road, despite the neglect and deprivation of wartime and the ugly gap where, like a row of clumsily pulled teeth, several houses were missing, gave a quite remarkable impression of prim respectability. Nervously Allie checked the address on the piece of paper she carried. What had she expected? A sleazy back street with shuttered windows and filth running in the gutters? She walked quickly, counting houses. Twenty-four, twenty-six, twenty-eight – there it was, a trim and tidy semi-detached with shiny tile path and polished brass doorknocker. It waited behind a clipped privet hedge, clean, neatly curtained windows looking out on the world like shiny, bland eyes. She stopped at the gate. This, surely, couldn't be the place?

The early September day was windy. A gust buffeted the street as she stood, uncertain, blowing her hair across her eyes and plastering her skirt to her bare legs. Number twenty-eight, Mortimer Street. This was Mortimer Street. And this, beyond doubt, was number twenty-eight. Her heart pounded sickly as she walked up the path. What was she doing here? What?

She stood in the sheltered porch, looking sightlessly at the door with its Thirties pattern of stained glass in a neat and stylized country scene, making no attempt to touch the shining knocker. The agonies of the past days, her own irresolution, Sue's utter and unshakable conviction had done nothing but confuse her more. In a nightmare of indecision it had seemed to her that nothing she might do

385

would be right. To Sue's despair she had left this, the final step, until the last minute: it was now, or never. Today, or nothing.

She reached to the knocker. Stopped. Drew her hand back, and half-turned to hurry away.

'Well, dearie, and what can I do for you?' The door had opened as if by magic and a stout woman with hair meticulously crimped and shining like lacquered brass stood watching her, unsmiling.

'I—'

'Miss – Smith – isn't it?' The voice was flat and a little harsh, the cockney vowels overlaid and distorted by an acquired accent that fell uncomfortably somewhere between the BBC and Bethnal Green. The woman was wearing a clean, faded wrap-around pinafore. 'I thought so. You're late.'

'I'm – sorry.'

'Well, never mind. Come on in now.' With an assumption of heartiness, the woman stepped back.

Allie stood for a moment as if rooted to the spot. The woman watched her with faint suspicion. 'Come on, dearie.' The thin mouth smiled encouragement, the beginnings of wariness moved in the flat, unfriendly eyes. 'Sooner we start, sooner it'll be all over . . .'

Allie allowed herself to be ushered through a dark hall that smelled of polish and into a small sitting room in which the beige-upholstered furniture was arranged with mathematical precision around the walls, cushions plumped and as undisturbed as if no one had ever dared – or would ever dare – to sit upon them, while a rug was placed precisely in the centre of the room, its fringes combed carefully and improbably straight, like the rays of an unnatural sun. The room was very cold.

'You can wait here for a minute, dearie, while I go upstairs and get everything ready.' The woman, however, made no attempt to leave, but stood, obviously waiting, watching Allie.

'I – thank you.' Allie's head was thumping. She felt very sick.

386

The woman did not move. She cleared her throat, delicately, held out a square, calloused hand, palm up.

'Oh – I'm sorry – of course—' Scarlet-faced, Allie scrabbled in her handbag, pulled out a rolled bundle of five-pound notes. As she did so, half the contents of her bag spilled themselves over the rose-patterned rug. She thrust the money at the woman who carefully unrolled it and began methodically to count the large, dog-eared white notes.

'It's all there.'

'Of course it is, dearie. Just making sure.'

Allie dropped to her knees and began gathering her fallen possessions. As she picked up her small gold powder compact, it fell open, and pale powder spilled messily onto the spotless rug. She heard the woman give a tut of impatient displeasure.

'I'm sorry.' Miserably she rubbed at the powder, making the mess worse.

'No, no! I'll do it.' Fussily the woman went to the fireplace, and picked up a small dustpan and brush. Allie sat dispiritedly back on her heels and watched as, with short, competent movements, the woman swept up the powder. Still tutting, she left the room, dustpan in hand. Allie wearily gathered the rest of her belongings and stuffed them haphazardly into her bag. Something rustled. She reached into the bag and pulled out a flimsy envelope that tore as it caught on the catch of the bag. Tom's last letter. The writing jumped at her, immediately recognizable, neat and positive, the downstrokes strong. She clambered to her feet, stared at herself in the mirror that hung above the cold, empty fireplace. The windows rattled in the wind. She heard the woman's footsteps, heavy upon the polished lino of the hall, listened as they passed the door and went on up the stairs. The floor boards above her head creaked. She shivered. The room was like an icebox, yet her face burned. In the mirror, she saw the hectic patches of colour on her cheekbones.

Tom's letter was still clutched, like a lifeline, in her hand. She looked at it. His writing brought him into the room –

not the lover, warm, and wild, and well-remembered, but the dispassionate cool-eyed man who had so often forced her to see things as they were, rather than as she would have them. She had told Sue that she would kill the child for his sake. When had he ever expected anyone to do such a thing? How could she have made such a mistake? The decision was not his, it was hers. Inexorably hers. Buzz's child had died; she had been too weak then, too shattered, too personally broken to know what it might have meant. This time she could have no such excuse. Unless simple cowardice could be called an excuse. What was she doing here?

With a sudden movement she grabbed for the bag she had left lying on the floor and flew to the door. The brassy-haired woman was coming down the stairs – she reached the last step as Allie came into the hall, and stood, stolidly, between Allie and the front door.

'Something up, dearie?' Her voice was deceptively pleasant, her expression hard.

'I've – changed my mind.'

'Have you now?' The too-bright head shook, sadly. 'Oh, no, dearie, that won't do. We can't have that, can we? Not after all the trouble – here—' She brought her hand from behind her back. In it was an opened bottle of gin, three-quarters full. As she stepped forward Allie smelt it, re-voltingly sweet, on her breath. 'Have a swig of this. Works wonders, it does. All part of the service, like. Most – young ladies – get a fit of the heebie-jeebies at the last minute. Nothing to worry about, dearie. Happens all the time. Come on, now, lovie, knock it back like a good girl. Be over an' done with in no time, I promise you.'

'No!' Violently Allie swept the bottle away from her, knocking it from the woman's hand. It fell against the wall where, although it did not break, it lay leaking its contents onto the polished floor.

'Silly cow!' The woman leapt for it, snatching it up. 'Stupid little bitch! What the 'ell d'you think you're playin' at, comin' 'ere, wastin' my time – what's your bloody game, eh? Look at this mess! Just look at it!'

Allie cowered from her rage. 'I'm sorry. I'm sorry – I'll pay for the gin – here—' She pulled a couple of pounds from her purse and almost threw them at the woman, who grabbed them from her and then, putting her hand in the pocket of her pinafore, drew out the bundle of notes that Allie had given her earlier. 'An' what about this eh? Expectin' it back, are we, dearie?' The words were venomous.

'I – no. Keep it.' Allie sidled along the wall, trying to get past the other woman. 'I don't want it.'

Her antagonist stood her ground for a moment, and for a split second, Allie feared actual physical attack. Then the woman stepped back, smiling unpleasantly. 'Well, now, aren't we the lucky one? A hundred quid an' she "don't want it".' She pushed the money back into her pocket. 'Get out, you silly little cow. Just get out. An' don't bring your troubles to me again, understand?' She grabbed Allie's arm as Allie tried to slip past her, grinned in her face as Allie recoiled from the gin fumes. 'An' no tricks, you. You keep your bloody mouth shut, you 'ear? You got nothin' on me. Nothin'.' She let go of Allie's arm, straightened her pinafore. 'Respectable war widder, I am.' She patted the pocket that held the money. 'You just try an' prove different.'

Allie was at the door. With a wrench spurred by desperation, she pulled it open, hearing the hateful laughter behind her.

'. . . come ter think of it, dearie, I could do with a few more like you. Easiest bloody 'undred I ever earned . . .'

Then she was out, and free and running in the clean, cold wind. She felt as if she had been let out of prison, as if the past, awful weeks of vacillation, the dreadful decision to which she had finally come, had been an illness from which she had miraculously recovered. She would not – could not, for the moment – think of the future, of the almost insurmountable problems that lay ahead. For now, she simply thanked God for the flash of clarity that had shown her her own responsibility. If Tom did not want the baby – and she knew that more than probably he would not – then so be it. For now, she was happy. She knew her decision had been

the right one, shuddered at the thought of what she might
have done while – what was the phrase? – while the balance
of her mind had been disturbed. Wasn't that what they said
about suicides? And wasn't the thing she had been contemplating – had so nearly done – a kind of suicide? Her
baby – part of her – might now, through her fault, be dead.
But it was not. It was living. Growing. Incredibly she found
herself humming beneath her breath as she swung from the
open platform of the bus onto the pavement, wind-scoured
dust, leaves and pieces of paper swirling about her legs. No
one could change her mind now. The decision was taken.

She did not notice the small red motorbike parked at the
kerb outside Rampton Court. Not until, running lightly,
she was half-way up the curving stairs did she glance up to
see the lad in a dark blue uniform, the bright yellow envelope in one hand, the other reaching importantly to press
the doorbell of Libby's flat.

Her heart stopped. 'Wait!'

He paused, turned in surprise, waited for her as she raced
up the last few steps.

He glanced down at the telegram. 'You Mrs Maybury?'

'No. She's my sister. I live with her. Please – let me take
it.'

The boy looked doubtful.

'Please. Look.' Allie slipped her key into the lock and
opened the door. 'There, you see? I do live here. I might
have opened the door. You'd have given it to me then,
wouldn't you?'

'We-ell . . .'

'Please. My sister's husband has been missing for over a
year. This may be news. It may be – I'm afraid it's very
likely to be – bad news. I'd rather give it to her myself.'

'All right.' He capitulated, handed the envelope to her.
'Hope it isn't as bad as you think.' And he turned and
clattered down the stairs.

'Yes. Thank you.' She stared at the envelope.

'Allie? That you? I thought you weren't due back till
tomorrow?'

'I wasn't. Change of plans.' Allie's voice sounded strained in her own ears. She shut the door.

'Have you heard? They're saying Italy's surrendered!' And in the same breath, 'Who was that I heard you talking to?' Libby had come into the hall, stood stock-still, her voice dying in her throat as Allie turned, the telegram in her hand. 'Is that for you?'

'No. For you.' Allie held out the yellow envelope. Her sister stared at it as if it had been a snake. She made no move to take it. 'Libby?' Allie bit her lip. Her own heart was pounding, sickly. 'You have to open it, love.'

Libby still did not move. Allie stepped forward and pushed the envelope into her hand. 'Libby, open it,' she whispered.

After a long moment's stillness, long white fingers, usually so neat and deft, fumbled with the envelope, tearing at it awkwardly. The yellow envelope, still unopened, fluttered to the floor at Allie's feet. Libby put her trembling hands to her face.

'I can't. Open it for me. Please, Allie, I can't.'

Allie dropped to one knee and feverishly ripped open the envelope, pulling out the scrap of paper it held. She stood up and held it out to her sister, who took a step backward, shaking her head. She did not even look at it. Her eyes were fixed with fearful intensity on Allie's face. 'Read it for me.'

Allie smoothed the telegram with her fingers. The faint, printed letters jumbled and blurred, then cleared into words. Wonderful words. She lifted a shining, smiling face, held out the scrap of cheap paper. 'Read it yourself.'

Libby grabbed it. There was a long, long silence. Then the fair head lifted, the lovely, pale face streaked with tears. 'I *told* you,' Libby said, 'I *told* you he wasn't dead. And now he's free. *Free!*' She suddenly shrieked the word and threw herself, sobbing as if her heart were breaking, into her sister's arms. 'And he's coming home! Allie – Allie – *Edward's coming home!*'

# CHAPTER TWENTY-FOUR

Edward's homecoming was, for Libby, ecstatic. The months that followed, however, were far from that. No one – not even the ever-optimistic Libby – had been naïve enough to expect him to return completely unscathed; but neither had anyone been prepared for how drastic, how totally devastating the change in him might be. It was not simply – nor even predominantly – his physical state that dismayed them all, though to be sure the first sight of his skeletal figure, the fair hair thinned and lifeless, the yellow skin stretched over bones sharp enough, it seemed, to pierce it, came as a great shock even to those already prepared for it. It was the mental and psychological changes in him that were the most savage and that were the reasons for the extended leave that they all knew would end in de-mobilization.

He was, for the most part, morose and silent, his temper hair-triggered and violent. He could not stand to be with people; abruptly, in the middle of a conversation, he would leave, locking himself into the bedroom for silent hours at a time. Crowds terrified him. He refused to speak in detail of what had happened to him; Libby gleaned only that he had been captured by the Japanese when Malaya had fallen, had spent five nightmare months in a prison camp, had been beaten, starved, worked almost to death until, in desperation, he and three companions had broken out. The seemingly endless months in the jungle that had followed, Libby could not bring him to talk about; she only knew that somehow, miraculously, he – the only survivor of the four – had stumbled at last, more dead than alive and purely by chance, into a guerrilla camp a few miles from Kuala Lumpur. It had been weeks before they had been able to get him out – one escaped prisoner, however sick, came very low in the priorities of an irregular commando group working behind enemy lines against a foe whose methods of warfare and reprisal owed nothing to the Geneva Convention. They had not even been able to communicate his name, since Edward had refused to give it, one of the symptoms of his mental disturbance being a paranoid distrust of every human being with whom he came into contact.

During those months of captivity and terror, Edward Maybury had become a stranger to his wife, to his family and – perhaps worst of all – to himself. That he was in desperate need of help was obvious to all of them, but even had they known how to offer it, Edward, it seemed, was past accepting it. And to make matters worse, he hated himself for it. After each violent outburst, each rejected attempt of Libby's to break through the barrier that stood between them, he would weep in her arms in the darkness, the desperate and inarticulate crying of a lost child. He slept hardly at all; his stomach would hold little food. In these austere days of shortages – of carrot cake and Woolton pie, of little meat and often no fish at all, of a stodgy diet of little variation and even less interest – Libby could find nothing to tempt his appetite. Physically, he improved a little, mentally, not at all; indeed, the black moods became blacker, the violent outbursts more frequent, and gradually – unsurprisingly – the never very patient Libby began to shout back. In the middle of one blazing quarrel, Edward caught her by the shoulders and threw her with frightening force across the room, sending her sprawling across the low coffee table and onto the floor. In a second he was beside her, trying to help her up. 'Libby – Libby, I'm sorry!'

'Get away from me!' she spat, enraged. 'You're mad!'

He buried his face in his hands. 'Don't.'

She scrambled to her feet, blazing with outrage, rubbing a bruised knee. 'What's the matter with you? What do you want from me?'

'Libby – I didn't mean to—'

'You never mean to! Edward – where *are* you, for God's

sake? Where have you gone? Don't you understand? You're safe now. You're *home*. Why can't you forget – at least *start* to forget – what's happened? Why won't you talk to me? Why won't you let me help? It's as if I – our life – doesn't mean anything to you any more. Oh, Christ, sometimes I wish—' She stopped.

He lifted his head slowly. 'What? What do you wish?'

'Nothing,' she said, shaken. 'Nothing.'

He looked at her from his changed, anguished face, bitterness in his eyes. 'Libby, what do you wish?'

The tears came suddenly. 'What do you think? I wish things could be as they used to be! Why can't they? Why?'

She did not see him turn from her but, hearing the frustrated violence in him as he slammed the front door behind him, she wept.


Allie had moved out of Rampton Court when Edward had returned, and, accommodation in London being almost impossible to find, had moved into the Kensington flat with her mother and father. She had still told neither her family nor Tom of the coming child. Letters from Tom arrived irregularly from 'somewhere in Italy', and she wrote to him, invariably, twice a week. September 1943, the month of Edward's return, had seen considerable problems in the engineering industry culminate, in the middle of the month, in the first offensive strike in the industry for two years. Against the wishes and instructions of their own union executive, engineers in Barrow, a town almost totally dependent upon the vast Vickers Armstrong Company, went on strike directly against a decision of the National Arbitration Tribunal, a body set up by the Minister of Labour as a final arbiter in industrial disputes. The men had been agitating to have part of their national bonus, paid for war work, consolidated into the basic rate for the job so that it could not be so easily withdrawn at the end of hostilities. The tribunal ruled that this should be so, and that one pound should be consolidated into the basic rate – but due to a lack of clarity in the ruling and to the incredibly complicated pay structure of the industry, this turned out to mean that, in fact, many piece workers would be taking an actual cut in their weekly wage. Many of the men greased their tools and packed them away even before they went to the meeting where the vote to strike was taken. A week later the women and apprentices of Barrow had joined the striking men, and production in the town was virtually at a standstill.

The whole industry felt the repercussions, with most workers solidly behind the strikers. George Jordan nearly had an apoplectic fit when he discovered that the Jordan employees were contributing to the strike fund. In October, the dispute ended in compromise, but a residue of bitterness was left that some took care to foster; the rank and file were unhappy that, in their eyes, the union executive had not supported them, indeed had actively taken sides against them, and strong feelings spread nationally through the activists of the union, especially the shop stewards. The short-term effect, so far as Allie was concerned, was that MacKenzie, who had supported the strike and had organized the fund collections, was more strongly entrenched than ever. It was not, however, until the beginning of November, with the Japanese fighting fierce and suicidal rearguard actions against the Americans and Australians in the Pacific and an air of perhaps dangerous optimism pervading the European front, that trouble threatened at the Jordan works in Coventry, and it had, in fact, nothing to do with the national controversy but was once more a direct clash between MacKenzie and George Jordan.

'George, for God's sake.' Allie was exasperated. 'Why didn't you mention this when I was with you the day before yesterday? And when will you understand that this isn't 1850? You can't just sack people because – oh, all right. Yes, tomorrow. No, George, I can't get there in the morning. Tomorrow afternoon. I'll see you then.' She cradled the phone, thoughtfully.

Her father, sitting by the tiny, dust-choked fire, looked up from his newspaper. 'Trouble?'

'And a half, I'm afraid. A girl has been behaving badly and George has dismissed her out of hand, and the union's up in arms. Unfortunately he's picked one of their new women members, and it's a heaven-sent opportunity for Alistair MacKenzie to refute the accusation that he's biased against women in the union. He's blotted his copybook once or twice in the past – he's bound to make a big thing of this. Needless to say, he and George have antagonized each other to the point where negotiations have broken down entirely.'

Her father lifted the paper again. 'Never thought I'd see the day the AEW opened its doors to women, I must say.'

'Something good had to come out of this bloody war.' Allie perched on the arm of his chair, leaning over his shoulder, glancing at the headlines. 'What news? Anything interesting?'

'According to this, the Russians are within seventy miles of the Polish border.'

'Heavens, that's good, isn't it? Anything else?'

'The fighting in Italy's still pretty bad. But it looks as if we'll make it. And there are more scare stories about this secret weapon the Germans are supposed to be developing.'

'Do you think it's true?'

Her father shrugged.

'Would they be allowed to print such rumours if there were no truth in them at all? I mean – do you think the government is – well, preparing us for something?'

'Who knows?' Robert leaned back in his chair and, not for the first time, Allie noticed how these years of war were beginning to age him. He looked drawn and tired. Impulsively she laid a hand on his arm and, without turning his head, he covered it with his own. She dropped to one knee beside the chair.

'Daddy?' She hesitated. He looked at her questioningly. 'There's something I have to tell you. Want to tell you.'

'What is it?'

How to say it? There could be no easy way. 'I'm expecting a baby.'

In the silence, a bus rattled by in the street below.

'I want to keep it,' she said.

Still he did not speak, but the hand holding hers was firm. Allie ploughed determinedly on. 'I've worked it all out. If you agree, I'd like to work up to about six weeks before it's due—' She held up a hand at his swift movement of protest. 'I *want* to, Daddy. I'm not ill. In fact, I'm very fit indeed. I've had umpteen checkups. Everything's going fine. There's no reason why I can't work, if you'll allow it. After the baby – well, I haven't quite thought that far yet.'

He made a small, helpless motion with his free hand.

'I've been in touch with Rose Jessup. Remember her? She looked after me when I was ill after – after Buzz died. Her son married again after her husband Charlie died, and young Stan's gone to live with his new mum and her two little girls. It's left Rose quite alone. She says she'd be pleased to come and help me. It was Sue's idea.' She waited for a moment for him to speak, tightening her grip on his hand. Still he said nothing. She went on, her voice stubbornly calm despite the hammering of her heart. She had not until this moment realized how much the re-establishment of her relationship with her father had meant to her. Was she about to shatter it again? 'I thought I'd buy a cottage, somewhere near Ashdown. If you and Mother don't mind . . .?'

'Mind?'

'My being – where people know you.' She spoke with difficulty.

'Don't be absurd. Where else could you possibly think of going?'

She stared at him. His voice was matter-of-fact, his expression showed pure concern. What had she expected? Anger? Pain? Disgust? He turned in the chair to face her, lifted her hand in both of his. 'Allie, darling – are you sure? About keeping the child? Do you know what it could mean? What you – and the child – might have to face?'

'Yes.'

'And the father?' Robert's voice was still quite astonishingly normal. 'What does he have to say about it?'

'He doesn't know. And I don't want to tell him yet.'

'I see.' Her father's face was pensive. 'How the world has changed. Am I allowed to know who he is?'

She had not intended to tell him – had not intended to tell anyone. Yet, somehow, she felt that he of all people had a right to know. 'It's Tom. Tom Robinson.'

His look was pure astonishment; in other circumstances it might have been comical.

'I love him. I can't explain it. I just do. I don't know how it happened—'

To her surprise, her father laughed, gently. 'Still trying to explain love? Allie, my dear, somewhere inside you is still, after all these years, that little girl who wants everything in black and white, everything neat, and tidy, and explainable. Don't tell me that you haven't discovered yet that life isn't like that?' He put a hand to her smooth hair. 'Don't worry, my darling. Everything will be all right.'

She felt as if someone had undone a tight and tangled knot in her stomach. 'You mean – you aren't upset?'

'I didn't say that. Of course I am. For you. For the circumstances. But I didn't spend the best part of twenty-five years bringing you up to have a mind of your own to throw a fit when you decide to use it. Don't you know me better than that?'

She hugged him, wordlessly and hard for a moment, then sat back on her heels, frowning. 'Daddy – please – don't tell Mother about Tom? I'll tell her about the baby, of course, but it's best she doesn't know – at least for a while – who the father is. She dislikes him so—'

'Then it's a pity,' Myra said from the doorway with some asperity, 'that you couldn't keep your voice down. You're quite right, Allie, I do dislike that young man. And with good reason, I begin to think.'

Allie stood up awkwardly. 'Mother. I thought you were resting.'

'So I was.'

'You heard?'

'Most of it.' Myra came into the room. She still limped

slightly and her movements were a little stiff as she favoured her damaged and still painful ankle. Her fair hair was fashionably swept up and away from a face that seemed to Allie to become more beautiful with each passing year. She was unsmiling.

Nervously, Allie waited. 'Do you mind terribly?' she asked at last, weakly, when her mother did not speak.

Myra lifted her head and stood perfectly still for a moment, her hand resting on the back of a tall chair. 'May I speak plainly?'

'Of course.' Allie's heart sank.

'Yes, I mind – fairly terribly.' Myra's pleasant voice was quiet. 'One cannot change one's feelings and opinions about such things from one moment to another. An illegitimate child is no more . . . acceptable or excusable now than it would have been ten years ago. To me, anyway. I know the difficult circumstances. I know too – as Allie so often tells us – that the world is changing about me. I don't have to like or agree with those changes. When this wretched war is finally over, they tell me that a new world will have emerged. Whether that world will be better than the old one I personally take leave to doubt. For myself – I have no intention of changing. Morals remain the same. Civilized behaviour remains the same. Disgrace remains the same—'

Allie flinched. Her father moved sharply in his chair. 'Myra!'

Myra ignored him. She was watching her daughter, and Allie suddenly realized that the expression on her face far from matched her harsh words. 'However, I'm not one to cry over spilt milk – and I have always been ready to recognize and applaud courage when I see it. I long ago gave up arguing with you, Allie, once your mind was made up. Once, I might have tried. Now – ' she smiled a little ' – you're a woman grown. Your life is your own. How may we help you?'

Allie repeated the words blankly, like an idiot. 'Help me?'

'Well, of course.' Myra was brisk. 'In heaven's name,

what did you expect? That we would turn you out into the snow and tell you never to darken our doorway again?'

'Well . . .'

'Ridiculous. Now – from what I heard, you seem to have made a good start on planning the future. Do you need financial help?'

'No. I have the money Grandmother left me, as well as my savings.'

'Good. But if you do need anything, then please ask, and let's have no silliness about that. It's an excellent idea to have Mrs Jessup take care of you. When is the child due?'

'At the end of March.'

'Then you'll leave Jordan's at the end of January.'

'But—'

'No "buts". You'll need a couple of months to get yourself settled and comfortable. Have you started looking for a house yet?'

'No.' Allie was bemused.

'Then it's time you did. You may have to rent, of course, at this short notice. We can furnish it from Ashdown, if you like. We'll start looking at the weekend.'

'Yes. Thank you,' Allie said meekly.

'You're sure you are well?'

'Perfectly. In fact I've never felt better.' And, with the weight of confession lifted from her mind, she knew it was true. Pregnancy this time had been nothing like the trial she had experienced before.

'There remains, of course, just one question.'

'What's that?'

'Tom. I won't question you about your reasons for not telling him now – but what will happen when he finds out, as he surely must?'

'I don't know. Truly I don't.'

'I assume that you are still – ' Myra paused, delicately ' – friends?' The word was imbued with an edge of distaste that brought a faint, uncomfortable flush of colour to Allie's face.

'Yes. We are. But if you're asking if we'll marry – I don't know.'

'I see.' Her mother's voice still held that slight acidity. 'Well, we must just hope that you know what you're doing.'

'Mother, I don't blame you for not liking Tom. Heaven knows I don't think I like him much myself from time to time, even now. But you mustn't blame him for this. Honestly, it wasn't his fault. It was mine. As the decision to keep the child was mine. As for marriage . . .' She shrugged helplessly. 'Truthfully, I just don't *know*. About him, or about myself. We haven't got to know each other well enough. I'm not going to force him to marry me. It simply wouldn't be worth it in the end. We must just wait and see. The war isn't over yet. Anything could happen. I'm not going to worry about tomorrow, about plans for the future' – about German fighters in an Italian sky fighting a savage rearguard action against opponents as war-weary as themselves. She did not speak the words.

Robert stood up and put an arm lightly about his daughter's shoulders. He was smiling at Myra in a way that softened the lovely face into an answering smile. 'We'll manage,' he said.

Myra lifted fine-plucked brows. 'Was there ever any doubt about that?' And Allie, happily, took the hand her mother offered.

Allie was not so happy the following afternoon. 'George,' she said, for what seemed the hundredth time, 'I understand how you feel. Clearly the girl has behaved badly—'

'Abominably,' snapped her cousin. 'You just met the Dexters . . .'

'And I agree with you. Obviously we must do something about the situation. The girl can't stay with them—'

'I should damn well think not. They're a decent, hardworking couple and they have two young grandchildren living with them. Out of the kindness of their hearts they offer this girl a home and, in return, what do they get?' He glared at Allie as if she were personally responsible for the situation. Allie, hoping the question to be rhetorical, tried remaining silent for a moment. George waited with grim self-righteousness.

Allie sighed. 'All right, George. We'll go through it again. She is alleged to have entertained men in her room, to have used foul language—'

'Constantly,' interjected George.

'—and finally to have indulged in a scuffle—'

'A damned free fight!'

'—with another girl in a pub, and arrived back at the Dexters' rolling drunk.'

'Right.'

'But she's never behaved particularly badly at work?'

George hesitated. 'Her language is intolerable.'

'George – so is a lot of the men's. We've had this out before. You can't have one rule for one sex and another for the other. You either sack the men for swearing too, or you sack no one.'

'If we tried that we'd have no workforce left.' George's voice was gloomy. Allie almost felt sorry for him. Whatever his faults, he did really believe in his own standards. She pushed from her mind the thought of his probable reaction when he discovered her condition.

'So – you have no complaints about Sheila Brown's work?'

'No.' Reluctantly.

'In fact I've been told she's a damned good lathe operator?'

George did not reply.

'George – you *know* what I'm going to say. You can't dismiss a girl because you don't like the way she behaves outside working hours. Are you going to sack every young man who gets drunk on a Saturday night and picks a fight with his mates?'

'Of course not.'

'Well, then, you can surely see the problem? MacKenzie jumped on this because he's out to show that he'll defend any of his people, regardless of sex. He needs to show it. The girls won't easily forget that he didn't give a tinker's cuss for them until the union at last agreed to let them in. He's got a lot of ground to make up, a lot of confidence to win. He's picked the battleground, and I'm telling you that we'll lose if we fight him. You've picked the wrong issue and the wrong time to stand against him.'

George stood up, wrathfully. 'I've told you before. I'm not being dictated to by some damned Red!'

Allie shook her head, her hand held pacifyingly up. 'George, I just don't believe that it hasn't occurred to you that there's a very easy way out of this? You don't have to sack the girl; just rebillet her. Find a room in a hostel. There must be one somewhere?'

'It isn't enough. I will not have such behaviour by a Jordan employee. She has to be taught a lesson. They all do.'

'You'll cause chaos in the works.'

His mouth tightened. 'There's something else. Something I had hoped not to have to bring up. I detest gossip . . .'

Allie waited.

'I believe the Brown girl to be pregnant.'

Strangely, the flat disgust in his voice came as a physical shock. Her stomach churned, queasily, and she stood straighter. 'Oh? Are you sure?'

'As needs be. It's all over the works. Apparently she doesn't even know who the father is.'

'I see.' Very calmly Allie walked to the door. 'I have to go. MacKenzie and the girl are waiting in the downstairs office.'

George's lips twitched almost into a dry smile. 'I'd lay money that you'll learn some words you've never heard before.'

Allie stopped at the door. 'I have to say it, George. You can't sack her. Not for this. It isn't worth it.' She closed the door on his suddenly frosty face.

Settled in the other office she regarded the two who stood before her with cool eyes.

'Miss Brown, would you say that your recent behaviour has been – reasonable?'

The girl watched her sullenly. She was very pretty, petite

403

and slim; the curls that sprang from beneath her turbaned scarf were dark and shining. Allie found herself keeping her eyes carefully upon her rebellious face, fighting the urge to look at her possibly thickening body. She could hardly believe such a pretty elf to be the subversive and unpleasant girl that George had depicted.

'Well?'

'What I do in me own time,' the girl said flatly, 'is me own bleedin' business.'

There was a short silence. Allie looked at MacKenzie. His face was impassive.

'I understand you had a stand-up fight in a pub?'

The girl's mouth twitched. 'Yeah.'

'Would you call that ladylike behaviour?'

'Would you call workin' a lathe for eight hours at a stretch ladylike behaviour, Mrs Webster?' MacKenzie asked, before the girl could open her mouth.

The girl smirked. Allie looked long and thoughtfully at her real antagonist.

'Do I detect a change in the wind, Mr MacKenzie?' she asked pleasantly, and was rewarded by the faintest, defensive flicker in his eyes. She turned back to the girl. 'Miss Brown, I'm not going to waste time and breath telling you what I think of this kind of behaviour. I will simply say this: Mr. Jordan has asked me to tell you that – against his strong personal inclinations – Jordan's will continue your employment. However – ' she interrupted the triumphant glance that passed between the two, ' – you will not, of course, be allowed to remain with the Dexters. I shall arrange hostel accommodation for you immediately.'

'No!' The smile had gone from the pretty face. 'I ain't goin' to no fu—' She caught MacKenzie's cold eye. '—No bleedin' 'ostel,' she finished defiantly.

Allie stared at her. 'You don't honestly expect to be billeted in another private house after this?'

'I'm all right where I am. I ain't goin' to no 'ostel.'

'You'll sleep on the street then,' Allie said, brusquely, and surprised a flash of something like admiration in MacKenzie's eyes.

'Them stinkin' 'ostels is rotten. Can't call yer life yer own – they run yer ragged wiv rules and fings . . .' The girl looked suddenly pathetic, a rebellious child.

Allie was beyond sympathy. 'Perhaps you should have thought of that before. You've obviously caused a great deal of distress to two kindly people whom I suspect, under other circumstances, would have been good friends to you. They took you in because they wanted to look after you—'

'Oo needs crappy lookin' after?' the girl muttered.

Allie regarded her with undisguised dislike. 'Clearly not you, Miss Brown. Now, this is my last word. You keep your job – on my terms – or you further this absurd charade and shut down Jordan's. If you do that then I assure you that my offer, and every detail of this conversation, will be made public. I don't think Mr MacKenzie would find that a worthwhile exercise.' She looked at the man, her fingers mentally crossed, by no means as certain as she sounded.

'We'll accept that, Mrs Webster.' The girl turned on him, fiercely. He shook his head. 'You've kept your job, lassie.' His face was hard. 'An' that's all you could expect. Off you go.'

She glared at him, muttered something that Allie, perhaps fortunately, did not catch but that brought a tinge of blood to MacKenzie's thin, fair skin, and started for the door.

'Miss Brown.' Allie's voice brought her up short. She turned and eyed Allie with hostile sullenness.

'Miss Brown – is there anything else you want to talk about?' Allie heard the absurd delicacy of the words and despised herself for it.

'No,' the girl said flatly.

'I've heard it said that you're pregnant?' Allie saw MacKenzie's brows lift – not, she was certain, in surprise at the information but at the fact that she possessed it.

The girl's attractive face was flaming. 'So what if I am? No law against it, is there?'

'Of course not.'

'Right then. That's it, innit?'

'You don't need . . .?'

'I don't need anythin' from you.'

Allie's temper almost took her breath away. 'I'm sure you don't, Miss Brown. But have you thought of the future? Of what you're going to do? How you're going to live?' She paused, watching uncertainty warring with suspicion in the other girl's face. 'If I could put you in touch with someone – someone who had nothing to do with Jordan's – a local organization, perhaps – would you accept help from them?'

The girl considered. 'Depends,' she said at last, warily.

'I'll see what I can do. That will be all, Miss Brown.' As the door shut behind the girl, she let out a pent breath and found herself looking into a pair of bright but not altogether unfriendly eyes.

'I'll be goin' then,' MacKenzie said.

'No – wait, please.' Allie waved him to a chair. He sat down.

'Did you know? About the pregnancy?'

'Aye. Och, the whole works knows. She's boasted about it. Doesn't even know which laddie knocked her up.'

'Bravado,' Allie said.

'Maybe.'

'It didn't occur to you to come to me – to one of the welfare people – before things went this far?'

'No.'

She looked at him wondering. 'Do you really care so little about what might happen to her? You've just fought to keep her job . . .'

He shook his head. 'Not *her* job. A job. Any job. It's nae my place to play nursemaid to any little – ' he caught himself ' – any daft fool of a lassie who gets hersel' into the family way.'

'I always understood it took two, Mr MacKenzie,' Allie said equably. 'And you really don't give a damn what might happen to her?'

'Aye.' He was watching her steadily, an odd expression

406

on his face. Allie could not for her life decide if it were compounded most of contempt or pity. She shook her head, defeated. Such total and cold commitment to an ideal with no gentling touch of humanity was beyond her. She detested the girl, as obviously did MacKenzie. But could she simply turn her back and leave her to her undoubtedly grim fate? With an illegitimate baby, no work – for she certainly would not be accepted back after the baby – no money, no home, what would become of her? Or – Allie tried to face the uncomfortable thought honestly – was it her own guilt that made her want to do something for the other girl? Her own child, with or without Tom, would be born into a world of safe and loving care, cushioned by money and family ties.

'Do you know if Miss Brown has a family?'

'Aye. They threw her out. Her da beat the living daylights out of her last time he saw her. So she said.'

'Mr MacKenzie, don't you think we ought to do *something* for her?'

He considered for a long time. 'Aye,' he said, reluctantly. 'Mebbe so.'

'Then, please – you know the city better than I do. Isn't there someone you could put me in touch with? Someone who might be able to help her? Someone she would accept help from?'

'Well – aye – as a matter of fact there is someone comes to mind.'

'Who?'

'A friend of mine. Iris Freeman. Local socialist worker. Seems to me that she'd likely know who to go to.'

'Would you arrange for me to meet her?'

He paused for a moment. 'Aye.'

'Tonight?'

He almost smiled. 'Aye,' he said again, 'tonight.'

Allie liked Iris Freeman very much indeed. She was a Londoner in her early twenties who worked in an arms factory in Coventry. The more-or-less self-educated daughter of a railwayman, she was of medium height and slightly built with a quick sense of humour and a directness of manner that could be positively disconcerting. When her initial mild suspicion of Allie had worn off, she proved to be an interesting, even inspiring companion. Alistair MacKenzie introduced them, a little stiltedly, in the poky and decidedly ill-stocked little bar of the small hotel in which Allie was staying, and then excused himself, leaving them together. The ice broken – Allie having convinced Iris that she was genuinely interested in the welfare work that was the other girl's life – they first arranged for Iris to be put in touch with Sheila Brown and then proceeded with the unstudied enjoyment of kindred spirits to dissect each other's beliefs and ideals. At the end of the evening, a sobered Allie strongly suspected that she had learned a lot more than she had imparted, and she said so.

'Rubbish!' Iris grinned as she stood up and pulled on her shabby coat. 'There aren't many women with your background in industrial welfare, you know. I've got some friends I'd like you to meet. Got time?'

Allie glanced at her watch. 'Now?'

The other woman laughed. 'When else? We're all working girls – got no time for get-togethers over afternoon tea. Still, thanks to the Jerries we're used to doing without our beauty sleep. Feel like staying up half the night? The company's good.'

She took Allie to a small two-up-two-down house in a shabby street not far from the hotel. Three young women were already there, huddled around a meagre, palely flickering fire, drinking steaming mugs of Oxo. 'Don't take your coat off,' Iris advised cheerfully. 'You'll freeze. Now – meet the Coventry branch of PAWS.'

'PAWS?'

'Poor 'Ardworking Women Socialists,' chorused the three from the fire. 'For Christ's sake, I, close that door,' added one.

Allie found herself the target for three pairs of eyes. A little uncomfortably she shoved her cold hands into her pockets and waited for her new acquaintance to introduce her.

'Look what I've found, girls,' said Iris, her grin at Allie friendly, 'a real live lady capitalist. Let's get to work on her . . .'

On the train back to London next day, Allie slept, on and off, despite the discomfort of being jammed between an enormous lady who insisted upon knitting all the way and a skinny young man in sailor's uniform who had the boniest elbows she had ever encountered. It had been a long night, but the company, as Iris had promised, had been very good indeed. It had been years since she had been so mentally stimulated, so fired with enthusiasm – her own and others'. And the camaraderie of that small group huddled around a fire that had died long before the lively discussion had was with her still. She could not remember a gathering where she had enjoyed herself more. She fell asleep on the thought that she would certainly take them up on their invitation to join them again the next time she visited Coventry.

She arrived in Kensington late in a dreary afternoon. Her eyeballs felt as if they had been sandpapered, and she ached with fatigue. Certain that if she put down her case and bag and rummaged for her key she would go to sleep where she stood, she leaned on the doorbell with her shoulder.

Myra opened the door, fresh-looking and immaculate. 'Hello, darling.' She kissed her daughter's cheek. 'You have a visitor.'

Allie had already seen him, through the open door of the sitting room. Perched on the edge of an armchair, a bone-china cup and saucer balanced precariously in his long fingers, was a tired-looking but smiling Tom Robinson.

'Tom!' She dropped her case and ran to him, flinging her arms about his neck as he rose to meet her, nearly knocking him off balance, cup and all. 'Tom! Where did you come from? How long have you got? When . . .'

'Whoa!' He put his cup on the mantelpiece, laughing, and laid his hands lightly on her shoulders. 'I've only got three days. Hitched a lift on a transport. Leaving again Sunday afternoon. Can you manage a couple of days off?'

Her face fell a little. 'Not tomorrow, I'm afraid. There's a meeting I have to go to. But Saturday – yes, all day.'

And all night? asked his quirked eyebrows.

She blushed. 'Where are you staying?'

He opened his mouth to reply.

'Why here, of course.' They both looked in surprise at Myra's composedly smiling face. 'It's next to impossible to get a room in London at the moment, and anyway, I wouldn't dream of allowing anything else. Of course you must stay here.'

Tom, for once, was caught wordless. 'Why, Mrs Jordan, I—'

'We don't have a spare bedroom,' Allie said.

'Oh, come now, darling.' Myra smiled her sweetest and most formidable smile. 'We have a very snug sofa. I'm sure Tom will find it as comfortable as any bed he's occupied.'

Allie winced.

'You will stay, won't you, Tom?'

Tom smiled. 'Of course. Thank you.' And Allie found herself wondering, ruefully, not for the first time, how it was that she had not managed over the years to perfect her mother's apparently effortless ability to get her own way.

'I'd better go and talk to the onion pie,' Myra said, brightly, 'tell it to stretch a bit.' And, having made certain that her daughter and her unlikely lover would remain well and truly under her eye, she left them alone.

Often during those three snatched, oddly dream-like days Allie was tempted to tell Tom about the baby, but she did not, and the longer she left it the more difficult it became. Tom was bright and cheerful, apparently light-hearted, but she sensed the strain in him, the tension beneath the easy armour of laughter. Instinct told her that to tell him now would mean nothing but harm for both of them. Tom, however, had no such qualms about surprising her, as she discovered on Saturday night, dining at the Savoy.

410

'What would you say,' he asked, grimacing over coffee that even the Savoy could not make truly palatable, 'to South Africa?'

Taken aback, she made a feeble joke: 'Hello, South Africa?'

He grinned. 'We've got a South African in the squadron. Great bloke. Great country, too, from the sound of it. I've been thinking – after the war it could be the place for a man to be. It'll be years before Britain's back on its feet again. Austerity, shortages, picking up the pieces. There's not much doubt now that we're going to pull through, but we'll break ourselves doing it. What about sunshine, servants, grapes, gold, diamonds . . .'

She tinkered with her spoon, not looking at him, not knowing how seriously to take the subject. The moment stretched, awkwardly, in silence.

He leaned across the table, half-laughing, but his eyes were wary. 'Don't look so miserable. It's only an idea.'

She lifted her head and smiled brightly. 'Of course.'

Watching her, his expression changed, warmed. 'Allie? I don't suppose . . .' He hesitated. 'There isn't somewhere we could go? Now? Before we go back to Kensington?'

She had known it was coming. Tomorrow he would leave and God only knew when she might see him again. But she knew without doubt that if she went with him, made love with him, naked, he would see the changes in her body and would know. She could not bear the thought. She shook her head. 'Tom, I'm sorry. It's – the wrong weekend. For me . . .' She found it easy to blush and hang her head. 'You – you understand what I mean?' She hated herself. Hated herself.

He looked at her blankly for a moment, then understanding crept into his face. Laughing despite himself, he grimaced. 'Oh, no!'

'I'm sorry.'

'Don't be silly. It isn't your fault.' He almost managed to mask his disappointment. 'Serves me right for surprising you.' He took her hand in his, kissed her fingertips, his tired eyes laughing. 'I'm not sure I could find the energy anyway!'

She wanted very much to cry.

Tom left Allie next day at the door of the flat, neither of them caring for the thought of goodbyes in public places. After a long, final kiss he picked up his small suitcase. 'In you go now. No point in hanging around. I'll write when I get back over there.'

She nodded, stepped back and half-closed the door, watching him as he walked with his light, quick step to the stairs. With his hand on the banisters, he turned. 'Allie?'

'Yes?'

'You'll be here? When I get back?'

'Here, or somewhere. You'll know.' Tear-blinded, she smiled and lifted a hand. When he had gone, she leaned a tired head against the door jamb. The bloody war! The bloody, bloody war!

# CHAPTER TWENTY-FIVE

It was obviously impossible to keep Allie's secret from the world for ever. She was, however – perhaps naïvely – absolutely unprepared for the storm that broke when, in December, while trying to cope with the disruption caused by one of the worst flu epidemics in years, she had an unheralded visit from George Jordan in the small office next to her father's that she used as a base while in London.

'George? What brings you here? Trouble?'

Very precisely George laid his gloves and hat upon her desk, leaned his rolled umbrella against a chair. Something in his expression, hovering between embarrassment and determination, rang warning bells in Allie's mind.

'Won't you sit down?'

'Er – no, thank you. I can't stay. I'm on my way to a meeting. It's just that I felt – that is . . .' Uncharacteristically ill at ease, he paused, cleared his throat. 'The fact is, Allie, that I'm afraid that the most – unsavoury rumour concerning you has reached my ears. It's nonsense, of course, and I regret dignifying such abusive gossip by taking it seriously, but I feel strongly that it is my duty to – that is – in the interests of yourself and of the company to stop such scurrilous talk at once . . .'

'Oh?' Not by the faintest tremor did Allie's voice betray the fact that her heart appeared to have stopped beating entirely.

'It's – hrrm.' He coughed again, clearly discomfited. 'I'm afraid that it's a rather – delicate matter for me to broach . . .'

'Broach it, George.' He frowned at her brusqueness. Allie was beyond caring. She did not know – probably would never know – who had guessed. But this, undoubtedly, was it. 'Well?'

'Allie, I have heard it rumoured – that is . . .' He coloured, then rushed on very fast, his voice clipped. 'Allie, I should simply like your assurance that you are not – pregnant.' The last word brought his clean-shaven face to the hue of a beetroot.

She regarded him in silence for a long time. 'I'm afraid I can't give you that assurance.'

She might have hit him. For a moment she thought he might actually choke. 'I don't believe it.'

'Believe it.' Her voice was crisp. 'It's true. The baby's due at the end of March. A second cousin for you, George. Won't that be nice?' She knew her savage flippancy to be unnecessarily provocative but, in sheer self-defence, could not suppress it.

The man's eyes hardened. To his credit, his self-control held. 'I see.' His voice was acid. 'Well, well.'

She said nothing. In frigid silence he picked up his gloves and hat. 'You'll resign immediately, of course.'

'I hadn't planned to leave for another couple of months, as a matter of fact.' She kept her voice cool and businesslike.

'No.' The word was icy. 'Oh, no. You go now. Immediately. It's bad enough that you should disgrace the family. I'll not have your – alley-cat morals tainting the reputation of Jordan Industries. You will resign now, Allie, or believe me I'll make you sorry you ever set foot inside one of Jordan's offices. I mean it. I'll call a board meeting. I'll bring it out into the open. I'll force your resignation. And that won't do your father any good. Don't think I can't.' He paused, his eyes raking her disgustedly. 'Don't think I won't.'

She did not. On the contrary she knew that he could and would. She regarded him in hostile silence.

'What an example,' he said slowly, 'what a shining example to set to our workers. Who look up to you. Respect you. Well, I'll say one thing – you've done me one favour.' He pulled his gloves on, smoothing them precisely to his hands. 'You have confirmed and exonerated my view that a

414

woman's sense of responsibility – or rather her lack of it – completely unfits her for the world of business.'

That was too much. She stood up abruptly, her chair scraping the floor. 'Just hold on one minute, George. I don't blame you for being angry. Knowing you, I don't even blame you for being disgusted. I wouldn't in any way expect you to understand, let alone condone what I've done. But – what do you think? – that I managed this on my own?' She saw the virulent distaste in the quirk of his mouth, but would not stop. 'Has it never occurred to you that for every unmarried mother there's an unmarried father? Are you honestly trying to tell me that you've never known a *man* in a responsible position to sleep with a woman he wasn't married to?' She stopped, aghast. Her father. Celia.

George placed his hat squarely upon his neat fair head and, unmoved, turned to leave.

'You're a poor thing, George,' she said more calmly. 'I feel sorry for you.'

He turned at the door, spoke quietly. 'Don't waste your sympathy. It isn't me who needs it. It is the poor bastard child you mean to foist upon the world. I intend to end this repugnant conversation here and now. I doubt we shall ever have cause to speak to each other again. I'll just say this: either you resign immediately, quietly and with dignity or I shall make it my business to see you are thrown out. That is all.'

It was indeed all. Neither Allie nor her father could stand against George's unrelenting and venomous hostility. Allie did not even work out her notice. She had, however, before she left Jordan's, two unexpected visitors, each of whom in their own way cheered her a little. The first was Iris Freeman who came with two pieces of news, the first that Sheila Brown had settled fairly well at the hostel – 'God, what a mouth that girl's got!' – and that she had been taken under the wing of an organization that took care of unmarried mothers and arranged the adoption of unwanted babies. Told in confidence Allie's news, she was torn between incredulity and, to Allie, surprisingly, admiration.

Her second piece of news was that the arms factory where she had been working had been damaged by an explosion and she and some of the other girls had been redirected to a factory just outside London. 'So it's an ill wind – p'raps we'll see something of one another?'

'I'd really like that.' Allie, delighted, scribbled down the address of the small house her mother had found for her in the village of Eastby, not far from Ashdown. 'Do come. I'm going to be bored stiff in the next few months.'

'You're leaving Jordan's?'

Allie grimaced. 'Not from choice.'

'Ah. Don't tell me. "Madmen, criminals and unmarried mothers not welcome"?'

'Something like that.'

Iris grinned and stood up. 'Come and join us, love. We're going to change the world, didn't you know?'

Allie's second visitor, who arrived as she was grimly clearing her desk for the last time was – astonishingly – Alistair MacKenzie. She did not hear his knock on the door but looked up when she heard him clear his throat, to find him standing watching her from the doorway.

'Mr MacKenzie. Do come in.'

'I came to tell you that we've settled the toolmakers' overtime rates.' His swift glance took in the disarray of the office.

'Yes, well, as you can see, I'm afraid that it no longer concerns me. A Mr Ralph Allard is taking over from me tomorrow. He'll be up to see you next week.'

'Aye. I'd heard.'

She waited.

'Jordan's'll be sorry to see you go, I daresay,' he said, dourly.

She stared at him in wonder.

'We've had our ups an' downs, you an' I, I'll no, deny that. But you've done a tough job the best you could. For a lassie.' She smiled at that. 'Aye, the best you could. I'll say that for you.'

'Good Lord,' she blushed. 'I mean – well, thank you.'

He held out a small, strong hand. 'I'll wish you good luck, then.'

She shook his hand. 'Goodbye. And thank you.'

His mouth twitched almost to a smile, his pale blue eyes gleaming between their sandy lashes. 'If you ask me, management's losing a damn good man, Mrs Webster.'

For the first time in two days, she laughed in genuine amusement. 'They aren't all convinced of that, Mr MacKenzie.'

'I daresay not.'

As he turned away, she stopped him with a smile. 'Mr MacKenzie?'

'Aye?'

'Don't be too hard on George?'

He lifted pale eyebrows, his face innocent. 'Now would I be, Mrs Webster? Would I be?'


A couple of days after Allie left London to move into Baywood Cottage, another unpleasant upheaval occurred in the Jordan family when Peter Wickham arrived at the Rampton Court flat to find Libby alone, crying hysterically, her face swollen and discoloured. He looked at her, horrified.

'Libby? What on earth's happened?'

She shook her head, sobbing wordlessly and wildly.

It took a moment for the obvious to sink in. 'Edward? He did this?'

She buried her bruised face in her hands.

'Good God!' Peter put a supporting arm about her, led her into the cold drawing room, sat beside her on the sofa, holding her hands in his, his damaged leg stretched awkwardly in front of him. 'Libby, where is he? Where's he gone?'

'I – don't know. I don't – care. He left – shouting – I don't know . . .' Her breath caught choking in her throat at every other almost unintelligible word. 'He – hit me! Peter – he hit me . . .'

'But why? What happened?'

'We – quarrelled – I said—' She could not go on, and the tears came again.

'Don't. Libby, my dear, don't.' With infinite tenderness he gathered her to him, brushed the strands of fair hair from her flushed and sweat-dampened skin, rocking her gently until her sobbing died. There was one still moment when she lay against him quietly before she lifted her head and sat up, moving a little away from him. One eye was purpling, her nose was swollen and there was a small bright smear on her lower lip. Peter restrained himself from taking her hand again. 'How long has he been gone?'

She shook her head. 'I don't know. An hour. Two, perhaps. I just don't know.'

He lifted a hand to her cheek, dropped it again. His face, usually so calm and kindly, was hard with anger. 'Would you like me to call someone? Your mother? Allie?'

Pathetically she put a hand to her battered face. 'No! No – not yet. Later, perhaps.' She shivered suddenly.

'You're freezing. No – don't move. I'll get you a jumper. Make you a cup of tea.' He indicated the empty grate. 'Have you any coal?'

She shook her head again, miserably. 'I couldn't get any. They said there'd be none till next week. There's a little electric fire in the bedroom, though.'

'I'll get it. Stay still. I won't be a moment.'

He busied himself with her comfort, watched as she sipped the mug of hot sweet tea he had made. She tried a smile. 'You must have used a week's sugar ration.'

'Just drink it.'

At last, calmer, she told him of the argument that had ended in violence. '. . . Peter, he's so unpredictable! I only started to talk about – about the old days. About the way things used to be. Before the war, when we were all so happy. Well – God! we have to talk about *something*, don't we? The present won't bear discussion, and as for the future . . .' She made the word a desolation. 'Oh, God, I don't know what I'm going to do.'

'It's that bad?'

'Worse. I'm living with a stranger. Nothing I do helps. Nothing I say is right. My own Edward is dead. A stranger has taken his place.'

He took her hand, his face sombre. 'Libby – is that what you said to him?'

She hesitated, then lifted her chin a little defiantly. 'Yes.'

In the silence, they both heard the key in the front door, the unsteady footfalls in the hall. Libby stiffened. Peter, very, very carefully, stood up. He managed without a stick for most of the time now, but balance was difficult.

Edward stopped at the door at the sight of them. He looked as if he had been dragged through a hedge backwards, his face stone-white, his eyes exhausted. As he came closer, the reek of cheap whisky filled the room.

He ignored Peter. 'Libby, I'm sorry.'

She would not look at him. Shook her head.

'I'm truly sorry.' His voice cracked painfully.

Libby at last lifted her head. Her husband flinched at the sight of her marked face.

'I think she should see a doctor,' Peter said.

'No.' Libby made a swift, negative gesture.

'But Libby—' He bent to her.

Edward grabbed his shoulder and hauled him upright, his eyes dangerous. 'Leave her alone.'

His friend staggered, recovered himself, looked at Edward in steady distaste. 'Are you going to hit me, now?'

'Stop it!' Libby leapt to her feet, her hands clenched to her ears. 'I can't bear it. Stop it! Both of you!' She ran from them and into the bedroom, slamming the door behind her.

The two men stood in silence. At last Edward turned away, leaned on the mantelpiece facing the empty grate, arms spread wide, head hanging.

'Edward, you're unwell. Very unwell.'

The other man lifted a haggard, tear-wet face.

'Someone has to say it. You need help. You need – treatment.'

'No.' Edward spoke through clenched teeth. 'There's nothing anyone can do.'

419

'You can't know that until you've tried.'

'I do know.'

'If you won't help yourself . . .?'

The other man straightened. 'There's only one way that I could help anybody. And that's to kill myself.' The words were so quiet, so matter-of-fact that at first Peter thought he must have misheard. When the meaning of the words did sink in he opened his mouth to protest. Edward stopped him with a fierce gesture. 'Oh, don't worry. I won't do it. I can't. I've already discovered that. The ultimate cowardice, eh?' He turned to face Peter. Libby's words came back to the other man – '. . . a stranger. My Edward is dead . . .' Looking at him, Peter knew the words to be the ineluctable truth.

'Edward—'

'And you know why I can't?' continued Edward bitterly. 'Why there's no peace? In case I'm wrong. In case – just in case – all that shit we had forced into us as children turns out to be right and this whole bloody mess we call life isn't, after all, some crazy accident. In case there really is a life after death. A vengeful God. Justice. I don't believe it, of course. The whole great fuck-up *got* to be an accident. It's the only acceptable answer, isn't it? But supposing – just supposing – it isn't? Suppose they're waiting for me? Beyond the pearly gates? What a laugh that'd be, eh?' The light in his eyes was not madness, but neither was it sanity. It seemed to Peter that Edward's wounded soul hovered somewhere between the two.

'Edward, what are you talking about? Waiting for you? No one's waiting for you—'

'How would you know?' Edward came very close to him. His breath stank. 'What would you know about anything? About what a man might do – might have to do – to save himself when the world's gone mad? What do you know of stinking jungle, of blind, sucking leeches, of starvation?' He stepped back, surveying Peter with raw hostility, his gaze lingering on the stiffened leg. 'What would anyone know? Thank your lucky stars, Peter, for a nice, clean, crippling wound. For King and country. Wows the girls, I should think. The gallant captain. Do you want Libby?'

Peter stared at him.

'Do you?'

'Don't be ridiculous, man. You can't just parcel people up and—'

'I'm leaving her. For good. I'll give her grounds for divorce.'

'You should be discussing that with her, not with me.'

Edward's wrecked, handsome face registered suddenly a blaze of self-derision. 'Talk to her? How can I talk to her? Didn't she tell you I'm dead?'

'She didn't mean—'

'I know what she meant. *And she's right.* She's bloody *right*! I'm going to hell. I don't have to take her with me. I'm leaving.'

'Peter.' Libby, in outdoor clothes, stood at the door, a small suitcase in her hand. 'Would you find me a taxi? I'm going to Mother's.' She had tried to repair her face with make-up. The effect was pitiful, almost clownish, yet her small figure, standing very straight, was oddly dignified.

Edward made no attempt to approach her. 'Libby, I'm truly sorry.'

'Yes.'

'I'll give you a divorce. Agree to anything that makes it easier.'

'Yes.'

Peter limped past her into the hall. For the space of perhaps half a dozen heartbeats, Libby and Edward Maybury looked at each other before Libby turned wordlessly away from him.

The four months between the trauma of Libby and Edward's final fight and the birth of Charlotte Anne Webster on the twenty-sixth of March 1944 were eventful, to say the least. After a miserable, war-weary Christmas of shortages and deprivation, as the nation dragged itself with grim determination into a new year, hoping – and praying – that

421

this one would surely see an end to the fighting, the Luftwaffe suddenly launched a vicious series of night raids on London, a 'little Blitz' that did nothing for Londoners' short tempers, and little for the peace of mind of the thousands of American and Commonwealth troops that packed the capital in preparation for the long-awaited invasion of northern Europe.

The south of England had once again become one vast armed camp, though this time the aim was openly offensive rather than defensive. Dunkirk was about to be avenged. The newspapers were full of the gallant landings at Anzio, the savage fighting around Monte Cassino. In the Pacific the Americans forged ahead with great courage and at great cost.

In London – a city under attack once more – the tube stations were again packed to capacity each night, the fires burned in gaunt and gutted buildings, and the guns thundered, torturing the nerves. Children, with the happy adaptability of the young, raced to school each morning collecting on the way streams of 'flutterers' – the silver paper strips that were dropped by the enemy raiders to confuse the city's defensive detecting devices, and which decorated trees and buildings as if a bizarre Christmas had come again. Then at the end of February, as suddenly as they had started, the night attacks stopped, and for a couple of weeks an uneasy peace reigned. Rumours abounded: of Hitler's new and deadly secret weapon about to be unleashed on the civilian population, of invasion, of yet more ration cuts.

To Allie, in those last weeks before the baby was due, the most shattering problem was a very personal one. Tom's letters had stopped. They had not petered out slowly, but simply, frighteningly, had just stopped arriving. Allie determinedly kept her nerves under control, told herself firmly that there could be any number of reasons for this sudden silence, and continued, with Rose, her preparations for the child's arrival. If something dreadful had happened, someone – surely? – someone would have let her know? But would they? asked a frightened voice somewhere in her head. Tom was not, even at the best of times, the most communicative man in the world. Did anyone even know about her? For three awful weeks she waited, faithfully sending her own letters, talismans against fate, tamping down her fears with logic. She spoke to no one apart from Rose of her terrors, not even Sue, who visited as often as she could, or Iris, who spent a considerable amount of time at Baywood Cottage. Her grim patience was finally rewarded when a letter addressed to her in a strange hand landed on the doormat. She lumbered down the hall and with difficulty bent to pick it up, ripping it open with fingers that were all thumbs.

'What is it, my dear?' Rose appeared from the kitchen, wiping her hands on her pinafore.

Allie suddenly sat on the stairs, supporting her swollen belly with her hands, the flimsy letter crumpled between her fingers. 'He's crashed! I knew it! He's in hospital! In Italy. He's too bad to be moved. Oh – Rose!'

Rose bustled to her. 'Now, now, don't take on, my dear. It's bad for you, and bad for the babe. Now – may I see the letter?'

'Oh – of course.' Allie handed it to her, seemingly unaware of the tears that were running down her cheeks. 'It's written by a nurse. Tom – asked her – to—'

Rose's eyes ran swiftly over the paper. 'But Allie, my love, this is *good* news! She says he's on the mend—'

'Well, she would, wouldn't she?' Allie asked with an absolute lack of logic. 'He's still too ill to write. He might have died. It says – he nearly did die . . .' Allie bit hard on the knuckle of her forefinger, the emotional instability of pregnancy unnerving her altogether. 'Oh, God, I *knew* there was something wrong! I *knew* it!'

'Oh, get along with you. He didn't die, and that's what matters. He isn't going to die. "Improving daily" the letter says—'

'But what if . . .?' Allie could not voice her worst fears.

'Fiddlesticks to "what if",' said the older woman briskly. 'Come on, my love – you've an address now – write to the man!'

Four days later, in a small cottage hospital, Charlotte Anne arrived, bawling and furious, seven pounds ten ounces of high-powered energy. The birth was fairly easy, the baby strong and healthy. Allie's only problem was with breast-feeding; after a couple of days of tears and trauma, Charlotte was put on the bottle – which in no way displeased Rose – and thrived. Within a few days Allie was back at Baywood Cottage, recovering her strength, enjoying being able to see her feet again, and listening to the constant roar of military traffic as it thundered down the Kentish lanes towards the coast and enemy-occupied France.

When little Charley was three weeks old, her father, well enough to travel at last, was transferred to a hospital-cum-nursing home in Yorkshire. Allie, impatient as she was to see him, had to wait another month, however, before she was equal to such a difficult journey, and before she felt confident enough to leave the baby for a couple of days in Rose's hands – although Allie was more than ready to admit that those hands were probably more competent than her own.

So it was not until mid-May, with Britain completely given over to invasion fever, that she set off to travel almost half the length of a country that had become something between a vast military warehouse and an invasion platform. Her figure more or less regained, she dressed carefully, for the first time really regretting those lost days before coupons and austerity. From the moment the day had been decided, her nerves had been frayed to breaking point, for this was it – Squadron Leader Tom Robinson would have to learn that he was a father. Telling him was not a task she relished. The journey was going to be bad enough: the thought of the possible cataclysm that lay at the end of it daunted her beyond telling. For the first time she wondered whether it might not have been more sensible to have told him in the beginning . . .

\* \* \*

The hospital was housed in an old mansion, one wing of which had been given over to convalescing servicemen. Spring rain mantled the grounds and drifted softly against the windows. A brisk nurse ushered Allie to an enormous room that was the size of a football pitch and that obviously, in better days, had been a ballroom. The vaulted ceiling, with its chandeliers wrapped inelegantly but safely in dust sheets, was two storeys high; at one end of the room, tall windows looked out to lawns that swept to a tumbling river. Two men in wheelchairs played a dextrous game of table tennis in the centre of the floor, while around a small table another group played cards noisily, and on the far side of the room a dartboard had been set up against a dark green baize board. A billiard table took up most of the space by the long windows. One corner of the room had been turned into a library. Beyond it a small bow window looked onto a pretty little courtyard, enclosed on three sides. A man in a wheelchair sat in this window, dark head bent attentively to the book that lay open on his lap.

'Squadron Leader Robinson,' said the nurse, pointing. 'Sister says would you please not make the visit too long. He still tires very easily.'

Allie walked steadily across the wooden floor, her footsteps echoing, as did the shouts of the table-tennis players and the laughter of the other men, to the high, concave ceiling. The table-tennis ball bounced over the floor towards her. She stopped and picked it up, tossed it back to the players with a smile. Tom did not look up until she stood in front of him, waiting. When he did so, she knew with absolute certainty that he had known of her presence from the moment she had entered the room. His expression was cool. Her heart sank.

'Hello there.' Awkwardly she took his hand and bent to kiss him. He looked very thin. There were two fine and still slightly angry-looking scars running across his forehead into the hairline, and a livid streak of scar tissue marked the left side of his jaw. One arm was still in plaster, as was the lower part of both his legs. All this she had been prepared for,

425

having by now heard by letter of the injuries he had sustained when his combat-damaged aircraft had crash-landed on a temporary airstrip outside Monte Cassino. The unmistakable chill of his greeting, however, was rather more unexpected. She had not thought that hostilities would begin quite so soon. 'How are you?'

'Fine, thank you. They're hoping to take the plaster off in a couple of days.'

'That'll be more comfortable.'

'Yes.' He made no attempt to hold onto her hand as she straightened.

She pulled a small, straight-backed chair close and sat down.

'How was the journey?'

'Pretty bad, actually. There are hardly any trains for civilians. The whole world's in uniform and on the move, it seems.' The clumsiness of that struck her at once, and it was all that she could do not to apologize for it.

'The Second Front,' he said.

'It looks like it, yes.'

'Not before time. If they don't get a move on, the Russkies will have taken the whole of Europe, and we'll be back where we started.'

'What do you mean?'

'You don't think Uncle Joe's going to let go of anything he gets his sticky hands on, do you?'

'I can't say that I'd really thought about it. You mean – you think the Russians will just keep what they take from the Germans?'

'Eastern Europe isn't being liberated. It's just changed hands.'

'Surely not?'

'Ask your new Commie friends. Perhaps they know.'

She stared at him. 'My new friends, as you call them, aren't Communists. They're socialists. As, I seem to remember, you once were.'

He shrugged.

Allie made a determined effort to smile, and to take the

426

undoubted edge off the conversation. 'Sorry I couldn't bring you any grapes. They're in rather short supply. But I did manage this.' She reached into her bag and triumphantly produced an orange.

He whistled, and for the first time really smiled. 'Good Lord, where on earth did you get that?'

Caught – unable for the moment to explain away a child's green ration book – she laughed. 'Libby. Who else? She still has friends in high places.'

'How is she?' Tom had heard, through Allie's letters, of Libby's troubles.

'Not too bad. It's hit her terribly hard though. I'm worried about her; she acts as if she believes the whole awful business is her fault. Peter Wickham sees quite a lot of her. I think he helps.' She did not think it necessary to mention the odd change in Libby's attitude towards her when she had discovered the identity of Charlotte's father. Allie had expected surprise but not something that to her astonishment could only be described as outrage. She had no doubt at all that her sister had been avoiding her since the disclosure. Libby had not even tried to disguise her fury: 'Well, of all the sneaky – you and – *Tom*? And all the time you pretended that you couldn't stand him – butter wouldn't melt in your mouth! Allie – how *could* you?'

'Will they marry, do you think? Once the divorce comes through?'

'I really don't know. There's no telling what she'll do. She's changed.' Allie leaned back a little tiredly in her chair. 'But then, who hasn't?'

'Quite.'

She looked sharply at him. There could be no mistaking the slight, unfriendly sharpness of the word.

'Tom, what is it? What's the matter?'

'Nothing.'

'Yes, there is. It's obvious. Here we are – the first time we've seen each other in months, and you keep biting my head off.'

For the first time in a year, he turned upon her that

sardonic, shuttered look that she so hated. It made her want to get up and simply walk away from him. She clenched her teeth. Since the baby, she knew, her temper had been short-fused. 'Exactly,' he said. 'The first time we've seen each other in months. I hardly expected you to swim to Italy. But Yorkshire isn't half a warring continent away. And I've been here for a month . . .'

'But – I explained in my letters . . .'

'Excuses. Why bother? You know me. Did I ever ask for half-baked excuses that a child could see through? What is it, Allie? Is there someone else?'

Her mouth was suddenly very dry, and all her careful, agonized planning, all her well-rehearsed words, seemed to have dried up with it. 'You could say that,' she said. 'I had a baby.'

'Game!' whooped one of the table-tennis players and spun his wheelchair in a perilous, victorious circle.

'Tom – did you hear what I said?'

His face was absolutely blank. 'I heard.'

'Our baby. Her name is Charlotte Anne, and she's very beautiful – at least I think she will be when she gets some hair.'

Still he said nothing.

'I'm sorry. I didn't mean to spring it on you like that. It was clumsy.'

Tom seemed at last to be coming to life again. He stirred, let out a breath. 'When was she born?'

'March. The twenty-sixth.'

She saw him work it out, saw too the recognition of deception. 'I see.'

'Tom, I couldn't tell you when you were here last. I just couldn't. Don't you see? After all that I'd said – all that I'd promised – it would have looked as if I were – as if I were trying to trap you. I'd promised I wouldn't tie you down. And anyway – I couldn't bear the thought of worrying you while you were flying . . .'

'Well, bloody hell,' he said, mildly, 'what do you think you've done now?'

428

She shook her head violently. She was mortifyingly close to tears. 'No! I'm still not tying you down. You don't have to marry me. I *know* it isn't what you want . . .'

'Oh?' He looked interested. 'What do I want then?'

'I don't know. South Africa?'

He nodded slightly. 'Can't deny it crosses my mind from time to time.'

An orderly, pushing a tea trolley, clipped briskly, cups rattling, across the floor. 'Tea, sir? Ma'am?'

'Yes. Please.' Allie felt as if he had offered her nectar. The man poured two teas and left. Tom stirred his, ruminatively, placed the spoon with care in the saucer and lifted the cup with his good hand, surveying Allie over the rim. 'A father, by God,' he said, a note of uncertain surprise in his voice.

'Yes.'

'A girl, you said.'

'Yes. Charlotte Anne – at least, that's what I'd like to call her. She hasn't been christened yet, of course. If you have any great objections to the name . . .?'

He shook his head. 'A girl,' he said, reflectively, and grinned suddenly, wincing a little as the smile hurt his unhealed face. 'Wouldn't you know it? A girl! Allie Jordan and daughter – what a combination!'

It took her a long moment to join in his laughter.

# CHAPTER TWENTY-SIX

Charlotte was almost eight months old before Tom was well enough to leave hospital. The summer of invasion had come and gone, and the grim job of liberating western Europe, inch by inch, sent the hospital trains northward in ever-growing numbers. But that summer's casualties included more than those trainloads of combat-wounded servicemen. In June, the population of southern England discovered that the fearsome whispers of a Nazi secret weapon had been, after all, more than mere rumour.

A week after D-Day the first V-1 droned, pilotless, across the Channel, a dehumanized killing machine designed to terrorize the civilian population with its random destruction and death. At first confusion reigned and casualties mounted, and three days after the first flying bomb had landed on London, the Minister of Home Security had to make a statement to the House of Commons explaining what the fearsome things were. From then on the city was in a constant state of alert, a condition wearing to the nerves and unconducive to calm. However, as so often before, the civilian population adapted to this new threat remarkably quickly, going about their business as the 'doodlebugs', as they were almost universally nicknamed, droned overhead, only diving for cover in the tell-tale silence that followed the cutting of the engine. If you heard the bomb go off, you were safe. If you didn't, you were probably dead. By August, seventy V-1s were dropping on London each day; the skies of Kent and Sussex, battlefield of four years before, had a new nickname – 'Flying Bomb Alley'.

In Europe the battle raged; the fortress, stone by painful stone, was falling, but at terrible cost. And while the doodlebugs continued to rain on southern England, a new rumour began to circulate, and a new fear turned eyes skywards. What was a V-2? Theories ranged from a giant version of the V-1 to an incendiary fog, and the unsettling anxiety did nothing to ease the nervous strain of a population too long at war. When, however, in September, a series of unexplained incidents occurred, people at first had no idea that Hitler's new secret weapon was actually involved. After all, inexplicable explosions, if not exactly commonplace, were at least not very much out of the ordinary – an unexploded bomb gone up, a fractured gas main – but then the truth dawned. London was under rocket attack. The V-2s had arrived: and the population, not surprisingly, detested them. They were worse than the flying bombs; there was no sound, no warning and, apparently, no defence. But at least, as the more philosophical citizens often pointed out, their victims had no time for terror. They simply never knew what hit them.

Those first months of Charlotte's life were marked by an escalation of violence, and Europe was once more in flames. In Warsaw the Soviet army stood shamefully by while the soldiers of the Reich butchered Polish partisans who might, had they survived, have believed themselves entitled to a say in their country's fate when the lunacy was over. Blood lapped the shores of the Pacific as it did those of the Mediterranean and the North Sea. Yet Baywood Cottage in that summer and autumn of 1944 was a small haven of peace for its three occupants. A doodlebug landed on the village in August, killing a woman and two children, the roads were still clogged with military vehicles, the trains decorated with red crosses that clanked over the level crossing were full of wounded, but still the sun shone, the birds sang in the woodland that edged the pretty garden, and Charley thrived. Allie watched her in wonder. Her hair, when it grew, was as dark, straight and floppy as her father's, darkly spun silk in the sunshine. She had the skin of a peach and eyes that promised to be as blue as her grandmother's. She laughed a lot, screamed with gusto when put out, and wound both Allie and Rose around one small pink finger.

Sue, bouncing the undisputed queen of Baywood Cottage

on her knee, was the first to coax a 'Ma-ma' from her. Allie, in quiet moments, gently teased her with a different word. 'Tom. Say "Tom", Charley . . .' But she stubbornly would not.

As the russet cloak of autumn spread across the countryside to herald the sixth winter of war, and the V-2s continued their nerve-racking bombardment, small, morale-boosting changes began to appear. The blackout was relaxed at last – for a rocket could just as well land on a darkened as a lit building – and trains and buses were lit once more, if still quite dimly. The signs and signposts that had been taken down reappeared, to the relief of those, like Sue, whose sense of direction was not their greatest gift. Preparations were under way to dismantle the Home Guard, for the fear of invasion was undoubtedly over. The Labour Party announced its intention, after the wartime years of coalition, of fighting the next election independently – and there were many, remembering Beveridge, who did not join in the cries of derision from those who considered a Churchillian defeat on the Home Front an impossibility. There was no denying it – above the smell of blood, of engine oil and of cordite, the faint sweet scent of victory was in the air. Many would die before the end came, much would be lost and much regretted, but few people doubted now that the Nazi wolf was on the run. Thoughts turned to the future, to the homes, the schools, the jobs of tomorrow.

Iris Freeman and her friends took to gathering at Baywood Cottage as much, Allie suspected at first, perhaps unfairly, to take advantage of warm and comfortable surroundings as for any other reason, and the coming new world was debated endlessly. Allie, starting by filling cups and watching the supply of logs for the fire, soon found herself taking an active part in the earnest discussions, and was amazed to discover how much she had learned in the past years, how eager she was to learn more. She watched with muted anger as, within British industry, moves were made against trade unionists as a precursor to another 1919. She found it hard to believe that people could be so blind;

moral issues and compassion aside, Britain could not – should not – after such a cataclysmic upheaval, simply shudder, sigh and sink back into the same rut of social inequality that had marred the years of the twentieth century so far. On the day that she joined the Labour Party, Iris sent her a telegram: 'WELCOME ABOARD STOP NOW GET ROWING.'

Tom was finally released from hospital in early November. He had been fretting for six weeks, anxious to be away, but a small complication concerning the slow healing of one of his ankles had kept him chained to bed and chair for longer than had been expected. Allie had visited him as often as she could, and they had corresponded regularly. She had sent him pictures of Charlotte, but had tried hard not to fill every letter or every conversation with anecdotes about her, for there was no denying that, as she had expected, Tom's acceptance of fatherhood was heavily weighted with a noticeable lack of fervour. His squadron was back in England; he felt keenly the fact that, because of the extent of his injuries, he would not be allowed to fly again, though he rarely spoke of it. On one occasion Allie arrived at the hospital to find a visitor already with Tom – a giant of a young man with blond-brown hair and a wide, ready smile. Having heard his accent she was not surprised to discover that this was Tony Partridge, the South African of whom Tom had spoken.

'Wonderful country, Mrs Webster,' he said, when she mentioned it. 'God's own land, believe me. Land of opportunity . . .'

It had not escaped her notice that Tom that day, after Tony had left, had been even less communicative than usual.

His first meeting with Charlotte was a nerve-racking occasion that went, perhaps predictably, awry from the moment they came face to face. Allie, standing at the cottage window, watched Tom, back in uniform, swing down the street with the slightly lopsided gait that his wounds had temporarily forced upon him, pause at the gate, checking the name of the house and then come down the long front path to the front door. Even from where she stood, she saw that his expression was guarded. She ran into the hall. 'Tom!'

There was nothing guarded about his kiss.

'How wonderful to see you away from that wretched hospital! How are you!'

'Fit as a fiddle. Fitter.'

She caught his hand and pulled him into the tiny sitting room, kissing him again. 'Charley's in bed at the moment, having a sleep. You'll meet Rose in a minute. She's in the kitchen, making some lunch. I thought we'd eat in here – in front of the fire?'

'Marvellous.' Allie was certain that she detected a gleam of relief in his eyes that the meeting with his daughter was postponed, for however short a time.

'Drink?' she asked, brightly. 'I've actually acquired some sherry. Not very dry, I'm afraid, but not bad.'

'Please.'

She poured two small drinks, brought one to him. 'Cheers—'

From above their heads, something closely resembling an air-raid siren sounded. Allie junped, put down her drink, laughing nervously. 'That's her. She has a pair of lungs on her like bellows—' She hurried from the room.

When she returned, she carried a struggling, still sleepy Charlotte who took one look at the unsmiling stranger who stood on the hearthrug and yelled as if murder were being committed.

'Oh dear,' Tom said.

Allie pacified the baby. 'Come on now, darling. It's Tom come to see you. You can say "Tom", can't you? Say it for Mummy? Say "Tom"?'

Charley's cherubic lower lip wobbled unhappily and she howled again. She would not stop. She screamed at Tom's every half-hearted attempt to make her smile and buried her small wet face in her mother's shoulder until Rose, tutting busily and beaming from ear to ear, bore her off to the kitchen, and silence.

Tom accepted his second, slightly larger, sherry with gratitude. 'Hardly an immediate rapport.'

'I can't think what came over her,' Allie said, distractedly unthinking. 'She's usually very good with—' She stopped.

'Strangers,' he supplied, unruffled. 'Oh, well. Cheers.'

Throughout the day Charlotte obstinately refused to be sociable. Allie, at her wits' end, finally and thankfully put her to bed in her little room and came back downstairs to find Tom sitting in the flickering firelight of the sitting room, gazing into the flames. Rose, the very soul of tact, had gone to visit a friend in the village. Allie stood by the door, studying his pirate's face with its sharp-drawn lines and fresh scars. 'I'm sorry. She's been a beast. I don't know what got into her.'

He did not reply.

She moved to him, sat at his feet, picked up the poker and prodded the smouldering logs. For a moment the room flared brightly with firelight. She felt Tom's hand on her hair. 'Allie?'

She had hoped – had planned – for this. She turned her mouth to his. It had been so very long since they had made love. His body, in the blood-light of the fire, was thin, and new scars had joined the one on his shoulder that he had brought back from Spain those long years ago. She loved him with every pulse of her blood, every nerve-end. With unhurried tenderness and care – for he was still not absolutely fit – they made love on the rug in front of the fire, scurrying draughts on their bare skin tempered by woodsmoke warmth from the crackling logs. He took her wordlessly, his face intent, his hands gentle; and she tried to show him by her giving the depth of a love that would let him go if that were the only way not to spoil it. He stayed still above her for a long moment, his body covering hers, his face in shadow. As he moved away from her, she shivered. He gathered her to him and they lay in silence, watching the racing shadows. At last he stirred, and turned. 'Cold?'

'A bit.'

'Best get dressed. I'll have to be going soon anyway.'

They dressed quietly. 'There's some supper in the kitchen,' Allie said. 'I'll get it.'

When she returned with a small plate of sandwiches, he was sitting fully dressed on the floor, his back against the chair, his legs crooked in front of him, his arms loosely circling his knees. He was staring once again into the fire, his face remote.

'Penny for them,' she said lightly.

He stirred, shook his head.

'Oh?' Laughing, she sat on the chair, offered the sandwiches. 'Secrets?'

He did not reply, nor did he smile.

'Tom? Is something wrong?' All day she had had the feeling of something withheld, some reserve in him. 'Darling, I'm sorry that Charley behaved so badly. She really is the sweetest thing most of the time.'

'It's all right. It wasn't her fault.'

'Then what is it? What's the matter?'

He hesitated. 'Allie – I want to ask you something. Something important . . .'

'What is it?'

'You may not like it.'

'Try me.' Her voice was more certain than she was.

'It's just – something I need to know – something that has to be explained between us . . .'

'Tom, what? What do you want to know?'

'Do you know – why you had Charlotte?'

A log slipped and rolled in the wide fireplace, sending a glittering spray of sparks up the dark chimney.

'Because – because I couldn't bear to—' She took refuge in sudden anger. 'What do you mean, why did I have her? I didn't get pregnant deliberately, if that's what you mean. God almighty, would I have done? But – once it had happened – would you rather I'd killed her? Had an abortion? Good God, I know she wasn't very well behaved today, but that's a bit harsh, isn't it?'

436

He was patient. 'You're misunderstanding me.'

'Explain then.'

'I wanted to know – do you think that there is no connection at all between the child you lost – Buzz's child – and this one?'

'No. Never.' Her voice was very calm. Liar! she told herself, savagely. Bloody liar!

'I'm not Buzz, Allie.'

'Well, for God's sake, I know that! I wouldn't want you to be. Nobody could be.'

He climbed to his feet. 'I'd better be going.'

'Wait!' She jumped up. 'You can't just say something like that and leave! I don't think I even know what we've been talking about.'

He sustained her angry look coolly. 'And I think you do.'

The air between them suddenly sang with the old antagonism. 'It's my turn to ask you a question.'

'Of course.'

'After the war – will you go to South Africa?'

He hesitated, noticeably. 'Possibly.'

'Alone?'

'Would you come?'

'You know I couldn't.'

He lifted his shoulders very slightly. 'Alone then, I guess.'

She knew she had pushed him to it, recognized the dangerous tilt of his head, the glint of anger in his eyes.

'Whatever happens,' he said, 'I'll support Charlotte, of course. We must make some arrangements.'

She glared at him. 'I don't want your money.'

'I'll give it anyway.'

'What for? I've got more than you have.' She had snapped the words before she could stop herself.

'True.' The word was cold.

'I'd hate to see you penalized for a biological accident,' she said, bitterly, and turned miserably from him.

The silence was awful. 'Is that how you feel?'

'No!' Dejectedly she sat on the sofa and stared sightlessly

437

down at the rug where not so many minutes before they had made love. She expected him to leave, but he did not. After an interminable pause he came and sat beside her. To her amazement he put an arm round her, and his voice was gentle. 'I'm sorry. For what I said. I didn't mean to upset you.' Very softly, he stroked her hair. 'And Charlotte is beautiful. It's just – she's an unexpected complication. And if that sounds cold, please believe me, I don't mean it to.'

'I know.'

He reached for her, turned her to face him, his expression deadly serious. 'Allie, I'm trying. Believe me, I'm trying. Just give me time.'

She nodded. Softly, he kissed her. Upstairs, Charlotte woke and yelled lustily for her mother.

That last dreary winter of war – for there was little doubt now in anyone's mind that it was the last – was bitterly cold and marked by a kind of national fatigue, another Christmas of miserable shortages and a hold-up in the Allied advances in Europe as the Germans broke through in the Ardennes and the last great battle began. Towards the end of January 1945, however, the news was once more heartening with both the Soviets and the Allies again advancing, the gap between them lessening with every step, and spirits began to rise. The collections and flag days now were as likely to be for the starving people of liberated Europe as for armaments and aircraft, for it came as a shock even to the tight-rationed, shortage-ridden British to discover that the civilian populations of their enslaved allies had fared even worse than themselves.

On the day the news came that the Soviets had reached the Oder river and were ready to link up with the British and Americans coming from the west, Peter Wickham visited Allie – the first time she had seen him for several weeks.

'Peter!' Her face lit with real pleasure. 'How lovely to see you! Come in – warm yourself . . .'

He rubbed his hands in front of the fire. 'No fuel shortage for you by the looks of it?'

'We're lucky – we've acres of woodland right next to us. There's always something to burn. Whoops – excuse me—' She dashed across the room to where Charlotte was, with great concentration and at some risk, trying to pull herself up from the floor by the tablecloth. Allie reached her in time to prevent an accident, scooped her up, laughing. 'Naughty girl!' She carried the child, perched on her arm, to Peter.

'She's lovely,' he said.

'Isn't she? But a tinker, I can tell you. She's so forward – she'll be walking before—' Allie checked herself, smiling. 'Oh, no, don't get me started on that. I can't stand doting mothers!'

She settled Charley on the floor with a saucepan full of spoons and a battered teddy bear. 'There – do try to stay still for thirty seconds.' She straightened up, to find Peter watching her with an affectionate smile.

'It suits you, motherhood.'

'Thank you.' She grinned at him. 'Though I can't say that I'm always so sure.'

Later, with the winter sun gleaming rose-red through the bare branches of the trees, they walked through the frosty woodlands, their breath fogging the biting air as they walked, their footsteps crisp upon the rimed carpet of leaves.

'How's Libby? I haven't seen her for a while.'

Peter did not answer at once. He held back a whipping branch so that Allie could negotiate the narrow path. 'To be truthful, I don't really know. She won't talk about anything. Oh – she talks all the time – you know Libby. Never stops. But . . .'

'She doesn't say anything.'

'Right.'

'She quite often didn't before.'

'I know. But this is different. She's more damaged than she appears.' They walked a little way in silence. Above their heads a robin sang as if his breath depended upon it. 'I asked her to marry me,' Peter said very quietly. 'When the divorce goes through.'

439

She glanced sideways at him. 'And?'

He shook his head, half-smiling.

Allie put out a hand to him. 'It's too early, Peter. Give her a chance. She's still – I don't know – in a kind of shock.'

'Yes.'

'You don't have much luck with the Jordan girls, do you?'

'I've never felt that.'

'Well, you should. One of us as good as proposes to you, and the other one turns you down.'

He laughed at that, as she had intended.

'It all seems so long ago,' she said, sobering.

'Yes.'

They paused as their footsteps disturbed a pigeon and it fluttered with its oddly clumsy movements through the trees. Allie was suddenly reminded of the Northamptonshire woods, and Buzz. It had been this time of year. 'Who needs spring?' she had asked. 'I'm sorry?' Peter had spoken, and she had not heard the words.

'I said at least it looks as if it'll all be over soon.'

She shook herself free of a laughing-eyed ghost. 'Pray God it will. Sometimes I think it's never going to end. It's funny, isn't it – I almost can't imagine what it will be like. Do you remember that first day? Saying goodbye outside Rampton Court?'

'Of course.' Their hands were still linked. He drew her to a halt. 'Let's make a pact? Friends – good friends – for ever?'

She laughed delightedly. 'Blood brothers without the blood?'

'Exactly.'

'Done.'

As they turned to continue walking, he glanced at her. 'May a blood brother ask a personal question?'

'Of course.'

'You and Tom. What's going to happen?'

She was silent a long time. 'I don't know,' she said at last. 'That's the simple truth. We're living in a kind of vacuum at the moment – as I suppose we all are – waiting for the war to end. After that – oh, I don't know, we don't seem able to talk about it. He's not flying any more, you know.' She paused, added wryly, 'A desk-bound Tom Robinson isn't the easiest creature in the world to cope with, I have to say.'

Peter did not comment.

'I think he'd marry me if I forced him to it. Threw hysterics, that kind of thing. Perhaps that's even what he wants me to do – I don't know. But I won't. It would be no good. It has to come from him, has to be his choice. Or he'll be hell to live with and we'll break up anyway.'

'Has it occurred to you,' asked Peter carefully, 'that—' He stopped.

'—that he'll be hell to live with anyway? Yes. But I'd take that chance. It's funny . . .' They had come to a gate. She leaned against it, digging at the soft wood with her fingernail. '. . . if it weren't for Charlotte I'd do anything to be with him. Go anywhere. It's she who somehow holds the key. Poor little devil. Hardly fair, is it?' She leaned on the gate, looking at Peter. 'You've never really liked Tom, have you?'

'Honestly? No, I never have.'

'He's a difficult man to like.' Allie kicked at a pile of leaves, looked up with a sudden smile. 'But I like him. I've only just realized it, but I do. There's a possibility that he might go to South Africa after the war, did you know?'

'South Africa?'

'Yes. Land of opportunity and all that. You can't blame him.'

'And you?'

She shook her head. 'I couldn't leave Charlotte. Besides—'

'You mean he wouldn't want her with you?'

'Almost certainly not. There's – a sort of wall between them. And it isn't just Tom. She's as bad as he is. Do you know, she won't even say his name? If I didn't know better I'd say it was pure perversity. She just won't say it, no matter how hard I try.' There was a note almost of despair

441

in her laughter. 'What a pair! Anyway,' she pushed herself away from the gate, pulled her glove back onto her cold hand, 'Charlotte isn't the only reason I don't want to leave the country after the war.'

'Oh?'

She hesitated. 'Peter, I haven't mentioned this to anyone else – but I'd appreciate your advice.'

'Of course.'

'A friend of mine has had tentative advances made towards her by the Labour Party. There'll be an election after the war. There'll be a lot of women voting, and more of them will know what they're voting for than ever before. The socialists want their votes. To get them they want to put up more women candidates. Iris is going to be one of them. She wants my help. And I want to give it. One day—'

'One day you might like to have a go yourself?'

'Yes. But I need experience. Iris is forming a local committee. She wants me on it.'

'And you want to be on it.'

'I want more than that, but yes, it's a start. It's a chance to do something – or at least to *try* to do something. Something I couldn't do in South Africa, however brightly the sun shone. Am I being absurd?'

'Good Lord, no. What's stopping you?'

'Tom's stopping me. I love him. And he'll hate this. Oh, how he'll hate it.'

'Are you sure? Shouldn't you give him the chance? Explain to him? If he can't – or won't – understand, then make a decision based on that. But give him the chance to say no.'

Tom would leave. She knew it. She would give him the excuse, and he would leave. 'I'm not sure I can face it,' she said.

Peter's voice was sympathetic, his words practical, as she had known they would be. 'You have to. Sooner or later. Why not now?'

\* \* \*

It was more than a month later before the opportunity presented itself for her to take Peter's advice. The Allies were across the Rhine. Iwo Jima had fallen. The British public, righteously angry as it was, had nevertheless felt twinges of disconcerted sympathy at the pictures of the bloody shambles to which the British and American bombing offensive had reduced cities like Dresden and Cologne. It was now only a matter of time. And it was Charlotte Anne's first birthday.

Allie and Tom were in the kitchen, she washing the crockery from their little tea party, he wiping it. Apparently inconsequentially, the conversation had turned to politics.

'Who was it,' asked Tom, 'who described democracy as the bludgeoning of the people by the people for the people?'

'Oscar Wilde,' Allie said shortly.

'Of course.'

'Just because it's clever doesn't make it right.'

He looked at her in surprise. 'I don't think I suggested that it did. The phrase just occurred to me, that's all.'

She swallowed, concentrated hard on washing a perfectly clean plate. 'Tom? I – wanted to talk to you about something.'

She sensed his sudden stillness. Very precisely he placed the cup he had dried on the kitchen table. 'Of course.' His voice was light.

'Us,' she said, bluntly.

The silence behind her finally forced her to turn. He had perched on the edge of the table and was watching her, waiting. 'Will you marry me?' he asked.

'I really think—' She stopped. 'What did you say?'

He was obviously enjoying himself. 'I said "Will you marry me?" You aren't the only one who's been doing some thinking. My darling, do shut your mouth – there's a bus coming. Say something.'

'I – you mean you don't want to go to South Africa?'

'Ah.' He looked down at his neat, narrow hands. 'Well now, I didn't say that exactly. What I had in mind was that we should get married and go together. We could send for Charley in a year or so, once we're settled—'

'No.'

'Allie – think about it – what is there here?'

'No!' She turned from him, blinded by tears, fiercely scrubbed at a saucer that was a blur in her hands.

'You won't even think about it?' His voice was frigid.

'I have thought about it. Constantly. You know I have. But it isn't just you and me. It's Charley. I won't leave her. No – ' as he began to speak ' – not even for a year. That could so easily turn to two, and then three. And there's something else.'

'Oh?' His voice was distant. He hardly seemed interested.

'Iris Freeman has agreed to stand as a Labour candidate in the next election. She wants my help, and I've agreed to give it. But that isn't all. I'm going to do my damndest to make sure that when the next election comes around, someone wants me. It may sound stupid, but I'm going to have a go. I've a life of my own to lead, Tom. I can't just trail around the world behind you, tying you down. You'd finish up hating me. I'd finish up hating myself. Yes, I love you. Yes, I want to marry you. But I can't leave Charley, and I can't give up my own life. I'm sorry—' She stopped at the violent slamming of the back door, stood staring at dark and greasy water miserably.

His disappointment and anger took him down the long garden path to the front gate. There he stopped. Charlotte stood by the garden gate on unsteady legs. Solemnly she watched him as he strode towards her. He hesitated, unable to open the gate without physically moving her out of the way. They stared at each other, blue eye to blue eye. Then, utterly unexpectedly, the child's face broke into a smile like summer sunshine and, balanced precariously on her own two pudgy feet, she lifted her arms to him.

Allie was still standing at the sink, torn between anger and wretchedness when she heard the door open behind her. She turned. Stared. Tom stood unsmiling in the doorway, Charley perched awkwardly upon one crooked arm, her fingers buried securely in his hair.

With some degree of competence, Tom shifted her to his

more secure arm, regarded Allie thoughtfully. 'There's every possibility,' he said, 'that one of these days you'll make someone an absolutely splendid MP. But something tells me you're going to make one hell of a stroppy wife.'

She dried her hands – and her face – composedly on a worn tea towel, kissed him, offered her finger to the laughing child. 'Serves you right,' she said.